PENGUIN BOOKS

THE GALLOWS CURSE

Karen Maitland travelled and worked in many parts of the United Kingdom before finally settling in the beautiful medieval city of Lincoln. She is the author of *Company of Liars* and *The Owl Killers*, both of which are available as Penguin paperbacks.

THE GALLOWS CURSE

KAREN MAITLAND

PENGUIN BOOKS

PENGUIN BOOKS

Published by the Penguin Group
Penguin Books Ltd, 80 Strand, London WC2R 0RL, England
Penguin Group (USA) Inc., 375 Hudson Street, New York, New York 10014, USA
Penguin Group (Canada), 90 Eglinton Avenue East, Suite 700, Toronto, Ontario, Canada M4P 2Y3
(a division of Pearson Penguin Canada Inc.)
Penguin Ireland, 25 St Stephen's Green, Dublin 2, Ireland (a division of Penguin Books Ltd)
Penguin Group (Australia), 250 Camberwell Road,
Camberwell, Victoria 3124, Australia (a division of Pearson Australia Group Pty Ltd)
Penguin Books India Pvt Ltd, 11 Community Centre, Panchsheel Park, New Delhi – 110 017, India
Penguin Group (NZ), 67 Apollo Drive, Rosedale, Auckland 0632, New Zealand
(a division of Pearson New Zealand Ltd)
Penguin Books (South Africa) (Pty) Ltd, 24 Sturdee Avenue, Rosebank, Johannesburg 2196, South Africa

Penguin Books Ltd, Registered Offices: 80 Strand, London WC2R 0RL, England

www.penguin.com

First published by Michael Joseph 2011
Published in Penguin Books 2012
004

Set in 11.34/13.04 pt Garamond MT Std
Typeset by Jouve (UK), Milton Keynes
Printed in England by Clays Ltd, St Ives plc

ISBN: 978-0-141-04744-7

www.greenpenguin.co.uk

Penguin Books is committed to a sustainable
future for our business, our readers and our planet.
This book is made from Forest Stewardship
Council™ certified paper.

ALWAYS LEARNING   **PEARSON**

Mandragoræ. Of Mandrakes. Known also as Satan's apple. A root dangerous for its coldness, being cold in the fourth degree. The root is dangerous.

Nicholas Culpeper (1616–54)
Complete Herbal and English Physician

Nous appelons notre avenir l'ombre de lui-même que notre passé projette devant nous.

What we call our future is the shadow which our past throws in front of us.

Marcel Proust (1871–1922),
French novelist, author of
A la recherche du temps perdu

Forgive your enemies, but remember their names.

A Norfolk saying

Cast of Characters

Narrator

Yadua – the mandrake

City of Lincoln, England

Gunilda – a healer
Warren – a Norman nobleman

The Village of Gastmere, Norfolk

Raffaele/Raffe – Gerard's steward and friend
Gerard of Gastmere – lord of the manor
Lady Anne – Gerard's widowed mother
Hilda – an embittered old widow and Lady Anne's maid
Walter – manor gatekeeper

Elena – a fifteen-year-old villein working as a field
    hand at the manor
Cecily – Elena's mother
Athan – Elena's seventeen-year-old lover
Joan – Athan's mother
Marion – leader of the field hands
Gytha – a cunning woman
Madron – Gytha's blind mother

Osborn of Roxham – Gerard's former commander in battle
Hugh – Osborn's younger brother
Raoul – a member of Osborn's retinue

City of Norwich, England

Mother Margot/Ma – owner of the house
Talbot – gatekeeper
Luce – a prostitute
Finch – a small boy

Town of Yarmouth, England

Martin – a French visitor

City of Acre, Holy Land

Ayaz – a Saracen merchant

Prologue
Anno Domini 1160

'I need poison . . . now . . . this very night. Poison that will kill a man for certain, but not too quickly; I can't risk being discovered with him when he dies.' The stranger hesitated. 'It must appear a natural death . . . one that'll arouse no suspicions when the corpse is discovered.'

'But why come to me?' Gunilda protested.

'I was told that if there is anyone in Lincoln, indeed in the whole kingdom, who has the skill to conjure such a substance, it's you.' The man reached across and grasped the edge of Gunilda's skirt, tugging it like a wheedling child. 'There's no one else I can turn to . . . help me, in your mercy . . . I beg of you.'

In the dim mustard light of the guttering tallow candle, Gunilda could see little of the man's expression, but she could hear the desperation in his voice. When a stranger comes knocking at the door of your cottage at the darkest hour of night, you can be certain it is not a cure for warts he's seeking.

The man leaned forward, lowering his voice still further. 'Your knowledge is valuable and the ingredients costly, I've no doubt.' He spread his hands wide. 'I'm a poor man, as you can see. I can't pay in coin. But I do have something that might interest a woman like you, something so rare and precious it is beyond price.'

He reached into the leather scrip hanging from his belt and pulled out a packet the size of his hand, bundled in rags. He began to unwrap it, but Gunilda caught his wrist to stop him.

'Have you any idea what you're asking? I'm not going to

help you to kill a man. I don't know what tattle you've been listening to, but I'm a healer, not a murderer. If you've some quarrel to settle, go to any of the alehouses and inns down at the quayside. You'll find a score of men hanging around those places only too eager to slit a man's throat or bludgeon him over the head for nothing more than the price of a flagon of ale.'

The stranger shook his head. 'Don't think I haven't considered that, but this man is a Norman knight, well guarded. He doesn't roam the streets alone.'

Gunilda snorted. 'And you think that's going to convince me to help you, do you? You're not merely asking me to murder some old midden-grubber or ship's rat. No, you want me to slaughter a Norman, and a nobleman no less. You're not just moon-touched; you're a gibbering cod-wit. I think you'd better leave now, before you put us both on the gallows for even talking about it.'

But her visitor made no attempt to rise. He leaned forward on the low stool, his face masked by the shadows from the bunches of herbs swinging above his head.

'You don't understand. The man I want to kill is the man who raped my daughter. She's not yet twelve years old. He hurt her, and she's beside herself with terror that he'll return. I can't accuse him without for ever defiling her reputation and besides, who would take notice of a poor man like me? If I brought such an accusation against a nobleman, he'd only deny it and the sheriff would believe him. Even if he didn't, what could the sheriff do? Fine him, if that, and then he'd be free to take his revenge on me and, worse still, on her. My child will never be able to sleep without fear until that monster is dead, and he deserves to die for what he's done.'

Gunilda glanced behind her at the small figure of her own daughter curled up asleep under a heap of rags. She was the same age as this man's child. If a man ever touched her daughter, she'd rip his throat out with her own teeth. Any louse who forced himself upon a child deserved more than mere poison.

The man had followed her gaze. 'For my daughter,' he begged.

He continued to unwrap the small package and this time Gunilda made no move to stop him. She gasped when she saw what lay inside.

'Can it be . . . is it genuine?'

But she didn't need him to answer that question for as soon as she took it in her bare hands she could feel it stirring to life. It was a black and twisted thing, a shrivelled root, shaped like a human with a body, two arms, two legs and a face as wrinkled as time itself. A mandrake! A genuine mandrake and here in her own hands. He was right; it was a creature beyond price.

'How did you come by this?'

'I . . . acquired it in the Holy Land, when I fought for the Cross.'

Gunilda knew that some blood-soaked tale must lurk behind that careful word *acquired*, but she didn't press him. There are some answers no one wants to utter or hear.

The stranger was watching her intently. 'So you will give me the poison . . . for the mandrake?'

Gunilda hesitated. It wouldn't be the first time she'd helped a man to die, though mostly it was some poor soul who, racked with pain or misery beyond enduring, begged her to help them speed their passing. They all came to her, those who could not afford the exorbitant fees of the apothecaries and physicians. She was well loved for her cures, and feared for her curses. But, though the physicians ranted against her, she did only good to the innocent and harm to the evil, so she was mostly left in peace.

Finally she rose. 'What he's done to your daughter he'll doubtless do to others. For their sakes – to prevent a greater evil – I'll give you what you need.'

Before the Nocturn bell had finished sounding from the priory, the stranger had slipped out into the stinking alley, a phial of poison safely lodged in his scrip where the mandrake had nestled.

Gunilda sat in front of the fire cradling the tiny creature in her hands, feeling the flutter of life beneath her fingers, the throbbing power rising up through her hands.

'What did he give you?' A sleepy little face appeared at her side.

Gunilda hugged her daughter tightly to her, thinking of another child. Then she held up the mandrake. 'It's something I've only ever dreamed of possessing. It has the power to cure every ill if used well, even to turn back curses upon the sender.'

'Can I hold it?' her daughter asked.

Gunilda shook her head. 'It's too dangerous; first you must learn how to use it well. Used wrongly, it can bring death and worse. I'll teach you all its secrets one day, but there is plenty of time for that. Go back to sleep now.'

Gunilda wrapped the mandrake carefully again and hid it in the darkest corner of the cottage, in the hollow under a stone in the floor where they kept their coins, on the rare occasions they were ever paid with money. She lay down beside her daughter, smoothing her hair and singing softly until she felt the child relax and heard the rhythmic breathing which signified sleep. Then she closed her own eyes. She slept without guilt for the nobleman whose death sentence she had signed. One tyrant less in the world was a blessing.

At dawn, nearly two weeks later, Gunilda was again awakened by a knocking at her door, but this time the visitors did not wait for her to answer it. Before she had even struggled upright, the door was kicked in and soldiers were pouring into the tiny cottage. Her daughter screamed and fought the men as they dragged Gunilda from her hearth, but they pushed the child to the ground, kicking her until she curled up into a ball and lay sobbing. The soldiers lashed Gunilda's wrists to a horse's tail and ran her up the great hill to the cathedral. She could hear her little daughter crying and calling out to her as, bruised and battered, she toiled up Steep Hill behind her mother.

Gunilda recognized only one man in the crowd who awaited her outside the cathedral, the stranger who had come in the night to her cottage. But he was not clad in a poor man's garb any more. And now it seemed he had a name, a name she would remember to her grave and beyond – Sir Warren. With trembling hand Warren pointed to Gunilda and feigned to weep as he betrayed her.

It took a while for Gunilda to understand the charge which had been brought against her, but eventually they told her that Sir Warren's wife was dead. The death had not been marked as suspicious at first. The deceased had been placed in her coffin while messengers went out to recall her poor grieving husband from London and to summon her brother from Winchester for her funeral, which, given her wealth, was to be a lavish affair.

But when Warren installed his comely, and obviously pregnant, young mistress in the house before his wife's coffin was even laid in the tomb, his brother-in-law began to suspect foul play. He insisted on the coffin being opened in the presence of witnesses. Despite the outraged protests from Warren and the parish priest, he commanded the tiring maids to lift the dead woman's clothes as he searched the body for the marks of violence he was certain he would find. He looked for stab wounds, bruises from strangulation, bumps on the head, but there was nothing.

He was about reluctantly to admit he had been mistaken, when a clerk pointed to the heap of maggots that had fallen to the bottom of the coffin as the clothes were disturbed. The woman had been dead a few days, so at first none but the clerk could see anything amiss in discovering maggots feasting on the corpse. Until, that is, the clerk pointed out that the maggots were no longer feasting; they were as dead as their dinner. And the unfortunate pig which was fed a morsel of the corpse's liver, the hounds having refused it, likewise sickened and died the next day. There could be no doubt; Warren's wife had been poisoned.

Although the brother now had evidence of his sister's murder, proving that his brother-in-law was the murderer was not so easy. Warren had been engaged on urgent business in London when his wife had died, and furthermore he swore that before he left, his wife told him she was intending to send for Gunilda to cure her of some woman's malady. No husband in the land could be expected to define precisely what a woman's problem might be. So no one questioned him further on this point.

A quaking servant in turn swore that he'd seen Gunilda visiting his mistress the very day she died. Gunilda denied it, of course, but who could she call upon to confirm her story that Warren had visited her? A nobleman, a Norman, creeping to her hovel in the night – it was a preposterous idea.

Gunilda was tried by ordeal of fire. She was forced, in front of the clergy, to carry a red-hot iron bar for ten paces. Afterwards her hand was bound and a seal put upon the wrappings and she was left to lie in the Bishop's dungeon for three days. Her daughter was permitted to stay with her, and for those three days, despite her mother's agony, they whispered and talked and slept little. There were so many secrets Gunilda had to entrust to her daughter, so much knowledge and so little time left. Just a few hours before, Gunilda believed she had years left to pass on all her skills to her child, now she knew she had only three days and three nights.

For Gunilda was certain of what they would discover beneath the bandages on the third day. There was no use hoping for a miracle. If she'd had time, a warning before the ordeal, she could have protected herself. She'd saved many others from the gallows over the years, for she could make unguents, almost invisible to the eye, which, painted on to the hand, would protect it from serious burns and help the skin to heal rapidly. But there had been no time to anoint herself.

When the seal was broken and the priest removed the bandages, the raw, festering wound proclaimed her guilt. The sentence was death by burning with the mercy of strangulation before the flames reached her, if she confessed.

She did confess. The falsehood made no difference now; she couldn't save her life, so why die in agony? She didn't fear going to the life beyond with a lie weighing down her immortal soul, for neither she nor her sobbing daughter believed in the merciful God in whose name these men were murdering her. Gunilda trusted in the old ways, the old goddesses of earth and water, fire and blood, and it was in their name that, with her dying breath, she cursed Warren and the unborn child his mistress carried, cursed every child that would ever spring from his loins.

Her daughter, alone now, quite alone, watched the body of her mother fired to ashes and smelt the stench of her mother's roasting flesh. No longer weeping now, she stood, aflame with hatred, as the white dust of her mother was carried up by the wind and fell soft as snowflakes upon her own dark hair.

✝

Anno Domini 1210

Periwinkle – This herb mortals call also *Devil's eye* and *Sorcerer's violet* for it is much used in spells and enchantments. Felons are crowned with a garland of this herb on their way to the gallows for it signifies death. If a mortal plucks it from a grave, the spirit of the corpse who is buried beneath that sod shall haunt him to his own death.

The leaves laid upon a boil will draw its venom. The green stems bound about the leg shall relieve the cramp and chewed shall ease the aching of a tooth or stop the bleeding of the mouth or nose.

But the plant is also much used in love potions. If man and woman eat periwinkle, houseleek and powdered worms together at a meal it shall kindle the love between them.

The Mandrake's Herbal

The Mandrake's Tale

You've no doubt been told that mandrakes scream when they are dragged from the earth. That's not entirely true. There is a scream certainly, long and agonizing, which can drive a human to self-murder just to escape the pain of it. But it is not we, the mandrakes, who cry out; it is our mother, the earth. Every woman moans and shrieks in childbirth when her baby is torn from her womb, so why should our mother not scream in pain when we are dragged squirming from the warmth and darkness of her belly into the bitter light? As they writhe in labour, mortal women curse the men who got them with child, but the curse of our mother is the most terrible of them all, for her curse lasts a hundred generations.

Our fathers never witness our births for their eyes have long since been plucked out by the ravens. Our fathers were a bad lot – murderers, traitors, forgers, warlocks, rich men, poor men, beggar men, thieves. Each of them danced on the gallows to pay for the pleasures they took in this world. You will no doubt tell me that innocent men too are hanged. But I will ask you this – is there any man alive or dead without guilty secrets? And as for those who condemn a man to be hanged, are they not the worst villains of them all?

But you must be the judge of guilt and innocence, sin and sinner. We mandrakes make no judgment for those you pronounce guilty are, after all, our own dear fathers. For the fact is when men are hanged, innocent or guilty, their semen, that salty white milk, falls on to the earth and there on that very spot we spring up, white and black, male and female, the monstrous offspring of the dead, the familial image of their dark souls. Yes, if you could only glimpse those wizened and twisted souls, you'd see there's no mistaking I am my father's daughter.

Why men should ejaculate in the throes of death is a mystery even to me. Perhaps death really is the consummation of life, or maybe it's the last act of the body desperate to bequeath a life that will go on even as its own is obliterated. But I like to believe it is a final one-fingered gesture of defiance at their executioners, the only obscene gesture they can make since their hands are tightly bound behind them. Whatever the reason, felons with their dying gasp impregnate our mother and so we, the mandrakes, are conceived.

Semi-human, demi-gods, they call us. Demi-gods? *Semi, demi, less than, partial, almost* – that, if you ask me, is a hemi-insult. We are gods, totally, fully complete. How could it be otherwise, when we are fathered by eternal sin and born of Mother Earth who was old when time began? We are the immortals and the mortal men who tear us up are mere midwives to our quickening.

You've heard of our powers, I've no doubt. How we can bestow children on the barren and make a man besotted with a maid. Ask that Jewess, Leah, if we did not bring Jacob to her bed and that very night get her with child? But remember this – we can also strike a woman barren and tear apart the most faithful of lovers. We can soothe the cruellest pain. We can conjure demons straight from hell. We can raise a woman to great wealth and cast a rich man into beggary. We can prolong the agony of those who beg to die, and snuff out the breath of those who plead to live. We can do all this for you. You think you can use us to gain whatever you yearn for, and you can. We don't judge if what you desire is good or evil. But never forget that we are gods. So have a care for what you wish – we might just grant it.

But there is one wish all men want us to grant them. It is the desire to know their own destiny. Men and women are so desperate for a glimpse into their futures, they will squander a kingdom for the knowledge – 'What will I become?' 'What will become of me?' – that we have the power to show them.

But knowledge always comes at a price, knowledge changes you, perhaps it can even change your destiny too.

You don't believe me? Let me show you. I have a tale for you, one that concerns me intimately. Hear it out and then you shall judge, for as I told you, we never do.

I was born, dragged from the earth, as you would say, in the hot, blood-soaked lands of the Saracens. Who my midwives were and why they risked their lives and sanity to pull me from the ground is another story, and perhaps I shall tell it to you one day, but the tale I want to share with you now begins many years after my birth. It begins in the cold lands far to the north, in England to be precise, in a piss-poor village called Gastmere, in Norfolk, during the reign of King John.

John has borne many titles, one such was Duke of Normandy, though he lost that to King Philip of France. But he has others; his toadying courtiers call him the true king of England. His nephew, Arthur, would doubtless have dubbed him thief, traitor and regicide, if he had lived to utter such words. The Pope proclaimed him apostate, the worst of the Devil's brood. John ignored them all for he had once had another title – John Lackland.

His own father, King Henry II, had bestowed on him that mocking epithet. For Henry had lands aplenty stretching from England to northern Spain. But when John, his youngest son, was born, Henry promised him nothing, not so much as a stinking village, for as the youngest of five lusty sons, John was surplus to requirements, his father's lands already pledged to his brothers. And what can you do with a babe that has no inheritance, no glorious destiny? Why, you give him to the Church, dump the infant in an abbey, and bid him pray for the souls of his royal father and lordly brothers.

But the boy without a future was determined to obtain one, steal another man's destiny if there was no other way. He lusted after his brother Richard's lands, those great domains of Normandy, Aquitaine and England. The premature demise of Richard Cœur-de-Lion might be considered by some a misfortune, but to his loving brother John, it was as if the stars were smiling on him. Fortune has blessed him, nudged along by a good sprinkling of cunning and a little dash of murder. For John has finally got his wish; he rules England. And the people of England have been granted their wish too; they finally have a king prepared to stay on English soil and govern their fair realm. So all is well, a happy ending you might think. Not so, not so at all. You don't need the powers of a mandrake to see that both king and people are deeply regretting their wishes now.

For the year is 1210, and it is not a good year for England. The land lies under Interdict; the churches are locked; corpses lie in unconsecrated ground and babies sleep unbaptized in their cradles. The cause is the problem that has always vexed the throne of England. The king believes he should have the right to name the Archbishop of Canterbury, and is determined to see the plump backside of his own secretary, John de Gray, sitting upon the most powerful ecclesiastical throne in the realm.

But Pope Innocent III has other ideas. He dared to send word to John declaring that his most favoured cardinal, Stephen Langton, had already been appointed to the post. King John replied with cordial greetings and begged to inform His Holiness that if Cardinal Langton should ever dare to set foot again on English soil, he would take the greatest pleasure in having him hanged from the highest gallows in the land.

So the Pope has ordered the Bishops of London, Ely and Worcester to lay an Interdict upon England. No church services may be held for the laity. The people are denied all the rites of the Church, save for baptism of infants and shriving of the dying, which might save their souls from hell. But these rites too have been snatched from the people of England, for John in his fury has seized the property of the Church, and the bishops and priests have fled the land or are hiding and dare not show themselves even to save the souls of their parishioners from eternal damnation.

So here is a merry England indeed. The populace are terrified of dying in sin; the Church is threatening eternal damnation; the barons are plotting rebellion and King Philip of France, with the blessing of the Pope, is planning invasion; but despite the army of entreaties and threats which daily assault his ears, King John remains obstinately defiant. And you have to admire him for that at least.

But our tale does not concern King John himself, though you might say he is the cause of much that occurs, if indeed you hold that any man may be blamed for the crimes of others. No, our story is about two of John's most humble subjects, Raffaele and Elena, both unknown to the king.

To be fair, if the name *Elena* means nothing to King John, his name likewise means nothing to her, for as a villein, it doesn't matter so much as a beggar's arse-rag to her who sits on the throne of England. It's the lord of the manor who has the power to make her life heaven or hell and, for all she knows, he will have that power in the next life too.

But the man, Master Raffaele, or Raffe as his few friends call him, knows King John's name only too well. He fought for him in Aquitaine. He knows him by sight and reputation. And just at this moment, Raffe is striding across the courtyard of Gastmere manor and cursing his sovereign lord to the foulest pit of hell. For Raffe blames John, the Pope and every cowardly priest in the land for what he is about to do.

1st Day of the Waning Moon, August 1210

Deadly Nightshade – which some call *Belladonna* or *Devil's berry*. A plant that befuddles the mind and brings death, for its other name is *dwale*, which means *mourning*. Since it is poisonous, it is sacred to the goddess Hecate who taught her daughters the knowledge of all plants.

Mortals make wreaths of the plant to cure horses that are witch-ridden and to ward off spells from their own persons. But the Devil jealously guards the plant for it does his bidding. So mortals who wish to gather it must first release a black hen which the Devil will not be able to resist chasing, and the plant must be quickly harvested before the Devil returns.

For a man who desires to accomplish death must first deceive.

The Mandrake's Herbal

The Chosen

Elena didn't notice Master Raffaele at first. Only when she became aware of the other girls jerking their heads in his direction did she glance behind her and see him standing just outside the barn door in a patch of dazzling light. The outline of the man shimmered against the sun, his form bleached to the pallor of a ghost.

The doors were wide open at either end of the long wooden barn to catch the slightest breeze and channel it between the walls. Inside, a circle of women shuffled around a large pile of sheaves. Marion was singing the chant, and the flails whistled through the air in answering chorus. The steps of the women had slowed to the pace of a hobbled donkey in the drowsy afternoon heat, but catching sight of Master Raffaele lurking outside, Marion took up a more lively song to quicken the threshers, knowing full well that the steward's fury would descend upon her if he thought the women were slacking.

> *. . . I heard a pretty maid making her complain*
> *That all she wanted was the saltiest grain . . .*

The women swung the flails in such a rapid, practised motion of the shoulders that a perfect circle hung for an instant above their heads as if drawn on the air, before they brought the shaft down to the ground, bouncing the full length of the swelpe across the ears of grain. After each blow the women took a single step sideways in unison as the flails were raised again, swing, thump, step, swing, thump, step, obeying the rhythm of the caller. Miss a beat, miss a step and it would be a human skull that was cracked instead of the ear of grain.

. . . Kind Sir, you're the man to do the deed,
To sow my meadow with the wanton seed . . .

The grain skipped and pattered in golden raindrops across the threshing floor and the dust rose in a dense cloud until the women seemed to be dancing on mist. The girls had masked their mouths and noses with rags to keep from choking, but still they coughed.

. . . then I sowed high and I sowed low,
And under her bush the seed did grow . . .

Several of the girls began to giggle. Marion shook her head at them, but though her mouth was covered against the dust, Elena could see that her eyes were watering with mirth. Had she chosen that song deliberately, knowing that Master Raffaele was listening?

Elena glanced over at the tall figure standing motionless in the hot sun. His expression had not changed. If he knew they were taunting him, he showed no sign of it. She felt a surge of pity for the man, but it was not without a shiver of revulsion.

Master Raffaele strode towards the barn.

Marion, watching him out of the corner of her eye, shouted, 'Cease flail!'

Like dogs whistled to heel, the women instantly lowered their flails. It was a command they never disobeyed. If a small child ran heedlessly into the barn or a woman stumbled and fell, those words could save a life.

All heads turned to Master Raffaele as the dust swirled around his knees. Marion took a step forward, expecting the manor's steward to address her with an instruction or complaint, but he ignored her. His eyes searched the circle. The women shuffled uneasily. Why didn't the man speak? Someone was in trouble, they could tell from his grim stare. It was typical of the old bastard to make them wait for the axe to descend.

Elena stared fixedly at the battered sheaves lying at her feet, praying she would not be noticed. She saw his thick leather shoes take a pace towards her, but she didn't look up. Her face flushed with guilt beneath the rag mask as she remembered the full flagon of wine she'd broken in the manor's kitchens yesterday. She'd scuffled the rushes on the floor to hide the spill and smuggled the smashed flagon out, hiding the pieces under a pile of rubbish in the yard. Surely he couldn't have found out? But what if one of the other servants had seen her and reported it? There were always those who sought to ingratiate themselves or divert attention from their own crimes by reporting someone else's.

She saw the brown shoes turn as if the wearer was about to walk away. In her relief she must have relaxed her grip on her flail. It slipped from her sweaty fingers and fell with a dull thump. The shoes turned back.

'You, come with me.'

He was addressing someone else, he had to be. She dared not look up.

'Did you hear what I said?'

His voice was as high-pitched as a little girl's, but booming from his great barrel chest, it echoed off the barn walls.

She felt the hand of the woman next to her pushing her in the back.

'Do as he says, Elena,' she whispered. 'Don't bait him. He's a bear with a toothache today.'

The field hands and servants might mimic the steward behind his back, but few dared do so in his hearing. Men knew from bitter experience that if he so much as caught them grinning, they'd be lucky to escape with their faces smashed to a pulp. He might sound like a small boy, but Master Raffaele had the temper of a charging bull and the bulk and strength to match.

The steward waited long enough to be certain Elena was following, then he strode from the barn. Elena stumbled after him. Her legs felt as if they were chained to the threshing floor, but somehow she pushed her feet forward. Every woman in the threshing circle was watching her, some anxiously, others winking at each other as if they thought he had called her out because he wanted a tumble.

Surely he wouldn't have taken her so publicly if that was his intention. Old Walter, the gatekeeper at the manor, had tried to drag most of the girls into the stables at one time or other, mostly when he was sheep-drunk after a night in the tavern. A knee in the groin and a threat to scream were always enough to send him reeling off to find other company. But she was pretty sure it would take more than that to drive Master Raffaele away.

The sun beat down hard on Elena's bent head, scorching her skin despite the cloth she had wrapped around her hair to keep out the dust. Master Raffaele lumbered across the court-yard ahead of her.

Even for a man he was unusually tall, with great long limbs out of all proportion to his body. Elena's mother, Cecily, had said that when he'd first returned from the Holy Land with Sir Gerard, Raffaele had been by far the best-looking man in the shire. There wasn't a woman in Gastmere, young or old, who hadn't dreamed of being bedded by him. With his heart-shaped face, delicate beardless chin and head of luxuriant blue-black curls, he seemed to have stepped straight out of the painting of the Annunciation on the church wall, a living, breathing Archangel Gabriel, clothed in flesh as soft and fragrant as a virgin maid's.

'Who wouldn't want to feel that between your legs?' Elena's mother had sighed wistfully.

And Master Raffaele was better than any heavenly messenger for he was, as everyone knew, a gelding, so unlike the Archangel Gabriel there was no danger of him leaving you with a bastard in your belly.

It was not uncommon for men to lose their testicles through getting injured in a boar hunt or having them cut off to relieve the agony of a hernia, and there were many whispered speculations about just how Raffaele had come to mislay his. Nevertheless, all the women were agreed on one thing: no other geldings of their acquaintance were blessed with such a wickedly tempting body as Master Raffaele possessed.

But it is impossible for the young to imagine their parents' generation could ever have been the objects of desire, for Master Raffaele was now approaching forty summers, so rumour had it, and old enough to be Elena's father – not that he could have fathered any brat. Even Elena's mother could scarcely believe she once lusted after him, for his angelic beauty had long since faded. His cream-soft skin was now scarred by battle and tanned to leather by sun and wind. His hair, though still thicker than most women's, was the colour of old lead. His belly, hips and backside were covered in sagging wads of fat, making his ridiculously long limbs appear even more gangling and spindly. To Elena he looked like a bloated spider.

She shuddered, feeling sick as she imagined those long fingers groping into her flesh. He wouldn't, surely he wouldn't. No one had ever said he'd forced himself on a woman. Quite the opposite in fact, for the alewives whispered that if he was capable of getting his prick up, which most of them doubted, his desire would surely be for the bull and not the heifers, for how else would you account for the hours he and Sir Gerard spent alone together? Besides, isn't that what you would expect from a grown man who had the voice of a little boy?

They were approaching the stables and Elena's stomach tightened, but Master Raffaele strode on past and entered the small, dusty inner courtyard leading to the great house. Elena was following so closely behind him that when he stopped and turned, she almost fell into his arms. He stared down at her, then reached out his great hand towards her. She flinched back, but he merely tugged the rag mask from her face.

'Brush the dust from your kirtle, girl. The Lady Anne wishes to see you.'

Elena stared at him in horror. 'Master Raffaele . . . the wine, I didn't mean . . . it was an accident . . . I swear.'

He frowned at her as if she was babbling in a tongue he didn't recognize.

'Wine? This has nothing to do with wine.'

The expression in his hard brown eyes suddenly softened. He squeezed her shoulder and she shrank under his grasp. He spoke more gently.

'No need to be frightened. The mistress is pleased with what she hears of you, a good modest girl, mannerly. She's a mind to take you into the house, as one of her tiring maids.'

Elena gaped at him. She couldn't believe that the Lady Anne even knew of her existence. She had seen her often, but Lady Anne had never spoken to her. Why would she? Any instructions she had to give to a villein would be passed on through the steward, reeve or bailiff. And Elena mostly worked in the fields, as her own mother had done and her grandmother before that.

The closest Elena had ever come to the house was the kitchens outside in the courtyard where she was sent to take herbs and vegetables for the cooks. She hated going there, a great noisy place with people flashing knives and rushing about bellowing orders. Worst of all was the stifling heat from the fires, and the smoke, steam and burning fat so thick in the air that it made your eyes sting and water before you'd even set foot through the door. She always imagined that the torments of hell would be just like the manor kitchens. Holy Virgin, surely they weren't going to make her work in there?

She stared down at a daisy struggling to grow in the dust between the cobbles. 'How . . . how does she . . . Lady Anne know me?'

'I knew she was looking for a new tiring maid, since that foolish girl got herself with child.' He smiled. 'I've been keeping an eye on you. I think you'll do very well.'

Lady Anne was standing at the window of the chamber, her greying hair covered by the soft folds of a linen wimple. The afternoon light streaming in cruelly exposed the dull flaking skin and sharp bones of her face. She was not yet in her sixtieth year, but to Elena she looked ancient, older even than her grandmother, which she probably was. Deep lines were gouged around her eyes and mouth from years of anxiety, and little wonder, Elena's mother said, for the poor soul had been a widow for nigh on twenty years. Cecily knew all about the sorrows of widowhood, for hadn't her own husband died of the marsh fever before Elena was even weaned?

Elena glanced only briefly at Lady Anne as she dropped a wobbly curtsy, for she was far more fascinated by the room than by its occupant. The chamber was vast in comparison to cottages in the village, with high ceilings and heavy tapestries. Heavy carved wooden chairs and even bigger chests stood against walls. The wooden floor was not strewn with rushes but with several rugs gleaming like water in the sun. Elena had never seen silk before. She longed to run her hands over them and trace the intricate patterns of blue, red and yellow flowers which spiralled into one another till you could not see where one ended and another began. They were not like any flowers that grew in the meadows of Gastmere.

A large bed stood in the far corner. It was hung with drapes which were pulled back into graceful loops to reveal a richly embroidered bedcovering. Elena guessed it to be where Sir Gerard, Lady Anne's son, slept when he was at home, for surely such a magnificent bed could only belong to the lord of the manor? The bed looked as wide as the entire room in which Elena and her mother lived, cooked and slept. Rumour in Gastmere was that Sir Gerard had recently been laid low with the fever. A wicked thought popped up in Elena's head that she too would declare herself sick, if she had a bed like that to lie in all day. She hastily crossed herself to ward off the evil she had tempted.

Like his father before him, Gerard had been away fighting for many years, first for King Richard in the Holy Land and then for King John in Aquitaine. Cecily said it was a wanton shame for an only son to leave his poor mother with the burden of running manor and village. But all the village women and not a few of the men were forced to concede that in her son's absence Lady Anne ruled the manor as well as ever her husband had done – better, in fact, some whispered. 'She's the spirit and tenacity of a sow-badger,' Elena's mother confided to Marion, and Cecily was not known as a woman who scattered her compliments freely.

From outside the open casement came the distant hum of voices, the clatters and bangs of dozens of people going about their work, but inside the chamber only the buzzing of bluebottles which had wandered in through the open casement broke the silence. Elena shifted uneasily, suddenly aware that Lady Anne's gaze had not left her since she entered.

'M'lady?' Master Raffaele prompted.

Anne jerked, then seemed to realize she should speak. 'Master Raffaele tells me that you are a good girl. You say your prayers each day?'

Elena glanced at Master Raffaele, unsure if this was a statement or a question. But Lady Anne did not wait for an answer.

'How old are you, my child?'

'Fifteen summers, m'lady.'

'So young,' Lady Anne sighed. 'And you are unwed? A maid still?'

'Yes, m'lady.' Elena had uttered the words before she realized she was lying, well, half lying. After last night with Athan she could hardly call herself a maid any more, but it wasn't a lie that could matter to anyone except herself. She blushed at the memory. It had been the very first time she'd made love to him, to anyone. Surely no one had ever adored a man as fiercely as she loved Athan? She had not known that her body could give her such pleasure, but almost better than that moment of passion had been the warmth and comfort afterwards of lying in his arms under the stars and wanting him never to let her go. She was Athan's wife now, in all the ways that really mattered.

'But I hope to wed as soon as . . . when the priests return and the churches are opened again.'

'Of course you do, child. Every woman hopes to wed and why should you not? You're young and comely, such pretty red hair. I'm sure a husband can be found for you in time. But in the meantime, Master Raffaele tells me you want to work for me in the house. Good.'

There was something strange about Lady Anne's smile, as if she was forcing herself into a cheerfulness that she did not feel.

'Your duties will not be onerous. After your labours in the fields, I doubt you will even think them work at all. And of course, we must find you a pretty kirtle to wear, one more suited to your new station. You'd like that, I dare say. But time enough for that, you must be hungry and thirsty after the threshing. Come and eat, we can discuss your duties when you are refreshed.'

Elena looked around her. The long table was bare save for a long band of half-finished gold stitch-work and a pair of small silver scissors such as might be used to cut threads. Lady Anne motioned to a large chest in the far corner of the chamber. It was covered with a white cloth on which had been placed a tiny wooden dish of salt, together with a pitcher, and a platter whose contents were protected by a wicker cover from buzzing flies. A low stool had been drawn up next to the chest.

Elena hesitated. She was ravenously hungry, but she couldn't understand why she was being offered food. Was this some kind of test of her table manners? She'd never eaten in the hall, but she knew from those who had waited at table here that the manor had a whole mountain of rules to be learned – not to scratch your head at the table; not to belch; not to dip your fingers too deep in the shared dish.

These were not rules observed by the men and women with whom she shared her midday bite or her supper. What if she made some dreadful mistake – would she be bundled out in disgrace?

She felt a hand take hold of her elbow and Master Raffaele guided her gently but firmly across the room and seated her on the stool. Flapping his hand to drive away several flies, he lifted the wicker cover to reveal a hunk of bread and slices of cold mutton. Raffaele poured a measure of ale into the beaker and set it beside the bread. Elena glanced up at him, on the verge of saying she wasn't hungry.

As if he knew what she was going to say, he shook his head and murmured in a low voice, 'You must at least taste each thing set before you or Lady Anne will take it as a great insult.'

'But if I do it wrong . . .' she whispered.

'Break the bread, dip it in the salt and bite a piece off. Then take a morsel or two of the mutton, and when you have swallowed it and your mouth is empty, drink from the beaker.' He smiled encouragingly. 'That's not difficult, is it?'

Slowly and carefully, Elena did exactly as she was told, trying to eat as daintily as she could and not drop a crumb or spill a drop. It was hard, for as soon as she tasted the food, it made her more hungry than ever and she longed to stuff her mouth with the dough-soft wheaten bread and sweet herbed mutton, which seemed to deserve far grander words than mere *bread* or *mutton,* for they bore little resemblance to the coarse, hard ravel bread and tough salt-meat she was accustomed to eating. Although she promised herself she would only take one bite, she devoured every scrap of the food as if she hadn't eaten for weeks.

She drained the beaker and rose, dropping a half-bob. 'Thank you, m'lady.'

It was as if Lady Anne had been holding her breath, for she answered with a great sigh and sank into a chair, gripping the sides so tightly that the knuckles on her hands turned white.

'You've done well . . . but I am weary. This insufferable heat . . . go home now and come back tomorrow at Prime. My maid, Hilda, will show you your duties.'

Master Raffaele nodded and led Elena out of the chamber as far as the set of steps on the outside of the building leading from the hall down into the courtyard. She looked up at him anxiously, trying to judge if her sudden dismissal had been a sign of displeasure.

'You did well,' he echoed. But as she turned to go, he grasped her shoulder, pulling her back round to face him again.

'If ever you have need of me . . .' He hesitated. 'I am . . . fond of you, Elena. I would protect you as my own sister or daughter, should you ever find yourself in need of such care.'

There was such a hungry expression in his eyes that Elena felt a shiver of fear. Young girls sense when an older man desires them, far more readily than if it is a boy of their own age. And where love is not returned, which it seldom is, such girls cruelly mock the poor man. But it was not in Elena's nature to mock, and so she did the only other thing she could, she convinced herself it was not so. She lowered her gaze, wriggling out from under his hand even as she stammered her thanks. She did not look back as she ran lightly down the stone steps, even though she was sure he was watching her.

As soon as she was out of sight, fear turned to anger at herself for being afraid. How dare they test her to see if her table manners were good enough to wait on them? What did they think, that the villagers troughed their food from the floor like a pack of hounds? As if she'd ever have need of Master Raffaele as father or brother! She'd managed for years without either and besides, if she needed help, she had Athan now.

Athan! She must find him and tell him the news. Her indignation rapidly turned to excitement and she hugged herself in delight. She had been chosen to serve her ladyship. That would surely mean money and gifts; Lady Anne had already mentioned a new kirtle. She'd heard that maids were given all kinds of things by their wealthy mistresses – dainty food, gloves, trinkets and even purses of money when they married. Of course Athan would wed her without any of that; what village lad expected a dowry from his bride? But if it was offered, just think what they could buy with it. What they had done last night already seemed blessed by God. Any thoughts of unease vanished as she raced like a small child across the courtyard and down the track, bubbling over with the joy and excitement of the day.

Raffe stood at the top of the stairs looking down at Elena as she ran out through the gate, lifting her skirts high like a little girl. Her long thick plaits, bouncing against her tiny waist, flamed red-gold in the bright sunlight. She was by no means the most beautiful woman Raffe had ever seen. Most men would have thought her gawky and homely compared to the raven-haired succubi who had been the ruin of many a godly knight in the Holy Land, but Elena possessed something those women had never had, not even as children. It was an air of pure innocence, an expression of guilelessness in those periwinkle-blue eyes that seemed to swear on her immortal soul that she was incapable of betraying any man.

Raffe set a goblet of hot milky posset, well laced with strong wine, on the small table next to Lady Anne. She was slumped sideways in the high-backed chair, her eyes closed, her forehead resting in her hand, but Raffe knew she wasn't sleeping. She would not permit herself to sleep tonight.

'You should drink this, m'lady.'

Steam rose from the goblet, carrying with it the tantalizing aroma of cloves, cinnamon, ginger and nutmeg. Raffe's stomach growled rebelliously, but food would have to wait.

He crossed to the chest from which Elena had eaten and carefully removed the flagon, trencher and beaker that still lay on top. Then he pulled off the white cloth covering the chest, steeling himself before he opened it. The heavy lid swung back with a creak.

Raffe stood looking down at the corpse hunched inside the chest. The body lay curled up on its side, the arms wrapped across its chest. A putrid stench was already rising from it, though Sir Gerard was barely a day dead. Fortunately it was not yet strong enough to penetrate the thick oak wood, but in this heat they could not delay burying him much longer. As if to confirm this, the flies buzzing among the rafters descended like a flock of miniature doves. Crawling over the face of the corpse, they refused this time to be deterred by the mere flapping of a hand.

'You must make the announcement of your son's death tonight, m'lady, in the hall. Tell them we have already washed and prepared the body, so that no one examines it.'

'No!' Anne wailed, 'I need more time.'

Raffe turned away, unable to bear the anguish on her face, but he could not afford to spare her feelings.

'He must be buried tomorrow, m'lady. Leave it another day and the body will start to bloat in the heat. I'll give orders that they're to work through the night to prepare the coffin and the grave.'

Anne raised her head. 'Where?' she demanded savagely. 'Where am I to bury my son? With the church locked, he cannot be laid in the family vault. What would you have me do, bury him under the midden?'

'The prison chamber beneath the undercroft. I went to examine it this morning.'

'The undercroft!' Anne blazed angrily. 'You think I want my son dumped among the stinking bundles of dried fish and barrels of pickled pork?'

Raffe slammed his great fist against the wall. 'God's teeth, woman, do you think that I . . .' he bellowed, but with a great effort managed to stop himself before he finished his utterance.

The wars had taught him that the men thrown into the hastily dug mass graves were the lucky ones. At least their humiliation was over. The severed heads staring sightless from the ramparts and the rotting corpses of mutilated men dangling from the walls soon taught you that even the meanest burial affords a dignity that is beyond price.

Raffe took a deep breath and tried to speak gently. 'That part of the prison chamber shall be walled up after the coffin is placed there. I'll do it myself. Then Sir Gerard may lay undisturbed until the Interdict is lifted and the coffin can be interred in the church.'

Lady Anne's head sank again into her hand.

'Why . . . why was he taken now?' she whispered.

Raffe turned his face away. Hadn't he screamed that very question into the hell-black heavens all night long, and received no more answer than she had?

'All those months and years when my son was away fighting in the Holy Lands and in Aquitaine I was driven to my knees in prayer a dozen times a day for him. I felt guilty if I laughed or even slept, imagining that Gerard was lying mortally wounded on a battlefield, or being tortured by the barbarous Saracens, or even drowning in the roaring seas, his ship torn apart on the savage rocks of the French coast. And when you and Gerard finally came home, and Gerard swore to me on his knees that he would go to war no more, you cannot imagine the joy and relief I felt. My son would live to see me buried, as it should be.

'What did I do wrong? Did I not show enough gratitude for his safe return? Did I neglect my prayers? Is God punishing me for my presumptuousness in daring to believe that my son was safe? Why has He taken him now?'

Raffe struggled to force words from his own tightened throat. 'At least you know how your son died and where he will be buried. Many mothers in England would give all they have to know that much.'

'Do you really think I need to be reminded of that?' Anne said bitterly. 'My own husband lies rotting in a mass grave in Acre. I know I should be grateful to have my son's corpse to grieve over. But it is no comfort. My husband died under the Cross in the Holy Wars, with all his sins absolved, but Gerard . . .'

Raffe turned back to the open chest. He pulled at the corpse, bending low so that he could heave the body over his broad shoulder, then staggered across the room and deposited him on the wooden table, carefully easing the head down on to the boards so that it did not thump on the wood. He crossed the arms over the body, and slid a large crucifix between the waxen fingers. Now that rigor had worn off, the face looked at peace, as if a terrible burden had been lifted from him. Their plan had surely worked; here was proof of it.

It had been more than a week since Sir Gerard had fallen ill of a fever. For days he had been racked with vomiting and the flux. He'd writhed in agony from the violent pains in his gut and his belly was so distended that it seemed the skin would burst open like rotten fruit if anyone so much as touched it. It was as if a demon had crawled inside him and was tearing his entrails apart from within.

For days Lady Anne had sat by his bedside, not daring to move, for the physician had warned her that her son could be taken from her at any hour. The worst of it was Gerard had known he was dying. Each time he was roused from his delirium he had grasped his mother's arm, begging for them to bring a priest. 'I must have . . . absolution . . . I must . . . confess.'

Raffe had turned away, slamming his fist against the stone wall in frustration. How far off was the nearest priest – four days, a week? Men had been sent in every direction to find one. But the servants who returned all told the same story. Church after church was boarded up and locked, the priests banished or fled before they could be seized by the king's men.

God's teeth, why hadn't Gerard died on the battlefield along with the thousands of others whose bones were even now bleaching under the burning desert sun? Priests were not needed there. The Pope had sworn that anyone who died fighting under the Holy Cross would die with all his sins absolved. Yet even so, every man in that army had prayed each dawn that they would still be alive to see the sunset over

Acre, and at every sunset they begged their God that they might live to see another dawn. Be careful what you pray for, Gerard had once told him. It was a lesson they both should have heeded.

Gerard had vomited, blood pouring from his mouth, the twisting muscles of his stomach screaming in protest. He lay back on the bed, shivering and sweating with the effort. 'There's . . . no priest coming, is there?' he gasped, gritting his teeth as the pain welled up again. 'Raffe . . . you can't let me die in my sin. We swore to each other . . .'

Anne clasped her son's hand to her face, her tears wetting his skin. 'My son, there's no man more honourable than you. No man who has ever made his mother more proud of her son. You've lived a pure life, fought in the Holy Wars. Those few venial sins you may have committed since must surely be outweighed by that. I promise you that I will pray day and night for your soul, and when the Interdict is lifted, which it must be soon, then we will have Masses said for –'

Gerard seized her wrist. 'Prayers will not be enough . . . I have to confess . . . we did a terrible thing . . . Raffe knows . . . I cannot die with it upon me. I shall be carried straight to hell.' His eyes rolled back in his head as if he no longer had control over any part of his body.

Raffe lumbered across to his friend's side. Clumsily he knelt beside him, seizing his other hand.

'Open your eyes, man! You can't sleep yet.' He shook Gerard, trying to force him to stay in this world, as you would pummel a drunk to keep him awake. Raffe wanted to scream at him – *If you die there will be only me to carry it. You can't leave me alone with this.* But although the words were written in his eyes, he dared not utter them aloud.

It was like holding on to the hand of a man who was hanging over the side of a cliff. Raffe could feel the life slipping away, as if the dangling man's fingers were sliding inexorably out of his grasp. This was his dearest friend, the man who had rescued him from the abject shame and misery of a mutilated life, the master who had raised him to companion and steward. They had protected each other in battle so often that they had long since forgotten who was in whose debt. And that night, a night that for ever haunted both of them, had bound them together with chains forged from a horror that was stronger than any affinity of family blood.

Did that bastard, Osborn, relive it night after night in his sleep? Raffe knew he did not. Even when Lord Osborn had issued those orders which other men were forced to carry out, he had given less thought to them than a boy snapping the neck of a snared bird. He knew Gerard would have to carry out those commands. Osborn was Gerard's liege lord and Gerard was bound by the oath of fealty to serve him. To refuse to obey his command on the field of battle was unthinkable. Any man who did as much would be branded a coward and a traitor.

That night, after it was all over, Raffe had watched Osborn with his younger brother, Hugh, tossing down a flagon of sweet cypress wine, already planning the next day's sport, and it was plain he had already forgotten the whole incident. But then it is easy to forget if you only have to say the words and don't have to look into terrified faces or hear the screams echoing again and again through all the long dark nights.

Raffe grasped his friend's icy hand so tightly that he could feel the bones grate under the skin. Gerard's eyelids briefly fluttered in protest against the pain. Gerard's hand still wore his father's ring, a heavy gold band with an intricate knot of gold filigree that held in place a single lustrous pearl. It was Gerard's most precious possession. Still kneeling at his bedside, Raffe bent his head and kissed the ring.

'I swear on your father's ring and by all the saints in heaven. I swear upon my immortal soul, Gerard, I will not let you carry that evil to your grave. I will not let it drag you down to hell.'

Gerard lifted his head and stared unblinkingly into Raffe's dark eyes as if he was trying to impale Raffe upon that oath.

Though Raffe had never flinched from any man's gaze in his life, he shuddered, suddenly terrified of the words which had fallen from his mouth.

Gerard drew in one last rasping breath which caught in his throat. Then Raffe felt his hand fall limp. He didn't have to hold a feather to Gerard's lips to know that his life was over.

Raffe looked down again at the corpse of his friend and master lying on the table. He reached out a hand and smoothed the ruffled hair.

'I have kept my word, Gerard. You will go to your grave now as guiltless as if you had been shrived by the Pope himself. I have done as I swore to do.'

He was turning away to fetch a cloth to cover the body when he felt his sleeve grasped tightly. Anne was standing beside him, staring up at him, her bloodshot eyes searching his.

'What have we done, Raffaele? What terrible burden have we forced that poor child, Elena, to carry? I insist you tell me what my son did. I have a right to know.'

Raffe looked down at Anne. Her body seemed to have shrunk over the past few days, shrivelled into itself as if it was withdrawing from the world. This woman who'd fought to keep the manor intact for her son, who'd faced every new disaster and threat with her eyes flashing defiance and a sword-sharp mind, had not been able to stand against her son's death. How could he tell her now what she demanded to know? It would destroy her. If she knew the truth of it, she too would bear that burden to her grave. Knowledge of sin devours the soul as voraciously as the sin itself. He couldn't bear to see her love and respect for Gerard shaken for even an instant. She must go on believing that he was a good and honourable man, as in truth he was and would now remain so for ever.

Raffe turned his face away and felt the grasp on his arm slacken. Anne had known him long enough to realize that there were some things not even she could command.

She gently lifted her son's cold limp hand and slid the pearl ring from his finger. She fumbled for Raffe's hand and before he realized what she was doing, she pushed the gold band on to his finger.

'No, no, m'lady, I cannot . . .' Raffe protested, trying to pull it off.

But she folded his fingers around the ring. 'It belonged to Gerard's father and, when he died, to Gerard, but he has no son to wear it in his memory. His lineage dies with him. You have been more than a brother to Gerard. That makes you my son. Take the ring. Wear it in memory of them both. They would want you to have it.'

Raffe felt as if the gold ring had tightened on his finger, burning into it, like a red-hot copper mask that is bolted on to the face of a traitor. Nothing, nothing she could have done could have caused him more misery and guilt than this and yet he knew it was being done innocently in love and gratitude.

Lady Anne softly caressed the cheek of her dead son, as if he was again an infant sleeping in a cradle.

'Tell me this, Raffaele,' she whispered. 'Are you sure, are you absolutely sure that the girl will be able to carry this sin without causing harm to herself and her family?'

'She doesn't know what she carries,' Raffe answered dully. 'It will be no burden to her. She is a virgin. Just as when, in the ordeal by fire, the hand of the guiltless is unwrapped and is found to be unharmed, so the sin-eater cannot be tainted by the sin, not if that person is pure.'

'And if Elena is not a virgin?' Lady Anne persisted.

'She is!' Raffe's assertion came out more vehemently than he intended. Lowering his voice, he added, 'You heard her say so herself, m'lady. Besides, it was for the soul of your son that we did this, your son and my friend. Is the life and soul of a villein worth more to you than that?'

Lady Anne gazed down at her son's wasted face. As she looked up at Raffe once more, he saw the same ferocity of passion in her own eyes as he had once seen in her son's.

'I swear to you, Raffaele, there is nothing I would not give in this world or the next, and nothing I would not do, to save my son from the fires of hell, even to the damnation of my own soul.'

He thought of the copper-haired girl running away from him down the steps. Although she didn't know it, Elena was bound to him now. No marriage blessing, no consummation could tie them closer than this. Marriage was only until death; together they would carry this sin to the grave and into the life beyond.

Quarter Day of the Waxing Moon, December 1210

Mistletoe – which some call *All-heal, Muslin-bush* or *Kiss and go.* It is hung in houses all year round to bring peace and fertility, and to ward off thunder and lightning, evil spirits, demons and the faerie folk. If it is hung over the entrance to a house or above a hearth, a guest knows that his hosts bear him no malice and he may enter with their pledge for his safety. If mortal enemies find themselves under a tree which bears it, they can fight no more that day.

Mistletoe is cut on Christmas Eve and hung on Christmas Day when the old sprig is burnt. But if new sprigs are cut before Christmas Eve it brings ill fortune, and if it is hung in the house before Christmas Day, a member of that household shall surely die before the next Christmas. It may also be cut on the Eve of Samhain or All Hallows, when a sprig is worn about the neck to keep the mortal safe from witches. But to cut it then, the mortal must circle the oak three times and cut the sprig with a new dagger, never before used.

Some call its twin berries the testicles of Uranus, which were severed and fell into the sea, becoming the blood and white foam from which Aphrodite was born. Thereafter men have kissed maids under the mistletoe, removing one berry for each kiss they have stolen, till no berries remain and kissing must cease.

But beware: if a mistletoe-bearing oak tree is cut down, the family who owns the land on which it stands will wither and die out, and their house shall fall and crumble into ruins.

The Mandrake's Herbal

The Fetch

The tiny room is dark after the bright sunshine, and crowded with pots, baskets and dyed linen strips hanging from the rafters. She can scarcely take a step without tripping over a box or tangling her head in the cloth. Just a store room, she thinks, no time to bother with it now. She turns, and is ducking through the low doorway when she hears a cry, the thin, muffled wail of an infant. It is coming from the far side of the room.

She impatiently tears down the cloth and kicks the boxes aside. She is looking for a cradle, but there isn't one. The wail grows louder. The source is only inches away, but still she can't see it, nothing but a stack of baskets covered with cloths like those hanging all around. As she stares, one of the baskets trembles. She rips back the cloth.

The baby is lying on a heap of rags inside the basket. Its face is scarlet and its eyes are screwed up tightly as it bawls. The toothless red mouth opens wide as if it would devour the whole world. Its tiny fists clench, beating the sides of the basket in frustration that no one is answering its insistent summons. It is ugly, a naked little rat. Now exposed to the light and cold of the room, its screams redouble, violent, arrogant, demanding to be served.

'Be quiet,' she orders, but the baby takes no more notice of her than if she was a fly on the midden heap. Her hand darts out and she grabs the threshing legs by the ankles, jerking the infant upwards, so that it dangles upside down, but even this does not make it stop screaming.

'Shut up! Shut —'

Elena jerked awake. Hilda was propped up on one elbow beside her in the truckle bed, shaking her hard.

'Quiet! Do you want to wake the mistress again?'

Elena could hear the irritation in her voice and small wonder — three nights in a row she'd wakened Hilda by calling out in her sleep. Elena glanced anxiously over at the great bed where Lady Anne now slept. It was still dark. But by the glowing embers of the fire, she could just make out the heavy drapes pulled round her mistress's bed. She heard the whimpering snores of Lady Anne, solidly asleep. Elena crossed herself in a silent prayer of gratitude.

Hilda turned over with a groan, yanking the covers from Elena and pulling them tighter around herself. Elena didn't protest; her body was drenched in sweat, despite the icy draught whistling across her from the shaft of the privy chamber. She shrank as far away from Hilda as she could in the bed, trying desperately not to fall asleep. She couldn't afford to wake her again.

The old widow had bitterly resented Elena from the beginning, grumbling to all, except of course Lady Anne, that she 'didn't know what had possessed her mistress to employ a field hand as a tiring maid. Next they'd be dressing up a pig in robes and sitting it at the high table.'

Ever since that first morning, when she'd been compelled to show Elena her duties, the sour-faced Hilda had watched her as keenly as a hunting hawk, waiting for some fault that she could swoop down upon. Only that evening, as Elena had undressed to her shift, she'd been aware of Hilda staring suspiciously at her belly as if she knew what was concealed beneath the folds of linen.

Elena had fallen pregnant that very first night they'd made love. Indeed, it had been the only night they had made love. Elena could have slipped away when Lady Anne was resting in the afternoon and Hilda was snoring over her stitch-work, but what was the use of that, for Athan had to work in the fields or coppices from dawn to dusk, as he had done for the past ten years, ever since he was a little lad of seven. And when he was free in the evenings, Elena was waiting on Lady Anne and could only steal away from her chamber for long enough to fetch a dish from the kitchen.

So the fragments of precious time she and Athan had been able to spend together had been snatched in barns and byres or in the dark corners behind the manor. They clung to each other, drinking in the smell of each other's skins and the heat of their bodies, alternating fierce kisses with whispered conversations. But all the time they were constantly on the alert for the sound of approaching feet and the ribald taunts of the other servants that would follow if they were discovered alone together.

When they did meet, they spoke mostly of the baby. To hear Athan talk you'd think no man had ever accomplished such a miracle before. It was all Elena could do to stop him crowing his prowess to everyone in the village.

'It's only been four months. Wait just a few more weeks,' Elena had begged him, 'till we've a bit more put by.'

The tiring maid she replaced had been sent packing the moment Lady Anne discovered she was with child. Elena had no illusions about being kept on once the news got out and she had no wish to return to the fields in her condition, not in the winter freeze.

'Besides, there's your mam to think of,' Elena had reminded him.

Athan had flushed to the roots of his sandy hair. 'She's always wanted a grand-bairn . . . She'll be happy as a fishmonger's cat when it's born,' he added, though it sounded more like a desperate prayer than a certain belief.

'Aye, she'll want the bairn all right,' Elena said, 'but not with me as its mam.'

The whole village knew that Joan regarded any woman under the age of seventy who so much as looked at her son as a wicked temptress hell-bent on snatching her boy's affections from her, and any girl who did succeed in ensnaring him would earn Joan's undying enmity.

Athan grimaced. 'I know Mam's tongue is a mite on the sharp side, but she doesn't mean it, and when she sees you with our bairn in your arms . . .' He trailed off – even he couldn't finish that lie. 'Anyway, who cares what Mam wants?' He pulled Elena close to him. 'I want you, that's all that matters.'

Elena wriggled her thin body closer against his chest and felt the same shiver of bubbles run up her spine as it always did when he held her. The muscles on his shoulders and arms were as strong as an ox's from his work in the fields, but she had never known anything except gentleness in his arms. Some girls might giggle about his coarse, sandy hair that constantly stuck up like the feathers of a hedge sparrow after a fight, and some might think that his nose was far too flat and squat to make him handsome, but Elena saw none of these imperfections. She wanted nothing more than the bairn she carried to be a miniature of Athan in every way.

Athan had seen the sense in keeping the pregnancy quiet in the end, but even so he'd come close to blurting it out to the other lads more than once, and as soon as the twelve days of Christmas were upon them and Athan was doing the rounds of the village with all the other mummers, swilling down cider, mulled ale and wassail at every croft, Elena had no doubt that the secret would soon be out. Besides, how many more months could she keep her swelling belly concealed?

She saw again the baby in her dream, the baby that would not keep quiet. Suddenly she shivered. She felt cold now, bitterly cold.

Although it was late afternoon, patches of frost from the night before still rimmed the corners of the courtyard and the water on the horse trough was beginning to freeze over again. A young scullion ambled towards the bakehouse, dragging a basket of turfs behind him. He started violently as a voice roared out from a doorway.

'Pick it up, you lazy little toerag; don't drag it. If you rip the bottom out of that basket, I'll flay the skin off your arse to match it.'

The terrified boy, trying to bow his head respectfully and at the same time hoist the basket on to his shoulder, only succeeded in tipping the basket over and spilling half the turfs on the ground. He cringed as Raffe lumbered towards him, but the towering man bent down and collected the turfs, then hoisted the basket on to the lad's shoulder before sending him off with a gentle cuff and an amused shake of his head.

Aware of a movement behind him, Raffe turned to see Elena, muffled in a heavy travelling cloak against the cold, picking her way across the slippery cobbles.

'Going far, Elena?' He glanced up at the pale sun that was already touching the tops of the trees. 'It'll be dark soon.'

Her cheeks flushed scarlet in the cold air. There was something about that first look she gave him whenever he called out to her, the innocent upward flash of her blue eyes, the soft mouth half-opening to reply, her arms thrust forward like those of a child waiting to be embraced. He longed to keep that moment frozen for eternity. Then it was gone and the girl was stammering and staring at the ground as she always did, but it did not displease him. It was how a modest young girl should behave with a man old enough to be her father.

'I have to run an errand.'

'For Lady Anne? Surely one of the page boys could . . .'

He stopped, seeing the anxious glance she darted up at the casement of the great chamber. No, Lady Anne had not sent her.

'You're going to see your mother.'

The girl hesitated, then nodded.

Raffe smiled indulgently. For all the comfort the manor could offer them, at heart these village girls would sooner be back in their squalid little cottages, living squashed together like hens in a basket bound for market. They missed their families and they were always running back to see them whenever they could sneak away.

'Wait there,' he commanded, striding towards the kitchen. He returned carrying a string threaded with dried apricots, fragrant as rose petals. 'You can't go to see your mother empty-handed.'

For the second time, she lifted her head and met his eyes,

murmuring her thanks, but there was more than blushing gratitude in her eyes. What was it? Guilt? Fear?

She lowered her head, but he caught and raised her chin, tilting back her face so that she was forced to look at him. His eyes were hard.

'You swear to me, girl, it is your mother you go to see, you are not running to meet some man?'

'No . . . I swear I'm not . . . not a man.'

He held her face for a few moments, then, satisfied, relaxed his grip, his fingers gliding gently over her throat as he let her go.

'Don't stay long. Be sure and be back before dark – that track isn't safe for a young girl alone. Besides, you must return before Lady Anne starts calling for you. It doesn't do to anger her.'

She nodded, and he watched her hurry through the wicket gate in the great door. Maybe he should have offered to go with her, just to see her safely there. He shook his head, reminding himself that she'd been roaming these tracks all her life. She knew how to take care of herself, more's the pity. He'd have given anything in this world to see those blue eyes pleading for his protection. He felt a familiar ache in his throat. He knew it was foolish to think about her in that way, it could only cause him pain, and yet however firmly he was determined to shut her out of his thoughts, he had only to see her for his resolve to vanish like a single drop of water falling into a roaring fire.

Raffe was half-way up the stone staircase leading to the Great Hall when he heard the rumble on the track beyond the walls. It was not the rattle of a trundling ox-cart or an ambling flock of sheep, it was the sound of armed horsemen riding swiftly. That always signified trouble. There came the clatter of iron horseshoes on stone and the whinnying of horses being sharply reined in. Raffe was already bounding back down the steps when a thunderous hammering sounded at the huge wooden door. The manor's hounds all began barking and howling together.

Walter, the gateman, alerted by the sound of the riders, had opened the small grill set into the iron-bossed door to enquire of their business, and whatever reply he received made him race to wrench the great doors open. He scarcely had time to get them wide enough before five mounted men trotted into the courtyard. Walter, bellowing for the stable lads, ran forward to take the reins which the leading rider tossed to him as he swung from the saddle.

The horse pawed the ground nervously, rolling its eyes back. Raffe at once saw the cause of its restlessness. Something was tied behind the beast, being dragged along the ground. For a moment he thought it was a pair of poles with a bundle fastened between them, such as might be used to carry a bale of dried fish or hay. But as the beast shifted sideways, pulling the bundle over the ground, Raffe saw the smear of scarlet blood on the white frosted cobbles.

It was not a bundle of stock-fish. It was a man, tied by his wrists to a long rope fastened to a horse's tail, or rather, what is left of a man after he has been dragged face-down over a frozen stony track. What few clothes the poor wretch had been wearing clung in shreds to his battered limbs. Every inch of visible skin had been grazed and ripped, till his flesh resembled a slab of fresh raw meat on a butcher's block.

Old Walter stared down at the seemingly lifeless man, his toothless mouth gaping wide in horror, then he looked helplessly up at Raffe, silently asking what he should do. Raffe gestured to Walter to back away. Until they knew the men's business it was prudent not to interfere. Most likely the man was a wolf's head, an outlaw or a murderer, and had been captured by these men who were taking his body to a sheriff to claim the bounty. Whoever the man had been, he was beyond help now.

The stranger who had dismounted first strolled towards the steps of the Great Hall, beating the dust of a long hard ride from his dark blue tabard. He came to a halt at the front of the steps and stood squarely, gazing up at Raffe. Raffe descended the last few steps with caution, his gaze, like any trained soldier's, assessing not the man's face but the position of his hands relative to the hilt of the sword slung about his waist. But the man's fingers were not creeping towards his blade, nor to the knife dangling from his belt. Instead, the stranger was pulling off his gold-trimmed leather gloves, slowly and casually, like a man standing at his own fireside.

He was not as tall as Raffe – few men were – but what he lacked in height, he made up for in the broadness of his frame, strong square shoulders, and a bull's neck, thick and corded from years of wielding the massive weight of a sword and jousting lance. A razor-straight scar pulled at the side of his mouth, carving a fat white line through the clipped, grizzled beard, grown in a futile effort to hide it.

The memory is slower than the eye, but Raffe felt a convulsion of loathing shudder through his frame even before his mind could put a name to the face before him. The man had gained weight since Raffe had last seen him, and lost what little hair had still clung to his pate, but there could be no forgetting the expression of mockery in those cold grey eyes, as pale as slug slime against the sun-ravaged skin.

'Osborn of Roxham. My lord.'

A bow or, at the very least, an incline of the head should have accompanied these words – it was only courtesy after all to any visitor of rank – but Raffe's back had locked rigid.

'What brings you to our hall, m'lord? If you've come to call upon my master, I fear you are too late. Have you not heard –'

'That Gerard is dead. Yes, indeed I have. God rest his soul. A useful man in a fight, so I recall.'

Raffe's lack of deference, which might have enraged another man, seemed only to amuse Osborn. His beard twitched as if he was trying to conceal a smile beneath it. He turned as two younger men strolled across to join him.

'Raffaele, you remember my little brother, Hugh. And Raoul here has newly joined my company.'

Raffe's jaw clenched so hard that it was a miracle his teeth didn't shatter. He barely glanced at Raoul for his whole attention was fixed on Osborn's brother.

Hugh curtly nodded his head at Raffe, somehow managing to invest the gesture with utter contempt. But Raffe's back remained obstinately rigid.

Hugh was slightly built, a hand's length shorter than his brother, and clean-shaven. Unlike Osborn, he still boasted a full head of crow-black hair. There was no disputing that women, on the whole, found Hugh handsome. His features were altogether finer than his brother's, as if he had been painstakingly carved by a master craftsman. In contrast, Osborn's face appeared to have been roughly hewn by an incompetent apprentice. A man seeing them apart would not have noticed the family resemblance, but put them together and there was no mistaking the fraternal bond. For Hugh seemed to have made a study of his elder brother's mannerisms and wore them self-consciously like a little boy walking in hand-me-down shoes.

Now the same barely suppressed smile hovered on Hugh's face. 'If it isn't the gelding, and now without a rider. We shall have to take steps to rectify that.'

Raffe fought to keep his temper. He'd been made to learn early in life that bridling at insults from men of higher rank was not worth a bloody back or the humiliation that went with it.

Osborn plucked at his beard. 'I hope you're not suggesting I should ride him, little brother. School him to the leading rein I will most certainly do, mount him never.'

Both Hugh and Raoul laughed, but Osborn's lips merely flickered in a smile.

Raffe had only ever heard Osborn laugh once, but the sound of that laughter had been seared into his soul, burning more fiercely than any executioner's branding-iron. He remembered every detail of that night at Acre. When he closed his eyes, he could still hear it, taste it, smell it.

It had been a blistering day and the darkness had brought little relief from the heat which still shimmered up from the sun-baked rocks. The air was thick with the stench of rank goat's meat spit-roasted over fires of dried dung. The foot-soldiers sprawled on the ground with their mouths hanging open, trying to suck in enough air to breathe. They were too weary to stamp on the scavenging cockroaches, or brush away clouds of mosquitoes gorging on bodies slippery with sweat. Some had fallen asleep as they ate, pieces of flat bread still gripped in their hands.

It was the silence that Raffe remembered most keenly. For once, there had been no buzzing of gossip or banter across the camp, no shouts of triumph or angry curses as men diced for spoils. Even the horses were too sapped by the heat to flick the insects away with a toss of their heads. The silver stars hung motionless as drowned herring in the black sea above his head.

Raffe had been watching them through the open flap of the tent: Osborn, seated at a low table, Hugh leaning across him for a flagon of wine, Gerard facing them, making his report. Three thousand dead. Gerard was trying to hold himself upright in the chair; trying to stop his hands from shaking as they clenched around the stem of a goblet; trying not to vomit again, though he had retched so many times since his return to camp there was surely nothing left in his stomach. Illuminated from within by the flickering red torchlight, the tent glowed like the pit of hell in the darkness binding the shadows of the men in ropes of flame.

Gerard was murmuring so quietly that Osborn and Hugh had to lean forward to hear him. A question, an answer, another question, another weary response. Raffe could not hear what was being said, but he didn't have to, he knew. He'd been there. The questioning continued, but then with-out warning Osborn laughed, a deep belly-rumble of mirth, slapping his hand on the flimsy table so hard that it almost collapsed beneath the blow. Gerard leapt to his feet, his hand darting to his knife. The blade flashed in the torchlight. Just as swiftly Osborn ducked, bringing his arm up to shield himself, but it was Hugh who had saved his brother's life, grabbing Gerard's wrist and twisting it until the knife clattered on to the table. For a moment none of the men moved. Gerard stared down in horror at the knife, unable to believe how close he had come to murder. Then, gabbling incoherent pleas for pardon, he staggered from the tent and ran out into the night.

As if his exit had been a signal, the howling began as first one starving dog threw back its head, then another and another until the whole valley was echoing with the raw, wretched grief of them. It was as if every poor beast in the world was screaming out against what they had witnessed that day.

Even now as he stood there on the steps of an English manor hundreds of miles from that place and thousands of hours from that night, Raffe realized for the first time that it was not the order which had been issued that he could not forgive, nor even what they had been forced to do, it was that single bellow of laughter. Raffe would never forgive Osborn for that.

Osborn's leather gloves flicked hard across Raffe's chest. 'Come now, Master Raffaele, must I start breaking in my new mule so soon? Don't keep us standing here with our tongues lolling to our knees, show me to the Great Hall, and bring us wine, and quickly, but the good wine, mind.'

Osborn already had his foot on the steps, when an anguished wail from old Walter, the gatekeeper, made him turn.

'Sir! Sir! Please, m'lord, I know this man . . .'

All the horses had been led into the stables, except the one Osborn had ridden. A terrified-looking stable lad held the reins of the horse, trying to prevent the powerful beast from dragging the still-tethered body across the yard. Walter was kneeling on the ground, cradling the man's bloodied head. Walter had turned him over and the man was staring up into the pale pink sky, moaning and shivering uncontrollably.

Raffe strode over to him.

Walter lifted his head, his rheumy eyes moist with tears. 'It's one of the crofter's lads, from backend of Gastmere. He's hurt bad.'

Raffe spun round to face Osborn. 'This is no outlaw. You've seized the wrong man. Any one in these parts will swear to that.'

Osborn's eyes narrowed. 'You've known me long enough, Master Raffaele to know that I do not make mistakes. I caught this thief with a brace of rabbits from this manor's warren. He was poaching and he didn't even trouble to lie about it.'

The tall, whip-thin man Osborn had referred to as Raoul waved a languid hand in the direction of the injured lad. 'Amazing stamina, these country-born villeins. Ran behind the horse for far longer than I'd have wagered any man could before he fell and had to be dragged. I warrant Hugh would have swapped him for one of his own hunting hounds, if the knave's nose had been as keen as his speed.'

Raffe could contain his temper no longer. Ignoring Raoul, he thundered at Osborn, 'What gives you the right to punish a villein from this manor? If . . . *if* a man steals rabbits from a manor's warren, then that is no one's business but the lord of that manor's. And if he needs to be punished, then it is up to the lord of the manor or his steward to dispense justice.'

Osborn and his brother, Hugh, glanced at each other, exchanging satisfied smiles.

'Exactly so, Master Raffaele,' Osborn said quietly. 'But perhaps, in the pleasure of becoming reacquainted, I omitted to mention that King John has seen fit to give this manor into my care. I am the lord of this manor now. So I will be dispensing justice here from now on.'

Every muscle in Raffe's body seemed to have been paralysed. Even his lungs had forgotten how to breathe.

Triumph shone in Osborn's pale grey eyes. 'What, Master Raffaele, no obeisance for your new master? We will certainly have to work on those manners of yours.' He raised his voice loudly enough for the whole courtyard to hear. 'Cut that piece of dung loose, but let him lie in the yard all night as a warning to others. No one is to tend him.'

Hugh, frowning, laid a hand on his brother's sleeve. 'There will be a hard frost come dawn. The man will die if he's left out here. Not an auspicious beginning to your rule here, Osborn. Perhaps in order to win the loyalty of the servants –'

Osborn's eyes were as cold as the North Sea. 'I have no intention of winning the loyalty of servants, little brother. Fear, that is what commands loyalty and obedience and that is why the man will be left exactly as I have commanded.' Osborn feigned a punch at his brother's chin. 'Stick with me, little brother, I'll show you how to rule men. Have I not always taught you well?'

Hugh smiled and inclined his head respectfully, 'I am what you have made me, brother.'

Osborn beamed at him with evident pride. Then, wrapping his arms round the shoulders of both Hugh and Raoul, he turned them towards the stairs.

'Come now, let's eat, that ride's given me the appetite of a dozen men.'

Raffe, trembling with rage, watched the three of them mount the stairs together. It was all he could do to stop himself charging after them and hurling them back down the steps. He strode back towards old Walter who was still cradling the crofter's lad.

'Never mind what Osborn says, go fetch a bier and we'll get him inside.'

Walter shook his head. 'Too late, Master Raffaele, lad's dead. And I reckon he's the lucky one, for if that bastard's really to be lord here, then God have mercy on the rest of us, especially our poor Lady Anne.'

The cunning woman's cottage was the last in the village, tucked among the trees, built hard against an old oak. In fact, you might say that the ancient tree was her cottage, for a great branch of the living tree came right through the thatch and formed the beam which supported the roof. Like Gytha herself, the cottage half belonged to the village and half to the forest.

It was a fair stride from any of the neighbouring crofts, for though land was scarce people were reluctant to build too close to her. Healer she may have been, but what might happen, the villagers asked themselves, if you accidentally crossed a woman like that? Supposing your chickens wandered into her toft and uprooted her seedlings, or your children broke her pots in a game of football? An ordinary villager might get angry and demand compensation, or might even break your own pots in revenge. But there was no way of knowing what dark magic a cunning woman might weave if she took against you and gave you the evil eye.

Although they were wary of her, that still didn't stop the villagers hastening to her door when they or their cattle fell sick, or they wanted a charm to protect their crops. Elena had been to Gytha's croft several times over the years. Her mother had taken her there as a baby when she'd fallen ill with the quinsy and later with agues and fevers. A neighbour had carried her as a child with a deep stab wound to her thigh when she had fallen on the prongs of a dung drag. If such a wound had festered, Elena might easily have lost her leg or even her life, as many a strapping man had done.

But Gytha had dressed the cut with herbs and then she had taken a rosy apple and thrust twelve thorns into it to draw the poison from the wound. And it had worked; the deep wound had healed without festering, though Elena still bore a silvery-white scar in the shape of a rosebud on her hip. A sign of hope and promise, everyone said. What better omen of future love and happiness could any young girl be blessed with?

Now Gytha sat sideways to Elena on a low stool, trying to catch the last of the fading winter light from the open doorway as she picked over a bowl of beans. She was a tall, lithe woman, with hair as dark as a raven's wing and slate-blue eyes, colder than steel in winter. Her mother occupied the single bed in the corner of the cottage which was heaped with blankets and threadbare cloaks piled over her against the cold.

The old woman, once a great healer herself, sat upright in the bed, her blue eyes now milky with blindness. She mumbled constantly to herself, her twisted fingers fumbling with a heap of bleached white bones in her lap, the vertebrae of cats, foxes and sheep mostly, though some in the village whispered that there were little children's bones among the pile. All the same, they pitied the poor old woman for her infirmity. Gytha and her mother had cures for every ailment a man could suffer, so the villagers said, but they had no cure for old age.

Gytha tossed a handful of beans into the pot bubbling on the fire in the centre of the earth floor. 'So how does this dream of yours end?'

'I pick the baby up . . .' Elena faltered, twisting a handful of her thick russet kirtle.

Gytha glanced sharply over at her. 'And then?'

'That's all. Then I wake up.' Elena watched the orange flames running lightly over the branch on the fire. She could feel Gytha's eyes on her, but she was afraid to meet her gaze in case Gytha read something in her face, something Elena did not want to hear uttered aloud.

'So in this dream you hear a bairn cry and you pick it up.' She snorted in disbelief. 'If that really were all, lass, you'd not have come to me.'

Gytha laid aside the bowl of beans and crossed to where Elena sat and pulled her to her feet. Before Elena could stop her, she was pressing Elena's belly.

'Thought as much. Three or four moons gone, I reckon. Was well timed. Green mist babies are born small, but they thrive better. Does that lad of yours know his seed's sprouting?'

Elena bit her lip and nodded. 'But no else knows in case word gets back to the manor. Don't want to leave afore I have to; we'll need all the money we can get when the baby's born.'

Gytha looked down at her, her already hard eyes narrowing. 'So you've not come to me to get rid of the cub?'

'No!' Elena stumbled backwards in horror. 'No, I'd never want rid of Athan's baby. I love him. He's so proud that he's to be a father. He says he'll love me all the more for giving him a child and I want to make him glad he chose me. I want his child more than I've ever wanted anything, that's why . . .' she gazed wildly round, as if the words that eluded her were hiding somewhere among the crocks and bunches of herbs, '. . . that's why the dreams frighten me. The same one night after night, it must be an omen. Something must be wrong . . . the baby might be in danger.'

Gytha pulled a stained and patched old cloak from her mother's bed and laid it on the floor. 'Lie down and I'll see what I can see.'

She took a shallow bowl carved from yew wood from the shelf, poured water into it and, motioning for Elena to pull up her skirts, laid the bowl on her bare belly. Gytha's fingers briefly touched the silver rose scar on Elena's thigh.

'You still have the scar from when I tended you as a bairn. So many moons ago that was, yet gone in an owl's blink.' She glanced over at her mother, and the old woman's fingers quickened as they scurried among her bones.

'Hold the bowl still, lass.' Gytha broke an egg into the bowl and then, pulling down the front of her kirtle, took her knife and slashed a small cut in her left breast, letting a few drops of blood fall into the water.

She swirled the mixture with an ash twig and stared down into the bowl. Elena watched the furrows between Gytha's eyes deepen.

'No, that can't be . . . the spirits must be wrong,' she murmured softly to herself. 'Rowan will speak the truth.' She rose and fetched another twig from the shelf. Then she bent over the bowl again, squeezing the cut on her breast so that more drops of blood fell into the mixture as she stirred with the new twig. Finally, she rose and took the bowl from Elena's hands, pouring the contents – water, egg and blood – into the supper pot of woodcock and beans bubbling over the fire.

'Did you see anything?' Elena asked fearfully, pulling her skirts down.

'You'll be safely brought to bed, you and the child. You've no need to fret on that score. You can tell your Athan that he'll have a fine son to his name,' she said, still with her back to Elena. She turned, scrubbing her hands briskly on the coarse homespun of her kirtle, as if she was trying to rid herself of a stain. 'I'll take the dried apricots in payment, and you'd best get yourself back to the manor now, afore it gets too dark to find the track.'

'No . . . you saw something else, I know you did. I can see it in your face. Tell me what else you saw, I have to know.'

Gytha glanced over at her mother in the bed. She had turned her sightless eyes in their direction and seemed to be aware for the first time of their presence.

'Madron, have the spirits spoken to you?' Gytha asked.

The old crone extended a trembling hand towards them. On her palm was a bleached white vertebra bone. It might have been the remains of the old woman's supper, except that it was stained with a wine-red mark, a single letter it looked like, though Elena, unable to read, could not make it out.

Gytha groaned and spat three times on the back of her two fingers. 'Three times – ash, rowan, bone – and each time the same. It is sealed. No power on earth can change it.'

'But what is sealed?' Elena demanded.

'There's a shadow on the heels of the boy.'

'Everyone has a shadow.'

'Not like this. Not a human shadow, the shadow of a fox. It's a portent of deception . . . a thing to be feared. The fox is the Devil's sign.'

Elena gave a little wail and crossed herself. 'My baby . . . what . . . what's going to happen to him?'

Gytha shook her head. 'The portent may not be about the bairn, but what will follow in his wake. The dream, you say you have it every night, and it's always the same?'

Elena nodded dumbly.

'Then you must finish it — see what happens to the child in your dream, then you'll know.'

Elena rocked back and forth where she sat, her face buried in her hands. 'But I can't finish it; I always wake up as I pick up the child. You can see the future. You have to look in the bowl again, please —'

'Wouldn't do any good, the spirits'll tell me no more. It's your dream, only you can see the way it ends.' Gytha crossed back to the fire, stirring the iron pot so that a rich aroma of woodcock and thyme rose from it in a cloud of steam. 'But I might be able to help you stay longer in the night-hag's world to see what you must see more clearly.'

Again she looked across at her mother as if silently asking her something. The old woman was leaning forward in her bed. She licked her lips like a hungry animal, and there was such an expression of greed on her withered old face that if she'd been younger you might have called it lust.

Gytha crossed to the end of her mother's bed and reached into the narrow space between the foot of the bed and the wattle wall. She seemed to be groping for something, and finally pulled out a small wooden box. She opened it and held up a shrivelled black root, roughly formed into the shape of two legs, two arms and a body, with a head made by the withered knot where leaves had once grown.

'Yadua. Some call them mandrakes. The male is white, but this is the woman, black and precious as sable. Comes all the way from the hot lands across the sea.'

Gytha was honest about that much at least. It was the genuine article. There are many bilge-spewers and piss-filchers who, through ignorance or greed, will try to pass off bryony root as mandrakes. Any fool holding them in his hands can feel they are as lifeless as drowned kittens and about as much use. But that cunning woman was no fool and she had enough respect for what we could do to give us our proper name, for an immortal deserves a godlike appellation.

Gytha cradled the mandrake in the palm of her hand as if it was a baby. 'You must take a drop of your blood drawn from your tongue and a drop of white milk from a man, smear them on the head of the creature, then hide her beneath the place where you sleep. She'll strengthen your dreams so that you will hear the spirits speaking to you and see the shadows more clearly.'

Elena scrambled up, holding out her hands for the mandrake, but Gytha swept it away from her reach.

'I told you, they grow only in the hot lands. Men risk madness and death to capture them, for they scream as they are dragged from the earth, a sound so dreadful that it shatters a man's reason. Yadua is costly, worth far more than a few dried apricots.'

'But I only want to borrow it for a night, if it shows me what –'

Gytha laughed. 'She can't be lent or borrowed. A fetch will only bring visions to the one who owns it. You must buy her from me and once she is bought, you can only rid yourself of her by selling her in kind, for the same price at which she was bought.'

'I have money. Lady Anne gives me coins and clothes, ones that she has finished with, and pretty silver pins too.'

Gytha shook her head. 'You think I bought Yadua with money or jewels? Where would I get such things? No, you may take her now and one day in the months or years to come, I'll ask you to perform some small service for me. That will be the payment. Are we agreed?'

Elena hesitated, as well she might. It's foolish to strike a bargain when you don't know the price. And everyone knows you must never fail to pay a cunning woman, unless you have grown weary of living. It's as dangerous as swimming in the mill race or killing the king's venison; worse, for even a slow hanging is quicker and less painful than the death that a cunning woman will send you. But, so Elena reasoned, Gytha had refused payment.

'Swear on the bones.' The voice from the bed was cracked and shrill.

Elena jumped. She couldn't remember ever having heard the old woman speak before.

The old lady was leaning forward, her white, sightless eyes fixed on Elena's own as if she could see right through to her soul. 'Unless you see where the shadow of the devil fox is running, you'll not be able to protect yourself or the bairn. You need Yadua. Swear you will do what my daughter says.'

Both women were watching her intently. Elena found herself nodding, and the old woman relaxed against the bed as though she could sense the movement of assent. Gytha took her wrist and led her, stumbling, to her mother's bed. The old woman fumbled for Elena's free hand and pushed it down upon the heap of bones so hard that it felt as if she was trying to impress her skin with the seal of them. Elena winced, but the old woman's hand held her fast like an iron shackle. 'Say it.'

'I sw . . . swear.'

They released her. Gytha wrapped the mandrake in a piece of rag and thrust it into her hands.

'Remember first you must feed her – a drop of his seed, a drop of your blood.' As Elena walked away, Gytha called after her, 'Yadua has other powers, great powers which she can turn against those who do not pay the price for her. I warn you, do not betray her.'

Gytha leaned against the door post of her little hut, watching the twilight gather up Elena's slender figure as she disappeared into the shadows. Then the cunning woman dragged herself upright and wandered over to the fire. She stood warming her hands over the flames.

'Have I chosen right, Madron?'

'The choice was never yours to make,' Madron spat. 'You

think you have that power? The day Yadua healed her, Yadua marked her.'

Madron heaved herself upright in the bed. From under the filthy covers she pulled a small wizen apple dried to the lightness of a feather over the smoke of the fire. A scrap of bloodstained cloth torn from a child's shift was tied about it. The wizened fruit was pierced with eleven black thorns. The twelfth thorn was now ash blowing about the land wherever the wind would drive it.

Madron held out the dried fruit in her wrinkled palm. 'Her apple. She was the one who came when you burned the thorns. Of all those girls you made apples for, she was the only one to come when you summoned her and on the very day the spirits warned us. She must be the one Yadua has chosen.'

Gytha took the pierced apple and rolled it in her hands, pressing the thorns deeper and deeper into the dried withered flesh. 'I can summon any living creature to me, be it man or beast, but getting them to act against their nature is not so easy.'

'You must make it her nature. She has Yadua now. So you must make her do what we need. Yadua will not let us rest in this world or the next till she does. It's not just Yadua's screams that send men mad, as well you know.'

'But how am I to make her, Madron? She's not –'

'That's your trouble, lass, always wanting to know how and why and when. Too impatient to let anything brew to its full strength. What have I always told you? You have to raise a skeleton one bone at a time afore you can set it dancing. We've waited many years, but now at last we've proof that the spirits are stirring. The first bone has come to us already, the next is yours to summon. Trust the spirits, they'll show you how.'

Gytha dropped the wizened thorn apple with its scrap of blood-soaked cloth into the ancient scrip hanging from her waist. She scowled. Madron still treated her as a child, even though Gytha was the one who had to nurse her now. But in their own way mother and daughter did have a fondness for each other, for who else did they have to cling to in life? And there were other ties that bound them too. Some bonds are much stronger even than love or death. For words are not the only gifts the dead bequeath to the living. Madron had suckled Gytha on the rich milk of hatred and now it ran like poison through both their veins.

The old woman turned her head, trying to sense what her daughter was doing. 'My supper? You fetching my supper? You've been at it long enough.'

'Patience, Madron, you'll just have to wait for it to brew, isn't that what you always taught me?'

Her mother spat angrily into the rushes. Gytha smiled and slowly stirred the pot, letting the rich aroma of the woodcock waft across to the hungry old woman. She had her own ways of tormenting her Madron.

Three Days before the Full Moon, December 1210

Salt – When a man eats of another man's salt, their souls are bound together and they are sworn to protect one another. When an oath is sworn on salt, if it proves false, the oath-taker will surely die. A prayer made near salt will be answered.

If mortals move to another dwelling they must leave behind a little bread and salt else bad luck will follow them and ruin come to the new occupants. If salt is spilled, it must not be gathered up, but the spiller must throw a pinch of it three times over his shoulder. But he should beware lest he throw it between himself and another, for salt which falls between two mortals is a sign that they will quarrel bitterly.

Salt is sprinkled in the cradle of an unbaptized infant to keep it safe from the faerie folk, and is placed on the body of the newly dead to guard the body from being possessed by a demon and the departing soul from being snatched by the Devil before the rites of burial.

Salt and water stirred three times and sprinkled over an object that has brought ill-luck will lift the curse from it, but if a mortal would curse land or a tree or beast that is fertile and render it barren, he should throw salt upon it as he utters the spell.

Salt can bless and salt can curse, for salt is salt until it falls into the hands of mortals.

The Mandrake's Herbal

A Whisper

'Just give me the name of one of the men!' Hugh demanded. 'Then I promise I will end this.'

'Can't . . . master. I swear on my life . . . I've told you everything. She's called . . . *Santa Katarina*, that's all I know,' the man sobbed.

'Which isn't enough,' Hugh snapped. 'I'm beginning to think you've invented this tale, just to save your miserable little neck.'

Hugh shivered in the icy wind cutting across the marshes. He was beginning to get bored with this. The light was rapidly fading from the sky and his belly was growling with hunger.

The man struggled to push himself up on to his hands and knees. 'It's true, every word of it . . . the French ship . . . everything.'

He screamed as Hugh's groom brought his whip down again on his bruised and bloodied back. Hugh's horse reared and snorted in alarm, pulling against the rein which tethered him to a nearby tree. Hugh took a few paces towards it, murmuring softly. He stroked the beast's neck gently, soothing it until it had calmed. The smell of fresh blood always makes young horses nervous until they become battle-hardened.

He and Osborn were enjoying the hospitality of a neighbouring landowner for a few days. That is to say, Osborn was enjoying it, but Hugh was bored witless by the unctuous little toad and his even duller wife who were so anxious to welcome their new neighbours they insisted on showing them every single hog and byre on their wretched little estate.

Hugh, mercifully escaping for a few hours with the excuse of exercising his new horse, had seen a man with a sack over his shoulder running along the edge of the marshes. More for sport than from any real suspicion of wrongdoing, Hugh had ridden the fellow down. But the sack, once opened, revealed two pewter platters. Not the kind of thing any marsh-man could afford to own. Hugh had threatened to drag him before a sheriff, but the man had started pleading for mercy, saying that he had information that was worth far more than the platters. Hugh had allowed him to talk, but the wretch had stuttered to a halt just when his story was getting interesting.

Hugh surveyed him with disgust. The man was lying on the sodden ground, panting like a dog. His nose and mouth were already so swollen that he was gasping to breathe. The groom glanced over at Hugh, plainly uncertain if he should continue.

Hugh gestured impatiently. 'Don't just stand there, you idiot, make him talk.'

The groom brought the whip down again, this time using the sturdy wooden handle. Again and again he struck the man about the head. Hugh, half distracted by what he'd heard, wasn't really paying attention to what the groom was doing, until he realized that the marsh-man had stopped screaming, stopped groaning, in fact, stopped doing anything at all.

Hugh kicked the body, but it didn't stir.

He rounded on the groom. 'You clumsy cod-wit, have you no idea how to question a man? One thing's for certain, I'll get no more from him now.'

'Maybe,' the groom said nervously, 'he knew no more to tell.'

Hugh scowled. The question was – did he believe what little the man had told him? If this marsh-man was speaking the truth, then it might prove to be the very opportunity Hugh had been seeking. But if it was the truth, he would be involving himself in a deadly game. He needed to discover more.

He beckoned to the groom, but when he approached, Hugh seized him by his throat and pushed him up against the tree.

'I will deal with the matter myself, and if you utter one word of what this man said to anyone, anyone at all, I shall personally rip your tongue out and feed it to my hounds. Do you understand?'

The groom nodded vigorously as best he could with Hugh's hand about his neck. Hugh dropped him.

The groom swallowed hard, tenderly massaging his throat. 'And what . . . what should I do with him, my lord?'

Hugh unloosed his horse's reins and swung himself into the saddle. 'Roll the body into one of the bog pools, of course, what the devil do you think they were created for?'

Day of the Full Moon, December 1210

Chicory – Mortals who carry this plant believe it will render them invisible to enemies and to evil spirits, and thieves swear that if it is held against a lock it will open any door or strongbox.

But chiefly it is used as an aphrodisiac to arouse a reluctant lover. Though do not think that it can be plucked from the ground by mortal hand. It must be dug up with a stag's horn or a disc of gold, such as resembles the warmth and fertility of the sun. To work its powers, the plant must be gathered on the days of St Peter and St James, but mortals must take heed for if the one who cuts the chicory should utter a single word as he digs he will die upon the instant.

A man must learn to keep silent if he desires life.

The Mandrake's Herbal

White Milk

The candles lighting the solar guttered in the draught, sending long shadows gliding across the deserted room. Elena hurried down the length of the solar to the door of Lady Anne's bedchamber at the far end. She was praying that Athan had received her message. They wouldn't have long; she just hoped that it would be long enough.

First, though, she had to retrieve the mandrake from where she had hidden it beneath the linen in her little chest. This might be her only chance to use it. And she had to do it this evening. She had to finish the dream. She couldn't face another night of hearing that infant's wails in her dream, that awful sick sensation of dread which made her heart race and her stomach turn sour. A fear that was nameless and faceless was a thousand times worse than the demons and beasts that leered from the tower of the church. If she could just see the end of her nightmare, then maybe it would cease to torment her.

She grasped the iron ring on the door of the bedchamber and was just about to turn it, when she froze. Voices were coming from behind the wooden partition that separated the Lady Anne's bedchamber from the solar. Frustration and something bordering on panic welled up in her. She'd been so sure the little room would be empty.

Lady Anne and Hilda were both occupied in the Great Hall. Lord Osborn had returned from visiting a neighbouring estate, together with his brother and a dozen men. Not that Elena had yet seen any of them. As soon as the messenger had arrived to warn the manor to make preparations for his immediate arrival, Lady Anne had sent all the young girls to the kitchens or on errands to the village to keep them out of the way of Osborn's men. And it was just as well, judging by the shouts and gales of laughter coming from the hall below. The men were in such a boisterous mood that their voices almost drowned out the clatter of dishes, swords and spurs and even the barking of their favourite hounds which fought and snarled around their masters' feet. The men were settling themselves in for a night of eating and hard drinking by the roaring fire.

So who could be in the bedchamber at this time? She knew Hilda would never leave her mistress alone in the Great Hall. She'd be flapping around Lady Anne like a mother partridge protecting its brood, despite her own fear of the raucous men. In any case it was a man's voice she could hear behind the partition. Servants trying to avoid waiting on Osborn and his men? Elena pressed her ear to the wood.

'And this Faramond will be aboard?'

'He will,' a second man replied. 'He's best, so they say. None more experienced nor skilful in the service of France. He can take a city with his tongue, even before a single sword's been raised.'

Elena didn't recognize either of the voices, but she knew they weren't servants. No one from Gastmere spoke like that.

'And you're sure of the place they will land?'

'Land, no,' the second voice said. 'But it will be an easy matter to arrange for you to meet with Faramond. Once the *Santa Katarina* sails up the channel from the North Sea and around the island of Yarmouth into Breydon Water there're a hundred little inlets cutting in across the marsh, all of them hidden from the view of a man standing even a few feet away. The marsh-dwellers know them like the faces of their own children. As soon as those Frenchmen are off the ship and in the coracles, they'll be able to get clean away. They can go to ground anywhere.

'No,' he continued, 'the only danger for our friends lies in sailing through the channel between Yarmouth and Gorleston, but come spring those waters will be thick with ships bringing in cargoes and men too. What's one among so many? If you want to hide a bone, put it in a charnel house.'

'Why not land at Yarmouth? Now that it is a free port, King John no longer has a garrison there.'

'But he does have spies in the town. More so now that it's no longer under his rule. He wouldn't trust the Virgin Mary herself if she came from Yarmouth.' He gave a snort of mirthless laughter. 'The ship will moor in the town eventually, pay its tolls and let the Yarmouth men examine its trade cargo, but it will have discharged its real cargo long before it sails into harbour.'

'We can trust this informant, you're sure?' the first voice asked anxiously.

'He fought in the Holy Land with us. He's more than a brother to me and we believe in the same cause, with good reason, as you well know. He hates the whole Devil's brood of the Angevins even more than you do and won't rest till he sees that bastard John's murderous head on a pike. Besides, you cannot know a man for so many years without becoming privy to a few secrets that he would not want spread abroad. It never hurts to remind one's friends of that from time to time, don't you find?'

'Are you threatening me? Because if you are I swear I'll cut your treacherous tongue from your mouth!' There was a loud crash as if a chair had been violently kicked over on to the wooden floor. The noise startled Elena and she jerked back, hitting her elbow against the iron ring on the door, and she cried out in pain before she could stop herself.

At once she heard the sound of footsteps hurrying towards the door. She turned and fled across the candlelit solar.

She had just reached the tapestry that concealed the entrance when she heard the door of the bedchamber flung open.

A voice behind her bellowed, 'Wait! You there, what's your name? Come here!'

But Elena did not stop or even turn her head to see who

was calling her. She slipped behind the tapestry and stumbled as fast as she could down the spiral staircase as if the Devil himself was flying after her.

She fled across the darkened courtyard towards the kitchens, narrowly avoiding knocking a laden dish out of a scullion's arms, though she did not escape his curses. The kitchens resembled a wasps' nest that had been kicked open. Men and women were screaming and bellowing at one another as they ran back and forth, basting, stirring, pouring and slicing. Sweat poured down the faces of the boys turning the spits on the great fires on which whole carcasses of fowls and beasts roasted, their skins bubbling and spitting as the juices ran from them.

Elena wriggled her way to the back and pretended to busy herself arranging lampreys in a pie dish, while darting anxious glances towards the open door, but whoever it was who had called out to her from the chamber had either given up the chase or lost her before she reached the kitchens, for no one but the servants hurried in or out.

Though she was still fearful of encountering the man in the courtyard, Elena dared hide no longer. If Athan couldn't find her, he might leave believing that she couldn't get away after all, and she had to meet him tonight. Something . . . something in her head with the persistence of a wailing infant was demanding it must be tonight.

She scurried across towards the barn, pulling back hastily into the shadows as she glimpsed a man caught momentarily in the light from one of the blazing torches on the wall of the courtyard. But he was hurrying out towards the manor gate and did not so much as glance in her direction. He looked like a friar from his robes, the sort that wandered from village to village begging. Elena wondered fleetingly how much alms a friar could have hoped to have begged from Osborn's drunken men. He'd probably been thrown out with a kick instead of a coin. As soon as he was occupied with old Walter, the gate-keeper, she made for the barn and slipped inside.

'Elena?'

Athan lifted the lantern high, throwing an oily yellow light about the barn as Elena hurried towards him.

'Hold it low, Athan, do you want the whole manor to see? You shouldn't have brought a light.'

'Don't care if they do, we're doing nowt wrong,' Athan muttered, but he lowered the lantern all the same.

Elena slipped her hand into his and led him towards some wool bales in the furthest corner. The field hands had deliberately stacked the bales proud of the wall to create a space behind it, large enough for a man to bed a maid in secret, two at once if he could find any lasses willing, and there were always a few who enjoyed such games. But there were no sounds of giggling coming from behind the wool bales now, all the servants were occupied with dinner in the Great Hall, either eating, cooking or serving it, so Elena prayed that she and Athan would be left undisturbed for an hour at least.

Safe behind the bales, Elena slipped her arms around Athan's waist and held her mouth up to be kissed. He bent and kissed her with such a hungry passion, it was as if they had not laid eyes on each other for years. Elena felt the same shiver of pleasure race through her body as the very first time they had kissed over a year ago at the Michaelmas Fair.

Athan gently fingered one of the flame-red curls of Elena's hair. 'Mam knows about the bairn.'

Elena stiffened.

Athan added hastily, 'But you needn't fret, she knows to say nowt in case the rumour gets back to the manor.'

'Is she . . . pleased?'

He gave her a wan smile. 'Course she is, course. Why wouldn't she be? Proud as a May Queen. It's her grandson in there.' He cupped his broad hand gently over Elena's belly. 'Or granddaughter,' he added quickly.

Elena wanted to believe him, but Athan was a hopeless liar. It was one of the many things she loved about him.

Outside in the yard there was a crash and clattering followed by a stream of oaths. One of the scullions had likely dropped one of the great platters down the stone steps. She hoped for the sake of his skin it was empty. But it reminded Elena they didn't have much time.

She snuggled closer into Athan's chest, revelling in the earthy tang of his skin. If she could get back up to the chamber straight away after they'd made love, she could feed the mandrake there. In many ways that might turn out better than if she succeeded in bringing it to the barn. Athan might have seen the bundle and become curious. She didn't want to tell him about the dream, not yet, not until she knew what it meant.

Athan held her face and kissed her tenderly again for such a long time it seemed as if his lips refused to be parted from hers, but his hands did not slide down to her buttocks to pull her closer, nor did he try to stroke her breasts as he had done when they were first stepping out together. It was as if he was suddenly afraid to touch her body.

Elena faltered. This wasn't going at all as she had planned. She'd thought this would be easy. When they were courting, she was the one who'd pushed him away when his hands wandered too freely. And even when they finally made love, she had only to respond to his caresses. She'd never had to arouse him before and she realized she had little idea how go about it. Athan had been her first and her only lover.

She pressed her body tighter against him, conscious of the swelling bump of her belly pushing between them. As if he felt it too, he drew away from her. A shiver of doubt made her tremble.

'What's wrong, Athan? I thought you'd be pleased to be alone with me. It's been so long since we got the chance.'

'I've been trying to see you, you know I have.'

'Then why won't you hold me like you used to?'

He looked down at her stomach, pressing his fingers to her belly reverently like a pilgrim touching a precious reliquary. 'Mam warned me not to go messing with you while you're in this condition. She says if a woman's blood gets hot it can addle the bairn inside her.'

'That's nonsense,' Elena said. 'If that were true there'd not be a babe born alive in this land. You think all the other men do without for nine months? Course they don't, and it doesn't do their bairns any harm.'

'Mam's only trying to do what's best,' Athan protested. 'It's her grandson after all and she'd be heartbroken if he should come to harm.'

'Your mam's only told you that to keep you away from me,' Elena snapped. 'Everyone in Gastmere knows she hated your father. I bet she told him sleeping with a pregnant woman would harm the baby just to make him take his hands off her.'

Athan shuffled uncomfortably. There was no denying that although his mother raged at him, at the neighbours and at any passing stranger that her husband was a 'whoring, feckless son of a strumpet', she could barely conceal her relief when he did stay out all night instead of lurching drunkenly home to her door.

Elena was shaking, but she took a deep breath and tried to calm herself. They mustn't quarrel. She mustn't drive him away. She wanted Athan desperately, wanted to feel his arms holding her, and his hot, bare flesh against her own. She hadn't realized how much she needed the physical intimacy of his body until he had kissed her.

But being kissed wasn't enough. If Athan didn't make love to her, where was she to get the white seed? Gytha had said the mandrake must be fed before it would speak – her blood and a man's white milk – or it wouldn't reveal anything. Tears of frustration began pricking her eyes, which only increased her misery.

Athan looked panic-struck, as young men do when faced with a weeping woman. He grabbed Elena's shoulders and held them tightly at arm's length as if he feared she was going to hurt herself or him.

'Please don't cry, Elena. I can't bear to see you miserable.

God in heaven, if you only knew how much I want you! You think this is easy for me? You've no idea how hard it is to resist you. You're all I think about when I'm working in the fields or lying in my bed at night. Half the time, I don't even know what the other lads are saying to me, because my head's that mithered with you. If you knew how many times I've made up my mind to march straight into the manor and carry you off right under their noses. And I would have done it too if I wasn't scared of hurting our bairn. Mam says . . .' He broke off, evidently realizing just in time that this was no time for another of his mother's famous sayings.

Elena scrubbed her eyes with her sleeve, took a deep breath and tried to smile. She lifted Athan's work-callused hand, cupping it to her mouth and kissing the warm palm. She drew his fingertips gently into her mouth, caressing the rough skin with her hot tongue, until she felt the powerful muscles of his arm soften a little in her grasp.

'But I need you, Athan. It's been so long. I lie in bed every night just wishing you were holding me. If you're gentle and I lie still, then it can't do any harm. I know it can't. And . . .' she couldn't stop herself from adding, 'I don't want you running off to my cousin Isabel because you can't get what you want from me.'

He opened his mouth to protest against this outrageous slur, but she hastily put her small hand over his lips.

'If you don't make love to me, I'll only fret myself sick that you're doing it with someone else, and that will be worse for the bairn, won't it?'

She put her head on one side and tried to look up at him coquettishly as she'd seen the other girls do when they were trying to wheedle a man round, but she wasn't practised at it and only succeeded in looking even more like a child. But the look was enough to make Athan laugh. Scooping her up in his arms, he laid her gently down on the hay and began to unknot the drawstring of his breeches.

*

'Where have you been?' The old widow Hilda stepped out of the darkness of the courtyard and grabbed Elena's arm, digging her sharp nails into the flesh.

No, no! Elena wailed to herself. Not now. What was the old witch doing lurking about out here? Why wasn't she waiting on Lady Anne? Her heart thumped in panic as she felt the slippery wetness on her thighs drying even as she stood there. She had to get back up to the bedchamber now, before it was too late. But Hilda was gripping her too tightly, and though Elena desperately wanted to push her out of the way, she dared not lay hands on a free-born woman.

'Answer me, girl!' Hilda shook Elena, trying to wrest out an answer to her question.

'The privy . . . I've been to the privy. Where else would I go at this hour?'

'Don't you take that tone with me, girl. I saw you creeping out of the barn. Don't think I don't know what goes on in there: the filth, the shameless acts of lust, girls fornicating with men, boys committing unnatural acts with each other. So who was he, this man you crept off to meet? One of the stable lads, I suppose. They're no better than the beasts they care for; they'd pant after a pig if it was dressed in a skirt.'

She thrust out her chin in disgust and the light from the guttering torches on the courtyard walls deepened every nook and cranny of her embittered old face, until you might have been forgiven for thinking that the church stonemason had used the old widow as the model for his malevolent gargoyles.

Elena glanced helplessly up at the window behind which lay her chest containing the precious shrivelled black root. If she didn't get to the mandrake now and wipe Athan's milk on it, all that effort would have been in vain. It had been hard enough to coax Athan to make love to her tonight, and even then he had crept away with a look of guilt and anxiety creasing his forehead as if he was already regretting giving in to her. He'd probably not trust himself to come near her alone again until after his son was born, thanks to that old termagant of a mother.

'Let me go, you've got no right . . .' Elena tried to prise the old widow's fingers off her arm, but Hilda grasped her more tightly.

'I've every right to ensure my poor mistress is not deceived by little cats like you. She is a good, pious woman. She doesn't permit harlots to remain in her service. So we'll see what she has to say about this, shall we?' She pulled Elena towards the stone steps, still shouting. Elena, trying to resist her, stumbled against the first step and would have fallen had not a pair of strong hands reached out from behind and caught her.

'Say about what, Mistress Hilda?' Raffaele asked sternly. 'You're so eager to drag this girl to Lady Anne that you almost dashed her brains out on the stones. So it must be important, whatever it is.'

In the light of the writhing yellow torch flames Hilda's eyes glittered with fury.

'I saw her coming out of the barn. What business would a tiring maid have in that barn at this time of night? I can think of only one. I warned Lady Anne she was making a mistake taking a base-born villein as a maid. What can you expect from such as them? Their kind are like feral dogs out to grab whatever they can, when they're not scrapping and snarling at one another, they're fornicating. I don't blame them, it's in their blood, but like a pack of hounds they need the whip to control them and that's your job, Master Raffaele. The servants are supposed to be under your authority. Yet you ignore the shameless debauchery that goes on night after night in there, right under the mistress's window. You know they all laugh at you behind your back, and is it any wonder –'

Raffaele shot out a great hand and, grabbing Hilda by her puckered neck, he pinned her against the stone wall, pressing down hard on her throat.

'You malicious old hag! Jealous, are you? Jealous that others are enjoying themselves when not even your poor husband was willing to bed you? No wonder the poor wretch died so young, he probably bribed the grim reaper to take him early just to get away from you. I doubt you ever gave him a warm word in his whole life. Your heart was shrivelled up like a dried pea long before the rest of you withered up to match it.'

Hilda was making a strange gargling sound and her eyes were bulging wide in fear. She struggled in vain to tear Raffaele's hand from her throat, but her movements were becoming more feeble.

Elena tugged at Raffaele's arm with all her strength, terrified he was going to throttle the old woman. 'Stop it, please, stop! You're choking her.'

The sound of Elena's voice seemed to snap Raffaele out of his rage and he slackened his grip. Hilda tipped forward, clutching the wall for support as she gasped for air and massaged her bruised throat.

Raffaele, breathing hard, seemed to be struggling to control himself. His fists clenched and unclenched, but his words to Elena were spoken softly. 'You should get yourself inside, girl, the mistress will be calling for you.'

Elena nodded gratefully and was half-way up the steps before Hilda lifted her head and snarled, 'You . . . you think she's so innocent, Master Raffaele, don't you, pure and pretty as a little white dove? Well, you take a good look at her belly. You feel it and tell me if the little whore's as sinless as you believe. She's taken you for a fool, Master Raffaele, right here in this manor, only you were too besotted with the little cat to see what was going on right under your nose.'

Night of the Full Moon, December 1210

Crickets – Twenty crickets steeped in white wine are said to cure the wheezing of the breath and, if eaten, ease the colic and also pains of the bladder.

A cricket thrown into the fire will not burn. If they enter a house and dwell there they must never be killed or driven out, for they will bring good fortune and their chirruping on the hearth will warn of a gathering storm. A cricket will even tell a mortal woman when her lover is approaching her house. But should the cricket suddenly depart, ill fortune will follow.

But take heed, if a white cricket should chance to appear upon the hearth, one of those who warm their hands around that fire will surely die.

The Mandrake's Herbal

The Turning

Walter, the gatekeeper, was never one to want to stir from his fireside after supper, even on a hot summer's night, and he certainly did not disguise his annoyance at being roused at this late hour in the bitter cold. He stamped his feet and blew on his hands, grumbling that the wicket door was very likely frozen solid and if he did manage to prise it open, he'd likely not be able to get it shut again for the rest of the night.

'You'd think folks'd have the wit to get their business done in daylight,' he muttered, 'not go traipsing around the countryside when they should be abed. Second time this night I've been fetched out of my cot. All these comings and goings, it's enough to daul a man to death.'

Raffe was in such a foul mood that he scarcely registered what Walter was saying, but the man's fumbling with the frozen latch only served to irritate him the more and he pushed Walter out of the way so hard that the gatekeeper slipped on the frosty cobbles and fell heavily to the ground. Raffe didn't even bother to apologize.

Elena bent to help the man, but Raffe caught her arm and pushed her out through the wicket door. He ducked under the frame, following her. Elena stood shivering on the path outside, clutching her small pack of belongings and staring back at the towering walls of the manor.

Raffe glanced sourly up at the swollen moon, which seemed closer and heavier this night as if it was taunting him with its belly-ripe fecundity. Holding the flaming torch aloft, he strode off in the direction of the village at a deliberately cruel pace, knowing Elena would almost have to run to keep up with him.

How could she have done it? How could she have betrayed

him, after all he had done for her? When he thought about how useless she was at almost any task in the house, her clumsiness, the pots and flagons she had broken – other stewards would have taken a stick to her long ago. But he had covered up for her, turned a blind eye to her slipping out of the manor whenever she chose, had even given her gifts to take home for her mother. By God, if he had a stick in his hand right now, that little fool would smart for it. If he'd a whip in his belt he'd have flogged her every step of the way from the manor to the village.

Raffe's fury was not soothed by the knowledge that it was entirely his own fault that he was having to put himself through this private agony of delivering Elena into the arms of another man. For Lady Anne would have willingly allowed Elena to stay until morning when a cart could have been sent to take the girl home, but it was Raffe who had insisted Elena leave at once and now, though he told himself he'd gladly drown her in the nearest ditch, he found he could not bring himself to let her walk alone at night without protection.

Raffe sensed Elena glancing fearfully up at him as she scuttled to keep pace, but he wouldn't look at her. He couldn't bring himself to speak. When he had dragged her into Lady Anne's presence, with that shrew Hilda triumphantly bringing up the rear, Elena had started sobbing. He didn't know if her tears sprang from her fear of Lady Anne's anger or from the pain of his vicious grip on her arm. At that moment he didn't care why she was crying, and he refused to slacken his grasp.

But Lady Anne had not been angry. Raffe knew she wouldn't be, whatever Hilda had hoped. Anne had shaken her head gravely, but said it was only to be expected. Elena had done no more than any pretty girl would do, especially now that marriage was impossible because of the Interdict. Then she had turned her face away and stared silently into the firelight for a long time, a silence no one dared to break.

Finally, she spoke without lifting her gaze from the flames. 'It is not that I disapprove of what you have done, my dear.

Young love is not a crime to be punished. But you must understand that I cannot bear to have babies around me. It is too painful for me. Even a pregnant woman reminds me . . . of what I have lost . . . seeing life go on as if my son had never existed. I cannot do it.'

Hilda, hovering protectively behind Lady Anne's chair, glowered at Raffe. 'You need your rest, m'lady. I keep telling everyone that, but they take no notice.'

Lady Anne absently patted her arm and glanced up again at Elena. 'Perhaps it is for the best. I don't like the thought of having young girls sleeping in the manor when Osborn and his men are here. There are many in his retinue who believe that any comely maid is simply there to be plucked for their sport, like a squab from a dovecote, no matter how much she resists. And I can't keep hiding you out of sight in the kitchens. For your own safety, Elena, it is as well you should leave now.'

Hilda crossed herself. 'I swear I'll not be able to close my eyes while those brutes are here.'

Raffe snorted. 'You can sleep soundly, mistress. There's not a man alive who wouldn't sooner bed his own horse than try your virtue.'

She flushed angrily. 'What do you know of being a man, you —'

Lady Anne rose. 'Enough! There is nothing else to be said, go now. Leave me, all of you. Can't you see there are far more pressing matters weighing on my mind than a pregnant girl? I have lost my husband and my son, and now I have lost my lands too. I cannot bear any more. You cannot ask me to!'

But as Raffe guided Elena from the chamber, Anne added more gently, 'God in his mercy grant you a safe delivery, Elena, you and the child.'

Lady Anne was a good woman, Raffe thought, a saint, and she did not deserve to have that bastard Osborn foisted on her by King John in her own home, a home she'd spent a lifetime defending for her son. Raffe savagely kicked a stone on the track and heard it crack against the ice in the ditch.

There was a shriek behind Raffe and he spun round. Elena was crouching on the icy path, rubbing her knee. At once he was by her side.

'Have you hurt yourself?'

She shook her head and Raffe lifted her to her feet. She stood swaying unsteadily for a moment. Raffe realized she was shivering. In the vastness of the darkness that surrounded them the tiny figure looked more fragile than ever. Her eyes, round and bright as the moon, glittered in the torchlight as she glanced fearfully up at him.

Placing the torch into her hands for a moment, he unfastened his cloak and wrapped it around her. Then, taking back the torch, he clasped her frog-cold hand in his own. She stiffened, trying to pull away, and instantly his anger came surging back.

'Stop that prudish nonsense! You're as bad as that old hag Hilda, thinking every man wants to ravish you. It's slippery. You've already fallen once, next time you might not be so lucky. But if you want to take that risk in your condition, go ahead.'

He turned away and started off again, but he had not taken more than a couple of strides before he felt a small arm burrow into the crook of his own. His anger dissolved in an instant. He drew Elena close and they walked on, slowly this time. He felt a surge of unexpected joy as he sucked in the closeness of her and knew for the first time the warmth of her small body pressed into his. He could feel the movement of her slender ribcage against his arm, the bones so delicate that a man might snap them with his fingers. Her sweet breath hovered in a veil of white mist as she panted in the icy air.

They were the only two people awake in the world, one tiny ship of frosted light floating through an empty black ocean. A faint breeze rippled through the branches of birch and willow and through the long-dead reeds in the ditch, making them sing like soft waves breaking on sand. From a great way off came the yelping scream of a vixen. Elena shivered and pressed tighter into him.

Looking down at the top of that small head hidden beneath her hood, Raffe knew the overwhelming desire of a father or a lover to protect something so small and innocent. But he was neither of these things to her and she wasn't innocent. He had not forced himself on her as other men in his position would have done. He had kept her pure and unsullied, though it had taken every grain of self-control he possessed when she was there under the same roof constantly, day and night. He had not touched her, but she had soiled herself anyway. Though he told himself he had been ridiculous to imagine she'd never take a man to her bed, all the same he felt like a child who'd been carefully saving a sweetmeat to savour, only to have it snatched from his hand and gobbled up by another.

'When?' he demanded so furiously that Elena jumped violently, almost slipping again.

Raffe steadied her and tried to control his voice, 'When did you get with child?'

'I . . . don't know.'

'Don't lie to me! You were a virgin when you came to Lady Anne's service, you told her so yourself. So it must have been after you started working in the manor that you started slipping off to the barn. How long did you wait – days, weeks? And was it just this *Athan* or did you have a stable of sweating field hands?'

He'd made her confess the name to Lady Anne, but it almost choked him to utter it.

She stopped and stared earnestly up at him, a look of astonishment on her face as if she couldn't believe anyone would accuse her of such a thing. 'It was just Athan . . . I've never been with anyone else and I never will, not even . . . not even if Athan said he didn't want me any more. I love him more than anything else in my life. I'm glad his son is in my belly, no matter what you or Hilda or Lady Anne think. I want this bairn! I want it, do you hear, because it's *his* baby!'

She turned her head away, but Raffe could hear the tears in

her voice, and he knew they were tears of indignation and fury, not remorse. They walked on in silence.

Elena struggled to keep pace with Master Raffaele, but she refused to beg him to slow down. She was so exhausted after the night's events that she couldn't even decide if she was devastated or relieved to be leaving the manor. She would be with Athan every day now, lying in his arms every night as she had longed to do. There was no question of returning to her mother's cottage. Now that she was carrying his bairn, she was, in the eyes of the villagers at least, Athan's wife, and a wife always moved into her husband's home to care for him and his kin. Her stomach lurched as she realized that meant she would be at the beck and call of Athan's mother, Joan, who made that sour-faced Hilda seem as kindly as a fairy godmother by comparison. But now that she was carrying Joan's grandson, surely the woman would soften towards her?

Elena glanced up at Master Raffaele. His face was turned away from her, staring ahead down the darkened road. There was no mistaking his anger, it pulsated from him, and yet she didn't understand why he was so furious with her. Unable to comprehend it, she tried to convince herself that his foul mood had nothing to do with her. As Lady Anne had said, with Lord Osborn taking over the manor, they had far more to worry about than the fate of a village girl.

She had been so anxious about Athan and then being caught by Hilda that the whole incident in Lady Anne's bedchamber earlier that evening had simply vanished from her head. But now she realized, with a little guilt, that perhaps she should have told Lady Anne what she'd heard. She had understood little of what had been said, except one thing: whoever the men in that chamber were, they were helping the king's enemies.

The villagers in Gastmere mocked their lords and rulers unmercifully behind their backs. They found ways to creep around the law when they could. They might hide a piglet or two, or a few chickens to avoid paying the tithes, or spirit away the odd fleece at shearing time before it reached the manor's barn. It was fair sport to hoodwink your masters provided you didn't get caught. But treason, that went far beyond a game. Treason meant torture and certain death in this world, and an eternal damnation in the next, for even Christ would never forgive the blasphemy of the subject who rebelled against God's own anointed king.

And to Elena such harsh punishment seemed only just, for though she had no idea what the cause of the quarrel was between England and France, like every man, woman and child in England, she'd heard the rumours that the hated French were threatening to invade and, if they succeeded, would rampage through the countryside burning the villages, raping the women and slaughtering the children. Any Englishman who helped the French must be as wicked as they were.

Elena glanced up at Raffaele's stony profile and swallowed hard.

'Master Raffaele,' she whispered.

He didn't give any indication he had heard her. She raised her voice a little.

'I heard two men talking in Lady's Anne's chamber this evening. She wasn't there and I'd gone to fetch . . . I thought the room would be empty. I heard men's voices coming from inside. I didn't mean to listen.'

Raffe turned to look at her, frowning. 'In Lady Anne's chamber? Were they trying to steal from her? You should have called me at once if there were strangers in the manor.'

'No,' Elena said hastily. 'They weren't thieves. At least, I don't think they were; they were just talking. But . . . it was about a ship, a French ship . . . coming here bringing men.'

Master Raffaele abruptly stopped and whirled to face her. 'Are you sure? Tell me everything. Tell me exactly what you heard.'

Elena told him all she could recall of the conversation she had heard. She knew her account was garbled and he had to prompt her many times to get the whole story, but she could remember all the names they had mentioned. She had always been good at that.

Finally, Raffaele asked, 'These men, would you recognize them?'

Elena shook her head. 'I could only hear their voices. But they didn't talk like Gastmere men. I think maybe . . . they came with Lord Osborn.'

'And you are sure they didn't know they were being overheard?'

Despite the bitter cold, Elena felt her cheeks grow hot. 'I don't know . . . I bumped into the door afore I ran off. They must have heard the thump, because one of them opened the door and called after me. But I didn't dare to turn round to see who he was.'

Raffaele grabbed her shoulders, almost lifting her off her feet. His face was creased with alarm. 'Are you saying that these men saw you?'

Elena flinched, trying to pull away from him. 'He couldn't have seen my face, but he might have seen my back. Will he . . . do you think they'll come after me?'

The thought had not occurred to her before. She glanced fearfully back up the road towards the manor. When the man had not pursued her out into the courtyard, she assumed that he had thought her not worth bothering with. But now, when she saw the fear on Master Raffaele's face, she realized that what she had overheard could put her in grave danger.

Raffaele relaxed his grip on her shoulders and awkwardly tried to pat her arm as if she was a child. 'They didn't see your face, that's good, but it is as well you left tonight. Sooner or later they would have run into you if you'd stayed in the manor, and if they'd recognized your kirtle or your . . .' He briefly touched her red curls.

Elena was shivering and not just from the biting cold.

'Come now,' Raffaele said in a more gentle tone than he had used all evening, 'I must get you inside before you freeze to death.'

Raffe did not trust himself to speak again until they reached the door of Athan's cottage. The village of Gastmere was silent, even the dogs were too deeply asleep or too cold to bother to bark at the footsteps crunching on the frozen mud. Here and there a few thin slivers of light from rush candles slid out between the shutters or cracks in the doors, but most had long been extinguished.

Elena hesitated before the door. 'Will you come in for a warm, Master Raffaele, afore you go?'

He backed away, bringing his hand up across his face as if to shield himself. It was more than he could bear to see that virile young man take Elena in his arms, to glimpse the bed where tonight they might . . .

'Elena, remember, I am still your friend. If you need help, if you need anything, come to me.'

The words blurted out of his mouth before he could stop them. He strode rapidly away, not even turning round to watch her enter the house.

His head was throbbing as if he had been repeatedly punched. He couldn't separate the hundred different thoughts that were darting through his brain – Osborn, the baby and now the French. If Elena was correct, then at least one, if not two, of the men who even now lay sleeping in the manor was a traitor to the throne of England, helping to smuggle spies into the country and laying the ground for Philip's invading army.

There were many in England who had reason to hate John, and would see a French king on the throne just to spite him, especially if it led to their advancement. God knows, Raffe had no love for John. But to betray England, Gerard's homeland, to an invading army, that was treachery he couldn't stomach.

Besides, no servants in the manor would have the wit or passion to plot against the throne, so one of the men at least must be from Osborn's retinue, for how else would he have got inside the manor and known the bedchamber was empty?

Elena said that they had talked of fighting in the Holy Land. Raffe tried to cast his mind back. Who in Osborn's retinue now had been with him in the Holy Land?

He and Gerard had not travelled there with Osborn, though Gerard's father had sailed with him, together with the bulk of King Richard's army. By the time Raffe and Gerard had caught up with them, the siege of Acre was already well under way. The Christian army had surrounded the walled city, trying to free it from the Saracens. Saladin, the great Saracen leader, was camped beyond the Christians, attacking them as they attacked the city, and trying to lift the siege.

Richard's army were hurling rocks at the ramparts from great siege catapults and slings. The defenders were throwing down lime and fire-filled pots on to the Christian army. You couldn't even recognize a man from his chevron or emblem, for everything was covered with a thick, choking dust. It was chaos; half the time you couldn't see the man fighting next to you for the smoke and sand blowing in the wind. Any one of the men riding now with Osborn could have been with him in that hell that was the Holy Land.

Besides, even if Raffe could identify the man, what could he do without proof? All he had was the word of a villein, and if the traitor, whoever he was, discovered that Elena had overheard him, he would find her and kill her without a moment's hesitation. No, there was only one thing to be done, he had to catch the traitor in the act of meeting these Frenchmen – that way he could bear witness himself and Elena need never be mentioned. There was just one man who might be persuaded to help him in this. He owed his life to Raffe, and Talbot was a man who did not forget a debt, especially one owed in blood.

But there was nothing that could be done tonight. Raffe tried to push the problem from his mind. The ship was not due until Spring. They would have to be patient and watch. In the meantime Elena was safe, that was the only thing that mattered. If the traitor was searching for her, it would be among the servants, not in the village, and if Raffe waited, as wait he must, then as time passed, the man would come to believe that whoever the girl was outside the door, she had heard nothing and was no threat to him.

As the icy air tore painfully at his lungs, Raffe realized that he had been striding away from the village at a furious pace. He stopped to catch his breath. The marsh pool at the edge of the track was frozen over. Frosted brown bulrushes bowed in permanent obeisance, their heads caught fast in the pond. The torch flames glittered in the ice. He caught sight of his reflection as he peered down, the sagging flesh around his jowls, the grotesque body. He had rotted from youth to old age without even fleetingly enjoying the body of a man in his prime, and his flesh would only become frailer and more repulsive as the days hurtled by.

Even at this moment, that fragile, flame-haired girl lay in the arms of a strapping young lad with all his life before him, a man who could give her the gift of a child. Life as a freed woman, money, even love itself, nothing that Raffe could have offered Elena was more than a stinking heap of dung, compared to one thing he could never give her – a child of her own. His own mother had once told him that was what every woman wanted more than anything else. She said, every woman longs to hold her infant in her arms and cannot feel complete without one. But when the next baby comes along, when her first-born is too big to be carried, what does a mother feel for her child then?

Somehow he had never really blamed his father for what they did to him. His father had paid the money. How much he never knew, but it wasn't a small sum, as his mother constantly reminded him when she told him how grateful he should be for the sacrifices they had made for him. His father had laboured night and day on the farm and at his pots, but he had done it without complaining. It was an investment not just for the boy, but for the whole family, that much Raffe understood. All their futures were pinned on Raffe, and he had betrayed their hopes. But his father alone had been the only one not to fling those words in his face, though Raffe could see them written in his eyes each time he looked at his useless son.

Men are forced to see their sons suffer much. Their boys are sent to mortify their flesh in cold cloisters of the monasteries, or to suffer the rope's lash on ships that lurch from danger to peril and back again. Young lads are killed in battle or plunge from cathedral towers, their mason's chisels still grasped tightly in their hands. Men and boys, fathers and sons, suffer and die side by side, but are not mothers supposed to plead and beg and try in every way to soften those blows?

His mother hadn't. She'd taken him to his executioner herself when he was just eight years old. He remembered as if it was yesterday the searing heat of that afternoon and twin puff balls of dust around his ankles as he scuffed his bare feet in the white grit of the path, dragging on his mother's hand, reluctant to be pulled away from a game of football with his friends. His mother tried to hurry him through the drowsy village, putting her finger to her lips as he whined to know where they were going. Flies crawled in the sweat on his upper lip. He was thirsty from playing football and the long hot walk. He remembered that vividly, a raging thirst, and when he saw the cold bath, that had been his first thought. He simply wanted to put his head down and drink the water.

They'd given him something to drink in the end, but it was not water. It was bitter, but he'd gulped it down so fast that he swallowed it before he had tasted it and it was too late to spit it out. His mother had been forced to help him undress, though she had not done so for years. He'd been mortified by that. She scolded him sharply as he fumbled with the strings of his breeches, slapping his hands away and undoing the knots herself, grumbling that he was keeping the good gentleman waiting. But he couldn't hurry, because his hands seemed to be floating away from the rest of his body, as if they had turned into butterflies. He staggered sideways. The floor was tipping. An earthquake! He must run outside. That's what his father had always drilled him to do, but he found he couldn't make his legs move and no one else seemed to feel the room spinning.

He couldn't remember if his mother had stayed to watch what the man did to him, but he relived it a thousand times in his head. Someone had picked him up and dumped him into the icy water. His teeth chattered in the sudden shock. Too late he'd seen the knife, felt the searing pain in his groin as it cut him. Fingers probed into him through the bleeding cuts, then the unimaginable fire of something being ripped out of his insides, once . . . then twice.

There had been others in the room, he was dimly aware of that even through his terror. But he knew for certain that his mother was not there when he woke up in the dark and found himself alone in an unfamiliar bed with his legs stretched wide apart, tied to the bed so that he couldn't move them. His wrists had also been tied so that he couldn't touch himself, couldn't feel with his fingers what they had done to him, what they'd taken from him, how they had mutilated him. He lay there alone in the darkness in the worst pain he had ever known in his short life, screaming and sobbing, not even able to wipe the snot from his own nose. And somehow, that seemed like the greatest betrayal of them all, that his mother had not been there to comfort him and soothe away his tears. Would Elena walk away from her crying child? Was that what all mothers did in the end?

The moon hung below the ice in the small bog pool, swelling up even as he stared down at her, as if she would burst open and thousands of baby stars would come tumbling out and wriggle away like tiny silver fishes into the black waters. Was Athan wriggling his way into Elena even now in the darkness, his sweat running over her pale skin, his hands on her breasts, making her giggle, making her moan and beg? Her face floated in front of him. He could see her naked body thrusting up towards Athan.

In a fury Raffe raised the torch and smashed it down on the moon in the water. The ice splintered and stinking muddy water splashed up his legs and on to his face. The flames were doused and he shivered in the cold hard silver of the starlight.

But like a good sharp slap, the cold water had done its work; it had brought Raffe to his senses. Elena was gone now and that was for the good. He might glimpse her from time to time in the village, but she would not be living under his nose, for ever reminding him of what he couldn't possess; and in a few years, after she'd borne more brats, when her figure had thickened and the children and her husband had cut wrinkles into her face, why, he'd probably not even recognize her, much less want her.

Trying in vain to convince himself that he no longer cared, Raffe strode fiercely back towards the manor, the moon obstinately keeping pace above him, lighting his path and mocking his attempts to smash her. With every stride Raffe took away from Elena, he tried to make the picture of her in his head more bloated, aged and unlovely. He painted her red hair grey. He gave her sagging breasts and a huge mole, and then pulled out even her grey hair, making her as bald as an egg, but still he couldn't wipe the girl from his mind.

Mortals are fools to a man: they believe that if only they can convince themselves of anything they will make it so, but they can never quite convince themselves enough.

✝

Day of the New Moon, April 1211

Yew – Mortals do not sit in its shade, nor place their beehives near it, lest the bees make poisoned honey. Nor do they drink from a bowl of its wood.

For those who would use a yew sprig in magic, the sprig must be not owned, bought or begged, but stolen in secret from a graveyard. If a maid would dream of her future husband, she must sleep with the stolen sprig under her pillow. If a mortal loses anything which is dear to him, he must hold a branch of yew before him as he walks and the yew will lead him to that which he seeks. When it is close upon the thing that is lost, the yew branch will wriggle in his hand as if he held a serpent.

For in the wood of the yew the spirits of the earth, both malicious and benevolent, may be bound fast and imprisoned for a hundred years.

The Mandrake's Herbal

The Quickening

The tiny room is crowded with pots, baskets and dyed linen strips hanging from the rafters. She impatiently tears down the cloth and kicks the boxes aside. She is looking for a cradle, but there isn't one. She is determined to find the child. How dare they try to keep it hidden from her? The wail grows louder. The source is only inches away, but still she can't see it, nothing but a stack of baskets covered with cloths like those hanging all around. As she stares, one of the baskets trembles. Did they really think such a foolish hiding place would conceal the brat? She jerks the cloth from the basket.

The infant blinks up at her in the sudden light, but it hasn't got the sense to stay quiet. It's messed itself. It lies wallowing in its own stench and excrement. Its face screws up and it bawls. It doesn't even look human, an animal, vermin, a stinking demon from the foul filth of hell. She seizes its ankles and jerks it up out of the basket; for a moment the child dangles from her fist, wriggling and writhing like a fish dragged from the river, then, as if it is a fish, she swings it violently, dashing its head against the stone wall. The silence is instant.

She stands quite still, watching the great splash of scarlet blood running down the white wall. The baby hangs limply from her hands, its eyes and mouth wide open, frozen. Then she notices for the first time that the baby's eyes are blue, deep and lucent as the waters of the ocean. They are the eyes of an angel.

Elena arched her back, trying to ease the ache of it, but her belly was so heavy she almost toppled backwards off the keg on which she squatted and had to press her hand on the wall of the dairy to steady herself.

The land was too wet from a week of heavy rain for any good to come from working in the fields, so Marion had rounded up some of the women to help with the work in the dairy. For most of the year the three dairymaids could milk the cows, feed the calves and piglets, and make butter and cheese. But now, with all the calves being weaned and the cows in full milk, extra hands were sorely needed.

Elena's belly was too big even to allow her to grasp the paddle of the butter churn at the right angle, and her ankles were too swollen for her to stand on them all day, so she was left to sit and fill the stomach bag of a newly killed bull-calf with water infused with boiled blackthorn and herbs to produce the rennet needed for cheese-making. It was greasy, messy work and her skirts were already soaked, but she made no complaint.

There was an indignant wail in the doorway and Joan, Athan's mother, marched in, struggling to hold the black dairy cat in her arms. The cat knew from experience what was coming and was trying to claw his way to freedom, but Joan had a firm grip on the scruff of his neck. One of the dairymaids grabbed the poor creature's tail and, parting the fur, searched for white hairs beneath the black. She took hold of a pinchful of hairs and yanked them out. The cat screeched. With a frantic wriggle it leapt out of Joan's arms and raced out of the dairy as if the hounds of hell were in pursuit.

The dairymaid circled the room, dropping three white hairs from the black cat's tail in each of the shallow stone troughs in which the milk had been left to separate. As every woman knew, the cat's hairs would help the cream to rise and counter any mischief evil spirits might have wrought. And it was well they did, for Gastmere abounded in evil-wishers, both spirit and human, just waiting for a chance to cause trouble.

'Has the fire been salted yet?' the dairymaid asked Joan, winking at the other women. They exchanged sly grins. She already knew the answer and was only asking to tease Joan.

Joan's chin tilted up with evident pride. 'Of course, I always do it first thing, before any other work is begun, else nothing will go right. You needn't fret that anything'll go amiss while I'm here.'

According to Joan, no one, not even the dairymaids, knew better than her the charms which would keep witches from spoiling the cheese or preventing the butter coming. And no one was more diligent in ensuring that such precautions were taken. As Elena had discovered, living under the same roof as her mother-in-law for these past four months, Joan had every reason to fear the evil eye, for there wasn't a man, woman or child in Gastmere who hadn't smarted under the lash of her tongue and cursed her under their breath.

Elena saw her mother-in-law casting her sharp little eyes about the dairy, and tried to shrink back out of sight, but with a belly as great as hers it was impossible to make herself invisible. Joan spotted her and pushed through the women towards her. Her lips were pursed as tight as the cat's arse-hole before she even reached Elena.

Shrinking from whatever spiteful remark she knew was already in Joan's mouth, Elena's grip faltered and the greasy calf's stomach slipped out of her swollen fingers and plunged to the floor, where all the liquid gushed out over her shoes. Elena tried to struggle off the keg to retrieve it, but Joan snatched it up.

'Such a wicked waste! The stomach can only be filled six times afore its juice is too weak to use. And you've already lost the first and strongest filling through your clumsiness.'

Marion took the stomach from Joan's hand and deftly poured more blackthorn water into it.

'Stop mithering the poor lass, Joan. There's no harm done, bag's not even been put to soak yet.' She winked at Elena, who smiled gratefully.

Joan's face flushed with indignation.

But Marion ignored her. 'How goes it, lass? You bearing up? Not long to go now, I'm thinking. Last weeks are always the worst, but it'll be worth it when you hold your own babe in your arms. You'll be cursing your Athan to Norwich and back when the pains are on you, but the moment they put that bairn to your breast you'll not remember a thing about sore backs or birth pains, isn't that so, girls?'

The other women smiled, murmuring their agreement.

'But you make the most of these last weeks, lass,' Marion said. 'Once the bairn comes, that'll be the end of a good night's sleep for years to come, 'cause even when they're weaned, they'll still keep you awake worrying about them.'

'My poor son hasn't had a good night's sleep since that girl moved in with us,' Joan snapped, still smarting from Marion's intervention.

Marion raised her eyebrows, grinning. 'Is that right? Keeping his pike well oiled are you, lass? Good for you.'

'No she is not!' Joan spluttered furiously. 'In her condition, I'd never allow it. I know my duty to protect my grandchild, even if its own mother doesn't. No, it's her dreams keeping us all awake. Night after night, moaning in her sleep. I've scarcely been able to close my eyes these past months. It's a miracle I've not been driven to my grave.'

'Bad dreams, is it, lass?' Marion asked sympathetically. 'Every woman gets those, 'specially with the first one.'

'Not like hers,' Joan said tartly. 'Same dream over and over she gets, or so she says. She hears her baby crying and goes to pick him up, only he won't stop so she dashes his brains out.'

Several women gasped and spat three times on their forefingers to ward off the evil that might follow such words, and even Marion looked troubled.

For a moment no one spoke, then Marion said with a forced cheerfulness, 'I used to dream I'd put the baby down in the field and when I came back he'd turned into a mushroom, with eyes and a mouth bawling fit to bust. Put me in mind of the lad's father, dead spit of him, now I think on it.'

Several of the women chuckled. Every one of Marion's brood had a different father, but none of them ever stayed around long enough to discover they had offspring.

'I dreamed I dropped mine in the wash pool,' one of the other women said. 'Sometimes I wish I had. Might have knocked some sense into the little brat.'

The women murmured their heartfelt agreement. Her son

was the torment of the village. His mother wore herself out with scolding him, but if anyone ever went to her cottage to complain about him, she stood up for him more fiercely than any sow-badger defending her cubs.

Marion nudged Joan with her elbow. 'You had dreams too when you were carrying your Athan. I remember you telling me. Didn't you dream you baked your babe into a pie thinking it to be a hare?'

The women exchanged sly grins and Joan flushed. 'Maybe I did, but I've never harmed so much as a hair on my dear boy's head.'

That wasn't entirely true and the whole of Gastmere knew it. Athan could still painfully recall the sting of his mother's switch which she had wielded vigorously on numerous occasions, whenever she fancied he was in danger of turning out like his feckless father.

'There, you see,' Marion said, patting Elena's shoulder heartily, 'every woman has these strange fancies when they're with child, and nothing comes of it.'

Elena smiled wanly, and tried to look reassured, but she was grateful when one of the maids called out that the milk was ready for churning. At once all the women set about their tasks and soon the steady slap-slap of the churn paddles filled the small building.

When Elena had confided her fears to Athan, he too had agreed that the dream signified nothing, although later when they were alone he had whispered to Elena that perhaps his mother had been right after all and they should not have made love in her condition. No doubt that was what was causing the night terrors. But Elena was not convinced by any of the women's tales. She had never in her life dreamed anything that seemed so real to her.

Ever since the first night she had used the mandrake and seen the end of the dream, she had tried repeatedly to dream it again, praying each night that it would end differently this time. She had become obsessed by the dream. Even in daylight she could think of little else. Days began to drag by as she waited impatiently for the night to come again. She was terrified by the dream yet, like someone with a sore tooth who can't leave it alone, she convinced herself she had to try again, and again. This time, this night it would be different. Once more, just once more, and it would surely change, it had to.

Even if she had not been pregnant, Elena could never have brought herself to make love to Athan with his mother in the same room, but neither could she persuade Athan to make love to her in the barns or fields, after she revealed her nightmare. However, she quickly came to learn that no matter how faithful men are when they are awake, they are helpless in their sleep. That wanton temptress, the night-hag Lilith, came often to Athan and seduced him in his dreams, so that Elena would waken to find the milk seed she needed was already spilling from him. She had learned how to steal a few drops, gently catching them on her fingers so as not to wake him, and slipping out of bed whilst Athan and his mother were still snoring in unison.

Day after day she fed the mandrake, and night after night she was rewarded with the same dream until she knew beyond any doubt or reasoning that she would murder the baby she was carrying in her belly, though how or why she did not understand. Perhaps she would do it in a moment of madness or hatred or revulsion, for she felt all those things in her dreams. But one thing she knew for certain, whatever Marion, Athan or Joan said, she would not be able to stop herself. There was nothing she could do. She would kill her own son, because she had already seen herself do it.

Raoul was feeling distinctly uneasy. Osborn had retired to the solar with Hugh and dismissed all his men, save Raoul, to talk, it seemed, about the manor. At least, that was how the conversation had started, but Raoul had spent enough time at court to know that just as a viper may lie hidden in a basket of roses, so the most innocent remark can conceal a deadly trap.

Osborn leaned back in the carved chair which creaked in protest at his weight.

'Do you really imagine I want to spend days kicking my heels in this midden? Why do you think John gave me Gastmere? It wasn't for my own amusement. He knows half the barons in the land are plotting rebellion against him and he wants the land in the hands of loyal men he can trust, strong men who can put down any sign of discontent.'

Raoul still couldn't see where this conversation was leading. To cover his confusion, he rose and refilled his goblet from the flagon on the side table. He glanced towards the casement of the solar where Hugh was standing gazing morosely out at the rain which was falling harder than ever. Even though he had his back to Raoul, it was plain from his hunched shoulders that he was sulking. Hugh considered a day without hunting or hawking was a day completely wasted. Raoul hadn't known either of the brothers long, but he'd spent enough time with Hugh to realize that hunting was the only thing that filled his head, whether he was awake or asleep.

Osborn's eyes narrowed. 'John gave me this land, because I am one of the few men he trusts, so the question is, Raoul, what does John think to gain by sending you here?'

Raoul flinched. So that was it. Osborn wasn't stupid, far from it, and he'd been long enough in the service of kings to know that when a monarch invites you to take one of his courtiers into your service, it isn't to teach him table manners.

There was little to be gained by lying to Osborn, not that Raoul wasn't a master of fabrication. You didn't claw your way up to becoming one of the king's favourites without learning a few useful skills. But he suspected Osborn had already half guessed the truth and he couldn't afford to alienate him by letting him think he was being treated as a fool.

Raoul wandered back to the long table and sat down on one of the benches opposite Osborn.

'You know that ever since the Interdict was pronounced the Pope has made no secret of the fact that he was backing the cause of Philip of France against John?'

'The Pope has no right to try to impose his cardinal on an English Church!' Osborn snapped. 'Now he thinks to plot with England's enemies.'

'Yes, yes.' Raoul waved a long, elegant hand. 'But the Pope argues that John is Philip's vassal and John did wage war against Philip in Aquitaine.'

'Aquitaine belongs to John; it was his mother's land. We fought to take back what was stolen from England.' Osborn swung forward in his chair and glared at Raoul. But Raoul had faced worst tempers than Osborn's.

'No one doubts your loyalty, my lord,' he said calmly. 'But every day John is receiving reports that England is swarming with Philip's spies who are reporting back on where and how he might best land his army. Now John has learned Philip is planning to send *agents provocateurs* to stir up the population to fight for him when he does land, as well as envoys who will try to persuade the rebel English barons to side with France.'

'Does John think I would side with France, after all I did for him in Aquitaine?' Osborn burst out furiously. He leapt from his chair and paced up and down the room. 'It was my skill and experience that helped him capture the castle at Montauban. It was me who ordered the escaping rebels to be hunted down before they could join forces with Philip's men.'

'I can swear to that,' Hugh said, turning back from the window, having at last been distracted from the rain. 'I served with my brother and I can assure you there was not a rebel left alive when we were done. We even rooted out those who'd gone to ground in the monastery, and then burned the monastery to ashes as a lesson to teach all of Aquitaine what happens to men who rebel against their lord. It was my brother who gave the orders and taught John's subjects the duty they owed to their king. There's not a man more loyal to John than Osborn.'

'Which is exactly why John put this manor in his hands,' Raoul said, trying to keep the note of exasperation from his voice. Hugh praised his brother more often than a love-sick maid extols her swain, but then Hugh didn't have a thought in his head that Osborn hadn't put there.

Raoul turned back to Osborn. 'This is the part of England he fears for the most. The sea voyage from France to Norfolk is many days longer and more dangerous than the voyage across to the southern ports, and for that very reason most of John's advisers believe that Philip will try to land the bulk of his troops in the south. But there are some who believe that the spies are not being landed through the southern ports; they are too closely guarded. Anyone being put ashore in these parts could dissolve into the marshland mists in the blink of an eye, but they would have to have a contact here. No stranger could find their way through the marshes alone and they'd need someone who could help them find the people they want to meet. John believes . . .' Raoul hesitated, then decided he might as well tell all. 'John believes that there is a traitor in these parts, perhaps even in this manor. He sent me to root him out.'

Hugh's hand jerked so violently that it sent Raoul's goblet spinning down on to one of the silk rugs. Hugh ignored the dark red puddle of wine sinking into it.

'The gelding! I knew it. I never trusted him. Raffaele's a foreigner; he's bound to side with England's enemies. What else can you expect but cowardly treachery from a man who isn't even a real man at all? You should dismiss him at once, brother.'

Raoul shook his head. 'No, if it is him, we need to keep him close till we have proof. Dismiss no one, whatever your suspicions. Sooner or later they will show their hand, and when they do, God have mercy on their souls, for John will show no mercy to their miserable bodies.'

But heaven knows when that will be, Raoul thought bitterly, for the truth was that however confidently he had assured John he could discover the traitor, he had no more idea how to go about it than of how to bake a pie or wash a shirt. So far, he'd discovered precisely nothing. Even if the traitor was Master Raffaele, how on earth did one set about getting him, or anyone for that matter, to betray themselves? One could hardly walk up to the fellow and ask him outright. Raoul only hoped that now he knew, Osborn would do the job for him . . . oh, and, of course, leave Raoul to claim the credit.

Day of the Full Moon, May 1211

Beans – a distillation of the bean plant when drunk will make a plain woman beautiful. If a mortal has warts, he rubs the wart on the lining of a bean case then buries it. As it rots, so will the wart fall from his skin.

But the scent of a bean flower will cause evil dreams and if any should fall asleep in a bean field he will suffer terrifying visions and after go mad. And if one bean in a row should come up white, then there will be a death in the household of he who planted it.

Beans must be eaten at funerals to keep the ghosts of the dead from lingering about the living. And the dried pods are rattled to drive away evil spirits.

In ancient times, when a human sacrifice was chosen, lots were drawn and the one who drew the black bean from the pot of white beans, drew forth his own death. What think you then: does death lie in his own hand to choose, or do his fingers reach for it because it is ordained they must?

The Mandrake's Herbal

Birth and Death

'No, no, take it away. I don't want to hold it.' Elena turned her face away from the bundle Gytha was holding out to her, and stared at the rough wattle wall.

'Bless you, the bairn's not an *it*,' Gytha chuckled. 'You've a boy, a beautiful, healthy boy, just like I told you. He's a mite on the scrawny side, babies born at green mist time always are, but he'll fatten up nicely on your milk once you get some good fresh meat inside you.'

Elena's mother-in-law, Joan, sniffed disparagingly. 'It's well known May's the unluckiest month to birth a bairn. You'll never rear a May baby, that's what my mother always said; too sickly. If Athan had listened to me –'

'Hush! Don't be telling the poor lass that,' Marion muttered, but Elena could see from her anxious expression she agreed with every word.

Her mother-in-law's tiny cottage was heaving with women. Her own mother, together with Joan, Marion, Gytha and two clucking neighbours, all bustled over her where she lay in the single room. Elena felt as if she was a small child again, lost among the legs and wheels of the crowded market place.

She lay on the beaten earth floor, her arms and legs too heavy to move. Her mother still supported her against her chest as she dabbed away at Elena's sweaty forehead with a rag, making little crooning noises as if Elena was herself a newborn again. Elena's buttocks were sore and numb from pressing against the hard, cold floor.

When the pains had come hard upon her, the women had hauled her off the low bed, scraped back the rushes and, pulling her shift up to her breasts, laid her bare loins against the cold, damp earth, so that she could take strength from Mother Earth from whence all men spring. It was how Gastmere women had given birth for generations and even Elena knew better than to protest against it. Now she was desperate to return to the bed, to curl up with her pain and misery and shut them all out, but she was too exhausted to drag herself there.

'Come on, my sweeting,' Gytha coaxed. 'I know you're worn out, but just let the bairn suckle, then you can sleep. He needs his mam's first milk. I'll help you hold him if you're afeared of dropping the mite.'

Gytha tried to push the mewling infant towards Elena, but she lifted her arm, warding him off as if he was a stick raised to beat her.

'Get him away from me,' she sobbed. 'I don't want him. I don't want to look at him.'

The women gasped and spat on their fingers to ward off the evil that would surely follow her words.

'That's a wicked thing to say,' her mother scolded, pinching Elena hard on the arm, as she used to do when Elena was a child and shamed her mother by misbehaving in front of the neighbours. 'Do you want to tempt the faerie folk to take him and leave you a changeling?'

She glanced over at the empty cradle into which Gytha had already laid a mistletoe twig and sprinkled salt to prevent the faeries from abducting the child.

'I do, I do, I want them to take him,' Elena wailed.

Her mother gasped in horror, crossing herself and moaning, 'Mary the Holy Mother and all the saints defend us. She doesn't know what she's saying.'

Gytha rapped Elena sharply three times on the mouth. 'Don't speak so, they'll hear you and take him.'

Joan pursed her lips. 'I knew it! I knew she'd never make a good mother. I warned Athan, but did he listen? You should have heard some of the wicked things she was saying before the poor lamb was even born. It was enough to mark the babe in her belly for life. It's a wonder he hasn't come out with two heads and a tail.'

'She'll feel different when she feels the bairn pull on her teats,' a neighbour said soothingly. She patted Joan's shoulder as if to comfort her for the distress of having such an unnatural daughter-in-law.

Although the women had wiped the baby, Elena could still smell the stench of birth mucus and her own blood on him. They wouldn't wash him with water. *Never wash a child's hands until he's a year old, else he'll not be able to gather any wealth.* Joan had kept reminding her of that and a hundred more commandments besides in these past few months, as if that would somehow allay Elena's fears about the child she was carrying.

But nothing could do that. The mandrake had done all that Gytha promised. It had shown her the end of her dream, and she was certain now, as she had been for weeks, that she was destined to murder her own child.

Elena lay on the cold floor as Gytha scrubbed the blood and mucus from her thighs with a hank of straw.

Her mother-in-law came bustling back into the cottage carrying a small pestle. 'I've just been to tell my bees there's a new babe in the family. Now we must smear her paps with honey and butter. Should be the first thing the poor bairn tastes, so the bees'll lend him strength and sweeten his nature.'

Elena felt the front of her sodden shift being pulled open. She tried to push them away, but her mother firmly held her hands, as her mother-in-law roughly anointed her sore breasts with a sticky mess of honey and butter.

'Butter to bless him with good health. And honey to keep the poor mite from the faeries.' Joan shook her head grimly as she said it, as if the precaution would be quite unnecessary if Elena hadn't so wantonly tempted the evil ones.

They held Elena tightly so that she couldn't push the child away. She felt the tiny face held against her breast, the warmth of the cheek, the nuzzling, then the soft lips fastening on her nipple. The hot little mouth pulling at her sent waves first of pain then of pleasure through her, like Athan had done that very first night. She felt her body relaxing towards this tiny, warm little bundle pressing into her bare belly. She pulled her arms free and cradled her son in her arms, as her resolve not to touch him melted away like butter in the sun.

But even in that moment as she fell hopelessly in love with her precious baby, even then, she heard herself screaming, 'No, no, I mustn't. I mustn't hold him. I'll hurt him, I know I will. I will kill him. I will murder my own little son.'

Raffe squinted up at the cold grey sky through the newly leafed branches of the trees. Thick clouds were tumbling across the flattened land and the light was beginning to fade. From his vantage point on the small rise he could see the cog-ship rolling at its anchor in the haven of Breydon Water. Wriggling forward, he peered down into the marshes that fringed the edge of the solid land, but could see nothing moving among the tall rushes. He didn't really expect to, a dozen little boats could have been hidden in the deep marsh gullies and you'd never see them until they emerged into the open waters of the bay.

'They'll not stir till it's good 'n' dark,' a voice growled behind him.

Raffe whipped round and was mortified to hear a deep chuckle. He hadn't heard Talbot creep up on him. The old soldier's legs were bowed as a barrel hoop, but he could still move as quietly as an assassin.

Talbot, his hood pulled low over his craggy face, shuffled his backside into the shelter of the trees next to where Raffe lay. By way of a greeting he punched Raffe on the arm with his great fist.

'I remember a time when you'd have had a knife across my throat afore I got within a lance's blow of you.'

'I knew you were there, you great ape,' Raffe lied. 'You make such a racket, they will have heard you coming out on the *Santa Katarina*.' He jerked his head towards the cog-ship out in the bay.

They'd known each other for twenty years, but the old

rogue hadn't changed since they'd first met at Acre. Talbot had been a sapper, one of the worst jobs in the Crusaders' army. Sappers burrowed under the walls of the city and lit fires beneath the stones to weaken the walls to make them collapse, while the defenders in the city hurled down any weapon they could on to their heads. And the Saracens would tunnel towards them from inside the city. If they met, the two sides would fight each other in the pitch darkness of those narrow tunnels. You had to be as tough and fearless as a mountain lion to survive that, and Talbot was.

Raffe grinned affectionately at him. 'But I didn't think to see you here. Your lads impatient for their money, are they?'

Talbot bridled indignantly, 'I came to watch your back, Bullock. If the marsh-men catch you spying on them and their cargo, your miserable carcass'll be lying at the bottom of some bog pool afore you can utter a curse. Whereas I can tell them you're a just a poor simple clod who wouldn't know his own arse if I wasn't there to kick it. They've only got to look at you to see the truth of that.'

If any other man had said as much to Raffe he would have laid him out cold, but instead he merely grinned. What Talbot couldn't fight his way out of with his great fists he could talk his way out of, at least with ordinary men. He wasn't quite so skilled in talking his way out of trouble with the nobility. Back in the Holy Land, Talbot would have found himself swinging from the gallows, hanged by his own commander, if it hadn't been for Raffe. It was the kind of debt that forged an instant and eternal friendship between the most unlikely of strangers.

And Raffe had known he could rely on Talbot to get him word when the *Santa Katarina* was sighted off the coast. He had a network of street urchins and boatmen who knew every inch of the river from Norwich to Yarmouth. A dog couldn't fart in Yarmouth without Talbot getting wind of it in Norwich. Through this web of rogues, Talbot could obtain anything that a man could pay for, though it was wisest not to enquire as to the source, that is, if you wanted to keep your guts safely in your belly.

'Any sign of this man you're looking for?' Talbot asked.

'Not yet, but he'll be here. As soon as I discover who the traitor is, I'll swear on oath to the sheriff in Norwich about what I heard him say and he'll be in chains within the day. With luck this night's work will rid us of Osborn too. John is bound to take the manor back from him, once this traitor is arrested. After all, a lord who doesn't even possess the wit to discover that his own men are plotting treason is hardly competent to have oversight of the king's lands. And John will take it very ill, that Osborn has allowed this rebellion to fester under his roof.'

Talbot squinted at him. 'Way I see it, you wanted rid of that bastard Osborn from the outset, so why didn't you tell what you knew straightway? If you heard this man so plainly, how is it you didn't recognize the voice? Even if you didn't know it then, you've surely heard it since.'

Raffe hesitated. He wouldn't trust Talbot with a clipped farthing if money was involved, but he would wager his life on the man's ability to keep his own counsel.

'If you want the truth I didn't hear what was said. It was a girl in the manor, a villein, she reported it to me. But she thinks one of the men may have seen her, glimpsed her anyway. If he's still at liberty when he discovers that he was overheard, her life wouldn't be worth the dirt on his shoe. That's why I need proof before I can act. I'll tell the sheriff I heard what was said, and I won't need to mention her.'

'So you'd lie for this lass,' Talbot grinned. 'Pretty, is she?'

'I'd lie to save a life,' Raffe snapped. 'And we both know it wouldn't be the first time I've done that, don't we?'

Mortals are strange creatures; they cling to life even when that life is nothing but pain and misery, yet they will throw away their lives for a word, an idea, even a flag. Wolves piss to mark their territory. Smell the stench of another pack and wolves will quietly slink away. Why risk a fight when it might maim or kill you? But humans will slash and slaughter in their thousands to plant their little piece of cloth on a hill or hang it from a battlement. We mandrakes can give them victory, but on whom shall we bestow it? For both sides will pronounce their own cause just. And which is the brave man and who is the traitor? You must choose; we mandrakes never do. We simply give them both what in their hearts they truly crave – the illusion of a glorious death, which the poor fools imagine is immortality.

You don't believe me. Let me show you. Two old soldiers lying side by side on the hill watch the little ship bobbing out in the bay. The sailors on the ship watch the shore. They all wait impatiently for the blessed cloak of darkness to cover their wretched little deeds, but the sun will not be hurried by the whims of men.

The cog-ship shuddered as the racing tide twisted her against her anchor ropes. Hunched under the castle of the ship, Faramond shivered miserably in the wet wind, which had grown sharper as the light began to fade across the Norfolk marshes. Although they were sheltered from the great ocean waves behind the sandy island of Yarmouth, the lurching of the ship seemed even worse now that they were at anchor. The three rivers raced into the basin of water and the sea tide pushed hard against them, creating a turbulence that felt more violent than any at sea.

Faramond tried to shuffle downwind of the breeze which blew charcoal smoke and the stench of pickled pork across his face, but he could not leave the safety of the shadows in the ship's stern and the best he could do to escape the nauseating stench was pull his cloak over his mouth and nose. As soon as the *Santa Katarina* had come within sight of the English coast, the five Frenchmen had been forced to spend the daylight hours squatting in the stern under the castle of the ship, well out of sight. Even had they dressed in the thin, patched clothes of the sailors, a casual observer would see from the way they staggered like newborn calves across the rolling deck that they were not accustomed to life at sea.

The captain cursed as he struggled to reach round the huddle of men to grab a coil of rope.

'How much longer must we sit here?' one of the men grumbled loudly.

The captain grabbed him by the shoulder. 'I told you, keep your mouth shut. Sound travels across water.' He squinted over to the horizon where the pale sun was sinking beneath the waves. 'Be a while yet before we get the sign, they'll not risk crossing open water till it's good and dark. So you'd best settle down and get some sleep. It'll be the last chance you'll have to close your eyes tonight. Once you're on the move, your head will think your eyelids have been hacked off.'

Another man grasped his shirt and whispered, 'They will come tonight, you're sure of this?'

'God's bollocks, those sons of bitches had better be here. I'm not hanging around with you lot on board, that I can promise you.'

The man's eyes narrowed with anxiety. 'But if something happens to prevent –'

'They'll be here,' the captain said firmly, as if he was trying to pacify a child. 'They'll have had watchers posted ever since we sighted land. They'll not risk leaving us here longer than they have to.'

He edged away and strode rapidly towards the bow, as if trying to put as much distance as possible between him and his unwelcome cargo.

The men made pretence at closing their eyes, but Faramond knew they could no more sleep than he could. It was not just the stiffness of their bodies, the hard boards and the cold keeping them awake; God knows they were used to worse than that. No, what would not let them rest was the fear of what might happen in the next few hours, days and weeks. They'd had plenty of time to think during the voyage, and imagine too – imagine just what could happen to a man trapped in a foreign land among his mortal enemies. Approach the wrong person or betray yourself by the wrong word and death would be the least of your troubles.

It was not for nothing that King John of Anjou was known far and wide as the worst of the Devil's brood. Rumour abounded in France that John had ordered Hubert de Burgh to castrate his sixteen-year-old nephew, Arthur, the rightful heir to Anjou, and to gouge out his eyes as the lad lay chained and starving to death in John's dungeon at Falaise. And when Hubert had refused, John had brought the boy to his castle at Rouen and kept him imprisoned there. One night at Easter, when John was drunk after dinner, he had slain his nephew with his own hand and, tying a weighty stone to the corpse, had cast it into the River Seine. If a man could so cruelly plot the murder of his own kin, the exquisite torture he might devise for a French spy, before death mercifully released the victim, was beyond any normal man's imagination.

And Faramond and his companions would be depending for their very lives on strangers whose loyalty was at best dubious, for hadn't they already betrayed their own king? A man who might have been on your side yesterday could just as easily betray you tomorrow. Some men change their allegiances swifter than birds in flight change direction.

Yet, as Faramond had tried so hard to convince his beloved wife, this was a just war, a noble cause to depose a wicked tyrant. Even the Pope had denounced him. Any man who rid the world of King John, an enemy of God and the Holy Mother Church, would be assured of the papal blessing. Of course, the Pontiff had not said as much in so many words, but his meaning was clear to all, and thus it followed that any man who helped to depose this tyrant would be blessed by God Himself.

Faramond had repeated these arguments to himself as he lay awake on the tossing ship, retching over and over again. *God was on their side.* And now, sick with fear at what the coming hours would hold, he tried to remind himself of that again, but he knew all the tricks of rhetoric and he could not convince himself this was God's work as easily as he could persuade others. All he could think of, as he sat shivering on that deck, was capture, humiliation, torture and then . . .

St Julian and all the saints, I beseech you protect me. He patted at the front of his tunic, feeling for the small silver reliquary containing a tiny fragment of the bone of St Julian of Brioude pinned beneath a piece of polished rock crystal. His wife had sold all the jewels she owned to buy the relic, so desperate was she to keep her husband safe.

One of the deckhands who had been keeping watch frantically beckoned to the captain, who was at his side in an instant, peering out towards the land. It was dark now and only the tiny red rubies of flame strung across the rise above the marshes marked out the village fires. The deckhand was pointing at something out on the marsh, and the captain nodded. He raised a lantern, allowing the light to shine out over the rail before lowering it hastily, repeating the signal several times in quick succession.

Then, sidling across to where Faramond and the other men sat, he shook the nearest man awake.

'Boats are on their way. So be ready to move quickly. And not a sound, not till they tell you it's safe. The marsh has many ears.'

As quietly as they could, Faramond and the others fastened their cloaks ready, and checked for the hundredth time that their scrips and bundles were securely fastened. They were travelling light, no papers, only a few spare clothes, and a bite or two to eat. They carried nothing which could slow them down if they had to run, except the round flat silver ingots strapped to their chests inside their shirts. Those were cumbersome, and already chafing the skin. But they were indispensable; men would have to be paid and paid well.

The captain, motioning them to keep low, beckoned them across to the gap in the rail, where a rope ladder was already being rolled out. Faramond was so stiff from the cold he could hardly stand up, never mind keep his balance on the rolling deck. In the end he dropped to his knees and crawled across it. Reaching the safety of the rail, he crouched, peering through the gap.

As his eyes accustomed themselves to the darkness, he saw three shapes below moving across the water towards the ship. He couldn't hear the oars of the little craft entering the water above the noise of wind singing through the rigging of the ship and the constant slapping of the waves against her hold. But the oarsmen were plainly skilled at their craft and that knowledge at least gave him comfort.

His stomach had tightened so much it hurt. He glanced over the rail. The rope ladder was flapping wildly against the boat each time she yawed. It seemed a very long way down. In the darkness, it looked as if the ship was riding upon a vast mass of writhing black maggots feeding on some gigantic beast that lay dead beneath. Faramond shivered, and not just from the cold.

The first of the boats was drawing alongside. A man was standing up at the back of the craft, rowing with a single oar that he rocked from side to side, trying to bring the little boat level so that the man in the bow could catch the rope from the ship. Just as the deckhand was about to toss it down to him, there was a sudden sharp pip-pip-pip call like that of a plover from the boat behind. Then Faramond saw to his alarm that just as swiftly as they had drawn alongside, the boats were retreating back into the darkness.

'Wait, where are you going?' Faramond yelled, completely forgetting the captain's warning for silence, but the captain was standing transfixed, staring up the haven towards the channel between the island of Yarmouth and the mainland.

He began barking orders. Before he realized what was happening, Faramond felt himself in the grip of powerful hands, being forced towards an open hatch.

'Get in there, hide, hide!'

He was pushed down the rickety wooden ladder with such force that he lost his footing half-way down and fell, landing in thick, slimy water. It was only a foot or so deep, but the planks beneath were so slippery he couldn't get a footing to stand up. For a moment he thought the fall had blinded him for he had rarely known such complete darkness, but he could hear the curses of his companions as they splashed around him in the filth. A foul stench engulfed him, making him choke. It was as if he had been thrown into a lake of rotten eggs. The air was rasping in his chest as he struggled to breathe. Then he heard the grating over his head being pushed back into place.

A voice that he recognized as the captain's yelled down, 'If you want to live, keep as still and quiet as dead men. There's a ship, one of King John's, bearing straight for us. If they board us . . .'

If the captain said more, Faramond didn't hear him, for a wooden hatch was slammed down on top of the grate and they heard the bolts being shot home.

The men in the hold did as they were bid: despite the misery of sitting in the freezing water, they instantly ceased splashing about trying to stand. The water sloshed back and forth over their backs as the ship rolled, and the crashing of the waves breaking on the wooden hull outside reverberated through the darkness. Above them they could hear shouts and bellowed commands, but the thick wood of the deck muffled the sound. Faramond was aware of the noisy gulping of the others around him, their lungs aching from the struggle to breathe through the gas that rose from the stinking water.

Then something heavy grated against the timbers of the hull. Had the ship caught up with them? Were the king's soldiers leaping aboard, prepared to search every foot of the *Santa Katarina*? Despite the captain's warning, Faramond crawled through the stinking water, feeling his way cautiously towards the hull, where no light would fall on him if the hatch was opened. Around him he could hear the others doing the same, cursing under their breath as their hands and limbs were grazed on the rough beams of the ship.

They were listening hard for the sounds of feet above them, boxes being overturned or arguments breaking out, but they could hear nothing above the sound of the water, not even voices. Perhaps the captain had managed to persuade the king's men that the barrels of wine and other stores on the deck were all the cargo he carried. It was so dark that Faramond's eyeballs hurt as he strained to see into the blackness above, searching desperately for that first crack of light that might give them warning the hatch was being opened.

Then he saw it, a line of orange so bright and yet so thin he thought for a moment his eyes were playing tricks because he was staring too hard. He saw another line of light flickering. He shrank back, wondering if he should duck his head below the water and how long he could hold his breath if he did. But the light was not coming from where he thought the hatch was, though in the darkness it was hard to remember. Then he smelt it, just a whisper of it; the stench from the water was so overpowering that it was hard to be sure and yet there was a waft of something new . . .

'Smoke!' someone yelled from the darkness. 'They've set the ship afire.'

Every man tried to beat his way through the water to the ladder. They were groping around for it in the darkness, catching hold of beams and the bodies of the other men, until with a cry someone felt it. Faramond himself grabbed hold of it just moments later and found other hands as cold as the dead also grasping the ladder and trying to force themselves on to the rungs. But the first man was already at the top. They could hear him battering at the grill, shouting and yelling.

Another climbed up, pitching him off into the water; he fell heavily with a single scream, instantly followed by silence.

'It won't shift. They've locked it! They've locked us in!'

'Let me try,' others shouted, but Faramond wasn't one of

them. He splashed and crawled his way back towards the side of the hull. Fumbling for his knife, he started hacking at the wood, trying beyond all reason to make a hole in the ship's timbers. As he did so, he knew it was useless. Even if he could chip his way through the wood with his small knife, what chance would he have of making a hole big enough to crawl through before the water poured in and dragged them all to the bottom? Yet still he slashed away, desperately trying to split the salt-hardened timber.

Around him he could hear men screaming or praying. Above them, louder by far now than the crash of the waves, was the roar of the flames as they raced through the oil-soaked and tar-coated timbers. Smoke was trickling down into the hold, mixing with the bilge gas. Faramond was choking. As the timber above their heads blazed, the heat rolled down as if they were trapped inside a vast oven.

Faramond clutched his reliquary through his shirt. 'Holy and blessed St Julian, save me, save me!'

There was a huge crash as the mast toppled into the sea, followed by another as the castle collapsed on to the deck, driving the timbers into the hold below. The last thing Faramond saw was the blinding orange flames licking over a great beam of wood as it hurtled towards his face. It struck him with a force that was almost merciful, sending the poor wretch instantly into the darkness from which there can be no return.

As soon as Talbot's sharp eyes had seen the three tiny craft creep out of the marshes and glide towards the ship, he had made his way gingerly down the hillside, the better to see where they might put ashore.

Raffe's whole attention was directed towards the land, trying to see if the traitor was also watching for the men to be landed. So it wasn't until he glanced back at the water to mark the progress of the little boats that he saw the king's ship. It was racing up towards the *Santa Katarina*.

The captain and crew on board the *Katarina* had seen it too. They had already launched their shore boat and were sculling away from their ship, but not before the crew had cut her anchor and tossed their blazing torches into rope and tar barrels they'd stacked on the deck. The shore boat disappeared up the River Bure and melted into the darkness as the flames on the ship took hold, lighting up the sea around. Later the captain and the crew would claim alms and shelter as poor shipwrecked sailors, for what could anyone prove against them, now that all the evidence was going up in smoke?

But aboard the king's ship the sailors and soldiers had far more to worry about than the vanishing craft. Every man aboard was racing to try to lower the sail and bring their vessel about before they collided with the drifting fire-ship. They finally managed to steer their boat clear of the *Katarina*, but only just. They dropped anchor at a safe distance where wind and tide would not drive the blazing ship into their own vessel.

There was no use in the king's men trying to board the *Katarina* now. The fire had taken hold from bow to stern, sending flames and smoke leaping into the tar-black sky. Only the sea could dowse those flames now and it would do so soon when the whole flaming ball sank beneath the waves for ever, carrying all her secrets with it.

This time Raffe heard the crackle of twigs as Talbot slipped back into the thicket beside him.

'It's too late. The crew got off the ship, but the Skeggs didn't.'

Talbot, like most Englishmen, had been born hating the French, calling their soldiers 'Yellow Skeggs' in mockery of their emblem the fleur-de-lis, but despite this there was a rare note of pity in his voice.

Raffe groaned. 'The king's ship must have been lying in wait, thinking to catch all involved, but how the hell did John's men find out?'

'Don't look at me! Maybe one of the marsh-men tipped

them off,' Talbot said. 'There's always those ready to take money from both sides, if they can get away with it. You can't trust a marsh-man, the only loyalty he has is to his own pocket.'

There were many who had cause to say the same thing of Talbot, but Raffe wasn't one of them, not yet, anyway.

Talbot nodded his head towards the ship blazing in the darkness. 'I reckon that bastard of a captain cut those poor runts' throats when he saw what was afoot. Didn't fancy being caught red-handed smuggling Skeggs into England and couldn't risk leaving them alive to talk after he scuttled off. Far as I could see, no one jumped overboard, and if they were alive they'd jump whether or not they could swim. Any man would sooner drown than burn.'

The two men were silent for a moment. They had witnessed the agony of flames before, had heard the screams, seen the blistered flesh, still saw it in their nightmares. The Saracens at Acre had a terrible weapon. Greek fire, they called it. They'd throw clay pots against the wooden siege towers and down on to the attacking men. The pots burst into flames and burned with a fire as fierce as a blacksmith's furnace. It stuck to wood, leather, metal, flesh, everything. Water wouldn't extinguish it, only vinegar, and where do you get that in the midst of a battle? They'd seen men reeling away, blinded, their faces aflame, roasting alive in their own armour, until they'd fallen on the mercy of a spear or sword. Both men knew only too well what a man would do to end the agony of burning.

Talbot tugged urgently at Raffe's arm. 'Look there, between those trees.'

Raffe glanced across at the rise. A lone figure sat on horse-back, watching the burning ship. Raffe, motioning Talbot to follow, crept forward. It was dark, but even so Raffe could see from the cut of the long, heavy cloak that this was no marsh-man.

The horse shuffled restlessly sideways. Its rider gathered the reins and turned the beast's head, preparing to leave. As he looked back for one last time at the ship, the light from the burning vessel revealed the full profile of the man's face. It was so familiar that Raffe could have drawn it from memory.

'God's blood,' he breathed. 'Do you see who that is? That's Hugh, that's Osborn's brother.'

Talbot threw his arm over Raffe, pressing his head down hard into the dirt, just as Hugh dug his spurs into his horse's flanks and cantered off straight past the thicket in which they were sheltering. As soon as the muffled sound of hoof-beats had faded, Raffe sat up, brushing dried leaves from his face and spitting out bits of twig.

Talbot whistled through his teeth. 'So that's your traitor. I always hated the bugger.'

Raffe shook his head in disbelief. 'Unless I'd seen it with my own eyes, I'd never have believed it. I knew it had to be one of Osborn's men, but his own brother! Satan's arse, Hugh fought for John in Aquitaine.'

'As did you,' Talbot reminded him. 'And it didn't make you love the bastard.'

'I loathe John, but I'd never give aid to England's enemies, not even to save my own life.'

Talbot grunted. 'Easy to say when your life's not at stake. Thing is, what are you going to do now? Seems to me it's still your word against Hugh's, or rather that girl of yours. And –'

Raffe smashed his fist into the palm of his hand. 'And I can't prove a bloody thing against Hugh. If I could have seen him with this Faramond, or the king's men had taken even one of the Frenchmen alive and questioned him, he might have given them Hugh's name. But Osborn will never hear a word said against his brother. If there's one thing in this world he has any feelings for at all, it's that little whelp.'

Raffe grabbed a clump of grass and ripped it from the ground in frustration. His hope of seeing the whole pack of them turned out of the manor had slipped so far from his grasp, he couldn't see how to retrieve it.

'Thing is,' Talbot said, 'sooner or later Hugh's going to

start wondering who tipped off the king's men, and I reckon he'll get to thinking that the girl did overhear what was said after all and told someone. If you've any feelings at all for her, you'd best see she stays well hidden out of his way.'

Raffe raked his fingers through his hair. God in heaven, how much more could go wrong? At least Elena was in the village, and Hugh was not likely to soil his boots by mixing with cottagers from Gastmere. He just prayed Elena would have the sense to stay away from the manor.

Both men stared in silence over the darkened bay. The flames reflected on the glassy black water danced around the stricken ship like imps at a witches' Sabbath. Even as the two men watched, the ship rolled over on its side with a mighty crash. As waves broke over the deck, the flames clawed higher in the sky as if they were desperately trying to escape the sea. But it was only for a moment, then the water closed over it and the *Santa Katarina* and all she contained was pulled down and down into the cold black depths.

7th Day after the New Moon, June 1211

Rowan – was once known as *raun,* meaning charm, for it is a powerful weapon against witches and the evil eye.

Raun tree and red thread, hold the witches all in dread.

The druids burn rowan to summon the spirits to battle, or to force them to answer questions. Mortals often plant the tree near the door of a house so that no evil may enter it. On Quarter Days, when the spirits of mischief are most active, mortals lay a rowan sprig over the lintel of doors and windows, so that evil spirits cannot enter. Some mortals wear necklaces of rowan wood and hang garlands of it in the cattle byres or over the horns of a beast that they fear has been overlooked by the evil eye.

Those whose milk is witched so that it will not turn to butter had best get themselves a churn made from rowan wood. If their horse is bewitched and throws the rider, it may be tamed with a rowan whip. But those who really fear the spirits seek out the flying rowan, the tree whose roots do not touch the earth, but grows in the cleft of a rock or on another tree, for its wood is the most powerful of them all.

But take heed, mortals, rowan will protect you from the evils of men, but it will not protect you from a mandrake's power, for we are neither witches nor spirits to be commanded. We are gods.

The Mandrake's Herbal

The Shearing

'You'll never wind the bairn like that,' Athan's mother declared, scooping the baby from Elena's arms and patting him briskly on his back.

The infant stopped grizzling and looked vaguely surprised.

'You'll join the other women in the barn soon as you've finished here,' Joan said. It was a command, not a question. 'They'll help you with the little one.'

What you really mean is, I can't be trusted to look after him, Elena thought, but she held her tongue and merely nodded. It was the first time since the baby had been born that she would spend the day away from her mother-in-law. With the sheep-shearing about to begin and ploughing still to be done and the first haymaking starting in the forward meadows, every man, woman and child was pressed into labour, no matter what their age or infirmity.

Athan had left for the fields at ghost light, before the sun was even visible above the dark fringed marshes. Every precious hour of daylight had to be used while the weather held fair. But his mother continued to linger at the door, still watching Elena as a fox watches a rabbit, waiting for it to come close enough to pounce.

Please just go, Elena willed her.

'Remember to take clean rags, he'll need changing.'

Elena nodded to the bundle she'd made ready. 'I have them. Hadn't you better make haste? Marion'll not be best pleased if you're late.'

Joan sniffed. 'Just because that harlot is keeping the bailiff's bed warm, doesn't give her the right –'

She broke off abruptly as Marion and some of the other women called out to her as they passed the open door of the cottage. Pausing only to issue a further list of instructions about the care of her grandson, she sped off to catch up with them, only too eager to regale them with the latest of Elena's failings as wife and mother.

Peace seemed to roll in through the open door in the wake of Joan's departure. Elena took her son in her arms and gently kissed his face. His eyes were heavy with sleep, but the lids were almost transparent so that the blue of his eyes glowed through them like a jewel through gauze. She stroked the soft apricot down on his warm head and slid her finger into the tiny fist, feeling the fingers curl tightly round her own as if he knew without looking that it was his mother's hand.

The bairn, that's what they all called him. Athan said he had chosen a name, but Joan declared it was bad luck to say it out loud before the baptism in case a stranger or the faerie folk should learn it and use it to witch the child before his name was sanctified by the Church. At his baptism Athan would whisper it to the priest at the font, but only when the priest proclaimed it to the congregation would Elena knew what they were going to call her baby.

She already had a name in her heart for him, though she would never be allowed to use it. She whispered it sometimes when she was sure no one would hear her, a secret name because she adored him and he was *her* son. But she knew that any name she gave the child would not keep him safe, only the Church, only baptism could do that. But when would he be baptized?

With the Interdict and all the churches closed and half the priests fled or imprisoned, no infant could be christened. How many months more would they have to call him *the bairn*? And all that time he would be unprotected from witches who could cast the evil eye on him and faerie folk who might snatch him, and from demons and monsters who would devour his soul. If he died before he could be made a child of Christ, his soul would wander lost for ever; he would be buried at the crossroads or the hundred boundary where all the suicides, madmen and murderers lay.

Once, years ago, Joan had told her, a girl in the village had given birth to a boy and kept it hidden in mortal fear of her husband for he had been away at the Holy Wars when it was conceived, so he would know it was none of his getting. The poor little mite had died not long after. The sexton had found the mother trying to bury the tiny body in the churchyard, and had torn the corpse from her arms and buried it at the crossroads outside the village bounds, for he knew that if they did not take it out of Gastmere the soul of the unbaptized infant would wander through the village every night, rattling the doors and shutters trying to find a mother who would take it in.

Ever after travellers who had the misfortune to find themselves at that crossroads at night heard a baby wailing in great distress. If they were foolish enough to go closer to try to find the child, they saw a little infant white as bone, with large hollow eyes, burrowing out of the earth and crawling towards them on one leg and one arm, screaming so piercingly that horses and men alike were driven mad. Locals avoided the place after dark and if they had to travel that way always carried a sprig of rowan and a horse shoe to beat the creature away with, but many an unsuspecting traveller had been thrown from his horse, which had bolted at the shrieks.

Elena gazed down at the softly rounded cheeks, the tiny nose and pink plump lips wrinkling as if he still suckled in his sleep. She would never let them bury her son at some lonely crossroads in an unmarked grave. She would not have horses trample the ground above him or carts drive over him. She would not have them curse her beautiful angel or watch his decayed corpse crawling up out of the ground. But if she killed him, they would bury him there. They would drag his little body from her arms and bury him deep and alone in the cold, hard ground, without even a twig to mark where he lay.

As each day passed she loved him more and she knew it would only get harder to do what she must do. It had to be today. She could not wait for another. She must do it now, before it was too late. She must keep him safe – safe from them and above all safe from her, his own mother. Tying her baby tightly to her chest with her shawl, she slipped out of the house. The track was deserted. Everyone who was fit enough to walk was already at work in the fields or barns, but Elena was not making for the barn, she was walking as rapidly as she could in the direction of the forest.

A soft, warm breeze had sprung up with the setting sun. It rustled the leaves on the currant bushes and stirred the bright green shoots of the onions in their beds. Elena gently removed one of the two young pigeons from the little wicker cage hanging under the apple tree and carried the bird back into Athan's cottage. She sat down on a stool by the rough wooden table. The pigeon was struggling, flapping its wings fiercely in an effort to get away, but as she caught the wings and smoothed them back into a resting position with her fingers, the bird calmed and lay passively in her grip. Its bright black eye looked sideways at her and blinked. She could feel its tiny heart thumping beneath its soft warm feathers.

'Hush now,' she murmured, 'I'm not going to hurt you.'

Outside in the small wicker cage, its mate cooed in the hot evening sunshine. For a moment or two, Elena stroked the bird gently, calming it almost to a point where it was falling asleep in the warmth of the fire. Then Elena's right hand moved up to the bird's neck. In one deft movement, she twisted and pulled sharply. The pigeon flopped limp in her lap.

She began to pluck it at once. It is always easier when the body is still warm. She ripped the feathers out, letting them drift into a soft mound on a rag she had spread out at her feet. When the bird was clean, she took her knife and ripped open the belly, pulling out the guts before tossing the carcass whole into the iron pot that was already bubbling on the hearth.

Then she went outside to the little wicker cage where the second bird still cooed, its hope undiminished, as if expecting an answering call from its mate. Elena reached inside and gently removed it, soothing it in her hands as she carried it back to her stool next to the steaming pot.

Preparing meals was something she had done ever since she could walk, like every girl in Gastmere. Her mam had taught her, just as her mother taught her before that. Most days Elena hardly wasted a thought on it, as long as there was food to be prepared. Her hands worked steadily as her mind drifted off to other places. But now she suddenly recalled how as a tiny child she had watched her own mother cleaning a bird. The picture was as clear in her head as if she was still there in her mother's cottage, though she had never remembered it before. Fascinated, Elena had pulled herself up on to her wobbly little legs by clutching her mother's skirts. Then, standing unsteadily, she had watched, with the wonder that only a child can know, as the soft grey feathers drifted down in dizzy spirals over her mother's legs, only to be caught by the breeze and lifted again, like a thousand tiny birds in flight. She remembered how she'd reached out her chubby hand to catch them and had overbalanced and tumbled on to the rushes. Her mother, laughing, had bent down to haul her upright again, with big red-raw hands smelling of feathers and onions and blood.

Tears suddenly poured down Elena's face and she realized that she would never feel her own son's dimpled little hands clinging to her skirts as he pulled himself up, never hear him laugh as she blew a dandelion ball for him so that the seeds danced in the shaft of sunlight, and never fashion a little boat of bark for him to bat across a puddle. There were a thousand inconsequential things she would never do for him, trivial things that did not put food in his belly or warm clothes on his back. Silly, time-wasting things, that somehow at this moment mattered more than anything else in her life.

She heard the sound of voices outside and hastily scrubbed the tears from her eyes as the door opened. She tried to compose her face, pressing her hands together to stop them shaking. But she need not have troubled, for Joan didn't bother to glance at her.

'What possessed you to shut the door?' Joan snapped. 'That cooking fire'll have us all roasted alive.'

The older woman sank wearily down on the stool, looking every one of her forty-five years and more. Her face was caked with dust and sweat, and her grey-streaked hair had come loose from its bindings and clung damply to her forehead. Elena, still trembling, pushed a beaker of ale into her hand, while Joan fanned herself with the other. Her mother-in-law just about managed a curt nod, which Elena was willing to believe might be a thank you.

Joan gulped thirstily at the ale, draining the beaker before she spoke. 'You want to be grateful, my girl, you could work in the shade of the barn today. It was as hot as a baker's oven out in those fields, not so much as a pant of wind all day.'

Joan glanced out of the open door. The light had almost faded, and in the cottages opposite theirs, rushlights were already being lit.

'They'll have finished the shearing for the day. I thought my son would be home by now.'

'He's probably stopped off at the alewife with his friends,' Elena suggested quietly.

Joan immediately bridled. 'Would you begrudge him a drink to quench his thirst? You want to be thankful you don't have the husband I had. He'd have slept in the inn if I hadn't gone round to haul him out. You've got a jewel in my son and you want to remember that and count yourself lucky. I hope that supper's ready, the poor lad'll be famished enough to eat a horse and its cart.'

Elena was too drained to reply. She felt as if she was going to vomit each time she tried to think how to tell them what she'd done. She tried not to think, and concentrated on ladling out the pigeon and bean pottage into a bowl, which she handed to Joan. Joan sniffed at it dubiously and took a sip from her horn spoon. She wrinkled up her nose in distaste.

'Too much salt. We've haven't got it to waste, my girl. Not at the price those thieves are charging in the market.' She pulled out her knife and speared a piece of pigeon breast, stuffing it into her mouth.

Elena hung her head, saying nothing, but she noticed that for all Joan's grumblings the pottage was disappearing fast enough down her gullet.

Joan thrust the empty bowl at her to refill. 'At least you got my grandson to sleep before Athan comes home.' She nodded towards the hooded wooden cradle in the furthest corner of the cottage. 'You see, you can manage the bairn well enough when you try. You just give up too easily, my girl, that's your trouble.'

Both women glanced up as Athan's bulk filled the doorway. He stumbled across to the fire, rubbing his aching shoulders, pausing to plant a kiss first on his mother's cheek, then on his wife's.

Joan flapped her hands impatiently at Elena. 'Stop pawing him, it's food my son needs, not your kisses. Quickly now, before the poor lad faints with hunger.'

Elena filled the bowl from the steaming pot and Athan tucked in, grunting in appreciation as he shovelled the food down. As Joan had predicted, he was ravenous. His mother beamed and affectionately ruffled his hair as if he was still a small boy, though she had to reach up to do it.

Elena watched him too, her heart aching with love for him. Even now that the first flush of youthful excitement had worn off and they were in all but name an old married couple, she could not look at him without a little jolt of pleasure. She even loved the foolish things about him, like the way his sandy hair, slick with grease from the shearing, glistened in the firelight, or the childlike way he ran his finger round the wooden bowl to catch every drop of the juices.

He must have felt her watching, for he glanced over at her with a smile, his blue eyes vacant and untroubled, like a dog who is thinking only of a juicy bone. How could she start to tell him? How would she begin? Her mouth was dry. He'd understand, of course he would. He loved her. If she could just speak to Athan alone, then he could explain the whole thing to his mother. Athan would stand up for her. She knew he would . . . when it really mattered.

Joan was already nodding off, exhausted by the long day in the fields. Her head lolled against the wall. Her mouth hung open. Elena caught hold of Athan's hand, and with her finger pressed to her lips began to tug him towards the door. Athan, with a glance back at his sleeping mother, grinned broadly, and followed Elena outside.

The wind, which had been sleeping in the heat of the day, had finally begun to blow in earnest and was skimming the clouds across the moon. Before Elena could speak, Athan pulled her round into the dark space between two cottages and drew her into his arms, his breath hot on her neck.

'I've been missing you all day, my angel,' he whispered.

'Athan, I . . .' She had meant to explain she urgently needed to talk to him, but Athan stilled her lips with a long and hungry kiss.

Feeling his warm, tender mouth on hers, Elena couldn't help but respond. Her body ached for him. They had not made love once since she'd come to live in the cottage and she was as desperate for his touch as he was for hers. Today, more than ever, she longed for his comfort. She wanted him to hold her and tell her everything was all right. She needed him to clasp her so tightly in his arms that all the pain and misery would be pushed away. She clung to him, and he to her. Even if she'd still had the strength left to speak, no words came into her head except *I love you, Athan.*

It may have been a log spitting on the fire or just a mother's instinct that her son was up to no good which eventually woke Joan, but something made her start up and almost at once they heard her shrill voice calling them from the door.

Athan, a pained expression on his face, tried to ignore her, but it was useless. His mother's voice was like a dousing of icy water. They quickly pulled apart, straightening their clothes without looking at each other, and returned inside. Joan stared at them as they came in, a look of growing bewilderment on her face.

'Where's the bairn?' she demanded. 'You've not left him out there, have you? You've no business taking him out there at all. Night air's dangerous for a bairn.'

Athan shook his head. 'He's in his cradle asleep.'

'He's not,' Joan said adamantly. 'See for yourself, cradle's empty. That's why I thought you had him with you.'

Athan rushed over to the cradle, and threw back the covers. Then he lifted it, shaking it upside down as if the child was a lost coin that might have somehow rolled to the bottom. He stared wildly round the tiny, single-roomed cottage.

'Someone's taken him. A peddler!'

'Not while I've been home, they haven't,' Joan said. 'You think any peddler could get past me?'

'But you saw him in his cradle when you got home?'

'No . . .' Joan said thoughtfully, her eyes narrowing. 'I didn't see him. Elena told me he was asleep in the cradle, but I didn't see him.'

They both turned to stare at Elena who hadn't moved from the doorway. Athan rushed over to her, grasping her shoulders.

'After you put him down to sleep, did you see anyone near the cottage? Did you leave him to go to the privy?'

But Elena just stood there, her arms wrapped round herself. Athan shook her slightly to bring her to her senses and she flopped back and forth in his hands like a rag doll.

'Think, my angel, think! When did you last check the cradle?'

But still Elena couldn't speak or look at him. Only now that he had found the cradle empty did it finally seem true that her baby was gone. Up to then she'd almost been able to convince herself that her son was still safely lying in the corner asleep. But now that Athan had turned the cradle towards her and thrown the heap of coverings on to the floor, there was no pretending any more. Even her love could not conjure the shadow of her baby in that starkly empty wooden box.

Athan wrapped his arms round Elena and hugged her tightly. 'It's all right, my angel, we'll find him, don't you fret. Whoever took him can't be long on the road. We'll catch up with them and I promise you'll have our son back in your arms afore cockcrow.' He turned to his mother. 'You take care of Elena. I'll go and raise the hue and cry. I'll get the whole village out looking for him.'

He was almost out of the door before Elena managed to force the words out.

'The baby hasn't been taken. I tried to tell you. I tried . . . but you wouldn't listen. I had to do it. The dream . . . it kept warning me. So I had to, you understand that, don't you, Athan? I had to do it. Please say you understand.'

But Athan was staring at her in bewilderment. 'Understand what?'

'She's murdered him, that's what.' Joan's eyes were glittering with hatred.

Athan's jaw dropped open. 'Mam, how could you even think such a foolish, wicked thing? Elena worships our son. She'd not harm a hair on his head. You can see how upset she is.' He flung an arm across Elena's shoulders, drawing her to him protectively. 'I know Elena's never been good enough for you, Mam, but you've gone too far this time. You've no call to go accusing her of anything. I know you're my mam, but she's my wife and I won't have you saying such things about her.'

Joan lifted her chin defiantly. 'Go on then, son, ask her. Ask her what she's done with my grandson.'

8th Day after the New Moon, June 1211

Elder – Mortals love this tree for they believe it cures many ailments from the bite of a mad dog to the toothache, and from sore eyes to melancholy. Its shoots make a tasty herb for the pot; the young branches make pipes for merry music; its buds are pickled for capers; its flowers give flavour to the pies and its berries make a fine wine.

But mortals beware if you try to take her wood without asking leave of the Elder Mother whose spirit dwells in the tree. For if you do any chair or table made from the wood will surely crack and break. This you should say to the elder tree, *Ould girl, gi' me of thy wood, and I will gi' thee some of mine, when I grow into a tree.*

But know this: a witch may often assume the form of an elder tree. If there is witchery in the village, then upon Midsummer's Day you must hold a feast and cut a branch from the elder tree. If blood runs from the tree when it is cut, then it is a witch tree, and if then you spy a woman with a cut on her limbs, you will know her for the witch.

A child must never be laid in the elderwood cradle for faeries will pinch them black and blue. An elderwood log must not be turned on the fire or the Devil will be drawn into the house. The wood is never used for building ships for a witch may ride upon an elder bough as if it was a horse and would ride a ship into a storm that would crack it in two. But planted near a grave the elder is said to protect the body from those who would seek to dig it up for harm.

For an elder tree may bring forth the fruit of healing and death on the same bough, but few mortals can tell the fruits apart.

The Mandrake's Herbal

The Trial

'Bring her closer.' Lord Osborn gestured impatiently with his gloved fingers.

He reached to caress the breast of a peregrine falcon that perched on his left arm. The bird turned its yellow-ringed eyes towards Elena, glaring at her as she was dragged towards the dais at the far end of the Great Hall. She shivered, staring wildly around her like a cornered doe in the hunt.

It seemed nearly every woman in Gastmere had crowded into the hall and now they stood pressed together, murmuring darkly and casting black looks at Elena. How they had all gathered so quickly was a mystery, but as is often said, 'a trouble shared is . . . all around the village in an hour'.

Osborn's dining table had been removed and he sat in the centre of the dais in a large, ornately carved chair. A clerk sat on a stool beside him, a slanted writing table pulled up in front of him. A shaft of bright afternoon sunshine slanted down across the polished wood of the dais; tiny fragments of dust swirled and danced in it. At any other time, Elena would have thought how beautiful it was. Now she could see nothing but the cold, sea-grey eyes of the man who glared down at her.

'This had better be important enough to keep me from hunting or backs will smart,' Osborn said sourly.

Turning back to the falcon, he slipped a leather hood over its head and gestured for a servant to remove the bird.

'Don't feed her, I want her keen for the hunt. And keep my horse saddled, we'll ride out as soon as this business is done. So?' he demanded, turning to Raffaele without drawing breath. 'You are incapable of dealing with a village squabble, are you?'

Raffaele stepped forward, his face flushed with anger. 'The girl stands accused of murdering her own infant. As you are her lord —'

'Murder? Interesting. Who brings such a charge?'

'The girl's mother-in-law, Joan. She came to me at first light and said that Elena had killed her grandson.'

'Is this woman present?' Osborn stared at the crowd of women at the far end of the hall, trying to guess which might be the mother-in-law.

Raffaele beckoned and Joan came hurrying up to the dais, throwing a look of loathing at Elena as she passed.

'I came home from the fields last night, my lord . . .' She faltered, realizing she had neglected to curtsy in her haste to blurt out her story. She made an awkward half-curtsy, half-bow which nearly pitched her head-first on to the dais.

'Are you drunk?' Osborn demanded. 'Then do stop jiggling about, woman. You came home from the fields and what? You found your grandchild dead?'

Joan shook her head vehemently, then stopped abruptly as if she feared this might be counted as jiggling.

'She said my grandchild was asleep in the cradle. I didn't look for I was afeared of waking him. Let sleeping babes lie, my mother always said. And I was that worn out, what with the hay harvest and getting up a dozen times a night to see to the bairn. It's me that's had the care of him; that wicked girl didn't even want to suckle him. She would've left the poor bairn to starve to death if I hadn't been there. I kept telling her —'

Osborn drummed his fingers impatiently. 'So you're saying the baby died of neglect and hunger?'

'No, my lord, no, she murdered him in cold blood. Dashed his brains out, poor little mite. She'd been threatening to do it since afore the baby was born. Said she dreamed of doing it. Now she's gone and done it, killed my poor innocent little grandson. She's a wicked evil murderer, that's what she is. I warned my son about her. I told him she was no good.' Joan sobbed noisily.

For a moment or two Osborn stared at her, a look of disgust on his face as she continued to moan and wail. Several women in the crowd began to weep too, as if their own babes had been snatched from them.

Finally Osborn gestured to Raffaele. 'Fetch the body, Master Raffaele. I've seen enough men, and children too, killed in war to know if she speaks the truth.'

'But there is no body, m'lord,' Raffaele said. 'Joan apparently found the cradle empty. She claims Elena confessed to having murdered her baby, as she'd threatened to do, but we've only Joan's word for that. We've searched the cottage and the toft. There's no sign of a body or of blood come to that.'

'So we only have the word of this villein that any crime has been committed,' Osborn said, pressing his fingers together. 'She wouldn't be the first mother-in-law to quarrel with her son's wife.' He leaned forward, frowning hard at Joan. 'But if you've been wasting my time, woman, making malicious accusations out of spite, I'll make you wish you'd never drawn breath. I'll have you flogged to the bone and –'

Terrified, Joan fell to her knees. 'No, no, my lord. It's the truth, I swear it on the Blessed Virgin's robe. My . . . my son, he'll tell you. He heard her threaten the bairn many times afore he was even born, and he heard her confess to the murder last night.' She swivelled on her knees, pointing at Elena, 'And if she hasn't done away with my grandson, where is he? Tell her to bring him here and prove herself innocent.'

Osborn nodded. 'She may be a garrulous halfwit, but she has a point.' He stared at Elena. 'So where is your baby? Did you kill him, like this woman says?'

Elena's throat was so swollen from pleading and crying half the night that she wasn't sure she could speak.

'I . . . didn't kill him, I swear,' she whispered.

'Speak up, girl,' Osborn barked. 'If you are telling the truth, let's hear it.'

Elena longed for just a sip to drink, but she dared not ask for it. She tried to speak up, but she couldn't seem to make her voice loud enough. Osborn leaned forward impatiently, straining to hear her.

'I was afraid that I would kill my baby . . . I kept having these dreams about harming him, Joan's right about that, but I didn't hurt him. I didn't. I tried to protect him, to keep him safe.'

'Then I will ask you again, girl, where is the child? It's a simple enough question. Any fool could understand it, surely. WHERE IS YOUR BABY?' he said with exaggerated clarity, as if he thought she was deaf or stupid or both. 'Just tell us where to find him, then all this will be over and you can return to your sheep or your spinning or whatever it is you do.'

Elena tried to moisten her dry lips with her tongue. 'My lord, I didn't harm him, but I was so afraid I would that I took him to the cunning woman's house near the forest, to Gytha and her mother. Gytha promised to find a wet nurse in another village to take care of him until he is older, then she will bring him back to us when the danger of the dream is past.'

Fierce muttering broke out behind her as the crowd of villagers tore apart this new morsel.

Osborn held his hand up for silence. 'Which village? Where was she to take the child?'

'I don't know,' Elena wailed. 'She wouldn't tell me in case I was driven to go there to find him and the dream should in that way come true. She said she'd known such things to happen and the only way to prevent it was if I didn't know where to look.'

The villagers excitedly debated the truth of this amongst themselves, but whispering this time, fearing Osborn's anger.

Osborn glared at Raffaele. 'Am I the only one who has any wits left in this manor? Why didn't you go to this woman Gill or whatever her blasted name is, and ask her to tell you where the child is to be found? It seems plain enough to me that either she can produce the infant, in which case the girl is innocent, or she cannot, in which case we may safely assume the baby is dead. It should be a simple matter to prove, even for you.'

The effort of keeping his tone civil showed plainly in Raffaele's face. 'I *did* go to the cunning woman immediately I heard Elena's story. But Gytha and her mother have gone and taken all their possessions with them, what little they had, anyway.'

'When did they depart?'

'They lived out near the forest, well beyond the last crofts in the village, and no one recalls seeing them for a week, but that signifies nothing for the villagers only go to them when they have need. Gytha could have left yesterday or even this morning before we arrived.'

Several of the villagers nodded in agreement.

Elena broke in. 'I gave my bairn to them yesterday morning. So they must have gone to take him to the wet nurse. When they come back they'll tell you, I know they will.'

Joan, who had scrambled to her feet, stepped closer to the dais, her fear replaced with a look of triumph now that she could see things were swinging her way.

'That's certain proof she's lying, my lord. Gytha's mother was blind and couldn't even stir from her bed, hasn't walked for years. What cause would Gytha have to drag the old woman on such a journey if she was only going to deliver the child and then return to the village? And why would she take all her pots and stores? No, they've done a flit, gone for good, left a week ago, which that witch Elena knows right well. She's an unnatural mother. There's plenty of women in Gastmere can swear that we had to hold her down and force her to suckle her own babe when he was born. Even Elena's own mother will tell you that. What kind of a mother doesn't want to nurse her own child? What manner of woman begs the faeries to take her child?'

Several women in the crowd crossed themselves and hissed their hatred of such wickedness. Elena's mother was sobbing loudly, in the arms of one of her neighbours, telling any who would listen that she couldn't understand what had come over her daughter and that she had tried her best to raise her to be a good girl. Neighbours sadly shook their heads; the shame of this would surely send the poor woman to an early grave.

Joan, spurred on by the outrage of the crowd, bellowed her words out as if she was a priest in the pulpit. 'Elena murdered my precious little grandson just to spite me, and she pretended the bairn was with Gytha, 'cause she knew right well that Gytha and her mother had already gone from the village days ago, so they wouldn't be here to gainsay her.'

Raffaele opened his mouth as if to protest, but nothing came out and he stared down at the floor, his face grim with misery.

Osborn leaned back in his chair and addressed the assembled company. 'Then, unless anyone else has proof to the contrary, there can be no doubt the girl is guilty.'

Elena was trembling violently. She stared wildly around the hall, desperately searching for someone who would say something to defend her, but all she received in return were cold stares from faces grim with shock and revulsion.

'Mam,' she pleaded, 'tell them I wouldn't do such a thing. Tell them I'd never hurt my own bairn.'

But Cecily only sobbed harder, turning her face away from her daughter into the comforting arms of her friends.

Elena took a few steps towards the crowd, who as one drew back from her as if they feared she was going to attack them.

'I didn't hurt him. You have to believe me. I gave him away to keep him safe. Athan, tell them, please! You know I wouldn't do anything to hurt our son. You told Joan I couldn't have done it. Tell them, Athan, tell them!'

Even beneath his tan, Elena could see the blood draining from Athan's face.

Osborn jerked his head in Athan's direction. 'You, boy, are you the baby's father?'

Athan twitched rather than nodded, his face stricken with anguish, but Osborn took the movement for assent.

'Have you anything to say in this girl's defence? Did you give her permission to take your son to this cunning woman?'

Athan stared from his mother to Elena, his mouth working convulsively. Silent tears began running down his cheeks. He made a desperate gesture, holding out his arms as if he was reaching for Elena.

'I'm sorry, so sorry,' he whispered. 'I love you . . . even if . . . I'll never stop loving you.'

Then he bolted for the door, shoving through the servants clustered around it, and fled out into the sunlight.

Osborn raised his eyebrows. 'I think we can take that as a *no*. So we'd better proceed to sentence.'

'But surely,' Raffaele protested, 'Elena should have the chance to prove her innocence?'

'How exactly do you propose she does that, Master Raffaele? She cannot produce the living child, nor the woman to whom she says she entrusted him.'

'We could wait and question Gytha when she returns.'

Elena felt a surge of hope leap up in her, and she fixed her eyes on Osborn's face, praying that he would agree.

Osborn snorted. 'You should pay more attention to your own eloquent testimony, Master Raffaele. Was it not you who told us that this cunning woman had taken her infirm mother and all her possessions with her? Plainly she has no intention of returning to Gastmere, which leaves us with the problem of what do with the girl. If this land were not under the Pope's Interdict, then she could be tried by the ordeal of water or fire and I would not have had to waste a good day's hunting over this matter. But since, thanks to the Pope, there is not a priest left to administer the oath, I must be the judge of her innocence or guilt. By order of our beloved sovereign King John, I am commanded to keep the king's peace in these parts and see that those who break it are justly punished. The girl will hang at first light tomorrow.'

He delivered the last sentence in such a matter of fact tone, as if he was giving orders for his horse to be groomed, that Elena couldn't grasp what he had said.

'Wait!' A voice rang out from the minstrels' gallery at the far end of the hall. Everyone turned and stared upwards. Lady Anne was gripping the gallery rail.

'It is the Church's teaching, is it not, that an infant who dies before baptism is not counted a human creature for he has no soul? Therefore a woman who does away with her newborn child before baptism is not guilty of murder.'

Osborn smiled the smile of a torturer who revels in his work.

'How gracious of you to take an interest, Lady Anne. But as I was just explaining to my steward here, who like you seems to be woefully ignorant of such matters, we are suffering under an Interdict. Who knows how long it will be before children may be baptized again? Why, these babes may be men themselves by then, and are we to say that if they are then murdered their killers should go unpunished?

'And please, mistress, do not waste my time in pleading that the girl was acting in a fit of melancholy and did not know what she did. On her own admission she had been dreaming about committing this crime for months, even torturing her poor mother-in-law by openly threatening it. But even if that was not the case, I am not punishing her for murder alone.'

Osborn turned a faintly amused glance on Raffaele, as if he was deriving a great deal of pleasure from Lady Anne's challenge. 'I take it neither this girl nor her husband were born freemen. They both are villeins?'

Raffe nodded dejectedly.

'Then the dead child was a villein also and as such belonged to the manor. This girl has not only deliberately murdered her own baby, but in doing so has destroyed manor property, *my* property, mistress. The death of a midden brat does not concern me overmuch, but the loss of a future workman does, not to mention the generations of villeins he might have fathered. By rights I should hang her twice, once for murder and again for theft. But I am inclined to show mercy. I will merely hang her once. That will suffice. Take the girl away and lock her up till morning.'

Someone was screaming. Elena didn't know if it was herself or her mother who was shrieking, for her legs buckled under her and she crumpled senseless to the ground.

9th Day after the New Moon, June 1211

Bluebells – Some call them *Deadmen's bells*, for a mortal who hears a bluebell ring is listening to his own death knell.

A bluebell wood is the most enchanted place on earth and mortals should never venture there alone for it is full of faerie spells. A child who picks bluebells alone will vanish, never to be seen again. An adult will be pixie-led and wander round and round in circles, unable to escape the wood, until he dies of exhaustion, unless someone should find him and lead him safely home.

There is a game that mortal children play in innocence, laughing as they weave through each other. *In and out the dusty bluebells* . . . they sing . . . *I am your master.* They should not play such dangerous games so lightly or wantonly, for the master they name is none other than the Faerie King himself who will lead them on a merry dance from which there is no return to this life.

The Mandrake's Herbal

Retribution

Raffaele grasped Elena's arm so hard she thought he would snap the bone. He tugged her towards the open metal grill in the floor of the undercroft beneath the Great Hall.

'Down there,' he ordered, indicating the rickety wooden ladder which plunged into the dark pit below. Raffaele held up his lantern to illuminate the first rungs. Although the sun had not yet set, in the far corner of the undercroft behind the kegs and barrels it was already dark. Elena peered down. The pit was twice as deep as a man's height. The bailiff stood at the bottom, staring up at her, holding up a short iron chain which was fastened at one end to the wall, while from the other end of the chain dangled an open iron collar. The flame from his lantern flickered across the beaten earth floor covered with dirty straw, and over the stone walls green and slimy from the damp. A stench of decay rose up on the cold, wet air that seemed to come from an open grave. Elena shuddered, trying to pull away.

'No, please don't put me down there, please, I beg you.' She turned desperately to Raffaele. 'You could chain me up here in the cellar.'

'And have you rescued?' Raffaele said harshly. 'You choose, you can either climb down that ladder yourself or I'll throw you down, and I can promise you lying there with broken bones will be a thousand times worse.'

Raffaele was holding her so close to the edge that she knew the slightest flexing of his arm would send her crashing down. The violent way he had dragged her from the Great Hall left her in no doubt that he was angry enough to do it. In the Hall he had seemed to be on her side, the only one who believed her. She couldn't understand why he had turned against her. Did he too now believe what Joan had said?

Shakily Elena climbed down the ladder and offered no resistance when the bailiff pushed her against the wall and bolted the iron collar around her neck.

'You'll be in good company down here.' The bailiff inclined his head towards a rough stone wall on one side of the cell. 'Sir Gerard's mouldering behind there. You'd best make friends with his corpse; you'll soon be one yourself.'

He tugged hard on the chain, to test the fastening, jerking the collar so that it bruised her throat, almost choking her. 'Not that you'll be resting in some fancy leaded coffin. Osborn'll have your body hanged in a gibbet cage till you've rotted away to bones, then they'll pound them to pieces and toss them in the marsh. And good riddance too, that's what I say. Nowt more evil creature on this earth than a woman who murders her own innocent bairn; 'gainst all nature, that is.'

Satisfied the chain was secure, he picked up his lantern and started up the ladder.

As the shadows rose up from the floor around her, Elena cried out, 'Leave me the light, for pity's sake.'

The bailiff paused at the top of the ladder and laughed. 'What do you need a light for, girl, there's nowt to see, save the rats and old Gerard's ghost when he comes for you.'

Raffaele's fist struck as swiftly as a viper's fangs, catching the bailiff on the side of the head and almost sending him crashing back into the pit.

'*Sir* Gerard to you, you son of a whore. And don't ever let me hear you speak of his ghost in front of her ladyship.'

But the next minute Raffaele was reaching out his hand and hauling the stunned bailiff up on to the floor of the cellar as if he was his closest friend.

'Come on, man, there's a flagon of wine waiting for us in the Hall. Leave this murdering witch to the rats. With any luck, they'll finish her and spare us the trouble of a hanging.'

The two men hauled the ladder up through the hatch. The iron grill slammed shut and Elena saw the glow of their lantern light grow fainter as they walked away. At least they hadn't closed the wooden trapdoor on top of it; she couldn't bear to think of being sealed in as if she was in . . . a coffin.

She was to die. She knew it and yet such a thing didn't seem possible. She couldn't make herself grasp the reality of it. In a few brief hours she would be dead, sent to the next world, and then what? Torment and torture without any end, like those pictures on the church wall of men and women being forced into the flames, boiling helplessly in cauldrons, their limbs hacked off or pierced with knives. She found herself retching in fear. No, no, she couldn't think of it, she mustn't think.

She crouched on the damp, mouldy straw in the corner of the tiny cell. Even had she not been chained to the wall, she would have crouched against it, too terrified to let go of the solidness of it and drown in the nothingness beyond. She had never known darkness so thick, so complete, as if she had been blinded.

She strained, trying to hear any rustling in the straw, but she could hear nothing except her own heart pounding. She tried desperately not to think of the corpse lying no more than a foot away, behind the loose rocks. Would she hear the coffin lid grate open?

Only yesterday she was stirring Athan's supper over their fire and now she was here, and they meant to hang her. They couldn't. It wasn't possible. She was innocent. Didn't they understand she'd given her child away to keep him safe? They must believe her. Gytha would return before morning. She'd tell them the baby was alive. Gytha must come back and tell them. She must.

Elena drew her legs up to her chin, wrapping her arms tightly about them and resting her head on the wall behind. Suddenly aware of the burning throbbing of her breasts, bursting with the milk her son would never drink, she tried to ease them, but they hurt so much she could hardly bear to touch them. She was so tired. She had not slept at all last night and all she wanted to do now was to sink into the oblivion of sleep, but if she did, then her last few hours of life would be gone and the morning would come instantly before she had time to prepare herself. If she could stay awake she could somehow stretch out those hours and give Gytha time to return.

She must pray. She must say the words that would save her from the fires of hell. But she couldn't remember what the dying were supposed to say. Maybe she'd never known. It had been three years since the churches had been open for services and she couldn't recall any of the words the priests had recited. She always said her prayers, of course, for things that no priest would ever pray – *Make Athan love me*. But those were her words, not the right words, not the Latin words, and she knew only the magic words of the priests had the power to save a person from hell.

Holy Virgin, Holy Mother, save me. But Mary was a mother, a good mother. She hadn't dreamt of killing her son. Was the Holy Virgin as disgusted with her as her own mam was? Would she refuse to listen because Elena was in her heart a murderer? To think about doing something, the village priest had once told her, was as wicked as actually doing it. It was the same sin. She had murdered her baby, because she had thought about murdering him, over and over again. She was guilty.

She holds the baby dangling from her hands, like a dead rabbit. The scarlet blood from his head is dripping down on to a piece of white cloth. The fat drops of blood spread out on the cloth, merging into one another, until the white is lost entirely. Now the cloth is as red as hawthorn berries, as if it had always been red. Her rage has slowly trickled away with the dripping blood and now she is staring at the tiny corpse, unable to believe what she has done. Not believing that she has done it. She knows she must have done it. She knows she wanted to. She was consumed by hatred, burning up with the desire to smash, to hurt, to destroy. But she doesn't remember killing him.

All she knows is that she is holding the dead infant and she is alone. Her legs give way and she falls to her knees, the baby drops from her grasp on to the bloody cloth. She turns and vomits. Shakily she wipes her mouth on the back of her hand, and when she turns back, the baby is lying there, looking up at her with wide blue eyes which do not blink. His soft lips are parted as if he has opened them to suckle, but no breath comes from them.

She hadn't meant to hurt him. That's all she can think. She hadn't meant to do it. She hears a creaking, a door opening behind her. She whirls round.

The iron ring caught her hard across the throat as she moved, jerking her awake with a cry of pain. Something was creaking open, something was grating towards her. She heard the sound of rasping breath. Elena sensed something moving beside her – the wall, the stones, were they being pushed outward? Was Gerard's corpse . . . ? She screamed.

'Be quiet, girl, do you want to wake the whole manor?' a boy's voice whispered from the dark.

Then came the faint glow of a lantern muffled beneath a cloak and she realized the wooden ladder was sliding down towards her. Minutes later the wood groaned under the weight of a heavy man descending cautiously into the pit.

Raffaele set the lantern down and reached out towards her. She was certain he was going to hurt her, probably rape her. She kicked and pushed him, struggling away from his long fingers until she was choking on the iron collar. She tried to scream again, but his hand clamped hard across her mouth.

'Stop struggling, you little idiot,' Raffaele whispered. 'What are you kicking me for? Can't you see I've come to help you? But there isn't much time. They'll come for you at dawn and you must be long gone by then. We have to hurry. Now, will you promise to stay quiet?'

She nodded and he slowly withdrew his hand from her mouth and reached for a key in his scrip. Clumsily he tried to unlock the collar. Cursing her, he thrust the lantern into her hand. 'Here, hold it up so that I can see, and stay still.'

Dumbly she did as she was bid and moments later he was climbing the ladder and ordering her to follow. He helped her over the edge of the pit, then grabbed her wrist and dragged her through the darkened undercroft, weaving through the barrels and past the cart until they reached the archway leading into the courtyard. There he paused, peering out.

It could not be too far off dawn now, for torches intended to illuminate the courtyard were almost burnt away. Raffaele had timed it well. Crushing her between himself and the wall, he hurried her round the edge of the courtyard until they reached the huge bossed gate. The shutter on the window of the tiny gate lodge lay open, and from inside came the sound of pig-heavy snores.

Raffaele bent close to Elena. 'Here, take your scrip and your cloak, you'll need them. As soon as I open the door, you run. Run for the ditch on the other side of the track. Hide and wait for me there. Don't move, understand?'

He pushed her into position next to the opening of the small wicket gate set into the large, imposing manor gate. As carefully as he could, he eased up the beam and pulled the door towards him, but not quietly enough. A hound leapt up, barking furiously, straining at its chain. There was a grunt and a curse, as inside the gatehouse old Walter struggled off his cot. All at once every hound in the manor took up the cry of the guard dogs. Raffaele pushed Elena through the gate and slammed it behind her.

Elena picked up her skirts and ran stumbling and tripping across the grass over the cart-rutted track and towards the ditch on the other side. She could hear shouts and barks from behind the manor wall. Desperately she tried to look for some hiding place, but between the manor and the ditch there was only a line of slender birch trees and bushes that would not hide a rabbit, never mind a woman. She crouched behind them praying the darkness would cover what the trees would not.

Every sense was screaming at her to run, but he'd said to wait. She must wait, but for how long? Why didn't he come? It would soon be dawn and as soon as the light began to creep over the marshes, she'd have no hope of escape. She must go now before it was too late.

She tensed herself and stepped out from behind the trees, but instantly drew back again as the huge manor door swung open. Raffaele strode through, but he was not alone. Four men stumbled out after him, still rubbing the sleep from their eyes, and hard on their heels came two more who held the leashes of two pairs of hounds. The dogs were almost choking themselves on their collars as they strained forward, sniffing excitedly at the ground. The hounds were searching for her scent. Almost vomiting with fear, Elena looped the leather strap of her scrip over her neck and scrambled towards the ditch behind her. She dropped into it, trying to smother a cry as the cold water rose to her thighs. She crouched down till she was neck-deep in the stinking water and huddled into the reeds.

'Over here!' the gatekeeper shouted.

Elena could hear the hounds snuffling and barking above her. A few yards away a duck, unnerved by the dogs, flapped in fright along the surface of the ditch.

'Keep those hounds on the leash, damn you!' Raffaele yelled.

'But they've found something,' Walter protested.

'Water rats, that's all. I told you, I saw the thief head off towards the village. Now you take those mangy hounds and track him down. And if you come back without him, by God's teeth, I'll flay the hide off you myself for leaving that gate unfastened.'

'It was secure. I checked it myself, like always,' poor Walter protested. 'I swear by my right hand, I didn't leave it unbarred.'

'Find him,' Raffaele roared, 'or I'll keep you to your oath and take your hand, and the same goes for each and every one of you idle bastards.'

The men did not need telling twice; pulling their reluctant hounds away from the ditch, they set off hastily in the direction of the village, with Raffaele's curses and threats chasing them till they were out of hearing.

When the sound of the barking had died away, Raffaele came to the edge of the ditch and softly called out to Elena.

She struggled to clamber out, holding up her hand for him to help her. But instead of pulling her out, he took off his boots, tied them by the laces around his neck, and slipped into the ditch beside her. He hauled her towards him, but she was so numb with cold and fear she could hardly stand.

'I've friends waiting for us where the ditch meets the river, but they'll not wait past first light. We have to hurry,' he added, looking anxiously towards the marshes. 'Best keep to the ditch. They think the gate was opened by the thief, but if someone thinks to check the prisoner hole and they find it empty, they'll send the hounds after you. With luck the water'll throw them off the scent. Come on, we must be well away before they realize you're gone.'

Elena shivered and tried to wade forward, but her feet had sunk deep into thick mud at the bottom of the ditch and her long skirts were dragging her back. 'I can't,' she moaned.

'You'd rather face the hangman's noose? You'll be a long time dancing on that rope for I doubt even your own mother would pull on your legs to end your suffering.' He slipped an arm around her and tugged her forward, saying more gently, 'Just to the end of the ditch, then you'll be safe.'

They waded up through the tar-black water, their feet sucked back at every step by the mud. Every now and then waterfowl would fly out of the reeds and go splashing and squawking up the ditch. Something large, soft and wet washed against Elena's legs, and she clung more tightly to Raffaele, trying to console herself that whatever creature it was, at least it wasn't moving.

Suddenly Raffaele stopped and pulled her down until they were crouching among the reeds. The wind carried the distant baying of hounds towards them.

'Damn them!' Raffaele cursed. 'I think they're doubling back, or else Osborn's sent out more of his hounds.'

They crouched, hardly daring to breathe. Were the dogs getting closer or was it the wind playing tricks? Elena gave a yelp as something scurried out of the reeds and across her head, its sharp claws digging into her face; she wildly beat it off and it fell into the water with a splash. She could hear a heart pounding, but she wasn't sure if it was her own or Raffaele's.

He glanced up at the lightening sky. 'We daren't wait. If the boatmen leave before we reach them, you and I are both dead.'

All caution abandoned, he splashed through the water as fast as the sucking mud permitted, dragging Elena with him.

Light was ghosting across the marshes, pale as buttermilk. Ahead of them they could hear the river thrashing between its banks. And, as if eager to join its bigger sister, the water around them in the ditch suddenly quickened its pace and began to buffet against the backs of their legs.

Raffaele pulled Elena towards the bank, almost flinging her against it. 'Out quickly. If you're tipped into the river, you may be swept away.'

Elena, her hands numb with cold, fought to drag her heavy sodden skirts out of the water and crawl up the bank. Her legs were trembling and she collapsed on to the top of the bank, trying to gain her breath, but Raffaele would not let her rest. Hauling her upright, he pulled her, crashing through the bushes and trees, towards the river. They burst out on to the bank and gazed wildly around. Light was just touching the far edge of the river. Already a dazzling orange rind was edging into the pale sky. The river was empty save for three swans floating serenely towards them on the glittering water.

'God's teeth, where's that blasted boat? I told them to meet me here.'

Elena caught Raffaele's arm and pointed to the bend upstream in the river, where she could just make out the shape of a long, flat craft slowly sculling away from them.

Raffaele started forward, and putting his fingers in his mouth gave three shrill whistles, but the boat had already vanished round the bend of the river. He groaned. 'I'll kill them if I ever get my hands on them, they swore . . .'

The deep, resonant baying of the hounds sounded once more through the silent dawn; they seemed to be getting closer. Elena glanced fearfully behind her, shivering in her wet clothes.

'You must go back. If you're missing they'll know it was you that released me. I can run.'

'By now Osborn will have ordered you brought up for your execution and they'll have already discovered you've gone.' Raffaele raked his fingers agitatedly through his hair. 'He'll send his men out searching for you on horseback. You'll never outrun them. We must —'

He was interrupted by a low whistle and glancing up saw the boat being sculled back towards them by two men, their faces half hidden under their hoods.

Raffaele crossed himself. 'The Holy Virgin be praised.'

As soon as the boat pulled alongside, Raffaele bundled Elena on board. He tossed a small leather purse to the elder of the two men whose face was tanned and as wrinkled as oak bark.

'Half the money you were promised. You deliver her unharmed to the house we agreed and as soon as word reaches me they've got her safe you'll get the rest.'

The man spat into the water and gave a toothless grin. 'They'll keep her snug and safe all right.'

There was something in that mocking tone that frightened Elena. In all her anxiety to get away, it had not occurred to her to ask Raffaele where he was sending her.

She half clambered back out of the boat. 'Where are they taking me?'

The men in the boat exchanged grins, but Raffaele ignored them, pushing Elena gently back in.

'To a friend of mine at Norwich, Mother Margot. She'll take you into her house. No one will think to look for you there.'

Elena breathed out in relief. Mother Margot, she would be the prioress of a nunnery. The boatman was right, she would be safe there. No one could search a nunnery, could they? She had always been a little afraid of nuns with their austere habits and even grimmer expressions, but if they could save her from Osborn and the noose . . . . she glanced up at the rising sun and shuddered. If Raffaele hadn't rescued her, by now she would already be strangling on a rope. Her fingers massaged her throat.

'Master Raffaele, I'll work, do anything. I'll repay the money somehow.' She touched his hand and gazed up at him with a grateful smile.

Far from being pleased, his expression suddenly changed to one of anger. 'I don't care about the money, but I told you that first day I brought you to Lady Anne that if you needed a friend you were to come to me. You should have told me about the child. I would have helped you. It didn't need to come to this. We are bound to each other, you and I. You should have trusted me, Elena.'

'But you have helped me more than I could ask. I –'

The boatman suddenly jerked upright. 'Horses coming this way, moving fast.' Before Elena realized what was happening the boatman had pushed her down flat in the bottom of the boat and was pulling a heavy, evil-smelling sail cloth over her.

'I'll come to you soon, Elena,' Raffaele whispered.

The men grunted as they dug their sculls into the water. Elena felt the craft inching slowly into the centre of the river. For a moment or two it hung there, then the boat gathered pace and slid quietly away into the dawn.

Walter was not at his post in the manor gatehouse when Raffe squelched into the courtyard, and as soon as he caught sight of the group of men standing beneath the undercroft, he knew why. He hesitated, trying to decide what stance he should adopt. Anger? Surprise? But he didn't get the chance to resolve anything for at that moment Osborn spotted him.

'Aah, here is Master Raffaele now. Perhaps he might shed some light on this matter.' He stared down at Raffe's sodden, muddy clothes. 'Have you been taking a bath, Master Raffaele? In the town it is customary to remove your clothes and use clean water, but perhaps you are more accustomed to bathing with the pigs in Gastmere. Or have you been doing more to those hapless sows than simply wallowing with them?'

It was a measure of the tension in the courtyard that no one laughed.

Raffe ignored the barb. 'I was searching the ditches for the thief, in case he was hiding from the hounds there. So, have you caught the rogue?'

Osborn took a pace forward, his ash-grey eyes narrowing as he searched Raffe's face. Raffe returned his stare without flinching.

'The girl that was to be hanged,' Osborn said dangerously quietly. 'She appears to have vanished. The bailiff swears he locked her in the neck iron, removed the ladder from the pit and fastened the grid above her. He says you were witness to this.'

Raffe glanced over at the bailiff's frightened face. 'It is as he says, and then we went to the kitchens together for a mug of ale.'

'If that is so,' Osborn said, 'someone came during the night and released her. She could not have escaped from the iron or that pit unaided. But if it was in the night, how did she get out of the courtyard without our faithful watchman hearing her?'

It was Walter's turn to look fearful, as well he might. A watchman who allows a prisoner to walk unchallenged through his gates could hardly expect to escape without punishment.

Walter twisted his hood nervously in his hand. 'Girl must have slipped out when I opened the gates for the men to give chase to the thief. I swear not a flea could have escaped afore that, 'cause my hounds –'

'Ah yes, this mysterious vanishing thief who appears to have stolen . . . what was it? Ah yes, precisely nothing. It was you who raised the alarm, was it not, Master Raffaele? What exactly did you see?'

Raffe didn't hesitate. This much he had already rehearsed

in his head. 'I saw someone coming round the back of the kitchen, but his face was in shadows. At first I thought him to be a servant, but as soon as he saw me, he ran for the gate, so I knew it was someone with no business at the manor. But it wasn't the girl, of that I'm certain, the figure was too tall and broad for that.'

'And what made you think –' Osborn began, but he was interrupted by shrieks and bellows from the track outside.

Several of the manor's burlier servants tumbled through the open gate. They were dragging a man and a woman between them, but they were having difficulty holding the man, who was wriggling like an eel.

Raffe's heart gave a sickening lurch. *Blessed Holy Virgin, let it not be Elena or the boatman.*

But as the servants gave the man a violent shove forwards, Raffe saw that their prisoner was Athan who, despite his hands being lashed behind him, was putting up a furious struggle.

The two servants behind were having an easier time of it, for their captive was putting up no resistance at all. Cecily, Elena's mother, was shuffling meekly between them, her head hanging so low it seemed that if they released her she would instantly burrow into the earth and hide from the shame of it all. But neither Athan nor Cecily was responsible for the noise. All the shrieks and wails were emanating from a third figure, Athan's mother, Joan, who was scurrying behind the servants and taking every opportunity to slap, bite and kick the men holding her son.

Osborn gestured to the ground and the two prisoners were forced to their knees in the muck of the courtyard. It had the effect of immediately silencing everyone, even Joan, who stood fish-eyed behind the group, her fists pressed to her mouth, gazing at Osborn.

He took his time, pacing back and forth in front of Athan and Cecily, staring hard into their faces until both were visibly trembling. Finally he spoke.

'Elena has run away from the manor. As villeins I trust

I need not remind you how serious an offence that is in itself, but if that were not bad enough, she is a convicted murderer and under sentence of death.'

Osborn continued to pace back and forth between Athan and Cecily. 'As you well know, anyone, *anyone* who assists a convicted felon to escape puts themselves under the same sentence as the prisoner they try to aid. Nevertheless, last night someone was foolish enough to help a murderer escape justice.'

As if his words were a child's counting game, on the word *justice* Osborn halted abruptly in front of Athan and, without warning, seized a handful of the kneeling man's hair, yanking his head upwards. 'You, as the girl's lover, are the obvious suspect.'

Athan's normally rosy face was ashen. 'On my life I swear I didn't, my lord. Remember . . . remember it was us, me and my mam, who told you that Elena had done away with my son. What cause would I have to rescue her?'

Osborn pulled Athan's head back so far, Raffe thought he might snap the lad's neck. 'Don't tell me what I remember as if I'm in my dotage, boy. What I remember is that you told me nothing at all. It was your mother who did all the talking yesterday. You were besotted with this girl. *I'll always love you*, wasn't that what you swore –'

Joan could contain herself no longer. 'My lad thought that harlot as wicked as I did. It was his own dear bairn that evil woman murdered. Poor lad's beside himself with grief. It's as certain as a stone wall to a blind man that he'd not lift a finger to help that murdering slut. Besides,' she added with an angry lift of her chin, 'he was at home with me all night, never left the cottage till daybreak.'

Osborn snorted. 'You can't really imagine that I would take the word of a doting mother as proof of her son's whereabouts? You'd no doubt swear your son could spin straw into gold, if you thought it to his advantage.' But despite his words, Osborn let Athan's head drop.

He took a pace towards Cecily, standing so close to the kneeling woman that his crotch was pushing into her face.

'I take it you are the girl's mother. It was you, was it not, who screamed when sentence was pronounced yesterday, the only villager who raised any protest to her hanging? A mother would do anything to save her own daughter, wouldn't she?'

Cecily raised a tearstained face. 'I couldn't believe my own bairn . . . my own flesh and blood would do such a wicked thing. I'd . . . heard her speak of this . . . dream, same as Joan, but it's well known pregnant women are often tormented in their sleep by demons who are jealous of the babes they carry. I never thought she'd really . . .'

'So you helped her escape,' Osborn said quietly. 'That was foolish, extremely foolish, but then all women are fools for their children.'

'I didn't, my lord. I swear I didn't!' Cecily wailed. 'No woman wants to see her own bairn hang, but what could I have done to prevent it? Even if I'd had the courage to help her, how would I have got the key to unlock the pit or her irons?'

There was an instant buzzing among the servants. Osborn held up his hands for silence.

'Your daughter admitted that she was in the habit of consulting a cunning woman. Doubtless you did the same and managed to release your daughter by witchcraft.'

Cecily moaned and swayed as if she was about to faint. 'No, no!'

Raffe, with a sick feeling of dread, knew exactly where this line of questioning could end. Desperate to stop it, he broke in.

'M'lord, the cunning women have gone from the village. Wasn't it their very absence that helped to convict the girl in the first place? So where would Cecily have got help to conjure such a powerful sorcery that would have made locks fly open without a key?'

Osborn took a step back from the sobbing woman; the expression on his coarse features was one approaching triumph.

'So, Master Raffaele, you are minded to pit wits with me, are you? If you are so certain that this is not witchcraft, then we must resume our search for mortal hands. So tell me this, who obtained the key to release the girl? Consider your answer carefully, Master Raffaele. For I promise you there shall be a hanging today, if not of the girl, then of her accomplice.'

Raffe swallowed hard, realizing too late what he'd said. He stared into those mocking grey eyes, trying to discover if Osborn already knew the truth and this whole exercise had just been a mummers' play designed to display Osborn's power and his own humiliation.

Raffe had never lied in his life to avoid just punishment, but to let Osborn hang him like a pickpocket, to have Osborn's laughter be the last thing he ever heard – he would not submit to that. And what of Elena? Osborn would surely try to extract her whereabouts from him before he hanged him. Raffe could bear pain better than most men – over the years he'd learned that the mind could force the body to fight almost anything – but Osborn was capable of inflicting hurt far beyond the imagination of most men.

Raffe, acutely conscious that Osborn was waiting, opened his mouth without the faintest idea what he intended to say, but before he could say anything, a voice behind him interrupted.

'I released the girl, Lord Osborn.'

Raffe spun round to see Lady Anne, composed but pale, her hands clasped across her stomach. 'I believed your sentence to be unjust. I know all the families of this manor – for years they were in my care and charge. Elena was my personal maid for a short time and I could not stand by and see her punished for something I am certain she did not do.'

For a moment Osborn just gaped at her, the colour rising in his face. 'Your maid?' Osborn crossed towards her in three swift strides, thrusting his bearded face into hers. 'Your son is no longer master here, I am, and by God, I will teach you what that means.'

Anne regarded him calmly. 'Even you cannot have a noble-woman hanged on your whim, Lord Osborn.'

'No, but I will make you wish I could. You were very close

to your son, weren't you, m'lady? How would you like to be even closer? Let's see if a month chained in the pit next to his rotting corpse will tame you. You won't look much like a noblewoman when you get out of there, that I promise you.'

Anne blanched visibly, swaying backwards. 'You wouldn't dare,' she blazed, but the quaver in her voice betrayed her fear.

Osborn's mouth curved in a humourless smile. 'You think not?' He turned to the servants. 'Take her to the pit.'

But no one moved. They all stood frozen, staring at him, shock on every face.

'No.' Raffe stepped hastily between Anne and Osborn. 'She did not release the girl. I —'

'He's right, m'lord,' a timid voice broke in.

Hilda was hovering by her mistress's side, her arm thrust out in front of Anne as if she thought she could simply flap away any man who approached.

'My mistress was sound asleep in bed all night.'

'No, Hilda!' Anne protested, but for once her faithful maid ignored her.

'Lady Anne was so upset about the girl, I knew she'd never rest, so I added a few drops of poppy juice to her posset. She wouldn't have been able to stir from her bed, never mind help that wicked girl. I knew that girl was trouble, taking advantage of poor Lady Anne's trusting nature. Evil, that's what she was.'

Anne gave a shuddering sigh. 'Hilda is confused, I didn't . . .' she began, but all the words seemed to have drained out of her. She swayed alarmingly and had to clutch Hilda's arm to stop herself falling.

Osborn spun around to face Raffe, his eyes flashing with rage.

'So!' he bellowed. 'It seems we come full circle. Who released the girl? As steward you are responsible for the conduct and discipline of my villeins, therefore you will decide. The girl's lover or her mother, which one will hang in her place? You may choose.'

Cecily, Athan and Joan all let out a shriek of anguish. Their horrified faces turned towards Raffe. For a moment he was too stunned to speak.

'No! No, you can't ask me to choose. You have no proof that either of them did it.'

'In that case I have no alternative but to hold Lady Anne responsible. After all, she did confess and her maid is doubtless lying out of a misguided sense of loyalty. Perhaps I should reward that loyalty by allowing her to join her mistress in the pit.'

Hilda whimpered in protest, but Osborn ignored her.

'Come now, Master Raffaele, do you really think a woman of Lady Anne's delicate breeding would survive a month in the dark, chained up in the cold and damp, with only bread and water to sustain her? I've seen men driven mad in half that time left alone in the dark. And next to her poor son's corpse too. What a torment that would be for a doting mother.'

Raffe's gaze flicked to Anne's face. She held her head defiantly high, but he saw the tremble of her mouth and the lines around her tired eyes. She would go into that pit with dignity if she had to, but they both knew she would not come out alive.

'So I repeat, Master Raffaele, it is your choice. Lover or mother, which shall I hang?'

In the courtyard none of the servants moved. The wind stirred their clothes, as if they were rags on stone statues. Athan's face was almost green, as if he was about to vomit. His eyes were closed and his lips moved frantically as he mumbled what sounded like a prayer. Cecily was crouching on the ground, her arms cradling her head, rocking backwards and forwards. Joan was twisting the cloth of her skirts, and gabbling frantic pleas for mercy. But she was sobbing so hard, it was impossible to tell if she was begging Raffe, Osborn or the Almighty to spare her precious son.

All the servants' eyes were fastened upon Raffe, but he couldn't look at anyone. He stared up. A flock of starlings, like a pillar of smoke, spun across the pale blue sky towards the marshes. Raffe knew what Gerard would have done, he'd have confessed in an instant. He'd never let someone else die for him, but then Gerard was of noble blood and would never have had to face the gallows. Raffe could not bear to lose his life to Osborn, to die ridiculed and disgraced. He had lived his whole life in humiliation until Gerard had found him, and he would not die in shame now, not after all he had been through. And who would protect Lady Anne and Elena? He couldn't leave them undefended to Osborn's mercy. He had a duty to stay alive for them.

If that spineless oaf, Athan, had ever stood up to his mother and defended Elena as he should have done, then none of them would be in this position. Elena would be safe and all would be well. That wretch had seduced her, fathered a child by her, and then hadn't had the guts to try to save the mother of his own son from the gallows. Athan hadn't rescued Elena, but by God's blood, he should have done! Elena adored him, yet Athan would have stood next to his witch of a mother and watched the woman he claimed to love hanged before his eyes. Any bastard who did that deserved to die.

Raffe whipped around to face Osborn. 'Athan! Hang him.'

'Not my son!' Joan screamed. 'You can't. Take her. Take Cecily. It's her daughter who's the murderer. She's to blame. She is Elena's mother, so it's her fault if the girl turned bad. Not my boy! Not my innocent little bairn!' She fell on her son, trying to cradle him as if she could protect him.

Osborn watched them, a look of triumph on his face. 'A wise choice, Master Raffaele, we'll have you broken to the bridle yet.'

He spun on his heels, pointing at the men holding Athan. 'String him up at once, and let's be done with this before some fool tries to rescue him.'

The men dragged Athan over to a thick metal hook that hung from the curved vault of the undercroft beneath the Great Hall. A stout rope already dangled from the hook with a noose at one end. Athan shrank from it, cowering and whimpering.

With a howl of anguish, Joan threw herself on the ground at Osborn's feet, clinging to his legs, begging and pleading. Osborn gazed down at her for a moment, then, as if she was a stray dog peeing on his leg, he kicked her away.

'Yesterday you were happy enough to see another woman's child hanged, so this is only justice, is it not? Perhaps you and the rest of the villagers will learn it is wiser to settle your petty squabbles among yourselves and not waste the time of great men.'

A bench had been placed beneath the noose, but Athan had collapsed on the floor, vomiting with fear. They tried to make him clamber up on to the bench, but he couldn't or wouldn't stand. In the end two men were forced to lift him bodily on to it and stand either side of him, holding him upright between them as the third placed the noose around his neck and drew the rope tight.

Athan's face was contorted in terror. He seemed to be mouthing something but no one knew if it was a plea or a prayer. All eyes turned to Osborn.

'What are you waiting for?' snapped Osborn. 'I said hang him at once.'

The two men holding Athan jumped down as the third kicked the bench from under him. He kicked and thrashed in agony, his eyes bulging, his face turning purple.

'Help him,' Joan screamed, 'help my boy.' She tried to reach him, but two servants held her back.

'Leave him,' Osborn ordered. 'Let him dance. It will be a salutary lesson to others. No one's to touch him till nightfall.'

Raffe, casting a furious glance at Osborn, ran towards the strangling lad and seized both legs in an iron grip. He pulled violently downwards. Instantly the jerking stopped. Athan's head lolled to one side in the noose. The eyes glazed and fixed. It was all over. Only Joan's sobbing broke the silence.

Raffe walked slowly through the crowd of silent servants without looking at anyone. As he passed, Osborn seized Raffe's arm and yanked him round to face him.

'You'll pay dearly for that,' Osborn growled. 'And if I ever find a way to prove that you had a hand in that girl's disappearance, by God, I'll make you wish it was you who had hanged this day, not him.'

Raffe tore himself out of Osborn's grasp, his face expressionless, and continued walking towards the gate.

Behind him he heard Osborn yelling, 'You needn't think this death wipes out the girl's punishment. I won't rest until she's dragged back here at a horse's tail. I'll find her, Master Raffaele, sooner or later I'll find her, you can be sure of that.'

10th Day after the New Moon, June 1211

St John's Wort – Mortals use this herb in love charms and to increase fertility. It is most effective when gathered on St John's Eve with the dew still wet upon it. If a maid shall gather it, fasting, it shall bring her a husband within the year, and if she places it under her pillow she shall see the face of the man she will wed. They also claim that if a barren wife desires a child, she should strip herself naked and go out to pick the flower on Midsummer's Eve, then she shall surely bear a child before the next feast of St John.

But beware lest you step on St John's Wort whilst it is growing, for a horse will rise up from the ground under you and carry you away. And though it rears and bucks, drags you through thorn thickets and stinking ditches until you are bruised and exhausted, you will not be able to slide from its back. You shall be forced to ride the beast until cockcrow, whereupon the faerie horse will vanish and you shall be left to walk home for many a mile.

The Mandrake's Herbal

Mother Margot

The two boatmen gripped Elena's arms on either side, hurrying her up the darkened streets. They had reached Norwich before dark, but the men had moored up on the River Wensum a little way short of the town in the shelter of the marshes. They had offered Elena bread and onions, and strips of dried eel. But though she had not eaten for more than a day, she felt full and nauseous after only a few bites of the coarse bread. Her breasts burned and ached, so swollen with milk that she couldn't even bear the touch of the cloth of her kirtle on them.

As soon as it was dark the boatmen sculled up the river into the outskirts of the town and tied up near a decaying wooden jetty that tilted precariously into the oozing mud. Now they scuttled through a maze of alleys and snickets, avoiding the main streets where the flames of the torches guttered and danced in their brackets on the walls of the houses. These little alleys huddled in darkness save for the dagger-thin blades of yellow light that struck out between shutters or under doors.

In Gastmere most villagers lived in tiny one-roomed cottages, separated from their neighbours by wide tofts where vegetables, herbs and fruit grew, and chickens, geese and pigs wandered freely. Elena had not dreamed that any place could have so many streets or houses so squashed together.

The men finally halted in front of a large wooden house. Elena guessed they must have looped back towards the river again, for she could feel the sharp, damp breeze on her face, though she could not see the water. The dwelling, though large enough to be owned by a merchant of some property, was not in the sort of street any man with money would choose for his wife and children. The ground was ankle-deep in bones, vegetable peelings and worse, thrown out by the inns and alehouses which lined it. The music of the hurdy-gurdy and frestelles tumbled from the windows, and bawdy songs and raucous laughter spilled from the casements.

One of the boatmen pulled on a rope, and somewhere from deep inside the building a bell tolled. Almost at once, as if he had been waiting behind it, a small panel behind a grill opened and a man peered out, holding up a lantern to illuminate his visitors.

The boatman moved closer to the grill. 'The Bullock said to bring this package to Mother Margot.'

'Did he now? Then we'd best take a look at it, hadn't we?'

After much fumbling, the door swung open and the boatman pushed her inside.

'Meet me in the Adam and Eve tonight, we'll reckon up then,' the gateman said. The two boatmen nodded tersely and, with a rapid glance up and down the street, retreated back into the shadows.

Placing a hand on her shoulder, the gateman guided Elena into a long, narrow room. A fire burned brightly in a pit in the middle, the smoke meandering to the blackened roof beams far above. Around the top of the walls were carved grotesques, masks of green men and other leering faces, like those Elena had seen on the church in Gastmere. At the far end of the hall was a long table set on either side with benches. The table was laden with flagons, leather beakers and half-eaten platters of cold meats, roast fowls, pies, bread and slabs of yellow cheese. It appeared that a great company had sat down to dine here, but had been served with more food than they could possibly eat. Another wave of hunger and nausea rose up in Elena at the sight of the meats. She swallowed hard, and tried to focus on something.

The gateman was looking her up and down with a great deal of curiosity. He was a stocky man, with thick, bowed legs that gave him a rolling gait. His nose had been badly broken and had mended crooked, and the thickened ears which bulged out from under his grizzled hair bore witness to their owner having engaged in numerous fist fights. But he had the cockiness of stance which suggested he usually came out of a fight victorious, whether by fair means or foul.

'I wonder . . . tell me, lass, did you work at the manor with Master Raffaele?'

'For a little . . . as a maid.'

An oddly satisfied grin flickered across the gateman's crocked face. 'So you're the girl he was so keen to protect. You certainly have a knack for getting yourself into trouble, lass.'

He nodded to himself. Then he glanced towards the far end of the hall as if someone had attracted his attention, though Elena could see nothing except the carved grotesques.

'You wait here,' he ordered.

The gateman disappeared through a narrow doorway on the opposite side of the room. Elena heard the creak of stairs, then silence. Finally the stairs creaked again and the gateman was standing in the doorway beckoning to her.

'Best follow me, lass, Mother Margot doesn't like to be kept waiting.'

Elena shuffled towards him, clutching her scrip tightly against her stomach, as if it would afford her some kind of protection. Although she had never seen a nunnery in her life, as soon as they had entered the building she had recognized that this was no convent. But some part of her still tried to cling desperately to the notion that it was, for if it was not a convent, what was it?

The gateman led the way up the stairs, holding the lantern down by his side so that Elena could see the steps. The stairs ended at a stout door. He knocked before reaching down for Elena's arm and pulling her into the room.

This upper room was smaller than the one below, with a casement overlooking whatever was behind the house, though the shutters were firmly closed. A large bed with thick hangings around it occupied one corner and much of the remaining space was taken up by a table covered with a pile of ledgers and quills and the remains of a supper – a good one too, judging by the wine dregs and goose bones. A huge carved chair stood behind the table, but it was set too deep in the shadows for Elena to make out more than a shape and something that glittered green. Only a single wax candle illuminated the room, so that at first Elena thought it unoccupied.

'A fresh little bub to see you, Ma.'

'Ah, the Bullock's girl.' The voice seemed to be coming from behind a thick woollen cloth screening off the corner of the chamber. 'So, what brings you here, my darling?'

Thoroughly disconcerted at being addressed by someone she couldn't see, Elena stammered, 'Master . . . Master Raffaele said you'd take me and I'd be safe here . . . I'll work hard, Mother, I'll do anything.'

'I'm glad to hear it. Very glad, but why should you need to be kept safe? Why should you not be safe where you were? Tell me the truth, my darling. I can always tell when someone is lying and I don't like liars, do I, Talbot?'

The gateman jerked his head in a vague gesture of agreement.

Elena stared at her feet, desperately hoping she was about to do the right thing, but Raffaele said Mother Margot was a friend of his and he'd not have sent her here if he thought the woman would turn her away.

'I had a baby, a boy. I was afraid for him so I gave him away, but they said . . . they said I'd killed him. But I didn't . . . I swear. You have to believe me,' she added desperately.

'I don't have to believe anyone, my darling, and I seldom do. So it's here or the gallows, is that it? That should sharpen your appetite for work. Now, let's see what Master Raffe has sent us.'

The cloth billowed as someone stepped from behind it.

Now Elena was naive, but she was not stupid. She was no longer expecting the figure which emerged to be dressed in a nun's habit, but nothing in her life thus far had prepared her for what she now saw.

The woman was a dwarf, no more than three feet high, with a massive head, so that it looked as if the head of a giant had been placed on the body of an infant. She was dressed in a long, loose scarlet robe, which though stained and a little threadbare, must once have been as costly as any gown of Lady Anne's. Heavy gold bracelets squeezed around the bulging muscles of Ma's arms. Her oiled black hair was coiled up like a snake on top of her head and fastened with long gold pins topped with jewels that glowed blood-red in the candlelight. Ma's yellow-green eyes, bulging like a frog's, ran an appraising glance up and down the length of Elena.

'Well, we know she'll not pass as a virgin, not now that she's been stretched by the baby. How old are you, girl?'

Elena was gaping at Mother Margot in such shock that for a moment she couldn't grasp the question, never mind remember the answer. Finally she managed to whisper, 'Sixteen.'

Mother Margot glanced up at Talbot hovering in the doorway. 'She looks much younger, that'll please some, those that like them looking innocent at the start of the night anyway.'

Talbot eyed Elena shrewdly, as if he was appraising the quality of a horse. 'Bit on the scrawny side if you ask me, Ma, most want a bit of flesh they can grab on to, still there're some that like them boyish-looking. You want me to get her started?'

Ma Margot shuffled forward and walked around Elena, then reached up a hand and without warning pinched her swollen breast. Elena gave a sharp cry of pain as milk soaked the front of her kirtle.

'No, not yet. For now she can earn her keep as a maid, till we hear from Raffe. He may have something special in mind for her.' She looked up at Elena. 'I'll give you something to dry up that milk. Our customers don't want reminding there are consequences to their sin. They like to think the good

Lord created breasts for their pleasure. If they wanted milk they'd sleep with a cow, or their own mothers. Isn't that right, Talbot?'

He snorted. 'I reckon some of them do just that.'

Elena's face was burning. She had been trying to pretend, trying to cut her mind off from the truth, but even little innocents like her can't keep thought out once it has wormed its way in. Master Raffaele, the one person she had trusted, had sent her to this place . . . this . . . she couldn't even think of the word for it, but there was no mistaking what they did here. How could he have betrayed her like this? How could she have been so stupid as ever to believe he would protect her? She should have known from his anger the night she had been dismissed from the manor, and again by the violence he had threatened when he sent her down into the pit, that he hated her. He believed that she had killed her son. This was his way of punishing her, but why? Why this? Why hadn't he simply left her to hang?

She turned and ran to the door, but Talbot stood barring the way.

'Let me go! You can't keep me here!'

Her only thought, for she had nothing that resembled a plan, was to run from this place as fast as she could. She tried to push past Talbot, but though he made no attempt to restrain her, he would not move from the doorway. Ma Margot caught her by the wrist, twisting it at the same time, so that before Elena could do anything to resist, she found herself being forced to her knees. Ma pushed Elena's arm up behind her, hard enough to leave her in no doubt that this tiny woman was capable of snapping a bone as easily as a twig if she chose to.

'And just where do you think you are going to run to?' Ma said, ignoring Elena's whimpers of pain. 'Do you think I didn't know that Osborn was searching for you, long before you set foot through the door? I know when a beggar farts in this town, before they've even smelt it themselves. You're wanted for murder and furthermore you're a runaway villein. By tomorrow, criers will on the streets of every town and village within miles, offering a reward to anyone who brings you in dead or alive. And I can tell Osborn means business, for most men would sell their own children for the size of the purse he's offering. If that weren't inducement enough, he's threatened dire punishment to any caught sheltering you.

'You just be grateful, my darling, that I'm willing to take that risk for you, 'cause I tell you now, no other soul in this town or any other would take you in, not if Osborn's determined to find you.'

With her mouth still bitter from the draught of herbs Ma Margot had given her to dry her milk, Elena descended the narrow staircase again, and this time Talbot led her through a door to the left, which opened directly on to a courtyard. Elena shivered in the cold night air. The courtyard and the garden at the far end were both enclosed by the solid walls of buildings. Half a dozen doors led from the courtyard into what appeared to be chambers beyond. Instead of blazing torches, lanterns swung in the breeze. They were not bright enough to illuminate anyone's features, but cast just enough light through the horn panels for a man to pick his away across the yard without falling down the well or colliding with the several stout benches that were scattered about. To one side was a bigger door set into the wall which appeared to lead out of the courtyard to the world beyond.

Seeing Elena's gaze fasten on it, Talbot nodded his head.

'Behind there's the stables. Some of our gentlemen arrive on horseback, but it's no use thinking you can get out that way. Kept bolted on the other side. There's only one way in or out for you girls and that's the way you came in, through the guest hall. But you'd best not try slipping out that way unless Ma gives you leave. You never know when she's watching you, and if she catches any of her girls doing something she don't like, believe me, they soon wish she hadn't.'

The gatekeeper led Elena past several of the chambers. Light shone out through the shutters and from inside came the sounds of laughter, grunts and squeals. Elena shuddered.

Talbot grinned. 'Noisy bastards, ain't they? Always puts me in mind of pigs when you throw them a mess of swill.'

He stopped outside the last door in the far corner of the courtyard. 'This is where you all sleep. No customers to be brought in here, you understand?'

He pushed her inside.

It was hard to see much by the dim light of the lantern. Raised wooden platforms ran along either side of the room, on which were a number of straw pallets at all kinds of angles to each other, and between them Elena could see small boxes and rolled bundles, evidently their owners' meagre possessions. More clothes were heaped on top of the mattresses.

At the same instant as she pitied the women for the little they owned, it struck her for the first time that she now owned nothing except the damp, stinking rags she stood up in and her scrip. She pressed the leather to her, but she knew it was empty save for the wizened mandrake, and what use was that to her now?

She thought of the small chest crammed with the kirtles and trinkets she had received from Lady Anne, standing in her mother-in-law's cottage. What would that old witch do? Wear them? Sell them? Anger boiled up in her. Joan had never thought her good enough for her son, but to do all in her power to get her daughter-in-law hanged – how could any woman be that spiteful? She shuddered at the thought that if Joan'd had her way, she would even now be hanging in a gibbet with ravens pecking at her sightless eyes. Elena tried to remind herself that all that mattered was that she was alive. She knew she should be grateful for that. But then she remembered where she was, and the fear and revulsion engulfed her again.

Several women were already sleeping in the chamber. Some lay sprawled across their pallets with arms and legs spilling out from beneath the coverings, others were curled up in tight balls, furrowing their brows in their sleep as the light from Talbot's lantern brushed their faces. Talbot marched down between the platforms, stepping carefully across the firepit in the centre though there was no fire burning now. Towards the back of the room, the pallets were occupied by four or five young boys, who were arranged head to foot like a row of herring on the monger's slab, tugging the blankets towards them as they fought one another in their dreams.

Talbot paused by two women who lay side by side whispering to each other.

'Here,' he said in a gruff whisper. 'Ma's taken in another bub. Find her a corner, will you, Luce. Tomorrow, take her in hand and show her the rules. She's only to clean for now, nothing more. And, Luce, mind you treat her like your own sister. She belongs to the Bullock.'

A dark-haired girl, with large doe eyes, propped herself up on one elbow.

'Belong to Master Raffe, do you? Aren't you the lucky one! What's he like then, the Bullock? They say he's got tricks that not even a ship's whore knows.' She tugged at the wet, muddy hem of Elena's skirts. 'If we're to be sisters you must tell everything he does in bed, I want every detail, mind.'

Elena snatched her skirt out of her grasp. 'I haven't . . . I've never let him touch me. He's an old man.'

Luce laughed. 'You wait till you see some of the wrinkled old cocks we get in here, you'll think Master Raffe a pullet compared to them. What's your name, kitten?'

'El —'

Elena was stopped mid-word by a heavy cuff from Talbot. 'Goose-head! You don't ever give your real name to anyone in here. Here, Luce,' he said, shaking his head as if he despaired of her stupidity, 'you give her a name.'

The girl chuckled softly. 'Prickly little thing, isn't she, and with hair that red, we'd best call her Holly. Tell you what, with flame on top like that, there'll be no hiding her light under a bush, not even a roomful of bushes.'

Talbot laughed.

Luce glanced around the room, then pointed to a pallet opposite her own.

'Take that one, next to Apricot; just chuck her bundle on to the top of that box. She's always spreading herself out.'

Elena picked her way across to the vacant pallet and, struggling out of her sodden shoes, lay down fully clothed, her scrip still fastened around her waist. Her teeth began to chatter and she shivered uncontrollably.

'You not got any covers, Holly?' A coarse blanket came flying through the air, hitting Elena in the face. 'Get out of your wet clothes, you'll catch your death.'

Elena gratefully drew the blanket over her, but she still made no attempt to peel off her damp clothes, though she longed to be warm and dry. To be naked in this place would be to admit she was now one of them and she wasn't. She wouldn't ever allow herself to be.

Luce glanced at Talbot and shrugged. Talbot, shaking his head as if he could never understand women, lumbered from the room.

Ma poured a goblet of wine for herself and pushed the flagon across her table towards Talbot. He shook his head, as he usually did. Talbot could down his own bodyweight in ale of an evening and still remember every word of gossip he'd picked up in the Adam and Eve Inn, but he'd never had the stomach for wine.

He hovered uneasily in front of Ma's table. He knew the signs; that silent and too concentrated paring of an apple with her razor-sharp knife meant Ma was not happy, and if she wasn't happy, you could be certain she'd make damn sure he wasn't either.

'So, my darling,' Ma said. 'Why don't you tell me why I'm really risking my neck taking in this girl? And don't say you're just doing a favour for the Bullock.'

Talbot grinned. 'She's a pretty wench, has an innocence

about her some men would love to spoil in more ways than one. She'll earn you good money.'

'I never take in girls who don't bring me money. What else?' The rubies on Ma's stubby fingers flashed in the candle-light as she scraped her long talons down the pewter goblet.

Talbot's grin faded instantly. He knew when Ma's patience was wearing thin.

'All right, Ma, if you must know, back in the spring Raffe told me that a lass in the manor had overheard a man talking about bringing French spies into England. She didn't recognize who was talking, but it turns out the rat was none other than Hugh of Roxham, Osborn's little brother. Raffe wouldn't report it for fear Hugh would get to the lass first. And I reckon that little red-head downstairs is the same girl Raffe was trying to protect then. Now it seems she's fallen foul of the other brother too.'

Ma's yellow-green eyes opened so wide they looked as if they might explode out of her head. 'What! And you persuaded me to take her in here! I'll have your bollocks roasted for this – while you're still wearing them.'

Talbot took a step backwards, his hands held up in protest.

'Wait, Ma. Don't you see? This could be good for us. Sheriff is always trying to line his filthy little coffers with taxes and fines. And with that bastard John demanding more and more money from Norwich and the other towns for his wars, it won't be long before the sheriff's round here again finding some excuse to fine us again. Osborn's got a long reach and he's a favourite of John. If anyone could persuade the sheriff to leave us in peace, he could. We just need to give him a reason.

'The lass has only murdered her brat, not like she's killed a nobleman, so we could tell her John would pardon her if she delivered a traitor to him. He'd probably hang her anyway, but what does that matter? Thing is, Osborn's got too much to lose to risk his brother being accused of treason. Once he learns what this little red-head knows he might be persuaded to keep the sheriff off our backs and even to contribute a generous sum to our little convent here, just to make sure we keep the lass quiet.'

Ma's fingers tightened round the neck of the goblet. 'Blackmail is a dangerous game, especially when it involves the likes of Osborn. It could see us all on the gallows.' She fixed Talbot with an unblinking stare. 'Now, you listen to me, my darling, and you listen well. We'll keep this girl safe till we see which way the wind is blowing. If the time's right we'll play your game, but if I think the risks are too high I'll sell her to Osborn myself. But I'll decide. Until then you keep your mouth shut, you understand?'

Talbot nodded. It was the best he could hope for from Ma.

He was almost at the door when she said quietly, 'That nobleman back in the Holy Land who would have hanged you for thieving, I seem to recall you telling me once his name was Hugh. Not the same Hugh, by any chance, was it, my darling?'

Talbot scowled at her. 'Everyone was at it, filling their pockets, the nobles were the worst. I only took their leavings. And that fecking bastard Hugh had me searched and, brazenly as you like, pocketed all I'd taken. Then he told his men to string *me* up for thieving. He was the bloody thief. It was him who should have been hanged. Those were my spoils. I'd found 'em. They were mere chicken scraps to a man like him, but that bit of gold and silver would have set me up for life. Could've bought myself a juicy little business and been me own man, I could, if it weren't for that swine.'

'Now we're getting to the real nub of it.' Ma smiled, showing her sharp white teeth. 'The Bullock's been a good friend to us and I'll take this girl for his sake, but if I find you putting me or this house in danger just to take revenge on this Hugh of yours, I swear I'll make your life so miserable you'll be cursing Raffe to the fires of hell for ever saving you from that noose.'

*

Elena lay rigid on her back, listening to the groans, snores and mutters of the sleepers around her. She heard the last of the customers stumbling drunkenly across the courtyard, some singing, some calling goodbyes in hoarse whispers loud enough to raise the saints from their perfumed coffins. Every now and then the door would open and another woman or boy would stumble into the room and pick their way across the prone bodies to their own little space, slip off their clothes and slide naked under the covers, sinking into sleep almost at once.

Just a few hours ago Elena had prayed to be saved from the gallows and now . . . now she didn't know what to pray. How long would it be before she was made to join them out there in those other rooms, and what would they make her do? All the jokes and conversations she listened to between Marion and the other women began to echo again in her head, the way they giggled over what they'd done with men, things Elena couldn't imagine any woman doing or wanting to do. Half the time she'd thought they were making it up just to make the younger girls blush, now she wasn't sure.

She had only ever slept with Athan, and the thought of any other man lying on top of her, his hands all over her, made her gag, never mind the thought of what else they might want her to do. She turned over and winced as her tender swollen breasts pressed against the coarse straw of the pallet. She longed desperately to feel her baby's soft little mouth nuzzling against her, to hold him just one last time.

Elena's eyes burned with tears from exhaustion, hunger, fear, but mostly for the great ache that was the absence of Athan and her son. She loved Athan so much. But the face that rose up in front of her when she tried to picture him was distorted with the doubt she'd seen in his eyes when he'd last looked at her. Did he really believe she could have done it? Why hadn't he spoken up for her to Osborn? Why hadn't he even tried to come to her last night in the pit? He said he would always love her. Those were the last words he had spoken to her and she clung desperately to them. But could you really love someone and believe them capable of murdering your own little son?

Tears forced their way from under Elena's eyelids but angrily she rubbed them away. Of all of them, Raffaele had been the only one to help her in the end and she must believe he would continue to protect her. Who else was there she could trust? If she allowed herself to think that there was no one, she'd never be able to go on living.

That first day after he'd taken her to see Lady Anne, Raffaele had promised to be like a father to her and no father would let his daughter be used as a whore. He had sent her here to keep her safe, and it had been a good plan, for Osborn's men would never think to search here. And when Gytha returned to Gastmere and proved her innocent, she would be able to go home again to Athan and he would look at her tenderly the way he had that night they conceived their son. Everything would come right. It must. All she had to do was wait. Clinging to that single thread of hope, Elena finally drifted into an exhausted sleep.

✝

11th Day after the New Moon, June 1211

Ants – which some call *pismires*, for they stink of piss.

As many swellings or warts as a mortal has, he should take that number of ants, bind them in a cloth with a snail and burn it all to ashes and mix with vinegar. Then remove the head of an ant and crushing the body between his fingers anoint the juice on the swellings and they shall shrink.

Some say ants are Muryans or faeries who undergo many earthly transformations, getting smaller and smaller until they become ants before vanishing for ever. Others say they are the souls of unbaptized children who cannot enter either heaven or hell, therefore an ants' nest must never be destroyed. And if a piece of tin is placed in an ants' nest at just the right moment under a new moon it will turn to silver.

Ant eggs can be used to destroy the love of a man for a woman, or a maid for a lad, if they should desire that person for themselves. For mortals are fickle in all ways but this, that they burn most fiercely with love for another when that love is not returned.

The Mandrake's Herbal

The Stew

A wisp of lilac smoke filtered up through the bright green leaves of the great beech tree, dissolving before it could touch the pale dawn sky. Beneath the branches, Gytha turned the wizened apple in her hand, counting the thorns pressed into the flesh: *eena, deena, dina, das, catiler, weena, winna, was, eena, deena.* The counting was to strengthen the power of the fetch, but Gytha knew exactly how many thorns she had used – one to bring the girl, and one for the babe, and now to set them spinning. She plucked the third thorn and dropped it on to a stone in the glowering embers of the fire. It lay for a moment before suddenly blazing into a single flame. Then almost before she could draw breath it had vanished, leaving a tiny mound of ash in the shape of a little grey fox. Gytha smiled to herself as she blew the ash into the wind.

She added a few sticks to the fire and rocked back on her heels, gazing up at the canopy above. The sunlight trickled down through the branches, illuminating the tiny cobweb of veins in every tender new leaf. It was a good time of year to be living outdoors. She'd missed this.

Gytha sensed a movement behind her, but she didn't bother to turn her head. She knew a lad had been hovering out of sight in the forest since first light, trying to pluck up the courage to approach the clearing.

At last the boy cleared his throat. 'There's this lass.'

He added no further explanation, as if he thought those three words were more than enough for anyone to expect of him. He continued to study her intently as she mended the fire, as though he thought there was dark magic in the way she laid the wood or blew upon the embers.

'Can you do it?' he finally blurted out.

'Course she can,' Madron said.

The boy spun round as if an arrow had struck him.

'Who was that?' he asked, looking fearfully about him. 'Was it a spirit?'

'An evil old spirit,' Gytha muttered.

Then, seeing the boy's terrified expression, she relented and gestured towards a little bothy woven from branches and last year's bracken, half hidden under the trees.

'Just the old besom in there. She's blind. She'll not hurt you.'

The boy took several steps backwards, not at all convinced by this assurance.

He was one of the sons of the charcoal makers who lived most of the year deep in the forest, tending their fires night and day. Every inch of visible skin was grimed with smoke and burnt wood, and his clothes were many layers of mud-coloured rags. He was a tall, angular creature, thin as a sapling that has shot up too fast. His blond hair bushed out wildly from beneath his cap, grazing his shoulders. He fidgeted restlessly like a child, but the sparse growth on his lip and chin suggested he might be older than he looked.

Gytha sighed. 'So, this girl you're in love with, when did you last see her?'

With another fearful glance at the bothy, the lad wrenched his attention back to Gytha.

'At Michaelmas, at the Herring Fair on the isle of Yarmouth. M'father took us there to sell the charcoal to the ships. M'father and brothers sent me to buy us some supper first day and there she was, walking up the length of the sand selling oysters from a great pannier on her back. I went back the next day, and the next, to buy oysters, twice sometimes, till m'brothers said they were sick of the sight of them, but then I went just to stand and watch her. She was . . . like a queen, her hair . . . it was sparkling all over like she was wearing jewels. When I told her, she said they were fish scales blown there by the wind, and she laughed and these two little dimples –'

'Did you tell her you loved her?' Gytha interrupted,

knowing from experience that love-lorn youths can easily talk to a woman about their sweethearts all day, given any encouragement.

The boy hung his head and scuffed the deep leaf litter miserably with his bare toe.

'You didn't.' Gytha said.

'But this year when we go back I'll do it. I will this time, only . . . what if she's fallen for another afore I can tell her . . .'

'Then you'll need something to make her fall out of love with him and fall in love with you.'

'Can you give me something that'll make it happen?' the lad asked eagerly.

'I'll need something of hers to use in the charm. Do you have anything that she's touched or worn? A lock of this wondrous hair of hers? A scrap of ribbon?'

The lad hesitated, then reached into his shirt and pulled out half an oyster shell that dangled round his neck from a bit of twine.

'She opened this herself and poured the oyster into her own mouth. Then she threw the shell away. But I picked it up and kept it,' he said, touching the flaking shell as reverently as a holy relic.

Gytha was sure he was blushing beneath the grime. She pressed her lips tightly together to keep from grinning. Men, like dogs, hate to be laughed at. She held out her hand.

'If she's eaten from it, that'll do fine. Come back at sunset for the charm.'

Gytha knew that the affair was as doomed as the salmon and the swallow who fell in love. The lad was a creature of the forest; the girl belonged to the sea, so where would they build their nest? But the young foolishly believe love can overcome all obstacles.

'You'll not lose the shell?' the lad asked anxiously.

'I'll guard it like pearls.'

The boy carefully placed the oyster shell in her hand and bounded off.

Gytha turned the shell over in her hand, caressing the smooth iridescent lining. She tilted it to the sun, watching the silver, blue and pinks flash across its shining surface like minnows in the brook.

'You going to use the same charm as you used on Sir Gerard?' Madron called out. 'It'll not last. I told you to use Yadua then, but you wouldn't listen.'

Gytha rose angrily and crossed to the bothy, glaring down at the old woman who lay inside, propped up on a bed of dried bracken.

'I told you, I used no charm on him. He wanted me. He would have taken me as his wife, had it not been for his mother.'

Madron wheezed with laughter. She turned milk-blind eyes towards Gytha, sensing exactly where she was standing.

'He was happy enough to bed you, lass, but a man of his blood doesn't wed a cunning woman, not even a free-born one, less he's witched. I warned you, it'd take more of a snare than your spread legs to catch a stag like him.'

'You never wanted me to have him,' Gytha spat at her. 'Afraid I'd leave you to rot alone in your cottage with no one to cook and tend to you.'

'You were too old to be mooning around like a love-sick maid. Besides, you were quick enough to get your own back when Lady Anne stopped him coming near you.'

Gytha's head whipped up. 'I only spoke the truth.'

'You did that all right, but did the truth need to be spoken?'

Gytha turned away, striding out through the trees with little idea of where she was going except to get far away from Madron's words. But she knew she could never do that. Madron had used those same words twenty years ago and they had burrowed deep inside Gytha like a tapeworm and would not release their grip.

Gerard had loved her once. She was certain of that. She had been his first love, older than him by six years, but what did age matter, they told each other. She had led him in his first tentative fumblings, their bodies pressed close together in the warm damp grass on a hot summer's evening.

But after a few meetings it had been him who'd taken her with a frenzied wonderment, as she helped him discover every secret pleasure of her body and of his. When they rolled from each other exhausted and utterly satisfied, they had lain there staring up at the stars through the trees. He had taught her names for the constellations, names that were foreign and strange, that he'd learned from books: *Virgo, Leo and Scorpio*. She had taught him her names, handed down for generations, familiar, comforting names: *The Path of the Dead, the Plough, the Swan*. And they listened to the owl calling to its mate, the nightjar and the vixen screaming, until he took her in his arms again and they heard nothing and saw nothing but the fire in each other's hearts.

After his mother found out, he did not come to her for many weeks. When he finally appeared, Gytha had been overjoyed to see him, adoring him the more for defying his mother. She'd come running towards him and flung her arms about him, kissing his neck. But he had held her by the shoulders, thrusting her away from him.

'I cannot. I came only to tell you that I am to be wed as soon as my father returns from the Holy Wars. I thought you should know. I was betrothed when I was a child.'

'Betrothed?' she repeated, stunned. 'All this time you were whispering your love for me, you were promised to another woman?'

He'd had the grace to look uncomfortable. 'I barely know the girl. We haven't met since we were little children. I thought you would realize all men in my position . . . Besides, you knew we had no future together, it was just a pleasant way to pass the time.'

'Pleasant!' she shrieked at him.

He'd tried to stop her raging torrent of words with his fingers, but she bit them, hard enough to draw blood. He swore, clamping his hand under his armpit. He said other things, words that were meant to soothe and mollify. But she did not hear any of them. She did not *want* to hear any of them.

After he left, she had raged and cried, planning spells and poisons, curses and love charms in equal measure, but in the end she had done none of those things.

Madron was right, she could have bound him to her with Yadua. She could have witched him so deeply he would have married her in defiance of a whole army of mothers. But what use is it to win a man by magic? What joy is there to lie in his arms realizing that he only holds you because he has no choice, and knows not what he is doing? What contentment is there to wake every morning wondering if this will be the day when the enchantment fails, and that when he opens his eyes and looks at you, you will see only hatred in them?

No, Gytha couldn't soothe her pain like that. In the cold grey dawn, after many sleepless nights, she could think of only one thing to avenge the hurt she felt. It would not bring him back to her, but it would punish him far more cruelly than any earthly power could devise. For as Madron had always taught her – the taste of revenge is far sweeter than love.

Luce led Elena towards the first of the entertaining rooms, as she called them. She flung the door of the chamber open and set about pushing wide the shutters to let in the early morning light.

'You'd best start in here. Straighten the covers, see the oil lamps are filled and wicks trimmed ready. Then rake over the rushes on the floor and strew some fresh herbs in them. Ma likes the place kept sweet. You'll find the lamp oil and sacks of strewing herbs in the stores across the yard.'

The room, which last night had been filled with grunts of pleasure, this morning was empty and silent save for the gentle snores of a couple lying at the far end. They slept on, tangled in each other, naked except for a cloak which barely covered the girl's buttocks as she lay with one leg thrown across her client's groin.

Unlike the chamber where Elena had spent the night, this hall had low partitions dividing the pallets from each other, not for privacy, for they were open at one end to the narrow walkway between them, but to keep out the worst of the winter draughts and prevent the more vigorous of the customers from accidentally striking their neighbours or rolling on them as they flailed about in the throes of passion.

Luce sank down on the nearest cot and curled up, yawning.

'Best make a start, Holly.'

Elena moved awkwardly in the overlarge kirtle which Luce had lent her and began to smooth the covers in the first of the stalls. She was almost grateful for the work, for it was an everyday task, something any woman might do in her own croft. But this was not her own cottage, and as she bent she caught the strong, salt-sweet smell of stains on the covers and the thick stench of sweat, overlaid with musky perfumed oils. She recoiled, her hands trembling. Would a stranger force her down among these smells, these stains, till her hair reeked of them as Luce's did?

Attempting to calm herself, Elena looked around, trying to find something that did not shriek at her of what went on in this room. Nailed to the wall near the door she noticed a long board divided into squares in each of which there seemed to be a painting of sorts. Curiosity drew her closer and for a moment she stared, unable to comprehend what she was seeing, then, flushing scarlet, she turned away. She heard Luce chuckling. The girl slithered off the bed and, putting her arm around Elena's shoulder, turned her firmly round to face the board again.

'That's what's on offer, see.'

Each of the little squares depicted a crudely painted figure of two or sometimes three people in various strange positions. Elena was not unacquainted with sex; after all, she had grown up surrounded by all of nature's fecundity. Before she could even put names to the beasts, she had seen cocks fluttering on the backs of hens, rams tupping ewes, stallions covering mares and even other stallions. She'd giggled at lads and lasses rolling together in the pasture. It had seemed but a natural expression of life, the grunts and groans and squeals of its daily renewal.

In the cottages or even the Great Hall, most of these human couplings were little more than animal copulations, rapid, furtively hidden beneath blankets, the noise suppressed for fear of disturbing children, parents or some short-tempered bed-fellow. They required no thought or imagination beyond the basic urge to relieve the burning of nature's honest lust. But as Elena was about to discover, the human mind, if left unoccupied, can create such strange fancies as have never entered the head of a cockerel or dog.

Luce nodded towards the board. 'We get many foreigners coming here, sailors, merchants and the like. We don't always understand what they want, so they can just point at that. Mind you, we have to use the board with some of the local lads too. They only have to step in here for every word they ever learned since they were weaned to vanish from their poor little heads and they start to babble like babies.' She smiled fondly. 'One lad I had the other day, couldn't even remember whether he was asking for a woman or a boy.'

'A boy?'

Luce waved a hand towards the wall. 'Boys work in the chamber next door. Some of the men in here don't like to see a man with a boy, puts 'em off. Funny, that,' she added, almost to herself, 'how what sends one man into ecstasy sends another to vomit.'

'I thought those boys were the sons of the women.'

Luce snorted. 'They're somebody's sons all right. There's many a mother or father has sold their sons to work in here. But they don't belong to us, though some of the women in here are more mothers to them than their own have ever been.'

Elena closed her eyes as a sudden pain slashed through her head. What had become of her own son? What had Gytha done with him? Was he really being cared for somewhere safe, or had she sold him? Would he end up in a place like this? For a moment she was almost glad she was here, as if that would be enough to appease heaven and spare her son from such a place. She wanted to believe that whatever happened to her meant it could not happen to him. But deep down she knew that wasn't true. A woman and her child could easily be slaughtered together – they often were – but she clung to the thought all the same: *I'm doing this to protect him.*

Why do mortals think that suffering is a coin with which they can buy justice or salvation? We mandrakes learn wisdom from our fathers: life is a steal if you are a talented thief, and if you are not, then you may suffer all you please but it will buy you nothing but pain.

Elena could not prevent her face from screwing up into an expression of disgust as she glanced once more at the pictures on the board. She looked at Luce, trying to imagine which of these things she did.

Luce saw her expression and her face darkened. 'You needn't sneer at us. You're in here too, aren't you?'

'But I couldn't do that!' Elena said.

'You'd be surprised at what you can do when you have to, and if you bend a little, kitten, you might even get to enjoy it.'

Elena felt her face burning, knowing that Luce had realized exactly what she was thinking. But she still couldn't bring herself to imagine doing such things with strangers. She couldn't and she wouldn't. She was married in all but name. She wasn't like Luce. She would never be like Luce.

But she wouldn't have to be. Raffaele would come soon, maybe he'd even come today, and take her somewhere safe. She wasn't staying here. She didn't live here, not like the other girls. Today or tomorrow Raffaele would come for her.

Trying to avert her gaze from the mesmerizing pictures on the board, Elena threw herself into the cleaning and tidying, trying hard to focus on smoothing, straightening, tossing, turning, strewing, all those chores which back in Gastmere she had impatiently prayed to have done and over, but to which she now clung as fiercely as a beggar grasps his only coin.

Luce saw her fearful expression ease and smiled to herself. She had seen enough bubs enter Ma's gates to know that all they needed was time. Let her get accustomed to it gradually, she thought. So she did not tell Elena that these plain rooms, these anonymous rooms, were just public rooms meant for the poorer classes: the penniless journeymen and the pimple-faced virgin apprentices; the sailors and peddlers who wanted ale, meat and a woman in that order; and the minor clerics whose long hours spent freezing their bollocks off through dreary Latin services gave rise to fantasies so ungodly that they dared not confess them to any but a whore. But there were other rooms, secret rooms, of which, as yet, Elena knew nothing, but she would learn. Oh yes, in time she would learn, as all mortals must, that every soul has its own dark and hidden chambers.

7th Day after the New Moon, July 1211

Vervain – an ancient magical herb, which the druids revere almost as much as mistletoe. Christians say it was used to staunch Christ's wounds on the Cross and therefore it is used to sprinkle holy water. It is said to avert evil, and stop bleeding. Nevertheless, witches and warlocks use it often in their spells as a love charm, and if a thief should make a cut on his hand and press the leaf to it, he shall have the power to open locks.

If a mortal suffers from a tumour he should cut a vervain root in half and hang a portion round his neck whilst the other is dried over a fire. As the root withers in the heat, so shall the tumour wither away. But the mortal must make certain to keep the withered root safe, for if an enemy or malicious spirit wishes him harm, he may steal the root and drop it into water and as the root swells again so shall the tumour.

Mortals believe that if they put vervain in the water they bathe in they shall have knowledge of the future and obtain their heart's desire.

But know this, those who pluck the herb must do so only at certain phases of the moon. They must recite charms and must leave honeycomb in the place where they gathered it to make restitution for the violence done to the earth in taking such a sacred herb. Payment must always be made for everything wrested from the earth, for if it is not offered then it will be forcibly taken.

The Mandrake's Herbal

Little Finch

Even before Raffe had taken a pace into Ma's chamber, his head was reeling from the soporific heat and the heavy scents of the musky oils Ma Margot rubbed into her glossy black hair. Although the sun was blazing down outside, the shutters on the window were, as always, tightly shut. The room was illuminated by thick candles impaled on spikes on the wall. Beneath the spikes dripping wax grew up on the floor and walls like layers of sallow fungus on a decaying tree, becoming fatter and more twisted with each passing day.

A flagon of wine and two goblets were laid on the table along with trenchers of cold meats, roasted fowl, cheese and figs. Raffe guessed that Ma Margot had been warned of his coming even before he'd swung down from the saddle in her stable yard. With a flick of her beringed fingers, Ma indicated the empty chair and Raffe sank into it, facing her across the narrow table.

Ma's chair was higher than Raffe's, with a set of wooden steps in front so that the tiny woman could climb up into it, though Raffe knew she always made a point of being seated before Talbot showed him into her presence.

In truth *chair* was too humble a word for such a piece of furniture. Some might have called it a throne, for its back and arms were carved to resemble serpents, painted in yellow, black and with touches of gold. The protruding red tongues of the vipers were hinged on wire threads and they flickered up and down at the slightest movement of the chair's occupant. The eyes of the snakes were inlaid with chips of emerald glass. At least Raffe supposed they must be glass for surely not even Ma Margot could afford real emeralds. The green eyes of the serpents glinted in the trembling candlelight, so that their gaze seemed to be fastened upon the victim in the opposite chair, giving Raffe the uneasy impression that at any time they might dart forward and strike.

Ma Margot pushed a flagon of wine towards him and Raffe poured the dark ruby liquid into his goblet.

'You've come to see your little pigeon?'

Raffe started violently, spilling a few drops of the wine, and Ma Margot's lips twitched in a smile.

'Is she . . . in good health?' Raffe said, avoiding the question.

Ma shrugged. 'Had a touch of milk fever the first week, but she's over that now. Strong girl, but then these field girls usually are. She works hard enough, I'll give her that. No! Don't fret yourself,' Ma raised a stubby hand to forestall the question he was about to ask, 'she's only been put to cleaning and the like, no customers, not till we knew what you had planned for her.'

Ma glanced slyly at him and, removing a long jewelled pin from her coiled black hair, began scraping at the dirt encrusted under her pointed nails.

'Thing is, I can't keep the girl here indefinitely if all she's to do is cleaning. I've women aplenty who are past their prime and don't get so many customers now, so they'll gladly do a bit of cleaning rather than be thrown out on the streets. They've served me loyally over the years and I'll not see them put out for a newcomer. This girl of yours, she'll have to start bringing some money in, and more than pennies at that. I'm taking a huge risk, hiding a fugitive here when Osborn's got a fat bounty on her head.'

Ma Margot pulled a wooden trencher towards her and stabbed her hairpin into the tiny carcass of a roasted song-bird. She lifted it daintily to her lips. Her sharp teeth crunched through the bones as she devoured it whole.

'If any of my customers should recognize her . . .'

'Why should they?' Raffe demanded. 'She's never been out of her village before and the villagers who come here to market can't afford your prices.'

Ma smiled serenely at him and gestured at the food spread out between them. 'We give our customers what they want and they pay for it. There are plenty of cheap stews in Norwich where you can have a whore for the price of a beaker of ale, but you may end up with a few surprises you didn't pay for.'

Raffe knew it was true; whatever else you could say about Ma Margot's, no man ever got his purse stolen as he lay sleeping, or woke up to find himself being sold as a slave to the pirates.

Ma leaned back in her nest of serpents and regarded him shrewdly. 'So what will we do with her, Master Raffe? There's a number of customers have asked for her already, for she is quite striking with that red hair of hers. You know what some men say, flames on top mean there's a blazing fire below, and a few customers would pay good money to quench it for her.'

Raffe was on his feet in an instant. 'Shut your filthy mouth!' His hand shot out to grab Ma's throat, but he'd forgotten about the long gold pin in her hand. He yelped as the point was rammed with unerring accuracy into his palm.

'Manners, Master Raffe,' Ma said, watching with evident satisfaction as he sucked at the blood flowering in his hand. 'Here, sit down. Take more wine and some meats for your belly. All men act with too much haste when they're hungry.'

Still smarting with rage and pain, Raffe reluctantly resumed his seat, and Ma waited as he ripped the meat savagely from a roasted duck and stuffed it into his mouth. He continued to eat in stony silence until, finally replete, he pushed the trencher away.

'Now,' Ma said, 'let's talk business.'

Her tone was so calm and matter of fact, Raffe might have believed he'd imagined the violent exchange, if his hand hadn't still been throbbing from the pin stab.

'You sent the girl here knowing what my business was, so you must have had your reasons, Master Raffe. For if her safety was all that concerned you, she'd be in Flanders by now, but that would have put her right out of your reach, wouldn't it?'

'That's not true. I thought of nothing else but her safety. That was precisely why I didn't attempt to send her abroad. We might have had to wait for days to find a ship that would take her from these shores, and Osborn would have had a watch put on the harbours within hours.'

Ma threw back her head and cackled with laughter. 'Don't try to cod me. We both know Talbot could smuggle a whole whorehouse of girls on board a ship if you paid him to.'

Raffe's face flushed with anger. 'How is the villein who's never been further than the manor's field supposed to fend for herself in a foreign land? She'd have died a beggar on the streets in a month, or worse.'

'Milking a cow or tending a field is the same the world over. We both know she'd have found work easily enough, so don't let's waste words.' Ma was no longer smiling and her eyes had taken on a glittering hardness.

'You want her here within your grasp. But if she stays here, she must earn her keep. I can fill Elena's bed a dozen times over with girls who'll gladly do whatever I ask for a roof over their heads and a full belly.'

'You owe me,' Raffe snapped. 'If it wasn't for me, your brother would have hanged in the Holy Land and you'd never have come to know him. I swore to you I'd never tell him who you were and I kept my word *so far*, because we both know that if Talbot ever found out you and he were kin, he'd start thinking he was master here. He'd want a share of the profits, and a great deal more than a share.'

Ma smiled, though her eyes remained cold and hard. 'I won't deny the old ape is useful. But you and I both know I've more than repaid that debt to you these past twenty years. A life for a life I've given you and I owe you nothing more. So if your girl can't turn a good profit for me, she's out.'

Ma leaned forward and plucked a fig from the trencher, but her gaze was fixed unblinkingly on Raffe's as if she wanted to make sure he understood every word she was about to say.

'Our parents died when I was still a babe in arms. Talbot was almost ten years old then, and, as he's told you, my father had already given him to a ship's captain in payment for a debt. My uncle and his wife took me in, thinking to make use of me as a servant as soon as I could lift a broom. But when they saw I'd never grow like other women, they sold me to the first man that would pay a fat purse to bed a freak. Some men are like that, you know, want to try one of every kind of woman there is, just like some men faced with a banquet won't rest till they've sampled every dish. The more exotic and bizarre, the better it suits their tastes – dwarfs like me, women without arms or legs, giants, Jewesses, Moors, albinos. Some men think if a woman looks different, she'll taste different between his thighs.'

Ma clenched her fist so tightly that the juice from the fig in her hand ran down her arm. 'I was lucky, if you can call it that – the man who bought me had money, and so did his friends. I wasn't a fool. I saw I'd got two choices: resist them and know that they'd rape me anyway, or go willingly with a smile on my face and screw every penny I could from them by giving them all they wanted and things they hadn't even dreamt of.

'Ever since I was twelve years old, I've survived and grown rich by giving men what they desire, even if they haven't got the guts to admit what they want to their own confessors. I learned to know men better than they know themselves, so believe me when I say, a man doesn't put his prize chicken into a den of foxes unless he thinks that hen is really a fox. So whether you know it or not, Master Raffe, you brought this girl here to a whorehouse because that's what you believe her to be.'

Raffe leaned forward on to the table, his head in his hands, trying to master the feelings raging through him. He felt as if he was trapped between two charging armies. Every instinct in him wanted to keep Elena safe, pure, unsullied, just as she had been that day he bound her to him over the body of Gerard.

Yet she had betrayed him with Athan. He could imagine every detail of it. He had done so many times, some furtive sweaty groping in a stinking byre or stable. And if she spread her legs for that gormless youth, who's to say there hadn't been others? Even that, he persuaded himself, he could have forgiven her, if she had only trusted him. Why couldn't she have brought the baby to him if she wanted to be rid of it? He had offered her, stupid little girl, a base-born villein, his love and protection and she wouldn't even condescend to take that much from him.

He knew he only had to toss Ma a few coins and Elena would be his to do with as he pleased, for as long as he pleased. That was all the old hag wanted – money. But even now, even after all he'd risked for Elena, he couldn't do it. He couldn't bear to see her mouth curl in disgust when she saw him naked, the ridicule in her eyes, the mockery pouring from those full lips. He could not force himself on her, knowing how much she would hate him for it.

A smile of satisfaction hovered around Ma's mouth. She pushed the wine flagon invitingly towards him. 'Now, Master Raffe, let me tell you what I have in mind for the girl.'

Few gentlemen came to Ma's house in the early afternoon, for most were seeing to their own businesses. The women took advantage of the quiet time to sleep, wash and mend their linen, or primp in readiness for the early evening customers. But Elena, once her cleaning tasks were done, always spent the afternoon in the courtyard garden. Mostly she just wandered among the vervain and germander, lavender and bergamot, letting her skirts brush the bushes to release the scents. Often she would pull a weed or clip off a dying bloom to encourage more to blossom. It wasn't part of her duties, but she missed the fields and the forests of her village in a way she had never dreamed possible.

When she had been a field hand, back before that day when Master Raffaele had summoned her from threshing, she'd done her fair share of complaining about the back-breaking work of hoeing and planting, reaping and gathering. But she had not understood until now how much freedom she'd had to stop and stare up at the wide open skies, the ships of white clouds drifting through the blue sea above and the ragged flocks of rooks wheeling around the swaying trees. In all directions the land had rolled out away from her, shaded with every hue of brown and green growing paler and paler in the far distance until finally the colours dissolved into the ocean of sky. But in here she could see no further than the high walls of the courtyard and the square of blue cut out above her head, like a piece of cloth laid ready to be crimped and sewn and bound.

Back in Gastmere, she had been able to escape on solitary walks to pick blackberries or gather firewood, and find the space to be silent, listening to the piping of a blackbird or the wind creeping through the rushes. But here she was surrounded by women day and night, chattering, laughing, snoring. For all that she missed the land, there was one thing she longed for more than any of that. It was Athan. It was those precious moments when they'd walked hand in hand under the great dome of glittering stars, when there seemed no one else in the whole world save the two of them. Who was he walking under the stars with now? Tears pricked her eyes. Why hadn't Athan tried to find her? Did he even care what had happened to her?

She must have been muttering aloud, because a frightened little face peered round from behind a raised turf seat that was covered over with fragrant purple flowering thyme and wild marjoram. Then it disappeared at once. Elena tiptoed around to the back of the seat and saw a small boy sitting on the grass behind it, his knees drawn up to his chin, his arms wrapped tightly around himself.

He glanced up briefly, then lowered his head again, as if by not looking at her he could make himself invisible.

'Hiding?' Elena asked with a smile, but the boy didn't answer.

Despite the heat, the other young boys were kicking a ball of woven withies boisterously back and forth between them on the gravel path. The still air rang with their shouts of triumph and groans as one side or the other scored a point over their fellows.

Elena settled herself down on the turf bench, revelling in the cloud of perfume that momentarily enveloped her from the sweet crushed marjoram and thyme. But the little hunched figure didn't move. She reached down and gently fingered the unruly mop of ash-blond curls. His hair was as silky and baby-fine as her own little bairn's. The boy flinched away.

'Don't you want to play football or won't they let you join in?'

He made no sign that he'd heard her. She peered down at the soft rosy cheek, which was all she could see of his face.

'I'm El . . . Holly.' She still couldn't get used to the name and the other girls often had to yell it three or four times before she realized they were addressing her.

The boy slowly raised his head. A stab of pain went through her as she looked at the child. He was beautiful, with cornflower-blue eyes and long golden lashes. His flawless, milky complexion was marred only by a small silvery scar above one brow. But it wasn't his face which pained her, it was the expression in his large eyes, frozen, dead, as if his mind was completely cut off from the world. Though he looked like an angel, all she could think of was the tales she had heard of corpses risen from their graves who walk without recognizing anyone or anything.

'Do you have a name?' she asked him gently.

For a few moments the boy stared right through her, as though she was the ghost of the garden. Then he opened his hand and studied it as if the answer might be written there.

'F . . . in . . . ch,' he said, striking the palm of his hand with the other one on each syllable, as if the name had been beaten into him, sound by sound.

'Finch, like the bird, that's a good name.' Elena smiled encouragingly. 'Have you been here a long time, Finch?'

His face was expressionless. The question of time seemed incomprehensible to him.

She'd never noticed the child before, but perhaps he kept himself hidden away. She wondered how old he was – seven, eight? It was hard to tell, he was very small, but his fingers were long and thin, almost like a youth's hands. What would her own son look like when he was this age? Softly she began to sing as if she still held her own bairn in her arms.

Lavender's green, diddle diddle, Lavender's blue
You must love me, diddle diddle, 'cause I love you.

She felt a slight pressure on her leg and, glancing down, saw that the child was tentatively leaning his head against her. As if he was indeed a little bird that might take flight at the slightest movement, Elena sat quite still and continued to sing.

Call up your maids, diddle diddle, set them to work
Some to make hay, diddle diddle, some to the rock.

Finch snuggled closer, pressing his face against her legs.

Let the birds sing, diddle diddle, let the lambs play,
We shall be safe, diddle diddle, deep in the hay.

She stopped singing and for a while the two of them sat quite still, Elena on the seat of thyme, little Finch on the ground, both sunk deep in their own thoughts, not hearing the shouts of the children playing or the bees humming among the roses.

Elena shivered as a white cloud drifted across the sun, casting the garden into shade.

'You want to see a secret?' Finch suddenly asked, sitting up.

'Of course,' Elena said, smiling at him indulgently. 'Is it a treasure you have?'

She knew from her own childhood that all children have secret treasures – a blown thrush's egg, a river-polished pebble that shines like a ruby, a sharp black dragon's tooth – all carefully hidden from adult eyes.

Finch shook his head. ''Tisn't my secret. Come, I'll show you. But you mustn't tell.' He took her hand in his own warm little paw and made to drag her.

'There you are, kitten. I've been looking everywhere for you, I have.'

At once the little hand withdrew from hers as Elena wheeled round to see Luce sauntering towards her across the garden. She looked down to say something to Finch, but the boy had vanished.

'Ma sent me to say you've got a visitor, someone you'll be right glad to see.'

A bubble of joy shot up through Elena and her face broke into a beaming smile. 'Athan, is it Athan? Where is he?'

Raffe paced impatiently about the small chamber and finally settled himself awkwardly in a high-backed wooden chair. The room was sparsely furnished. A broad bed occupied one corner, mercifully for this meeting concealed behind heavy but somewhat threadbare drapes. A long, low bench was positioned in another corner and in the third was a tall wooden frame with leather straps hanging from it. Raffe eyed it with disgust. He could guess what implements lay hidden behind the hangings around the bed, but he'd seen too many men's backs laid open to the bone with the lash to find flogging a pleasurable game.

He gazed hopelessly around the room. On that day he'd chosen Elena from the circle of threshing girls to eat that little piece of bread and salt, how could he have foreseen that it would lead her here? If Raffe had chosen a different girl from the circle, would the outcome have been the same? Ever since he was a child, he had wondered whether you could ever really choose, or if something had already chosen you.

When Raffe was just six years old, his father's scythe had hit a stone hidden among the grass. That was all. That was all it took to change the whole course of Raffe's life, just an ordinary lump of stone in the wrong place. The scythe blade bounced off the stone and cut deep into his father's leg. The wound had festered and Raffe's mother was terrified that her husband would die.

A neighbour swore that St Gregory would surely save the poor man, if Raffe's mother would only seek his help. So his mother decided to make a pilgrimage to the abbey which housed a finger bone of the saint and offer the necklace of amber she'd been given on her wedding day, to secure the saint's aid. Raffe, she insisted, must go too, to pray for his father's life.

Raffe and his mother had set off before the sun had even risen above the hills. They arrived at the abbey church in the cool of the evening, just as the service of Vespers was beginning, and climbed the great white steps to join the throng of worshippers in the public part of the church. As Raffe entered that great building his thirst and belly-rumbling hunger vanished. His mouth fell open and he stood rooted to the spot in the doorway, unable to tear his gaze from the spectacle before him.

The tiny village church at home, where he sang in the little choir, was painted with scenes of brightly coloured angels and saints wandering through familiar fields and hovering over cottages exactly like his own. But here the towering walls and pillars were emblazoned with scenes of heaven and hell, of Creation and the Last Judgment. Angelic faces peered down at him from the great dome, and God Himself surveyed the whole church from his golden throne, his dark almond eyes staring directly into Raffe's own.

Raffe was too busy staring around him to notice the choir singing the psalms, until they began to sing the Magnificat. He had never heard such voices before in his own village choir, so much sweeter, higher and resonant than any boy's. Ignoring his mother as she frantically hissed at him to come back, Raffe pushed through the standing congregation until he was at the front. Still he could see nothing because of the carved screen. So he stooped down and crawled forward, edging around it until he could stare up at the beings making the sound.

He saw monks and novices kneeling in prayer, but this unearthly music was not coming from those plain creatures. He twisted his head around and then he saw them standing together. Some of them were mere youths, the others were men who might have been as old as his father, but they were smooth-cheeked, without a trace of beard. And the notes that were pouring from them sent shivers of awe and delight running up and down Raffe's spine.

He crouched there in the shadows, listening. Finally, when the service was ended and the monks had gone, the small group of beardless singers, laughing and chattering, began to amble out through a narrow door of their own. Raffe gaped up at them, shaking his head like a dog with sore ears, for he couldn't believe that girls' voices were coming from men's bodies.

As Raffe watched the girl-men saunter from the church, the last one turned and seemed to be staring right at the dark corner where Raffe was hidden, and then he smiled and winked. Only a demon could have the power to see him in his hiding place. Terrified, little Raffe scrambled to his feet and fled down the church yelling for his mother, not caring that the few people remaining all turned to stare as he tore past them.

His mother was deep in conversation with one of the

priests, and she turned in horror and shame at her son's sacrilege in such a holy place.

The priest stared down, frowning. 'Is this the boy?'

'Yes, Father, but I swear he is usually so well behaved. He's never before . . .'

But the priest silenced her with a wave of his hand. He grasped Raffe's chin, turning his face towards the candlelight. Whatever he saw in it seemed to satisfy him. He ran his fingers over Raffe's throat and down his chest, back, belly and groin. The priest pressed him hard between his legs. Raffe squirmed and tried to wriggle away, but his mother held him firmly.

Finally the priest straightened up. 'Promising, definitely promising,' he said to Raffe's mother, who beamed back at him.

The priest looked down at Raffe once more. 'Now, boy, kneel and make your prayers for your father's recovery to health. See you pray in earnest, for God knows if you are not paying attention and praying with all your might. Little boys who displease God go straight to hell; you know that, don't you? But St Gregory will listen to the prayers of children if they are pure and without sin.'

Raffe's mother pushed him down on to his knees, before a mass of tiny burning candles. The heat from them was so fierce that Raffe felt as if his own face would melt like the wax which ran down from them.

'You heard, son, pray hard for your father. He is depending on you.'

If they are pure and without sin. The whole weight of his father's sickness seemed to be crushing down on Raffe's tiny shoulders. All his guilty sins began dancing round him in the candlelight, tiny imps of flame, mocking and jeering. The stolen peaches; the lie about working when he was really climbing trees; the torn shirt he'd tried to hide; the countless nights he'd sworn he'd said his prayers when he hadn't. As he knelt there, each and every one of those wickednesses was leaping around him, rolling their eyes and thumbing their noses at him.

Little Raffe was certain that when they reached home the next day, his father would be dead. His mother's precious amber necklace that even now dangled beneath the saint's reliquary would have been sacrificed in vain. St Gregory had refused to listen because Raffe had sinned. God would kill his father to punish him. His mother would sob. His family would starve and all of it, all the misery in the whole world, would be his fault.

But his father did not die. In fact, he made a full recovery and little Raffe almost cried in his relief that his sinful state would not, after all, be revealed to the whole village.

He thought he had escaped God's punishment, but he hadn't. Two years later, the whole family retraced their steps to the abbey church. And it wasn't until that day when they handed Raffe over to the priest that he learned that, just like his mother's amber necklace, he had been part of her deal with God: her son for her husband's life. Only then was he told how mortal men could conjure those soaring angelic voices. And only on that morning, standing there in the abbey, did he finally realize why it was they had mutilated him.

The door was flung open and Elena burst through it in a flood of sunlight. Her copper hair gleamed in the light and there was such an expression of eagerness and joy on her face that Raffe almost started up and ran towards her. But as she caught sight of him, she stumbled backwards, the light instantly snuffed out in her eyes. After the briefest of moments, she tried to smile, but he knew it was courtesy, nothing more. That smile hurt him more deeply than he could ever acknowledge.

She looked much better than the last time he'd seen her when he'd thrust her wet and bedraggled into the boat. As well as cleaner, she was if anything a little plumper, as well she might be, for the food Ma provided for the girls was far more rich and plentiful than the diet of coarse bread, beans and herbs Elena was used to. The fear and misery which had been etched into her face the night he had rescued her had faded so that now once again she looked much younger than her sixteen years.

Her red hair, instead of hanging in braids, was rolled and pinned at the nape of her neck, though like the other girls in the stew, she wore no net or veil to cover it. Her dress was different too. Gone was the plain, drab homespun kirtle; instead she wore a faded but finely woven green kirtle falling to mid-calf and revealing the white hem of the linen smock beneath. The low, V-shaped neckline was tightly fastened with a cheap pewter pin. Where had she got that from? Not from Ma, that was certain. If Ma Margot had her way, that pin would be unfastened and the swelling of her breasts tantalizingly displayed, like fruit on a monger's stall.

Who had Elena been expecting to find waiting for her in the chamber? Who had that look of delight been for? His question was answered the moment she began speaking.

'Have you seen Athan? Is he well? Does he know where I am? Did he try to find me, when he learned I'd escaped?' She babbled like an excited child, not waiting for any answers. 'It was only Joan who thought I'd hurt my bairn. I know deep down Athan didn't; he was just too frightened to say so in front of her. He refused to speak against me at the trial, which proves he knew I was telling the truth. He knows I've never lied to him.'

Her face was bright and eager once more as she spoke Athan's name. Raffe could see the hope in her eyes and something more, something that made his guts knot hard inside him. There is no mistaking when a woman is in love. Raffe had seen it in others before, though never with himself as the object of that soft, longing look. Elena was still in love with that oaf Athan even now, even after the spineless numb-skull had let his mother denounce her to that bastard Osborn. Even that betrayal had not brought Elena to her senses.

For a moment Raffe came close to breaking his resolve

and telling Elena the truth – *Your precious Athan is dead, hanged in place of you*. In his head, Raffe watched that eager little face crumple, the tears well in her eyes, imagined her throwing herself into his arms, sobbing and clinging to him for comfort. But as he looked again at her face, he knew not even the knowledge of Athan's death would cleanse away her love for the boy. It would only bring despair and guilt, and Raffe had borne too much guilt in his own life to let her suffer that.

He stood up, turning away from her, and stared out of the open door into the sun-washed garden. 'I have come to tell you that you must start to earn your keep here. Ma Margot is a charitable woman, but she can't afford to keep you here unless you work.'

'But I thought you were coming to take me away from here?' He could hear the bewilderment in her voice.

Raffe slammed the door shut and rounded on her in exasperation. 'And where exactly did you imagine I was going to take you? You are a runaway villein and a convicted murderer. Yes, I know you protest your innocence, but in the eyes of the law you are a condemned woman. Unless you're going to tell me you've found this cunning woman and she can produce your child to clear your name?'

Elena hung her head miserably.

'I thought not,' Raffe said. 'Osborn has put a bounty on you. Declared you a fugitive from justice, a wolf's head. Any man in England has the right to kill you on the spot and claim the reward for your body. And believe me, there's not a man out there who wouldn't hesitate to do it for the size of purse Osborn is offering. Who do you think is going to take you in and hide you?'

'I thought . . . a nunnery,' Elena murmured weakly.

'Have you forgotten the whole of England lies under Interdict? Where would we find a priest to seal your vows? Where would you get the dowry to be admitted as a nun? If you couldn't be admitted to holy orders, you'd be nothing more than a lay servant and the nunnery would not be able to protect you. They'd have to hand you over to Osborn.'

Only when he saw her trembling did he realize how terrified she was.

He took a deep breath and tried to speak more softly. 'You must remain here for a year and a day; if you can do that undiscovered, you can be declared a free woman instead of a villein and . . .' He paused awkwardly.

What could he tell her? Should he tell her the truth, that being declared a free woman would by itself solve little? Unless she could also prove her innocence she might never be able to leave. He crossed over to her and stood looking down at her. He gently caressed her cheek with his thumb as a father might soothe his little daughter.

'You must accept that you must stay here for a year at least. But much may change in a year; who knows, this cunning woman of yours might turn up again with the child. But,' he added firmly, 'you will have to work for your keep.'

'I do work,' she told him. 'I clean and tidy and do all that is asked.'

Raffe sat down in the chair opposite her again, fixing her with a grim expression. 'That is not what Ma means by work. It merely pays for the food you eat, not for the risks she is running in keeping you here. She needs you to start earning money.'

He stared down at his hands, unwilling to look into her wide blue eyes. Once, in the Holy Land, he had witnessed the Saracens tie a man by his arms and legs to four rearing Arab stallions. The stallions, simultaneously struck by their riders, had galloped off in opposite directions, ripping the shrieking victim to pieces between them. He felt as if the same was happening to his own being. Part of him wanted to make her suffer for betraying him with Athan; for refusing to trust him; for that look of revulsion he could see in her eyes whenever she looked at him. He wanted to make her the whore she was, dirty, humiliated, to have men look at her and despise her, as she looked at him.

Yet the thought of another man pawing her, laying his sweaty body against that smooth flesh, was more than he could bear. Even now he wanted more than anything to protect her, to have her come running to him for love and comfort. He wanted to keep her pure and untouched, as he could pretend to himself she was, now that Athan was dead. He and Elena were bound together by bonds stronger than any wedding vow – why couldn't she feel that?

He swallowed and tried to keep his voice level and businesslike. 'You will not be expected to serve the ordinary customers, that much I have made plain to Ma Margot. But when she gets a special customer from time to time, you will attend to him.'

'Attend to? What . . . does that mean? What will I have to do?' Her voice trembled.

'Ma Margot and the gentleman himself no doubt will tell you what is required each time. All men are different in their appetites.'

'Appetites,' she repeated dully.

Was she deliberately trying to be stupid? Did he have to spell it out for her?

'Don't play the innocent with me, girl,' Raffe snapped. 'You've borne a child, so you can't pretend that you don't know what goes on between a man and a woman. Or are you now claiming it was a virgin birth and then your bastard miraculously ascended into heaven? Is that why we can't find him?'

Before Raffe had time to realize what she intended, Elena slapped him hard across his face, her cheeks blazing scarlet in fury. Raffe gaped at her, stunned. It was the second time that afternoon he had allowed a woman to take him unawares and assault him. Had he lost all his soldier's instincts? Ma Margot he knew of old and should have expected her to defend herself, but no villein had ever dared to strike him before, especially not a woman.

It took him a moment or two to realize Elena was shouting at him, her eyes flashing and her fists clenched in fury. 'I may not be freeborn, but I am not a whore. I will not sleep with any man except Athan. He is my husband in all but name. He knows I didn't murder his son and he will wait for me until I can prove it to the world. I won't betray him. I won't!'

Raffe caught hold of her wrist and dragged her towards him; grabbing her face in his other hand, he tilted it up towards him, lowering his mouth close to hers. She screwed up her eyes and tried to wriggle away as if she thought he was trying to kiss her.

Raffe tightened his grip and spoke with exaggerated slowness, to force her to listen. 'You will do exactly what Ma Margot asks of you, *all* that she asks of you. And you will do it with a smile on your pretty little face, because if she can't get her money one way, she'll get it another. You refuse and she'll hand you straight to Osborn and claim that bounty. Osborn will hang you and this time there will be no escape. And I know Osborn of old – before he hangs you, he will make you suffer in ways you cannot begin to imagine. The fact that you are Athan's betrothed won't stop him using you in any way he pleases, in fact that knowledge will only add to his pleasure.'

'But Athan,' she moaned faintly.

'Athan is already in the arms of another! Trust me – Athan is not waiting for you!'

He felt her go limp in his hands and lowered her down on to the bench. She sat there, her body trembling, but she did not cry as he expected and he grudgingly admired her for that.

'My cousin Isabel? Athan's with Isabel, isn't he?' she said, staring up at him.

Raffe didn't answer. She seemed to take that as confirmation. Was silence a lie? Perhaps it was the worst kind of lie, Raffe thought, and by God he was guilty of enough silences in his lifetime.

Elena stared at a fly that was dashing itself aimlessly against the wall. 'Isabel won't last long with Joan around; she's always called her a slut. She'll soon send her packing.'

'You're not listening to me,' Raffe yelled at her. 'He will *not* be there waiting for you. Stop playing the little fool and make up your mind to do as you are told, because make no mistake, you have to do this, and it'll go a lot easier with you if you do it willingly.'

Elena was shaking so violently, Raffe thought her body would break into pieces. He knelt down in front of her, gently taking her cold hands in his.

'Look, all Ma wants is for you to be pleasant to a rich merchant or ship's captain once in a while. Is that really so hard? Can it be worse than being raped or tortured by that bastard Osborn? At least you'll be alive. And believe me, nothing on this earth is worth as much as life itself, not your virtue, not your pride, not even your love for Athan. If you die unshriven, strangling to death on the end of a rope, there will be nothing except endless misery and torment spread out before you for all eternity. Whatever happens, you must cling fast to life with both hands, no matter what it costs you. You must stay alive for me, Elena. I need you to live.'

The Night of the Full Moon,
August 1211

Roses – If mortals dream of a red rose, they shall be granted the love their hearts yearn for, but if they should dream of a white rose, it is a bad omen, for they will know only sorrow in love. If a maid would bring back a faithless lover, let her pluck three roses on Midsummer's Eve. The first she must bury beneath a yew tree, the second in a new grave and the third place under her head when she sleeps. After the third night she shall burn the rose to ashes. Thus her lover will be tormented by thoughts of her and will know no rest until he has returned to her.

If a maid desires to find her true love she must pluck a rosebud on Midsummer's Day and lay it in some secret place till Christmas Day, then if it still be bright and fragrant, she must wear it and her true lover will pluck it from her, but if it has shrivelled and turned brown, she must beware her life, for it is an evil omen.

White roses signify silence, for Cupid gave a sacred rose to Harpocrates, the god of silence, so that he would not reveal the amorous secrets of Venus, Cupid's mother. Thus noblemen carve or paint a rose on the ceiling above the table where they dine, or hang a white rose from the beams where they meet to show that nothing which is spoken in that place must be revealed. So mortals speak of *sub rosa* or 'under the rose', when they desire to hold their discourse in secret.

But mortals beware, we mandrakes see all and will reveal all in time, for the rose has no power to stop our ears or our mouths. At the end of days we will break the silence of gods and mortals alike, for were we not birthed in a scream?

The Mandrake's Herbal

The Summoning

'It is time,' Madron said.

Her milky eyes swivelled towards Gytha as if she could see her in the darkness and beyond her into her very thoughts.

Gytha shifted uncomfortably on her bed of bracken, trying to ignore her mother. Once this business was done, they'd have to move on, and Gytha was happy here. She'd no wish to go traipsing into the city. She hated it. People staring at you suspiciously as if you were going to thieve from them, that's when they weren't trying to rob you themselves. You couldn't breathe, all those people jostling and shouting. You couldn't hear anything above the foolish clamour of their voices, not even your own thoughts.

'Take me outside.' Madron's tone was more querulous than usual.

Gytha sighed and struggled to her feet. It was a warm night. She needed no shawl over her coarse, threadbare kirtle. She bent over her mother and the old lady put an arm around her neck. Gytha scooped her up in her arms and, ducking low, carried her out of the bothy. Madron was as light as a bag of fish bones, but the thin arm locked around Gytha's neck had a grip as hard as ice in winter.

Gytha placed her gently in the centre of the clearing. The old woman's head lifted, turning her face towards the bright moon, as if she was seeking its coldness.

She pinched Gytha's arm. 'Fetch my bones and my black-thorn rod.'

Gytha returned once more to the bothy and fetched the objects, laying them in her mother's lap. This summoning would require greater magic than a thorn apple, for they had nothing of his which they could use against him.

The air was still and heavy in the forest. The trees were shaggy with leaves. They encircled the glade like great dumb trolls silently watching the stars glittering above: the Bear and the Swan, and the great arching bridge of stars over which the souls of the dead travelled. The Milky Way, Gerard once told her she must call it, but he would know it for its real name now, for his soul had walked that path. She had seen it.

Madron was squatting in the glade. Her hair glowed silver in the moonlight, her skin was turned to pearl. She had drawn a circle around herself in the leaf mould with the tip of the blackthorn rod. Then around the circle she had made four marks. A stranger might not have recognized the crude symbols, but Gytha knew them well, for her mother had taught them to her when she was still in her cradle: a serpent for the earth, a fish for the water, a bird for the air and a salamander for fire. The moonlight poured into the scratches in the earth, filling them with molten silver. Madron could not see them, but Gytha knew she could feel them just as well as she could feel her own hands.

Madron fumbled in the bag and drew out one slender bone, only as long as a woman's hand. She placed it before her, then from her sleeve withdrew a small posy of herbs, bound together by a scarlet thread – periwinkle, orpine, vervain, monkshood and deadly nightshade. She laid the bundle across the bone, so that it made a slanted cross.

Finally she turned her sightless eyes towards Gytha, extending her hand.

'Come, you must stand inside the circle, else you'll not be safe.'

Gytha stepped over the mark scratched in the floor of the forest, careful not to break the circle. Then she crouched behind her mother and waited.

The old woman threw back her head and lifted her face to the moon. She began to chant, ancient words long since forgotten by the world, words that women had taught their daughters since first the owl flew and the wolf hunted her prey. The hairs on Gytha's neck prickled.

Madron's chanting died away and silence flooded back into the moonlit grove, a silence as solid and lucent as glass. A cloud drew across the moon, plunging the clearing into darkness. The forest held its breath.

Then the ground around them began to tremble, shaking as if a thousand horses were charging by. As the cloud peeled back from the moon, Gytha could see something rising in front of them just beyond the circle. A wisp of mist was uncurling from the ground, pushing up the earth around it, like the first shoot of a plant. Then the column of mist burst out of the black earth with a thin wail like a newborn baby's cry. It whirled around and around, and as it turned there came a low moaning in the forest as if an icy winter wind was wandering among the branches of the trees, but the trees were quite still. The moaning grew into a shriek, rising higher and higher till the very darkness was vibrating with the pain of it. Then, just as suddenly, the shrieking stopped.

A naked infant stood in front of them, its body so thin the ribs stood out like the timbers of a wrecked ship. The lips were drawn back to reveal the toothless bones of its jaws, its empty eye sockets were as dark as black fire.

Madron turned her sightless eyes towards her daughter. 'Has he come? Do you see him?'

Gytha could not wrench her gaze from the little corpse in front of her.

'He is here, Madron, the babe is here,' she whispered.

The old woman lifted the bone and the bundle of herbs together and pointed them at the creature.

'Spirit, I command you to fetch Hugh of Roxham. Bring him here to us.'

The little corpse hopped towards her, the clawed fingers of its left arm scrabbling uselessly in the air, as if it was trying to snatch at something. Its right leg was missing.

'I command you,' Madron repeated. 'Fetch Hugh of Roxham. You will bring him here. You will bring him!'

The creature took another step towards her, reaching for

the bone, but it drew back as if burned as it touched the air above the circle. 'Give me, give me! It's mine. Mine!'

Madron lifted her head, pronouncing the words for the third time. 'I command you by the bone of your body, bring us Hugh of Roxham. Go, go now. Ka!'

As she pronounced the last word the corpse shuddered violently; it slumped down to the ground and for a moment Gytha thought it was going to disappear back into the earth. But as she watched, its ashen, waxy skin began to bubble all over, as if maggots were crawling out of it, covering it from its skull to its feet. The skin was erupting into soft white feathers. The child lifted its head, and in the dark empty hollows of its eyes were two black glistening pearls. Two long wings unfurled on either side of its body and as they beat, the pale creature rose silently into the air. The barn owl hovered above them for a moment, its wings outstretched against the moon, then it turned and glided away over the dark mass of the trees.

Madron slumped back, exhausted. She turned her head to Gytha. 'It is done. Carry me back inside. You know what to do when he comes.'

Gytha bent to lift her mother up. 'You're sure he will come, Madron?'

'He will come. Sooner or later, he will be drawn to us.'

Gytha laid her mother in the bothy and wandered back out beneath the trees, bathed silver in the moonlight. From under her shift, where it nestled between her breasts, she withdrew the wizened apple and plucked another thorn. Was it a waste? Should she simply wait patiently for Madron's spell to work? Her sixth sense told her that another little twist of the apple was needed. Something all of her own. She laid the thorn carefully in the embers of the supper fire. A shiver of pleasure stroked her spine as a tiny flame danced in the darkness. She watched it burn; she loved to watch them burn.

*

Raoul, yawning and trying to ease his aching shoulders, stumbled across the courtyard towards the steps leading to the Great Hall. The light from the burning torches on the walls flickered across the uneven cobbles of the courtyard, making it hard to see where he was putting his feet. God's bones, but he was tired and stiff! His backside was bruised and his thighs raw from a day in the saddle. He was starving too, but he wasn't sure if he could even manage to stay awake long enough to eat.

He heard a clattering on the stairs, and lifted his head in time to see Osborn striding down them. Raoul groaned to himself. He knew he'd have to see Osborn tonight to deliver the message, but he had hoped to get at least a goblet or two of wine inside him before he was forced to speak. His throat was as dry as old leather from the dust on the roads.

Osborn confronted him at the bottom of the stairs. 'And how fares the king?'

Raoul massaged his parched throat. 'In health His Majesty is as fit as a man half his age and has twice the energy. In temper . . .' Raoul winced at the memory.

The king's violent rages were legendary, and Raoul had felt the full force of the royal displeasure, having been forced to admit to John that he had so far failed to discover the identity of anyone engaged in aiding England's enemies. It was not an experience he ever wanted to repeat. The king's fury had only been slightly tempered when his latest mistress, a sweet, sympathetic girl who had smiled coyly at Raoul, reminded the king that the *Santa Katarina* had been prevented from landing her cargo thanks entirely to the brave and loyal Raoul.

It had not been thanks to Raoul at all. He'd never heard of the ship or its French cargo until he arrived back at court and he'd no idea who had alerted the king's men, but he certainly wasn't going to contradict the rumour. It was the only thing that was preventing the full measure of the king's anger from descending on his head.

Raoul sighed. He wasn't suited to this business of skulking around trying to uncover traitors and spies. All he'd ever wanted was a comfortable position at court and the only thing he had any desire to uncover was the breasts of a lovely young girl, someone like the king's mistress. Now she had a body just begging to be ravished.

He was jerked out of his daydream by Osborn. 'Speak, man, what did the king say?'

Raoul fumbled in his scrip for a roll of parchment bearing a heavy wax seal. 'His Majesty instructs me to give you this, but I know what it says, there are similar messages going out across England. John's called a council of the lords known to be loyal to him. He intends to draw up plans if Philip should attempt to land. You and your brother, and the other commanders who are experienced in the field of battle are instructed to attend. He expects you in three days' time.'

'God's teeth!' Osborn swore vehemently, his fists clenched.

He must have seen the startled expression on Raoul's face for he added quickly, 'I am, of course, honoured to wait upon the king in this matter. But I have just this day learned of something I had hoped to attend to personally.'

Osborn gnawed at his lip for a moment, then his face brightened. 'John has not commanded you to attend?'

Raoul tried to suppress a shudder. He was in no hurry to return to the king's presence in his present mood. 'I've never seen battle, unlike you. I would be of little use to His Majesty.'

'Then you may do me a service instead.' Osborn glanced around the darkened courtyard. There were only a few candles still burning in the casements for most of the manor's inhabitants were already asleep. Nevertheless, he drew Raoul away from the steps and into a corner of the courtyard as far as possible from any doors or windows.

'I received word from the sheriff in Norwich this afternoon. One of his men has heard a rumour that my runaway villein was taken to Norwich by boat when she escaped from here and is still in the city somewhere. I want you to go to Norwich first thing tomorrow and see if you can track her down.'

Every aching muscle and bone in Raoul's body screamed out in protest at the thought of another day in the saddle. 'My lord, surely the sheriff can order his men to search for her?'

'The man is a lazy, incompetent numbskull whose only interest is in filling his personal coffers. He says red-headed girls are as common as bird shit in Norwich, and he doesn't have the men to spare to go banging on every door of the city. So you'll have to do it. I'd go myself, but the king . . .'

'But I've never laid eyes on the girl,' Raoul protested. 'How am I to find her, if the sheriff's men can't?'

'The man who brought the news says he heard talk of it in an inn. The Adam and Eve, he called it. It's a place frequented by all the knaves, rogues and cutpurses in Norwich, or so he says. Take lodgings there. Drink with them. Flirt with their whores. Buy the customers whatever disgusting muck they throw down their poxy throats to get them drunk, so they'll talk freely. I don't care what you have to do, just find that girl. I'll not have any villein on this manor think they can defy me and live.'

Raoul's face brightened a little. Drinking and whoring, now that was something he was good at. A week or two in Norwich maybe wouldn't be so bad after all. And if he couldn't find this girl, he could always tell Osborn she'd been seen boarding a cart or a boat out of the city.

Raoul was still smiling to himself as he mounted the steps to his bed, picturing the slender, lithe body of the king's mistress, so deliciously young and helpless. Yes, he deserved a little treat and if the wenches in Norwich were half as enticing as the king's whore, this was one task he might actually enjoy.

†

1st Day after the Full Moon, August 1211

Fox – There are some mortal families which are descended from foxes, and if someone in that family is about to die, many foxes will gather near the house. A mortal who is bitten by a fox will live only seven years more.

He who would find courage must wear a fox's tongue to make him bold. He who would be cured of a swollen leg must carry a fox's tooth. The liver of a fox washed in wine and dried will sooth a cough. If a mortal has a thorn embedded in him, he should lay a fox's tongue on it through the hours of darkness and when dawn breaks the thorn will be drawn out. The ashes of a fox drunk in wine will cure a mortal of complaints of the liver. Bathing in the water in which a fox has been boiled will ease the pain of gout, and if a bald man rubs his pate with fox fat, his hair will be restored.

Witches may take the form of foxes and often when the fox is chased it will seem to vanish and the huntsmen will find only an old woman standing there.

For though its corpse heals men, the living fox is to be feared, for it is the symbol of the Devil, and if a fox should pass a mortal on the track, it is a dark omen that a terrible event shall follow.

The Mandrake's Herbal

The Cage

Osborn's scrawny little clerk looked like a helpless, naked baby bird behind the great wooden table which had been pulled into the centre of the manor courtyard. The sallow-faced man nervously shuffled ledgers and parchments from one side of the table to the other, then began counting the freshly cut quills in his pot, as if the exact number was of vital importance. Osborn, irritated, rapped on the table with the handle of his riding whip to get the little man's attention.

'I want every rent paid in full today, no excuses. If they cannot pay they leave the crofts or workshops this same day. Likewise their field strips, any man who cannot pay for land he is renting will have it ploughed up.'

The clerk opened his mouth to protest, but seeing the thunder gathering on Osborn's brows, thought better of it and nodded vigorously enough to show that he wouldn't dream of disagreeing. Raffe too stood silent. A few weeks before he would have tried to argue with Osborn, but he'd learned that only made the man more savage in his dealings. Better to say nothing and simply ignore the instructions. He could manage to hide the odd late payment, that's if the little scrivener could be trusted to keep his mouth shut and not go squealing to his master. But Raffe was confident that he could persuade the clerk, once Osborn was safely out of the way.

As if he could hear Raffe's thoughts, Osborn turned to him. 'See to it that you send men round the village to remind people it is Lammas.'

'I doubt there's a newborn babe in the village who doesn't know what day it is today. The crofters have been counting the days down till they can drive their stock to common pasture on the hay meadows, for some of the beasts are skin and bones and the grass is so parched there's nothing left for them to graze.'

'Then they should learn to make better provision for them,' Osborn said. 'But just you make sure that in their eagerness to get their beasts out to graze they don't forget their first duty is to me. I am leaving this morning with my brother to wait upon the king's pleasure, and in my absence you will ensure that every last penny is collected in. I will hold you accountable for any sum that is missing. So you'd better see to it that every man turns out with what he owes, and if there are any too sick or feeble to come in person, I expect you to go to their crofts and fetch it.'

He searched Raffe's face, looking for the slightest flicker of rebellion, but Raffe concentrated on keeping his expression impassive.

'Did you hear what I said, Master Raffaele?'

Raffe allowed himself a dangerously insolent pause, before saying calmly, 'Yes, m'lord, I heard you.'

The whip twitched in Osborn's hand. Raffe saw the warning but unlike the clerk, he did not flinch. He was thankful Lady Anne was away visiting a sick cousin, for she would certainly have tried to intervene on the villagers' behalf, and Osborn had still not forgiven her for challenging him over Elena and Athan. She could not afford to make him angry again.

Osborn, after another furious scowl at Raffe, bellowed to the gateman, 'Stop gawping like a halfwit, man. Stir yourself and open the gates.'

Walter, who had been standing with his hand ready on the beam for almost an hour waiting for his lord's signal, jerked into action and lifted the great beam off the brackets and flung the gates wide.

If Osborn had been hoping for a throng of eager villagers waiting to pay their dues, he was sadly disappointed. A couple of old men hobbled up to the table and began counting out their pennies with a painful slowness as their gnarled, swollen hands fumbled in worn purses. Osborn waited with growing impatience as his clerk re-counted the old men's pennies with equal slowness, terrified of making an error while his master was watching. Finally, Osborn turned on his heel and strode back to the stairs leading to the Great Hall, flogging each step with his whip as he climbed them.

Though the villagers were noticeably absent, there was no lack of activity in the courtyard. Osborn's men and servants scurried back and forth loading the small travelling chests and making ready Osborn's favourite hawks and Hugh's hounds for the journey, for who knew how long the king would keep his lords kicking their heels at court? Raffe reluctantly crossed towards the Great Hall. It was one of his many duties to see that nothing was lacking and to chivvy slow or clumsy servants, a duty he was increasingly coming to loathe when the brothers were in residence. He could barely disguise his delight at the news that Osborn and Hugh were leaving. He prayed the king would detain them for weeks, or even months, but that was probably too much to ask.

Raffe stopped as he caught sight of a young lad he didn't recognize mounting the steps before him. He stood out immediately from the other boys in the manor.

'You there, come down here,' Raffe ordered.

The lad turned and obediently retraced the few steps. He was barefooted, dressed in a pair of mildewed leather breeches with a curious smooth eel-skin cap stuck so firmly to his head that it looked as if he had a bald black pate.

'Marsh-man, aren't you?' Raffe said. 'What's your business here?'

'Come to see her ladyship.'

'The Lady Anne? And what makes you think you can just walk in here and expect a noble lady to see you?'

The boy scowled, thrusting out his lower lip. 'Weren't my idea to come, he said I'd to bring her a message.'

Raffe caught the boy by his arm and dragged him into the shadows beneath the undercroft.

'Now, who sent you and what's the message?' Raffe demanded.

The boy jutted his chin out obstinately. 'He said I wasn't tell no one 'cept her.'

'Lady Anne is away from the manor visiting her sick cousin. She'll not be back for three or four days.' Raffe's eyes flicked up to the Hall above. 'Listen to me, boy. The man up there, Lord Osborn, is dangerous, and there's no love lost between him and Lady Anne. If he discovers she's hiding something from him, her life will not be worth living. Now, tell me what you were supposed to tell her and I'll see she learns of it the instant she returns.'

Anxiety creased the boy's forehead. He gazed from Raffe to the stairs and back again, evidently trying to weigh up who to trust.

'It'll be too late by then. He said he must get word from her tonight.'

'Who, boy, who told you this?' Raffe urged.

The boy cocked his head on one side like a raven and looked slyly up at Raffe. 'He said she'd give me a silver penny for the message.'

Raffe seized the boy's jerkin and shook him impatiently. 'I'll give you a clip round the ear if you don't tell me, which is nothing to what Lord Osborn will do to you if he finds you here. He'll flay your hide to the bone to get the truth out of you.'

The boy's eyes widened in alarm. He tried to wrest his arm from Raffe's grip, but with little success. 'I'll tell you, master.' His eyes darted round the courtyard, fearful of being overheard. 'There's a man hiding on the marshes. Says he must get a boat to France afore he's discovered. Said he was told the Lady Anne would help him.'

'Who is this man?'

'He never said his name.' The boy's expression suddenly changed. 'I nearly forgot, he said I was to give her this.'

The lad fumbled for something under his shirt and thrust it into Raffe's hand.

It was a tin emblem in the form of a wheel, the symbol of St Katherine. Raffe's heart suddenly began to thump in his chest. This man on the marsh, could he be a French spy? Had one of them escaped the fire after all? But how had he come to know of Lady Anne and be so convinced she would help him? Her own husband and her son had fought for England. She would never betray her own country to the French, not her, Raffe would have wagered his life on it. So what on earth was she mixed up in?

The boy held his hand out, anxious, but plainly determined not to leave without his promised penny.

Raffe fished in the small leather purse that hung on his belt. The boy's eyes gleamed as he saw the silver penny in Raffe's hand.

'You came by boat.'

'Coracle,' the lad answered, not taking his eyes from the coin.

Raffe gnawed at his lip; a boy's coracle would not hold the two of them, especially not when one of them was Raffe's size.

'There's a place upstream where the river splits in two around an islet. You know it?'

The lad nodded.

'This silver penny is yours if you meet me there next to the water meadow at sundown. Wait at the back of the islet, the shrubs on it will hide you from the track. There'll be another silver penny for you if you guide me safely to this man and home again.'

The boy nodded reluctantly, gazing longingly at the silver as Raffe dropped it back in his leather purse. Raffe saw his disappointment and hesitated. Would he wait? It was much to ask of a young lad to be so patient for so many hours, and despite the promise of coins, he might easily get bored and leave. On the other hand, if he gave him the penny now, he might simply vanish anyway.

'Stay here,' Raffe instructed.

Raffe swiftly crossed to the kitchens, thankful that those inside were too preoccupied stirring and sweating over the fires to take any notice of him. He grabbed some bread, onions and a couple of fat mutton chops and, wrapping them hastily in a bit of sacking, returned to the boy.

Raffe thrust the parcel into his hands. 'To keep you from hunger while you wait. I'll bring more when I come tonight.'

The lad peered inside the sack and his mouth widened in a huge frog grin. 'Thanks, master!'

He was still grinning when he ran out through the gates.

The morning was half gone and still Elena didn't move from the turf seat in the garden. She crushed the leaves of the thyme and marjoram over and over, trying to fill her head with the scent, but almost as soon as she smelt it, it seemed to vanish again. It was like trying to hold a fistful of mist. She knew she should go back and finish tidying the women's chamber, but she couldn't.

The stench of sweat, the thick, sticky stains and the images of what they did in those stalls rose up in her throat until they choked her and she had to run outside to vomit over and over in the corner of the yard. She could not lie down in those stalls. She couldn't lie there and let a man climb on top of her, his wet lips on hers, his fingers probing and touching. Every morning as light crept too soon through the shutters, her first thought was, would it be today? *Not today, Holy Virgin, I beg you, don't let them make me do it today.*

She'd barely slept these last few nights since Raffe's visit and when she had closed her eyes, images whirled in her head: Athan in the arms of another woman; men pawing at her own body; Osborn walking towards her holding out a noose in his hands. And over and over a drumbeat of words pounded in her head: a year and a day, *a year and a day*!

She gave a convulsive sob and tore again at the herbs where she sat.

'Did a man hurt you?' a voice whispered. She jumped. Finch was crouching close beside her. She hadn't even noticed him.

She shook her head, her throat too tight to speak.

Finch pulled at some grass blades. 'They hurt boys some-times.'

'You, have they hurt you?' Elena's own self-absorbed misery vanished instantly in her concern for him.

Finch didn't answer, but continued tearing at the grass. Then he looked up. 'I could show you that secret now.'

She tried to smile. 'Not now, maybe another time.'

He touched the back of her hand lightly with his grubby finger. 'Please,' he begged. 'You'll not be sad then.'

She was about to refuse again, when she saw the pleading in his bright blue eyes. She was too tired even to think up a reason to refuse. Besides, it would delay the moment when she had to return to that chamber. She allowed herself to be pulled by the small boy, as a carthorse allows a puny human to guide it.

Finch led the way across the garden to the chamber where the little boys entertained their customers. Elena shuddered as she entered, and averted her eyes from the stalls, but the room was deserted, for it was too early for customers to come knocking. Finch stopped at one of the stalls, pushing his hand under the straw pallet and pulling out a small stick. At first Elena thought that was his secret treasure, and though she could see nothing special about it, was about to play along with whatever he was pretending it to be, when the boy set off again.

'Come on,' he urged. 'It's this way.'

Meekly she followed the tousled blond head until they reached the back of the room, where a great wooden pillar was set against one side of the wall. Finch tugged her into the alcove behind it. Even though she had cleaned this room before, Elena had never noticed that there was a low door-way behind the pillar, set at an angle which made it impossible to see from the rest of the room.

The boy glanced back to make certain they were alone, then he slid his fingers across the door until he found a small hole on one side. Now Elena understood the reason for the stick, for he wiggled it into the hole and she heard a latch being lifted on the other side. The boy slid in as soon as the door swung open, pulling Elena with him in such haste that she barely had time to duck to avoid hitting her head on the low archway.

She found herself standing at the top of wide curved steps leading downwards. A terrible stench wafted up from below, that instantly made her eyes sting and water. It was the stench of a midden – shit, urine, rotting meat and something else she couldn't quite recognize.

A single torch burned on the wall half-way down.

'Come on,' Finch whispered.

Seeing Elena hesitate, he slipped his little warm hand into hers. 'Don't be afeared. I'll look after you.'

Every instinct was telling Elena to back out as quickly as she could, but she firmly told herself that if a little boy was bold enough to go down those steps, there couldn't be anything much to fear at the bottom.

Elena pressed her hand to the wall to steady herself as they descended. The rough stones were dripping with water. They passed beneath the flames of the torch and at last she felt solid ground beneath her feet. They were in a long, low chamber that curved away to the left. The flames from the torch on the stairs barely illuminated the first few yards. The flagged floor tilted slightly towards a hole in the floor on one side of the chamber steps, more than big enough for a man to climb through, and the moisture from the walls ran in little rivulets towards it, falling in a pattern of loud, resonant drips into the dark maw below.

But it was not the sound of the dripping that captured Elena's attention. She could hear something moving beyond the curve of the cellar wall, as if someone was shuffling through straw.

'Is there someone here?' she whispered to Finch.

She was answered by a low, deep-throated growl coming from somewhere ahead. She started back, but Finch was quicker.

He darted past her and back up the stairs and, for a moment, Elena feared this was a trick, and he had lured her down to lock her in, but moments later he returned with a lit rush candle in his hand, carefully shielding the dim light from the draught of his movement with his other hand. He walked a few paces around the curve of the wall and held up the pitifully feeble light.

'Look there.'

The light did not penetrate far, but something caught it. Two great glowing spots blazed out in the darkness and, with an icy rush of fear, Elena realized they were a pair of eyes. The deep-throated growl rumbled again, echoing through the chamber, only to be answered by a snarl from somewhere deeper in the shadows.

Elena gasped in horror and tried to run towards the stairs. She slipped on the slimy wet flags and, tumbling over, landed in a heap. She scrambled to her feet, trying to catch the boy's hand and pull him up the stairs, but Finch resisted.

'But you haven't seen them properly yet. It's all right; they can't harm you. They're in cages. See?'

He edged forward and Elena, her legs trembling, followed him, her hand gripping the small boy's shoulder ready to pull him back out of harm's way. Finch swung the flame to his left. A stout iron cage was set against the oozing wall and inside a large creature was padding back and forth in the small space. The floor of the cage was littered with large gnawed bones and, by the stench of it, a good deal of dung.

Elena moved closer, trying to make out the grey shape in the smoking light of the rush candle. It turned its head towards her and snarled, baring its sharp white teeth. Elena had seen such a beast only once before in her life, and then it was dangling lifeless from a hunter's pole. As a child she'd been disappointed, for the dead creature had looked not much more fearful than a large dog, but now, as she saw the living beast and watched the muscles rippling in its shoulder, smelt its hot breath and felt the amber glow of its eyes fix on hers, she understood for the first time why men shuddered at the mention of a wolf.

Without warning the wolf hurled itself at the iron bars. Elena stumbled backwards into something hard. She felt something snatch at her skirts and whipped round, almost falling again as she found herself staring into a second cage. She had never seen anything like it before. The creature reared up roaring, its massive paws clawing at bars inches from her face. The great head of the beast was surrounded by a mane of yellowish-brown fur. A long, black-tipped tail lashed angrily back and forth. Elena ran from between the two cages and flung herself back against the wall of the cellar, her heart pounding in her ears.

'What is that beast?'

'That is a lion,' a voice answered, but it wasn't Finch's.

The tiny figure of Ma Margot was standing at the foot of the stairs. She held a lantern in her hand. In the light shining up from below her face became a grinning skull.

With a cry, Finch dropped the rush candle on the floor and rushed to hide behind Elena, clinging to her skirts.

'You're wise to hide from me, Finch,' Ma said sternly. 'You have not been given permission to come here.'

The boy gave a little whimper. Elena slid her arm behind her and held his hand.

'It's not the child's fault. I'm to blame. I made him bring me.' She tried to sound defiant, but her breathing was still ragged from the shock of seeing the creatures.

Ma smiled, as if she didn't believe a word. 'You want to be careful down here.'

She pointed to the great dark hole in the sloping cellar floor. 'Bottomless, that well is. They say the merchant who built this place thought his young bride was spending too much time with her confessor. He reasoned she couldn't have that many past sins to tell, so she must be committing new ones and he knew it wasn't with him. So he caught the young priest and brought him down here to do a little confessing of his own.

'He lowered the priest into the hole, to loosen his tongue, but when he came back a few hours later and hauled up the rope the merchant found it had snapped in two. The merchant's wife was beside herself when she heard the priest had drowned and threw herself down the hole after him. At least, that's what the merchant told everyone, which, like he said, proves they were guilty. But who's to say for sure, for their bones are still down there.'

Elena shuddered and Finch pressed himself into her skirts more tightly.

Ma watched them, a slight smile of satisfaction flitting across her mouth. 'I prefer it that no one comes here, for I would hate my poor creatures to be teased or goaded. But since you are here already you may as well see them.'

She raised the lantern and Elena saw that in her other hand she carried a basket. As she approached the wolf's cage, his snarls changed to excited little yelps. Ma handed the basket to Elena. Elena, thinking it light, having seen Ma carry it easily with no effort, staggered under the unexpected weight of it.

Ma pulled out a raw and bloody shank of mutton from the basket and tossed it over the top of the bars. The wolf seized it and dragged it off to the far corner of the little cage, where it began to gnaw at the bone.

Ma turned around to the lion whose pacing had become even more excited. It rubbed its shaggy head against the bars and Ma stroked the rough mane before tossing a haunch to it too. The great cat lay down with the meat between its paws, licking the flesh with a great rasping tongue.

'That is a lion?' Elena whispered. 'But I've seen lions on banners and they don't look like that.'

'The golden lion, no doubt, King Richard's standard.' Ma chuckled. 'Men have a way of making the creatures they fear into gods. They put them on pillars, cover them with gold, worship them and by doing so think they have tamed them, but they will not be tamed. Beasts and monsters, God or the

Devil, they're all the same, my darling, and they have only one purpose, to kill and destroy. Don't you ever forget that.'

Ma led the way further round the curving chamber. Beyond were more cages. An eagle flapped its useless wings in one, in another a brown bear sat upright on its haunches, its piggy little eyes staring with malice at them as they passed. Some of the creatures crouched in the shadows at the back of the cages, their fur as black as the tunnel itself, and Ellen could see little of them except their glowing eyes. But to each one Ma gave a portion of raw meat.

'Why do you keep them?' Elena asked.

'They're my guardians, my pets. But they have other uses. They earn their keep as we all do here. But I am fond of them and they are fond of me; they have to be for I am their god. I bring them food and water and they know it. Who knows,' she chuckled, 'maybe when I am late in coming they pray to me. *Panem nostrum quotidianum da nobis hodie* – give us this day our daily bread.'

There was one more hunk of meat in the basket and Ma lifted her lantern and led the way a little further on. The creature in this last cage was huddled down in the corner, not pacing impatiently like some of the other beasts. Even when Ma lifted the lantern Elena could not make out what it was, for its head, like that of the lion, was covered with a great mass of tangled dark hair and its body lay half buried in the straw.

'Your dinner, my pet,' Ma called, tossing the remaining piece of bloody meat into the cage.

The creature slowly lifted its head and Elena clapped her hands to her mouth for the blue eyes that glowed out at her from a face that was almost black with filth and grime were unmistakably human. He was naked, but Elena was scarcely aware of that for his body was so filthy that he might have been wearing a garment woven from mud.

The man tipped forward and crawled towards the hunk of meat on his elbows and knees. As he came closer to where

Elena was standing, she suddenly saw why he moved in such a curious way. His feet and hands had been lopped off. The skin was twisted and scarred around the stumps where the bleeding limbs had been dipped in boiling tar to seal the ends and stop him bleeding to death.

Elena had seen mutilations before. A hand or nose or ear severed for thieving or some other crime, but never had she seen a man so cruelly and deliberately maimed as this. The wretch sat up and using the stump of one arm to lever the meat up against his chest and his teeth to grasp it, he dragged his meal back away from the bars.

'You are well?' Ma asked, surprising Elena with the gentleness of the question.

The man did not speak. His gaze darted from Ma back to Elena. It lingered on Elena's face with such a miserable intensity that she wanted to turn away, but found she couldn't tear her eyes from his. Then, as if he was suddenly conscious of his nakedness, he hunched away from her, scrabbling with the stump of his arm to pull a few wisps of straw across his groin.

'Who . . . who is he?' Elena breathed.

'Have you learned nothing, my darling? We none of us own our names in here. Here he is known as my pet, nothing more. What does he need with a name?

'But come, I sent Luce to look for you a while ago. I've work for you tonight, my darling, important work, and we must prepare you well. For the gentleman is very particular in what he wants.'

The Evening of the 1st Day after the Full Moon, August 1211

Eels – Eels are creatures of water and thunder, for they are quickened from the slime of the fishes when the thunderstorms rage. Many mortals fear to swim where there are eels lest they suck the swimmers' blood.

The fat of the eel when rubbed on the eyes gives mortal men the gift to see faerie folk and those secrets which others would hide from their gaze. The livers of the eel ease childbirth and their blood cures warts.

If they be dried in the sun, softened with fat, then stuffed with thyme and lavender, they can be worn as garters to ease the pains of the joints which come with age, or the marsh ague.

But if a wife wishes to cure her husband of drunkenness, then let her put a live eel in his ale or wine and suffer the creature to die in there, and when her husband drinks it, he shall never desire that drink again.

The Mandrake's Herbal

The Marsh Creepers

Luce lowered the chaplet of white roses as gently as she could on to Elena's loose red hair.

'There now,' Luce murmured soothingly, 'they'll match that little white rosebud mark you've got on your thigh. If he's a passion for roses, he'll love that. Gentlemen love to find little hidden scars and moles, makes 'em think they've discovered a secret.'

She adjusted the angle of the chaplet and Elena yelped as the thorns pricked her scalp. Luce bit her lip and glanced at Ma, who merely shrugged.

'You heard what he said, he wants the thorns left on.'

Luce crossly examined her own hands which were scratched and bleeding from having woven the crown. 'Wants to see these'n' all, does he?'

'He can see anything he likes, if he pays for it,' Ma said tartly. 'Now then, let's have a look at you, my darling.'

Elena was finding it hard to breathe through the small holes in a wooden mask. She peered out through the eye slits, already feeling the panic rising as it pressed against her face. She couldn't understand why this man had demanded she wore it. It was painted white. No features, no detail, just a smooth, blank surface as if her face didn't matter, didn't exist. Only the flesh of her body was important.

Elena squinted down at the fine bleached linen kirtle she wore. It was plain, but hung smoothly to the floor, bounded by a girdle of scarlet silk. But she was painfully conscious that beneath it she wore no shift, nor hose, nor shoes, and she felt as if she was standing there already naked.

Ma nodded her satisfaction. 'Come then. He wants you ready when he arrives.'

'But please, Ma, tell me what he wants me to do,' Elena said desperately.

'Very little, I suspect, at least at the start. He'll do it all at first and then you do whatever he asks.'

She opened a door that led to a second chamber and waved her jewelled hand at Elena. 'Come along, my darling. In here.'

Elena stared at the open door as a prisoner might look at irons in a torturer's fire. She couldn't move. Luce slipped her arm through hers and tugged her forward.

'You'll see, it won't be half as bad as you think,' she whispered encouragingly. 'Some of the gentlemen can be real sweetings. Know how to treat a lady, they do.'

Elena shuffled forward. The second chamber was larger than the one she had been dressed in. Small tables were scattered around the room, bearing flagons and goblets, platters of meats and honey-covered pastries and fruit. On one side of the chamber was a raised wooden platform covered with a thick pallet that looked as if it might be stuffed with feathers, not straw. Elena saw it and shuddered. Was that where he would do it?

On the other side was a shallow marble basin shaped like a giant scallop shell, large enough for two people to sit inside. A pole was fixed in the centre of the basin, carved and painted with a riot of leaping dolphins, garlanded with strange fruits and flowers that never grew above the waves. On top of the pole was a giant carved fish, coloured gold and red. It hung over the basin, its fat gold lips agape. Luce crossed over to it and pressed down on the fin of its tail. At once a jet of water spewed from its mouth in a graceful arc on to the pole and ran into the basin below. Luce laughed.

'That's enough, Luce, don't waste it, or we'll have to refill it,' Ma said, but she was smiling with satisfaction. 'Now quickly, my darling. He'll be here soon.'

'You have to get into the bath,' Luce urged. She helped Elena to step over the side and then clambered in with her. 'Turn around and put your back to the pillar.'

Ma reached for something under a table, and returned to Luce carrying a long length of rope.

Elena suddenly saw what they intended to do, and pushed Luce away, gathering up her long skirts and trying to scramble back out of the basin.

'Hold her,' Ma barked.

Ma clambered in over the low lip of the basin, grabbing her arms and slamming her back against the pillar so hard that for the moment Elena was winded. Before she knew it Ma had pulled both her wrists back behind the pillar and Luce was tying them tightly. Elena struggled and screamed as the rope was looped around her waist and over her shoulders, cutting between her breasts and binding her body to the pole.

Breathless from the struggle, the two women clambered back out of the basin and surveyed their handiwork. In the struggle some of the thorns had pierced Elena's skin and thin trickles of scarlet blood ran down from her forehead over the white mask. She was sobbing now, panting for breath beneath the hot mask, begging for them to release her, but she could see from their faces they would not.

Luce grimaced. 'Stop fighting, Holly, please. You'll only hurt yourself. It's just a game, is all. Some men like to play the hero. I dare say all he wants is to pretend he's rescuing you. If you play along, you'll enjoy it, you'll see.'

'I won't, I won't,' Elena screamed at her, her voice muffled beneath the wood. 'If you want to enjoy yourself, you do this. But I won't play. I won't do what he asks. I'll fight him. As soon as he lets me go I'll rip his face off.'

Ma nodded to Luce. 'You'd best go see if the gentleman is ready and then get back and mind the gate. Talbot's attending to some business and he'll not be back till late.'

As soon as Luce had closed the door behind her, Ma took a step forward, her hands on her hips, and looked up at Elena.

'Now you listen to me, my darling. I've seen it all; tears and pleas don't move me. If you don't please this gentleman, then you'll find yourself in the common hall pleasuring the sailors and the shit-shovellers, most of them drunk and stinking of the midden. Half a dozen of them a day, and you'll soon learn to swallow your pride and that won't be all you'll swallow. But you can beg and plead as much as you like; the gentlemen enjoy that. It quickens their blood. But I warn you, the more you beg, the more he'll be spurred on to do.'

Ma looked sharply at the door, hearing the sound of a man's footsteps striding towards the door. With a final warning gesture, she slipped through the connecting door that led to the dressing room. Even as that door closed, the main door to the chamber burst open. A tall cloaked figure stood squarely in the open doorway, framed by the darkness of the passage outside. Elena bit back a scream, for in the guttering candlelight his face was not the face of a man, but the mask of a demon.

'You want me to come with you?' the eel man asked Raffe. 'I can show you where the best fishing spots are. But I'll not be telling you where my eel traps are laid, that's a secret I'll share only on my deathbed.'

His face creased in a weather-beaten, toothless grin and he tapped the side of his nose, from which a large chunk was missing.

He loved to tell in gory detail, as old men do, how it was that one day, many years ago, a giant eel had fastened on the end of his nose and bitten it clean off. He was so old that no one could remember if that was the truth or not, but as the years went by the monstrous eel grew so long and fat in the telling that each new generation of children marvelled that the beast had only eaten his nose, and not devoured the whole man.

'I want to go off fishing by myself. Get away for the night from Osborn and the noise of the manor,' Raffe explained.

The old man nodded sympathetically. 'I can understand that. I couldn't be doing with people mithering me night and day. Peaceful it is on the river with only your own thoughts for company.'

Raffe slipped the coin into the tanned old hands. It was far more than the old man could earn from eeling in a night and they both knew it. He took the coin gratefully, thankful no doubt for an evening in by the fire, instead of shivering his ancient bones out on the river.

Raffe pushed the end of the long pole down into the mud to steady himself as he stepped into the flat-bottomed boat. It was long and narrow, too easy to overturn if you weren't careful, but better for a man of his size than trying to paddle a small, round coracle. The boat began to rock alarmingly as Raffe tried to balance himself. It had been a while since he had used such a boat and even then he had only ever taken it out with Gerard.

The eel man watched him shrewdly, then slid a short blunt paddle into the boat. 'This might serve you better. Easier to balance when you're sat down.'

As soon as he was out of sight of the old man's cottage, Raffe found a likely spot and lowered a couple of stout lines into the water with a hank of tangled sheep's wool on the end, baited with worms. He fastened the lines to the willows growing at the water's edge. He'd had all day to think about how he might manage this escapade without getting caught. The wars had taught him that rash courage was no substitute for a careful plan. But fate does not always cooperate with the plans of men.

The sun was already below the horizon when Raffe paddled around the back of the islet in the centre of the river. The bank next to the water meadow was deserted, save for a grey heron which lumbered heavily into the sky, disturbed from its fishing. Raffe cursed himself for his foolishness in having given the lad so much food. The boy had plainly thought it payment enough for delivering the message and had not bothered to wait. But as Raffe's boat glided past a willow that overhung the water, he saw the small skin coracle in the lee of it, blending so perfectly into the mass of dark vegetation that Raffe would certainly have missed it, had he not been looking for it.

The boy was curled up asleep inside, but awoke on the instant he heard the splash of Raffe's paddle.

'You ready, boy?' The lad nodded, searching the boat for the extra food he'd been promised and smiling broadly when he saw a covered basket lying in the bottom.

'Lead on then. I'll follow, but mind you keep me in sight. I'm not as nimble as you are on the water.'

The boy set off into the gathering darkness. Raffe was right; the boy's coracle was an extension of his body. He made no sound as his paddle licked in and out of the water, and so swiftly did he move that he disappeared from sight almost at once. Raffe paddled as fast as he could, nearly crashing into the little coracle as he rounded the next bend, where the lad sat waiting for him.

'Wait,' Raffe said. 'We'd best fasten the boats together, else you'll lose me or I'll sink you.' There were several lengths of old rope lying in the bottom of the eel man's punt, so he tied the coracle behind his boat and helped the boy clamber into his own craft.

'Now, you lie flat in the bow and tell me where to turn.'

The boy did as he was told and after nearly an hour of paddling, he pointed towards a gap in the vegetation which Raffe would never have spotted in the darkness. With help from the lad who pulled and pushed against an overhanging birch tree, Raffe managed to nose the clumsy craft into the gap and found himself paddling into the thousand twisting waterways that ran through the marshes. Tall swathes of reeds rustled and whispered above their heads, in other places wiry sedges and bog myrtle formed little islands on the thick, soft mud. Raffe jumped as a bittern hidden somewhere in the reeds let out its harsh, booming cry almost by his ear. The boy giggled.

Oily black water snaked between dark mud banks, but

only the boy could tell water from land. The pungent stench of mud, stagnant water and rotting vegetation lapped over Raffe's nostrils until he was drowning in the smell. One false move, one false turn and they would be trapped in the sucking ooze. And all around them in the darkness the marsh was whispering, shrieking and croaking as if it knew an intruder had trespassed into its kingdom and it was determined to sound the alarm.

Each man measures his own hour, so while it seemed to Raffe that it must already be nearing dawn, to the boy it seemed no time at all when he turned to Raffe and whispered for him to stop. A moon had at last risen into the sable sky, casting just enough light for Raffe to see a stump of what might have been a mooring post or a piece of bog oak sticking up from the mud. He looped the boat's rope around it.

The boy leapt off into what looked to Raffe like just another patch of reeds. Raffe wobbled down to the bow of the punt, painfully conscious of his great girth, and prodded the ground with his stave. It was spongy, but the end of the stave didn't sink into it. Raffe picked up the basket of food and gingerly stepped off the boat, praying that the ground would hold his weight.

Pushing forward through the fronds, he discovered he was walking up a narrow little path through the reed bed, on which stones and dried rushes had been laid to raise the track above the marsh. He emerged on a slight rise, almost blundering straight into a hut, which though not large occupied most of the clearing.

The boy's arm appeared, beckoning Raffe round to the side of the hut. There he found an entrance screened by a leather curtain and pushed his way under it, ducking as low as he could for there wasn't room for a man of his height to stand upright under the reed thatch. A small fire burned in the pit in the centre of the floor and the tiny hut was choked with smoke as it wandered about trying to find its way out of the thatched roof. There was an oily, fishy stench too. Raffe soon saw the cause. A seabird had been impaled on a wooden spike in the ground and a wick made from stripped rushes was burning in its beak, the oil for the flame being drawn from the bird's own body.

A shape rose up from behind the fog of smoke. 'Who is this?' a man's voice shrieked in alarm. 'Have you betrayed me, boy?'

'No, Father.' The boy sounded hurt. 'He says Lady Anne's away from the manor, said he'd help you instead.'

'I gave no such promise, lad,' Raffe protested. He stared at the figure in the shadows, trying to see his face, but the man's hood was pulled far down over his head.

'I came to find out what business you have with Lady Anne, for if your message had reached the wrong man, it would have been to her ruin or worse. It's lucky for you the boy found me before he ran straight into the arms of Lord Osborn. Did the boy call you *Father*? Are you kin to the lad or a priest?'

The man hesitated. 'I don't know if I can trust you or not, but since you must have already reasoned I am a fugitive, it puts me in no greater danger to tell you that I am also a priest.'

Raffe's back was stiffening by the minute as he stooped almost double in the cramped hut. He sat down cross-legged on the rush-covered floor and the priest warily followed suit.

'You are trying to get to France?'

The priest nodded.

'So why come to Lady Anne?'

'She's a pious woman. I was told she has helped other men of God. Arranged for food and money to be smuggled to them and passed on messages to those who could help them. I thought she might know someone who could help me find a safe passage.'

'He has food,' the marsh-lad chimed in eagerly, pointing to the basket.

'That I have,' Raffe said, 'but let the priest eat his fill first; I warrant it's been longer since his belly was filled than yours.'

The boy looked crestfallen, but he dutifully passed the basket to the priest and was rewarded as the priest broke a pastry in two and handed half to the boy, pausing only to gabble an exceedingly rapid grace in Latin before devouring the other half of the pastry almost without pausing to breathe. Before he had even swallowed the last bite, his hand was already reaching back into the basket.

Raffe was content to let the man eat while he considered what to do. He'd never suspected that Lady Anne was playing such a dangerous game. Although he was sure she was not meeting these priests herself, but simply passing on messages, if any message should be intercepted or a man's loyalties turned by the promise of a fat purse, then Anne was risking not only her freedom but her very life. The giving of any kind of aid to an enemy of the king could be considered an act of treason. Her sex and title would not spare her, indeed the king would count the crime worse in anyone of noble birth. Had Gerard known what his mother did? He would have considered it good sport to take such risks himself, but he'd never have allowed his mother to do so, and besides, he would have confided in Raffe. More likely it was Anne's grief over her son dying unshriven that had drawn her into this dangerous web.

But there was something more here, something about the desperation of this man that didn't make sense.

'Tell me something, Father,' Raffe said.

The priest was thirstily gulping down the wine from the flagon he'd found in Raffe's basket, but he reluctantly laid it aside and gave Raffe his attention.

'Why are you so eager to get to France? John has done no real violence to the simple parish priests. He has imprisoned some who resisted him, but most have simply taken off their habits and gone into hiding or sought shelter in the monasteries.'

The priest remained silent for a moment and Raffe knew he was weighing up how much to confide in him.

'I have been in hiding up to now. But . . . I am no ordinary parish priest . . . I was chaplain to the Bishop of Ely.'

Raffe whistled through his teeth. He could see now why the little man was nervous. It had been the Bishop of Ely along with the Bishops of London and Worcester who, on the instructions of the Pope, had laid the sentence of Interdict on England when John had refused to consent to the appointment of Stephen Langton as Archbishop of Canterbury. John would revel in an opportunity to take his vengeance on any man in the bishop's circle that he could lay hands on. And a chaplain would surely know if the bishop had any dark little secrets that John could use against him to win his cause. This might be an insignificant little man in the Church's eyes, but to the king he would be a prize catch. And John's methods of encouraging reluctant men to talk were legendary in their exquisite cruelty even for a son of Anjou.

'So why didn't you stay safely in hiding?' Raffe asked him.

The priest shivered. 'They arrested my housekeeper. She was with child and her family could not afford the fine to get her released. She feared for her life and her unborn babe, so she told John's men where I might be found.'

Raffe barely suppressed a smile. Doubtless the babe was of the priest's getting. Everyone knew that a priest's housekeeper was in most cases the priest's mistress too, which is why John had arrested as many of them as he could, knowing that would make the priests smart even more than seizing their possessions. Usually they were released, but not until a hefty fine had been imposed to swell further John's denuded coffers. But in this case his men must have discovered to their delight that they'd caught a swan instead of a sparrow in their trap.

The priest leaned forward. 'Are you able to help me? I have money to pay for the passage.'

So not all of the missing church silver had found its way into John's coffers, Raffe thought. The priests had doubtless made sure they didn't flee empty-handed.

'I'll need money in advance to pay the river boatman to take you to the ship and the lads who can bring word of a ship.' Seeing the priest was about to argue, Raffe added, 'A steward's wages don't stretch to all the palms that have to be greased.'

'How do I know you won't just make off with it?' the priest said suspiciously.

'You'll have to trust someone, or cool your heels here till the Interdict is lifted, which could be months or even years, for John's in no mood to surrender to the Pope.'

The priest hesitated, then shrugged in a sullen gesture of acceptance. 'So does that mean you'll help me?'

Raffe stroked his beardless chin and studied the man closely. 'Do you swear on the Blood of Christ that what you've told me is the truth? That is the only reason for your flight to France?'

The priest crossed himself. 'By the blessed Blood and Body of our Lord, I swear it. What other reason could I have?'

Raffe snorted. 'To aid England's enemies?'

'Never, on my life!' the priest said indignantly. 'I am a priest, not a traitor.'

'There're many who have been both,' Raffe said. 'But I will help you get away. No, not so fast, wait.' He held up his hand to forestall the man's thanks. 'There is something you must do for me first.'

'I cannot say a secret Mass, I have no host or any –'

'A good, brave man, Lady Anne's son, Gerard, lies unburied at the manor. He died without rites for no priest could be found in these parts who would come to his deathbed. Before you leave for France you will come and bless his resting place and anoint him.'

'But if he died in sin,' the priest protested, 'I cannot anoint him. The Church does not allow –'

'I said he died unshriven, but not in sin.'

The priest waved his hand impatiently, indicating that they were one and the same. 'You may rest assured I will pray for him, and if you can get me safely to France I will say Masses daily for his soul in recompense to you for your services. Shall we agree three months of Masses for a safe passage?'

He squealed in alarm as Raffe suddenly reached across and grabbed the front of his tunic. 'You will come to the manor and give him unction, or I promise you will never set foot on French soil.'

The priest tried to prise Raffe's great fist from his clothes, but without success.

'Don't be a fool, my son, it's far too dangerous. You said yourself that Lord Osborn almost caught the boy – what if he should catch me? I can't simply walk into a bustling manor with a hundred pairs of eyes watching me. Besides, God will hear my prayers for Gerard's soul just as well in France as over his coffin.'

'But I cannot,' Raffe retorted. He let the man go, and the priest shuffled as far back in the tiny hut as he could get.

'Now,' Raffe said firmly, 'I will go and make arrangements for your passage to France. When all is ready I'll send word to the boy to bring you to the manor after dark. When you've done your duty by Gerard, you'll be taken to the boat. If you don't come to the manor when I send for you, the boat will depart without you. You have a choice, Father: freedom and safety, or starving out here on the marshes until I get tired of waiting and tell the king's men where to find you.'

'You would betray me?' The priest's eyes widened in alarm.

'I would not betray a priest, but if you will not act as a priest should, if your miserable little skin is worth more to you than another man's immortal soul, then you have abandoned your vows and you are no priest.'

Elena lay curled up on the turf seat in the darkened garden, but she wasn't sleeping. She was so drained and exhausted that she felt she might never again have the energy even to lift her head. But she couldn't sleep. She couldn't bear to close her eyes in case he came to her again in her dreams.

The green scales glinting in the candlelight, the long black horns and the sharp fangs protruding from the blood-red mouth. The only things that moved were his eyes, glittering in the shadow of his wooden mask.

She saw him over and over again walking slowly towards her, silent and expressionless. Just those cold green eyes flickering over her body. She felt again the ropes tying her to the post, keeping her helpless, tangled like an insect in a web, waiting for the spider to sink his fangs into her. She crushed her fists into her eyeballs till they hurt, trying to make them stop seeing what was burned on to them. The water, the cold water from the great fat lips of the fish, pouring down over her head, running over and under her mask, till she thought she was drowning, her lungs tearing as she struggled to breathe.

Far above, the stars prickled in the small square of hell-black sky caged by the high walls of the courtyard. Elena's cheek was crushed against the rough stems of the thyme, but she ignored the scratches. It was nothing to the pain that engulfed her whole body and burned between her legs.

Most of the women had already staggered back to their own chamber or else lay sleeping in the arms of customers who had paid to stay all night. The giggles and shrieks had long since ceased, but still Elena didn't stir from the garden.

She was shivering, but she couldn't bring herself to go inside, to be near hot human flesh, to smell the stench of sweat and semen on the women's bodies. She tried in vain to draw in the cleansing scent of the thyme to rid herself of his stench that returned again and again to her nostrils like an echo that wouldn't stop.

A year and a day, Raffaele had said she must stay. A year and a day to gain her freedom, but if she couldn't prove her innocence, who knew how long? And how many times in a year could that man come again, or others like him? If only she knew how long she had to endure this place, maybe she could teach herself to bear it. But what if she waited and hoped and never got out? Never again felt Athan's arms around her or saw her son's little face? She had to know if there would be an end.

Although she had thought herself unable to move, Elena pushed herself upright. Her knees almost giving way beneath her, she stumbled towards the communal sleeping chamber. Carefully stepping around the bodies of the prone women, so as not to awaken them, she found her own sleeping pallet and, lifting the edge, pushed her arm beneath it until her fingers felt the cold leather of her scrip. Sliding it out as quietly as she could, she crept back outside and crossed the moonlit garden to the turf seat. She froze as she heard the great door of the hall open and then close. But no one came into the garden. It must have been someone leaving the brothel.

Beyond the walls, she could hear a dog howling, but inside the courtyard there was no sound. Trees, gilded in silver, breathed softly in the warm night air, and the dark shadows of the branches glided as gracefully as dancers across the sable grass.

Elena needed no light to perform her task. How many times had she done this in Athan's cottage while he lay sleeping? She drew out the little bundle from her scrip and carefully unwrapped it. She lifted her knife and, steeling herself, drew the sharp blade across her tongue. His semen was crusted on her thighs. She pulled up her skirts and let the blood from her tongue drip on to her bare legs, until it mingled with the dried white crust. Then she carefully anointed the mandrake with the salty blood-milk.

It had been months since Elena had fed me. I had not drunk since her child was born and I was hungry. I was ravenous. The red milk in my mouth was like sweet wine is to men. It is easy to get intoxicated by it, giddy on the perfume of it, heavy as iron. But unlike wine-sodden mortals our wits grow sharper, our strength increases with each drop of the thick red curds we imbibe. I trembled in her fingers and she felt me stirring in her grasp.

I knew what she wanted, far better than she did, but she had to ask, all she had to do was ask. That is our code, our pledge — *Ask and it shall be given unto you.* That was our promise long before another usurped it; for there were gallows and crosses centuries before He bawled his lungs out in the byre. We are as old as murder itself, and only the Angel of Death can make claim to be our elder brother.

Elena held me close to her lips and whispered, 'Show me a dream. Show me what will happen. That man who came tonight, show me if he will come again. Tell me how I can be free.'

But I knew what she was really asking. I knew only too well.

2nd Day after the Full Moon, August 1211

Thyme – This herb gives courage to the faint-hearted and joy to the melancholy. The crushed leaves relieve the pain of bee stings, cure headaches, kill the worms of the belly and banish nightmares. Foolish ladies give sprigs of it to those who ride to the Holy Wars in the forlorn hope that their lovers will remember them.

The souls of the dead take shelter in thyme. When a mortal dies, thyme is brought into the house, and kept there until the body is taken for burial, but it is not used in the funeral wreath, for time means nothing to the dead.

But if a man or maid be foully murdered, the sweet smell of thyme shall haunt the place where they fell for all eternity, though no thyme plants grow near it. For the passage of time cannot undo the crime of murder, since the victim is gone from mortal reach and has no tongue or sign to forgive the one who wronged him.

The Mandrake's Herbal

Crime of Passion

It is dark, but she sees him standing there with his back to her, gazing into the flames of a small fire. He is mesmerized by the twisting orange light, as men are when they are exhausted. His head is drooping slightly. She advances, a knife in her hand, but she doesn't mean to kill him. Not murder, no. She has another use for him. Swiftly and silently as a cat pounces, she slashes him across the backs of his thighs.

With a cry of agony he falls forward, narrowly missing the fire. He rolls away and writhes on the ground, clutching at his legs. She is sure they must be bleeding, but it is too dark to see. She raises the hilt of the knife and brings it crashing down on the man's head. But the blow is not hard enough. He is still moving, still yelling. She must make him stop. Someone will come running, if she does not. She raises the knife to bludgeon him again, but he knows what is coming and lashes out with his arm as she strikes, dashing the blade from her hands and sending it spinning off into the darkness.

Now he is struggling to kneel, groping at his belt for his sword, but he is too stunned to act quickly enough and it is awkward for a kneeling man to draw a long blade from the scabbard. Even so, in time he will succeed in freeing the sword and then she will be at his mercy for she has no weapon. She cannot see her knife and she dares not waste time searching for it, for he is still yelling, shouting for help, and soon someone must hear him. She pulls the rope from her waist, the rope she meant to tie him with, but she knows now he cannot be tied. It is too late. She flings it over the kneeling man's head like a noose, pulling it tight against his throat. He struggles, trying to grab her hands as the rope tightens around his neck. If he does, he will be able to pull her over his head. She knows that, she has seen men do it.

Something rolls beneath her feet as she struggles with him. A kindling stick, not big enough to strike him with, but she snatches it up and thrusts it through the rope, twisting the rope tighter and tighter round the stick. She hears the rasp of his breath, sees the frantic and now futile beating of his hands. Still she twists the rope harder and harder. Finally she realizes that it is only the rope which is holding the man upright. His hands have fallen limp at his sides. His head lolls forward. He is not screaming. He is not breathing. She lets the body fall and this time he does not rise.

Raffe stayed away from the manor until he saw the early morning smoke rising from the kitchens and the first of the carts trundling in through the manor's gates. If he went banging at the gate for Walter to open up in the middle of the night, word of it would race round the manor quicker than a lightning flash. But if he strolled in through the morning bustle of servants, with luck he would not be noticed. He thanked heaven Osborn and Hugh were away.

He had not wasted the night. Even now a small boat laden with sacks of grain was being sculled upstream towards Norwich, by the same boatmen who had taken Elena to safety. They would carry the message to Talbot that passage was required on a ship for a gentleman who needed to slip away quietly from these shores. Talbot would know where to find a ship's captain who would ask no questions.

The few hours' sleep in the bottom of the boat Raffe had managed to snatch before dawn had been fitful and uncomfortable. Perhaps it was meeting the priest that made him think of it, but for the first time in many years, when he did manage to sleep he dreamed not of the wars, but of the abbey where he lived as a child.

Those years in the abbey choir had been the happiest Raffe had ever known. After the initial shock of being left there by his parents, given to the Church to pay for his father's life, he had found himself among friends, boys and men like himself, mutilated for the greater glory of God. He was taught to read and write, to sing in Latin and to study music. The laity who flocked to the abbey church treated the castrati like princes. Stout matrons vied with one another to bake them the most delicious treats; girls gave them flowers; and rich men bought them costly trinkets. Among the ordinary choir whose voices, though accomplished, were merely human, these rare and costly boys and men were the elite.

The boy castrati worshipped the beautiful young men in their twenties whose looks and voices surpassed the angels'. But they'd giggle and whisper about the older castrati who dragged their bloated bodies about, yet whose voices, behind the screen, could still move men to tears. It never occurred to them that one day their own bodies too would become as aged and grotesque.

Raffe loved the comradeship of this little band of chosen brothers. But his greatest joy was to sing, to stand among the choir and hear their voices rising together up to the throne of God. Daily he dreamed that one day the whole church would hold its breath as his voice ran like molten silver from the moon.

But though he prayed every night and tried to convince himself that he was one of them, he knew something was starting to go badly wrong. Even if he hadn't seen the singing master shaking his head and the choir members exchanging glances whenever he was asked to sing alone, he knew that his voice wasn't like the others'. The music was perfect in his head. He could hear exactly how each note should sound. He knew what was required of him, but when he opened his mouth, what came out now made even him cringe.

When he was eleven years old, they sent for him. The cart to take him back to his village was already standing at the abbey door. Sometimes with training the voice can be improved, they said, but his was becoming worse. It happens with some castrati. Unlike normal boys, their voices can never break, but they can crack as the child grows, and a bell that is cracked cannot ever sound a pure note.

Raffe begged them to let him become a monk or to take Holy Orders as a priest, so that he could remain among them and listen to those voices even if he could never be one of them. But they sadly shook their heads. Did he not know, had he not learned in his studies what is written in the Holy Bible – 'He that is wounded in the stones shall not enter the congregation of the Lord.' Eunuchs are unnatural. They are an abomination. They are unclean. He had been wounded for God, and for that very wound he would be cast out from God's sight.

When he returned home, his father said nothing. In contrast, his mother had plenty to say about the wicked waste of money and the dashed hopes of the whole family after all they had sacrificed for him. He had trampled on all their dreams by failing to study hard enough, by failing to be good enough. He found his sleeping place occupied by his younger brother. His tasks on the farm had been shared out among the others. They had not expected him to return. Like a stone lifted out of a pond, the water had closed over the gap where he had once been, leaving no trace. But all that he could have borne, for none of it had hurt him as much as his father's silence.

A swan alighted with a splash on the river, almost colliding with the boat. The ripples sent the slender craft rocking. Raffe squinted up at the sky; the sun had risen high enough now for Walter to have opened the gate and the servants to be about their morning tasks. He hauled himself upright, scratching violently at the swelling bites of the marsh midges on his arms.

Having returned the boat to the old eel man, Raffe made his way back to the manor. He could not suppress a yawn as he crossed the courtyard, weaving between the bustling servants.

'Weary already at this bright hour, gelding?'

Raffe whirled about to find Osborn's younger brother, Hugh, standing in front of the stables. God's teeth, when had he returned? Only yesterday he'd ridden out with Osborn and the rest of his men on their way to attend the king at court. What was he doing back here?

Hugh looked the steward up and down with amused

disdain. 'By the Blood, you look so draggled, had it been any other man I'd have sworn he'd spent the night in the arms of a whore, but we know you weren't losing your sleep in that cause, don't we?'

Raffe, aware of the barely suppressed grins of the other servants, turned away, trying hard to swallow his anger. It wasn't easy for his fist was itching to connect with Hugh's nose.

'I can see you still want for manners. Like a dog to a whistle you should come running to your masters when they address you.'

Raffe wheeled around and walked rapidly towards Hugh, his fists clenched. He stopped so close to him that, being a good head shorter, Hugh was forced to crane his head back to look Raffe in the face.

'Did you want something?' Raffe said coldly.

Hugh giggled. 'You know, however many times I hear you speak, I still can't get used to the voice of a little girl coming from a man's body. Well, I say man, but we all know that's not exactly true, is it?' His tone changed without warning. 'Yes, I want something, gelding. I want to know where you were yesterday. When I returned last night I was burning up with a fever, but the maids brought me nothing to ease it. I was kept waiting for my food for hours and when those feckless arse-wipes did finally stir themselves to bring it, it tasted like dog shit. I sent for you to speak to you about their neglect, but apparently not one of the numbskulls you laughingly call servants could find you. So where had you sneaked off to?'

'I am not a villein,' Raffe said coldly. 'I may come and go as I please. Since my duties were done, I decided to spend the night where the air was sweeter and the company had greater wit than I've been forced to endure these last weeks. So I spent it on the river with the fish.'

'Let's see, shall we?' Hugh's dark grey eyes flicked to Raffe's basket, the same one in which last night he had carried food to the priest. 'Open it!'

Raffe shrugged and unfastened the lid. A knot of three fat

black eels squirmed over one another in a nest of damp weeds. Just as Raffe had hoped, the eels had snapped at the worms on the lines he'd laid out in the river before meeting the boy and had got their teeth entangled in the mass of sheep wool. He had pulled them from the water at dawn in a matter of minutes, but how could any man prove how long it had taken to catch them?

Hugh scowled. 'So you were off enjoying yourself when you should have been here checking that the servants carried out their duties. It's as well I returned to see how my poor brother's manor is neglected the moment his back is turned.'

'The servants know their duties.'

'That's what you think, is it? Here, you! Come here, boy.'

A thin, hollow-chested stable boy crept out of the darkness, his head held down at an angle, cringing away from Hugh. Raffe could immediately see why. The lad's nose, encrusted with blood, was so swollen it was hard to tell if it was broken. His eyes were purple and one was so puffy he couldn't open it more than a crack. There were bruises on his scrawny arms, and from the way the lad was limping, Raffe suspected that his clothes concealed more injuries.

Hugh grabbed the lad's neck and pushed him forward to face Raffe. 'This wretch was instructed to tend to my horse, but when I came to see all was well with the beast, I found his hooves still caked in mud.'

'So you beat him?' Raffe demanded furiously.

If any of the lads had been so lazy as to neglect a valuable horse, Raffe would have taken a switch to them himself, but he would never have disciplined them like this. Besides, they all knew better than to leave mud under the hooves where it could cause rot. And this lad loved horses and doted on all of them as if they were his personal pets. Raffe knew that Hugh had beaten the boy solely to punish him for his absence rather than anything the poor lad had neglected to do. God's blood, he wouldn't rest until he'd found proof that Hugh was a traitor, and when he did, nothing would give him greater satisfaction than watching the bastard die as slowly and painfully as possible.

The boy stood shivering with misery. Raffe placed a gentle hand on his shoulder, shocked to feel him cringe under it. He called out to one of the scullions who was crossing the yard with an armful of fresh-cut herbs.

'Take this lad to the kitchen, and tell cook she's to mull him some ale. My orders. And get someone to clean the lad up, gently mind. I'll be across myself presently.'

The scullion laid a brotherly arm around the lad and led him off as quickly as he could, darting a scared glance over his shoulder at Hugh.

'You reward a lazy little midden-brat like him, when you should be thrashing him,' Hugh thundered. 'No wonder you can't keep order in this manor.'

Raffe's temper finally lunged out of his control. 'You are not master here and if you ever lay a hand on one of my charges again, I'll break every bone in it, one by one.'

Hugh was white with anger, two high spots of colour blazing on his pale cheeks. 'Have a care, gelding, I'll see you brought to the whip yet, by God I will.'

He stormed into the stable and, grabbing the reins of his horse from a boy, swung into the saddle and clattered across the yard and through the open gate, scattering terrified chickens and maids to the right and left of him.

Raffe, now that his temper had cooled slightly, cursed himself silently. Hugh would be watching him like a vulture from now on. How the Devil was he going to get the priest past him? He felt for Gerard's pearl ring which hung from a leather thong beneath his shirt. Whatever the danger he must do it. If there was the slightest chance that the priest's anointing would bring peace to Gerard's soul, then he must try even if it cost him his own life.

The serving maid waddled awkwardly across the courtyard at the back of the Adam and Eve Inn, trying not to let the contents of the slops bucket she was carrying splash on her skirts. She glanced up at the shuttered windows of the inn; the guests wouldn't stir for another hour or more, and even then they'd be lucky if they could crawl off their sleeping pallets, given the amount of ale and cider most had drunk last night. She thumbed her nose at the shutters behind which the innkeeper and his crabby wife still lay snoring. It was all very well for them, they could sleep on, but the old termagant would grumble all day if the chores weren't done by the time she deigned to wake.

The maid went round the back of the wooden shack where the meals were cooked over the great fire and flung the contents of the bucket towards the midden, without bothering to look. She didn't need to; she'd been emptying slops here at least twice a day for the past five years. There was a screech, and a cat with a wet tail raced past her ankles, spitting its indignation.

The sudden appearance of the cat made her glance down. For a moment she just stared at the ground without her mind being able to comprehend what her eyes saw. Then she began to scream and once she'd started, she couldn't stop. She carried on screaming until the innkeeper, naked save for a short shift which barely covered his scrawny thighs, came hurrying round the shack, closely followed by his wife who was armed with a heavy cudgel. Several of the guests trailed after them, grumbling at the disturbance.

The maid, her hand trembling violently, pointed at the earth next to the midden heap. A man lay on his belly in the filth, his head twisted to the side. Flies swarmed over the dark blood congealed in his hair and crawled over his purple, grotesquely swollen face, settling in the deep black bruise that encircled his neck. Only the buzzing of the flies broke the stunned silence in that courtyard.

Finally, the innkeeper shook himself, and seizing the maid by the shoulder, shouted at her to go and raise the hue and cry, and send someone to find the bailiff. She did not need any urging to run.

It took a while for the bailiff to appear and by that time half the street had crowded into the courtyard to see what was afoot.

The bailiff peered at the body from several angles, though he did not attempt to touch it.

'Plain as a pig's ear what's happened,' he announced to the crowd. 'Someone's whacked him across the back of the head with something heavy, maybe while he was drunk and taking a piss. That would have floored him. Then they throttled him to make sure he was good and dead. He wouldn't have put up much of a fight, not if he was already half-dead from the crack on the head, none at all if he was out cold from the blow. Wouldn't have taken much strength to kill him. A boy could have done it, just as easily as any full-grown man . . . or woman, come to that.' The bailiff stared pointedly at the cudgel in the innkeeper's wife's hand.

'I'll have you know I'm not in the habit of murdering my customers,' she said indignantly. 'What profit would there be in that?'

'One of yours, was he?' the bailiff said, as if that explained everything. 'There'll be no shortage of suspects then. Every rogue between here and Yarmouth passes through your doors. I wager it'll be a falling out among thieves.'

The innkeeper's wife was about to retort to this wicked slander on her respectable establishment when something caught her eye.

'What's that?'

It was half concealed beneath the corpse's hand, but it stood out vividly against the dark muck and filth of the yard.

With evident distaste, the bailiff crouched down and wriggled the object out from beneath the cold fingers. It was crushed and wilted, but it was still recognizable. It was a single white rose.

As they stared at it, the buzzing in the air grew louder. It seemed that every fly in Norwich was swarming towards the corpse.

The candles on the walls bled drop by drop on to the twisted mass of wax below. Ma Margot sat enthroned in her snake chair, a goblet of wine untouched on the table in front of her. She stared hard and long at Elena, her bulging yellow-green eyes unblinking in the candlelight. Elena felt sick and she longed to sink down into the chair in front of Ma's table, but she dared not do so without being invited. She grasped the back of it, trying to keep herself upright. Her stomach had been churning ever since Talbot had said Ma wanted to see her. Not another gentleman, not so soon, she couldn't.

'Please, Ma, I can't! I can't —'

'Wait till you're spoken to, girl,' Talbot growled. Elena jumped, not realizing that he was still standing behind her. But Ma continued to study her without making any attempt to speak.

Elena's head was throbbing. Back at the manor she had once drunk too much cider at a harvest-home and remembered the same dizzy, nauseous misery the day after as she felt now. But she had scarcely drunk anything at all last night, just a mouthful or two of the wine when the man had insisted. Could there have been some herb or potion in it?

Ma's fingers caressed the carved head of the serpent on her armrest. 'Where were you last night?'

Elena gaped at her, wondering if she had heard the question aright.

'With the gentleman . . . you dressed me, you and Luce.'

'And after he left?' Ma's voice was low, but sharp as a dagger.

'I was here, asleep.'

'You're lying. Luce swears you were not in the women's chamber when she went to bed and she didn't retire until after the watch called midnight. Your gentleman had long gone by then. Talbot says you were not abed when he made his rounds when he returned. So I'll ask you again, my darling, where were you?'

'I . . . I was sleeping out on the turf seat in the courtyard. I couldn't bear to be inside after . . . what he did.'

'Never mind what he did,' Ma snapped. 'It's what you did that matters.'

She beckoned to Talbot, the heavy blood-red ruby on her finger flashing like a warning in the candlelight.

Talbot lumbered round and stood beside Ma. His broken nose seemed even more twisted out of shape in the deep shadows cast by the candles.

'Tell her,' Ma ordered.

Talbot folded his thick, hairy arms, glowering at Elena. 'A corpse was found this morning in the courtyard of the Adam and Eve. Been murdered.'

'You know who that man was?' Ma asked.

Elena shook her head. They were both staring at her so intently that she found her cheeks burning with guilt even though she didn't understand why.

'The man's name was Raoul. He was in the service of Lord Osborn,' Ma said.

Elena's heart began to pound. 'Did he come to Norwich searching for me?'

Ma and Talbot exchanged glances.

'He'd been asking questions in the taverns about a runaway girl with red hair,' Ma said. 'He wasn't very discreet about it. But last night it seems he was just searching for pleasure.'

Elena's chest was so tight it hurt to breathe.

'And it seems, by chance, you were his pleasure,' Ma Margot added with relish. 'He was the gentleman you enter-tained last night.'

'But he never told me his name,' Elena said, horrified. 'I didn't know. I didn't who he was. He wore a mask, you know he did.'

'Told you,' said Talbot, 'no one ever gives their real name here. Not customers, nor girls. Now you know why. If he'd heard your real name last night . . .'

Elena clung to the edge of the table, her head reeling. She had been forced to pleasure one of Lord Osborn's men. Had Ma known who he was? But she couldn't have. Ma was trying to hide her, wasn't she?

'And now Raoul's dead,' Ma said. 'So, what happened, my darling? Did you let your name slip? Were you scared he'd recognized you, or did he tell you he was one of Osborn's men? Is that why you followed him after he left here? Is that why you killed him – to stop him talking?'

Elena's legs would hold her up no longer. She sank into the chair beside her, burying her head in her hands.

'I didn't . . . I couldn't have! I dreamed of a murder, but I couldn't really have done it. It was only a dream, a warning . . . about the future. It wasn't real.'

'What dream?' Ma asked sharply. 'When did you have it?'

'Last night when I was asleep on the turf bench . . . I dreamed I killed someone. I didn't mean to, but he was yelling and I had to stop him. But it was a dream, that's all. I've had them before. I dreamed of killing my baby – that's why I gave him away.'

'So you tell us,' Ma said tartly. 'But there are plenty who believe you murdered your child in the flesh, else you'd not be with us now. And if you've killed once, it makes it easier to do it again. In this dream of yours, how did this man die?'

'I . . . he was . . . strangled.' Elena looked up in desperation. 'That wasn't how Raoul died, was it? Tell me! Please, tell me.'

Talbot and Ma looked at each other again.

'He was strangled all right. Living breath choked out of him,' Talbot told her with a grim satisfaction.

Elena gave a shuddering moan. 'But it couldn't have been me. I don't remember doing it. I don't remember going out. I was asleep on the seat and when I woke again I was still there.'

'But no one saw you there,' Ma reminded her. She reached behind her back in the snake chair and pulled something out, dropping it on to the table. It was the white linen shift Elena had worn last night, crumpled and stained with dried blood. Ma fingered the stains and raised her black brows quizzically.

'But that's *my* blood,' Elena protested, '. . . from the thorns . . . it isn't his. It can't be his.'

'And the scarlet girdle you wore about your waist last night, my darling, where exactly is that? It wasn't found with the shift. Luce has looked all over for it, but it seems to have vanished.'

'Handy thing to strangle a man with, a girdle,' Talbot said.

Ma leaned forward, cocking her great head to one side. The candlelight flashed from the ruby-headed pins in her coiled black hair. 'I understand, my darling, murder is a terrible thing, a shock to a soul.'

'Aye,' Talbot said grinning. 'A bastard of a shock to the poor sod who snuffs it.'

Ma glared at him. 'They tell me that those who commit such dreadful deeds walk as if they are in a sleep, not knowing what they do, and after remember it as a distant dream. Fear can make us desperate, my darling. When you discovered that Raoul was Osborn's man, you panicked. I understand that.'

She gave what might have been intended as a sympathetic smile, but to the terrified Elena she looked more like a wolf baring her sharp white teeth.

'But you should have come to me or Talbot and told us what you feared. There's ways to sort such matters without leaving bodies all over the city to be found by prying eyes.'

'But I didn't know who he was, I swear,' Elena said desperately.

Ma ignored this. 'You've put us all in grave danger.'

'Dropped us right in the midden,' Talbot growled.

'If Raoul told anyone where he was going last night, then –' Ma was interrupted by a loud and insistent tolling of the bell at the door.

'By the sound of it they already know,' Talbot said.

Ma's heavy black brows flexed in a frown. 'Talbot, answer

the door. But delay them as long as you can before you bring them up here.'

Talbot, despite his bow-legs, could cover the ground as fast as a charging bull when he had to, and he was out of the door and clattering down the stairs before Ma had managed to scramble down from her chair.

'This way, my darling.'

But Elena was frozen to the spot with incomprehension and fear. Ma seized her wrist and dragged her bodily towards the curtain hanging across the corner of the room from which Elena had seen her emerge that very first night. The corner was in darkness and Elena could see nothing behind the drape, but evidently Ma didn't need light to find what she wanted. She was feeling for something on the floor. Elena heard a trapdoor being lifted. Ma tugged her across to the hole.

'Kneel on the edge and feel for the rungs of the ladder with your feet,' Ma instructed.

Elena, shuddering with the memory of the prisoner hole beneath the manor, used all her strength to pull herself out of Ma's grasp. But Ma Margot was as strong as Talbot. Exasperated, she gave a sharp twist on Elena's arm to bring her to her senses.

'It's down there or be arrested for murder. And just you think about this: if they were planning to hang you for killing a mere villein's babe, imagine what they will do to a base-born villein who murders a nobleman!'

'But I didn't, Ma, I swear I didn't,' Elena sobbed.

'You can swear all you like, but they'll no more believe you this time than they did last. Now, get down there and mind you keep as silent as the grave.'

'At least give me light,' Elena begged. 'I can't even see the ladder.'

'No time,' Ma hissed fiercely. 'Just seven rungs is all, then you'll be on solid ground. Hurry, I can hear Talbot climbing the stairs!'

As soon as Elena's head was below the level of the trap-door, Ma closed it, leaving Elena in total darkness. She stood on the ladder, too afraid to take another step down. But as she shifted her weight the wooden ladder rocked and creaked under her. Scared of it falling, Elena felt for the step below, then the step below that until, as Ma had promised, her feet touched solid ground.

As she turned, her hand brushed something furry, and remembering the caged beasts, she stifled a cry of fear, shrinking back against the wooden ladder. But whatever it was didn't move. She tentatively reached out again and felt thick, silky fur, as soft as melting butter, but it was cold to the touch and she knew that there was no animal beneath the skin.

As her eyes adjusted, she realized that the chamber was not entirely without light. Pricks of daylight were shining in through holes on the other side of the room. She saw dimly that she was standing in a wedge-shaped room, next to a sleeping platform covered with a heap of pelts over a thick mattress. Some of the furs were as pale as snow in moon-light, others dark as the night. She smoothed the skins with her fingers, marvelling at their sensual softness.

Footsteps padded across the wooden boards above her head, followed by the scrape of chair legs and a hum of voices. But although she strained to hear, she could make out no words. Gazing fearfully towards the ceiling, her eyes caught sight of evil, distorted faces in the darkness glower-ing over at her. She cringed. Were they bats or demons? She held her breath, staring fixedly up at them, but they didn't move. Holding her arms protectively overhead, she crept a little closer, then saw what they were. Around the top of the chamber was carved a series of grimacing grotesques as you might see in a church. Human faces with pig snouts, women with pendulous breasts and tangled beards, men with faces twisted into a leper's leer, owls with human heads and men with the heads of dogs.

Elena sank down on to the bed, trying not to look at the mocking faces glaring at her. Above her she could still hear the murmur of voices. What was Ma saying to them? Would she hand her over to them? Cold sweat drenched her body. Raffe had warned her that if Ma couldn't earn a profit from her then she might be tempted to give her up for the bounty.

She tried desperately to remember what had happened last night. She couldn't have killed that man. She'd wanted to, all the time she was in that chamber with him, every muscle and sinew in her body had been screaming out for his death. If she'd been able to get her hands free, if she'd had a knife or a staff or anything to defend herself, she would have lunged at him through sheer fear, of that much she was certain.

But she didn't even know where this Adam and Eve was, and even if she'd found it by following him, how could she have got there and back without remembering anything? And yet she could vividly remember standing behind him, feeling the panic as he yelled out, his hands groping for hers as she twisted tighter and tighter. She could remember feeling his dead weight sagging from her arms as he swung forward. All of that she could picture with painful clarity, as if his body was lying right here beside her in Ma's chamber.

The image had been as clear as when she saw herself murdering her own child. But she hadn't done that, had she? She pressed her hands to her eyes. She wasn't sure of anything any more. One thing was certain, Raoul was dead. The man who had raped her was dead. If she could kill him and not remember how she got there, then maybe Joan had been right all along and she really had murdered her baby. Perhaps she had only imagined she'd given him to Gytha. She didn't know what was real and what was the dream any more.

Footsteps echoed again on the floor above, and she shrank into the corner of the bed, but the trapdoor didn't open. Then she heard voices as if they were next to her. She slid over the furs and tiptoed to the opposite wall.

One of the carvings in the corner was set lower than the others, placed just above Elena's head. It was like a mask. But it was turned around, facing into the wall, so the hollow back was open to the room. A dim, pale light was streaming into the chamber through the pupils of its eyes and open mouth. There was a wooden shutter to one side of the mask, and a set of steps in front of it, like the ones Ma used to get into her chair. Elena stood on the bottom of the steps and pushed her face inside the stone mask. She could see right through the eyes into the room beyond and realized she was looking into the guest hall where Talbot had taken her that first night.

Three men were swigging the last gulp from beakers of ale, and one by one handing them to Talbot, wiping their mouths with the backs of their hands in appreciation.

'You'll keep your ear to the ground and let us know if you hear any gossip that might give us a lead.'

'Aye, you'll be the first to know, if I hear aught,' Talbot answered. 'What do you reckon this Raoul was doing at the Adam and Eve? Not the place for a gentleman.'

The leader shrugged. 'Maybe your girls were just a dish of dainties to him and it whetted his appetite for stronger meats. He fancied sinking his teeth into the juicy fat haunch of a street whore.'

One of the other men clapped his leader on the back. 'If you think these girls are dainty, you ain't had fat Alice here sit on your face. I warrant her haunches are meat enough for any man.'

All four men laughed.

'Besides,' the man continued, 'a noble like that would take a whore to his lodgings. He was no pimple-faced apprentice who had to have a girl against a wall for fear of his master.'

The leader nodded. 'There's something in that, but it's my guessing we'll not know till we find his killer. God's blood, I wish it had been anyone but a man in Lord Osborn's retinue. Any other man and we could have simply hanged the first knave we came across and called it justice. That would have been the end of the matter. But Osborn's already blaming us for not finding that runaway serf and felon. Any murderer we catch he'll want to put to the hot irons himself to be sure. Osborn will see me put out of my post for this, unless I bring him someone's head on a pike.'

Talbot eased the men towards the door. 'I'll keep an ear open, never you fear, though if I were you, I'd be asking around the moneylenders or the dog-pits. From what I hear, this Raoul liked a wager on the fighting dogs and the cocks too, but some men don't take kindly to a man who can't or won't settle what he owes.' He tapped the side of his nose.

The men nodded seriously to one another, as if Talbot had just given them the information they were looking for, and hurried away.

'Thank the star your mother birthed you under that Talbot's a good liar,' a voice said quietly behind Elena. She wheeled round to see Ma at her side.

Ma drew her away from the mask and pushed her down to sit on the bed. She stood squarely in front of Elena, her arms folded across her pendulous breasts.

'I hope you're grateful, my darling. Talbot's just saved your neck. If they start asking questions among the cock-fighting men they'll be sent round in such circles that by the time they're finished, their heads'll be stuck so far up their own arses, they'll be eating their dinner twice over. But it's far from over for you, my darling. They know Raoul came here. If they don't find someone to pay for his murder, sooner or later one of them'll want to talk to the girl who pleasured him and you'd better pray it isn't Osborn asking the questions.'

'But I didn't kill him, Ma,' Elena repeated woodenly, though she didn't really believe it herself any more.

The tiny woman looked at her and shrugged. 'You think that's going to make a flea's shit of difference?'

She grasped Elena by the shoulders. Elena cringed as Ma's fingers dug as hard as iron fetters into her flesh.

'Now, you listen to me, my darling. If you want us to go on

protecting you, you'd better see to it that you do exactly what I say. Next time you entertain, put your back into it and look like you are enjoying it. Give your customer all he asks for and more. Men don't have any imagination, but we do. We show them what they can't even dream of, and for that they're willing to sell their own mothers. In the meantime, if you still believe in such things, you'd best get to your knees and pray that no one comes forward who saw you near the Adam and Eve last night.'

✝

7th Day after the Full Moon, August 1211

Cuckoo pint – which some call *Devil's prick, Bloody fingers, Angels and devils, Wake robin, Wild arum* and *Jack in the green.* This is the plant we most loathe for its presumption. Unlike the mandrake that grows at the foot of the gallows, this weed claims to have sprung up at the foot of the Holy Cross, no less. Its dark leaves, so mortals claim, were spotted with red by the very Blood of Christ, whilst we may claim only the honest semen of dishonest men.

Further more, mortals declare it a certain remedy for poison. They say also that it brings down a woman's menses so that she might conceive even when she is past her child-bearing years and is a powerful love potion. And there is many a foolish mortal youth who before a feast or merry dance sings out, *I place you in my shoe, let all fair maids be drawn to you.*

Be not deceived, this Devil's prick is but a feeble shadow of what a mandrake can do.

The Mandrake's Herbal

The Corpse

Raffe pulled Talbot into the shelter of some willows on the bank of the river.

'I don't have much time, I must get back before I'm missed.' Raffe glanced over his shoulder in the direction of the manor. 'Hugh was supposed to be at court with his brother, but he left him on the road and returned here, some excuse about a fever, though I've never seen a man more fit and hale in my life.'

'Devil take him!' Talbot spat into the water. 'That queers things, 'cause I've come to tell you there's a ship in Yarmouth due to sail day after tomorrow, so you need to move your package downriver tonight. Can you do it with Hugh on the prowl?'

'I'll do it,' Raffe said grimly. 'Sooner the man's gone, the safer for all of us.'

Raffe was thinking of Lady Anne, but he had not mentioned her part in this to Talbot. Talbot loathed and despised every nobleman and woman simply by virtue of their birth and there was no point handing him information he might delight in selling.

A little way downstream, a boatman sat hunched in his craft, chewing a strip of dried eel and whittling away at a small piece of wood. From time to time he glanced over at the two men, but he knew it was safest not to be seen showing any interest in any business in which Talbot had a hand.

Talbot grunted. 'The boatmen'll be waiting near the jetty by the Fisher's Inn around the midnight hour. They'll take him down river to Yarmouth. Give the men this token. Otherwise they're liable to cut his throat. No one trusts any man, these days. See you get him to the inn tonight otherwise the ship'll sail without him. And with John's men keeping watch on every port, it could be weeks or months afore we find another captain willing to risk his neck.'

'He'll be there,' Raffe said. He turned to go, but Talbot grabbed his sleeve.

'Hold hard, there's something else. You know a man name of Raoul?'

'He's one of Osborn's men.' Raffe frowned. 'But now I think of it, I don't recall seeing him in the manor these past few days. I'm sure he didn't ride off with Osborn to court though. Why do you ask? What do you know of him?'

'I know he's dead, that's what, murdered. His body was found in the yard of the Adam and Eve Inn.'

'In Norwich? But what was he doing there?'

'Asking questions about that lass of yours. He seemed to think she was in the city.'

Raffe felt the blood drain from his face. He grasped Talbot's shoulder urgently. 'Did he find out where she was?'

'Now, that's hard to tell, but one thing's for certain, she found out where he was. It was your lass who murdered him.'

'No!' The word burst out of Raffe so loudly that the boatman's head jerked up and he stared at them, before he remembered he wasn't supposed to be listening.

'Your lass as good as admitted it. And there's proof of it too.'

'This is madness.' Raffe felt as if he'd been punched in the stomach. 'She couldn't. How . . . why would she?'

'This Raoul came to Ma's the night he died. And your lass entertained him. She must have followed him after he left, for he stayed a while drinking in the guest hall after he'd finished with her and no one saw him leave.'

Raffe couldn't believe what he was hearing. 'What possessed you to let him see her, never mind entertain him, when you knew he was looking for her?' He seized the front of Talbot's shirt, blazing with fury. 'You swore to me you'd keep her safe, you miserable little maggot.'

Talbot was unmoved. Even though Raffe was much taller,

Talbot had no doubts about who would come off best in any fight.

'I wasn't there. I was trying to find a ship for *your* friend,' he said pointedly. 'Luce was on the gate and she let Raoul in. But she'd no idea who he was for he didn't use his real name, who does? Even if he had, it would have meant nowt to her. Thing is, your lass was missing from the house that night and she knew exactly how this Raoul died afore she was told.'

'She could have heard someone talking about it or guessed . . .' Raffe protested feebly. 'But she couldn't murder anyone; she's just a young girl. She's so gentle she couldn't even kill a bird.'

'Murdered her own bairn, didn't she?' Talbot said gruffly. 'You and I, we've both seen plenty of women fighting to the death under the Cross in the Holy Land. There was that lass who took down a two-score of men with her long bow, afore the Saracens killed her, remember? Even Saladin admired her, though she was a Christian. When a woman's blood is up she's more ruthless than any man.'

'Not Elena.' Raffe felt as if the earth beneath his feet had suddenly turned to liquid. From the day she'd been accused, he'd tried to convince himself she hadn't murdered her child, yet hadn't there always been a tiny seed of doubt? Mothers did harm their children . . . But not Elena. He pictured those wide, innocent eyes staring up at him. Those were not the eyes of a murderer.

Then a thought struck him. 'What about you, Talbot? Where were you when Raoul died? You're always in the Adam and Eve, and if you discovered he was one of Osborn's men, you wouldn't think twice about killing him if you saw the opportunity.'

'I could ask the same of you. A man who's smitten with a woman would do just about anything to protect her, and if you found out this Raoul had tracked her down . . .' Talbot gave him a shrewd glance.

Raffe didn't answer. An even more alarming thought had

occurred to him. 'Do the sheriff's men think it was Elena? Are they looking for her?'

Talbot eyed him for a moment or two. 'They say this Raoul was in debt, owed the dog fighters a deal of money.'

'And did he?'

Talbot grinned. 'Who's to know? A whisper planted in the right ear, and afore you count the claws on a cat the whole town is certain it's true though no man can remember who told him of it. It'll take them a while to untangle those whispers. Thing is, if this Raoul was one of Osborn's men, I reckon that means Osborn knows his runaway is in Norwich. He doesn't know where yet, else his man would not have been asking questions. But when Osborn returns and learns his man's been murdered, he's not going to take that kindly. And he won't be so easy to cod as those frog-wits the sheriff has working for him.'

Gytha was pulling her bucket up from the spring when she heard a furious grunting and crashing in the bushes behind her. She whirled round. A great boar was standing not a man's length in front of her, his flanks heaving as he panted for breath. The beast's red mouth hung open, and his long yellow tusks curled up over his cheeks, dagger-sharp. He lifted his hairy black head and snouted the air.

Gytha stayed quite still. She knew those tusks could rip the guts out from her belly in one swift jerk of his great head. They said that when it was hunted, a boar's tusks grew so hot they would burn the fur from a hound. She had a healthy respect for the beast, but she was not afraid. She lifted her hand slowly, palm open, reciting a charm under her breath calling on the ancient ones, on Freyr and Freyja, whose sacred boar with the golden glowing mane illuminated the darkest storm. The beast blinked his tiny red eyes.

'Whist now, whist,' Gytha said softly.

The boar turned a little and as he did, she saw the blood dripping from a gash on his hind leg on to the green blades of grass. Gytha had heard the distant calls of a hunting horn earlier that morning and the excited baying of the hounds. This beast had doubtless been their quarry. He had been wounded, probably by a spear. Gytha knew by now he would be tormented by thirst. That was all the poor creature wanted, water. He could smell it.

Moving as slowly as she could, she tipped her bucket, letting the water trickle out towards the boar. Most of the water soaked away before it could reach him, but it was enough to make him lower his massive head towards the muddy trickle. Gytha used that moment's distraction to edge away to the side of the spring, leaving a clear path for the boar. Pulled by his raging desire to drink, the beast lumbered forward, pushing his snout deep into the clear, cold pool.

A boar's eyesight is poor, but Gytha knew that he could sense any movement and if he did, he would charge. So she stood quite still, trusting that once he had sated his thirst he would move off.

Both woman and beast lifted their heads as one as they heard the sound of snapping twigs and blundering footsteps. Someone was crashing through the bushes towards them. The boar swung round with an agility that belied his great bulk and squared himself to the direction of the sound, snorting and lowering his head for the charge. Whoever was coming would have their legs ripped open by those tusks before they even realized what was thundering towards them.

As she bellowed a warning, Gytha snatched up a stone and flung it at the rocks behind the spring; it hit them with a resounding echo, then splashed into the water. The boar whipped round in the direction of the sound. Whoever was in the bushes had the sense to stand still. The boar charged towards the pool, then stopped, turning his head this way and that, snuffling the air.

Again, Gytha held up her hand and recited the charm. Then, in the distance, she heard the blast of the hunting horn and the far-off baying of the hounds. With a grunt, the boar turned, crashing off through the undergrowth away from the barking dogs. And Gytha finally let her hand drop.

The bushes parted and a man stepped out. Gytha could see at once this was no charcoal burner. His fine red leather gloves and boots were not fashioned by any cordwainer in these parts. Nor was he a man who needed to hunt to fill his family's hungry bellies, for the flash from the gold thread on the trim of his tunic was enough to alert any quarry for miles around. He was limping. Gytha guessed he'd been thrown from his horse, for a man like that would hardly enter the forest on foot, and there was a long, deep scratch across his cheek, which still oozed beads of blood.

He inclined his head, but there was nothing respectful in those iron-grey eyes. 'I believe I should thank you for your timely warning, mistress.'

'You were hunting that boar?'

'My men were trying to put it up, but the fools lost it.'

'And your horse?' Gytha asked him.

A look of anger born of humiliation flashed across his face. No man, especially a nobleman like him, cares to admit they cannot master a dumb animal.

'A barn owl flew right in my face, in broad daylight. I'd almost swear it had been trained to go for my eyes.' His gloved fingers briefly touched the gash on his face.

A thrill shuddered through Gytha's frame, but she tried to conceal her excitement. Instead her tone was grave.

'An owl at noon. 'Tis a bad omen. An omen of death.'

His chin lifted in a challenge. 'If you think to frighten me, woman, you've chosen the wrong mark. I've fought in battles that would turn men's guts to water. I'm not going to start trembling like an old village crone over some bird.'

But Gytha could read the flash of uncertainty in his eyes.

'There are some things that can't be fought with a sword, Hugh of Roxham.'

This time his grey eyes betrayed something bordering on fear. 'How do you know me?'

'Every soul in these parts has heard of you and your brother. But they say Hugh is the handsome one of the pair.'

Hugh laughed. 'You heard right, mistress.'

'Yet they say Osborn is the more powerful.'

'Is that what they say?' Hugh muttered savagely.

Gytha knew that baiting such a man as Hugh was as wise as baiting a wounded boar, but it is sometimes necessary to goad a beast into charging before you can ensnare him.

'Osborn was born afore you, isn't that the way of it? The elder receives the title and property, while the younger is tossed his brother's leavings.'

Fury blazed in Hugh's face. 'My brother is a fool and treats me like some halfwit child. He has all the power and wealth and knows nothing of how to use either. He follows in blind obedience whoever sits on the throne, even if it leads to ruin. He was forced to borrow a fortune to finance Richard and his own men in the Holy Wars and he won back not a half of it in spoils. And now John demands more money for more wars.'

'But what can you do?' Gytha asked innocently. 'It's the way of it, the natural order for the younger to obey the elder, and the subject to obey the king.'

'John didn't sit around waiting for his divine right to inherit the throne,' Hugh said, his eyes glittering with malice. 'If he had, it wouldn't be his royal backside sprawled across it just now. But I promise you, my brother won't . . .' He seemed to realize what he was saying and seized Gytha's wrist, yanking her towards him. 'What is this to you? What do you want?'

Gytha did not betray even by the smallest grimace that he was hurting her. She had mastered that art as a child. She'd had to, for the offspring of cunning women are seldom treated kindly by their playmates.

'It seems unjust that the fool should lord over the wise,' she said evenly. 'I could help you get what a man like you deserves.'

Hugh snorted, looking down at her stained homespun kirtle. 'And what can a beggar offer a man such as me – money, soldiers, power? What could you possibly do to help me?'

'I've already saved you from death today,' Gytha said. She slid her hand into her scrip and pulled out a long thin band of black fur with two leather thongs dangling from either end. 'This'll guard you against the owl's curse and aid you in gaining the power you seek.'

Hugh, as if he couldn't help himself, stretched out his hand and fingered the fur. Then, shaking his head to clear his senses, he pushed it roughly away.

'Don't you dare take me for a fool. Do you really think I'm going to buy a mangy old piece of fur from you? This is how you make your living, is it, cheating the gullible with fake charms? I could have you flogged bloody for this.'

Gytha shrugged and pushed the fur back into her scrip. 'How do you think I could stand so close to a wounded wild boar and come to no hurt?'

She turned back to the spring and calmly dipped her bucket back into it.

There was a moment's silence, then Hugh asked suspiciously, 'What are you asking for it? I warn you, don't try to cheat me; I know what these things are worth.'

Gytha placed a tight coil of cloth on her head and swung the full pail up, balancing it on the coil.

'Nothing. I ask nothing now. When you have the power you seek, perhaps you will remember me.'

Hugh gave a harsh laugh. 'So when I have my brother's estates, you think I will reward you handsomely, do you?'

Gytha thought no such thing. But she knew only too well that men are suspicious of anything which is freely given and anyone who gives it. She smiled, then set the pail down again.

'Show me your hand.'

Hugh hesitated, then peeled off the glove. Gytha ran her fingers over his palm, turning the hand this way and that to the bright sunlight, as if she was examining it carefully. She was not. She knew what lay there would tell her nothing. She had already decided what she would say to him.

'You are a king-maker, Hugh of Roxham. And king-makers have more power than the sovereign himself.'

His eyes flew wide. 'You know this . . . you . . . you can see this?' He peered down at his own hand as if he had never noticed his arm ended in such an appendage before.

Gytha let his hand fall. Then she pulled out the strip of fur again, and held it up before his greedy eyes.

'You must wear this as a girdle about your waist, next to your bare skin. It will guide you. Do whatever it leads you to do. Follow the desires it awakens in you, for as you satisfy them so your power will increase. You will feel the hunger, you will feel the strength grow in you, as soon as you put it on.'

Hugh was about to speak, but she held up a warning hand. 'Listen, your friends are coming this way.'

He turned his head towards the sound. She was right; the barking of hounds and crashing of the horses' hooves were growing louder, coming straight towards them. He turned to say something to her, but she had vanished. Puzzled, he looked down and started violently as he realized that he was holding the girdle of fur.

Hugh would wear the girdle of fur about his waist, Gytha was sure of that. He wouldn't be able to resist the temptation, not if he thought there was the slightest chance it would give him what he desired. And when he wore it, he would be forced to satiate the desires it would awaken in him. He would have to act. He would be driven to it. It was but one small step, but each step leads to another. *You must raise the skeleton one bone at a time before you can set it dancing.*

Darkness stretches time, as wetting stretches a woollen cloth. A man waiting alone under the stars feels each passing hour drawn out so far he can no longer trust even the hourglass to mark it faithfully, and Raffe had no hourglass in his hand.

He was squatting in the concealment of some trees, gazing out on the twisting black waters of the river, his ears straining for the splash of a paddle. His limbs were so stiff, he was beginning to think that if the boat came now, he would be unable to stir a muscle to meet it.

His mind felt more numb than his legs. Although he'd thought of little else all day, still he could not digest the news that Elena had murdered Raoul. It was impossible to think that such a fragile, innocent creature could have killed a man. Yet Talbot said she had as good as admitted it. If she had realized who Raoul was, if he'd threatened to take her back to Gastmere, she would have been terrified. If he'd hurt her, forced himself on her, she might have lashed out in panic, like a cornered animal, not meaning to kill him, an accident. But Talbot had said the corpse had been found at the inn and she'd been missing all night. That meant she must have followed him and . . . no, Raffe couldn't bring himself to think that. He wouldn't allow himself to think that.

Osborn would tear the city apart when he discovered Raoul was dead. Raffe's head was pounding. He couldn't think about this now, he would drive himself mad and he couldn't afford to lose concentration, not tonight, too much was at stake. He must focus on the priest. If the priest was caught and started talking, both Raffe's and Lady Anne's lives would be forfeit. And there was Gerard's body. This might be his only chance to obtain holy unction for Gerard. Raffe would not fail his friend.

No, before he could even think about Elena, he must deal with the priest first. As long as Osborn was at court, Elena was still safe where she was. *Blessed Virgin, let John send Osborn to France, Flanders, anywhere, but just keep him far away from us.*

A chill wind blew off the marshes and Raffe drew his cloak tighter about him. God's bones, why was it always so damn cold at night in England? Even in midsummer, as soon as night closed in, you felt yourself encased in cold as if you were entombed in a cave.

When he'd been a boy in the mountains of Italy he could lie outside on a summer's night staring up at the great bright stars and the air was as silky and warm as a perfumed bath. It had been just such a night when he'd first laid eyes on Gerard.

Gerard had ridden into the farmstead near sunset, with all the bravado of a youth of nineteen years, scattering chickens to the four winds. Four other knights clattered into the yard behind him, their horses foaming at the bit. Sweat had caked the white dust from the road to the men's faces so thickly that one of Raffe's little sisters had come screaming into the cottage that dead men were attacking the house.

All of the men and boys in the household had grabbed up pitchforks and stout sticks and run outside to defend their farm to the death if need be, but Gerard had wearily eased himself from the saddle and walked towards them, his hands upraised in a gesture of peace. One of the horses had a loose shoe, he told them, which the beast was likely to lose altogether if they continued to the next town. So he announced that this household would have the pleasure of their company for the night.

Raffe's mother and aunts had whispered to Raffe's father that the knights must be sent away. They had not enough food to spare and where would these gentlemen sleep for they could hardly be asked to bed down in the byres?

Raffe's father sadly hushed the scolding women. 'What we don't give them, they'll take anyway and more besides. Have you not seen their sign?'

He gestured to one of the knights who carried a lance from which hung a small pendant in the shape of a scarlet cross on a white ground. Crusaders! The women crossed themselves, muttering and spitting on the first two fingers of their right hands to ward off the evil eye, for if rumours were to be believed, and they always were believed in those parts, Crusaders were the very demons of hell made flesh. If they rode into a village they were likely to ride out again with the cottages in flames behind them, and their scrips bulging with the looted treasure from the village and its church.

Raffe's mother seized Raffe's younger brother. 'You take

your sisters and female cousins through the cellar to the caves. Get word out to warn our neighbours.'

The cellars of every home and church on that mountain-side led into a series of labyrinthine caves, once home to their ancestors, but which now served as storage chambers as well as an escape route for any who might need to disappear from view. A man might enter one cottage and while his pursuers were keeping watch on that door, he was slipping out of another house a mile or more away.

Raffe's brother knew well what to do. He herded the five unmarried girls down to the cellars along with his pregnant sister, for her swelling belly would be no deterrent to a soldier whose blood was hot. The old women would have to pray to the Blessed Virgin that the Crusaders were not desperate enough to want them, for they would be needed to cook.

The men dragged trestles and benches out into the yard and called to Raffe to bring wine, while the women heaped onions and olives dressed with olive oil into wooden bowls to stay the men's hunger and buy them the time to add more vegetables and beans to their family's own meagre pottage.

The Crusaders picked suspiciously at the proffered bowls. Then one scooped up a handful of olives and angrily threw them at Raffe's head. 'God's arse, what are these, sheep drop-pings? Are you trying to poison us?'

Raffe wiped the drips of oil from his face. 'They are the fruits of the tree, very good to eat.'

The man stared at him then roared with laughter. 'What are you, a maid or a man? I do declare I've never heard a girl's voice come from a man's body. Did your mother think to dress her daughter like her brothers to protect you from our ravishings?'

The others joined in the mocking laughter, for a moment forgetting their impatient demands for food. Even Raffe's own brothers giggled. Gerard alone didn't laugh, but met Raffe's dark eyes with his own sapphire-blue ones. His face creased in a grimace of pain as if he had felt the barb himself.

'Are you the maid's mother?' the knight asked. 'Tell me

what you have bred here, for she's the mostly comely maid I've seen yet in this household, and I think I've a mind to warm my bed with her, if you've nothing better to offer me.'

Raffe's mother regarded her son with disgust. 'Do what you like with him, for he's neither man nor woman, and has brought us nothing but shame.'

'In that case, I'll throw him back, mistress. Once when I was a boy, I pulled a fish from the river that was covered in a furry white wool. "What's this?" I said, "Mutton you can eat on a fish day, now there's a miracle." But when I tasted it, it was *fowl* and I was as sick as a drunkard all night.'

The others snorted with laughter, but it only reminded them they were hungry and they roared again for food, banging with the hilt of their knives on the wooden table. Even the pottage did not satisfy them and they demanded meat. When Raffe's father protested they had none, two of the men went to the byre where the hens were roosting and returned with five of them dangling from their fists, their necks wrung. Raffe's mother wept as she plucked them.

The family spent the night huddled together in the byre while the Crusaders occupied their beds in the house. Raffe did neither. He could not sleep and wandered alone among the olive trees under the star-filled sky. What the Crusader had said had glanced off him like a deflected lance blade leaving only a flesh wound, nothing more. He'd swallowed such jibes ever since he had returned to the village. He scarcely separated the pain of each remark any more, for they merged like bruises. No, it was not the Crusader's laughter that made him punch his fists over and over again into the trunk of the olive tree. It was the burning pain of his mother's words that was tearing him apart from within.

'Can you beat a man with as much strength as you can strike that tree?'

The voice startled him and he turned around searching for the source, and eventually saw a man sprawling on the ground in the darkness under an almond tree.

'I can beat any man to pulp,' Raffe boasted through gritted teeth.

'Then don't wreck your hands on an enemy you cannot overcome. Ride with us, and try your strength on men who can be beaten.'

Raffe's face burned with anger. He took a step closer. 'Can you fight as well as you can mock? Get up and face me.'

'I have no wish to fight you.' The man held out one open palm towards Raffe. 'I am Gerard of Gastmere , and I don't mock you, my friend. I'm serious. I have no squire to ride with me.' He chuckled. 'Or rather I do, but I couldn't prise him from the arms of a doe-eyed beauty he discovered the first night we landed on these shores. I suppose I could have forced him to come with me, but I would have no man ride by my side or drink with me in a tavern who does not want to be there with his whole heart. So I told him to stay until he wearies of her or her of him.' He laughed again, an open, honest laugh and in spite of himself, Raffe felt drawn to this man.

'Now, what do you say, lad? Shall you stay here and be the whipping boy of your family for the rest of your life or do you ride with me and make men respect you for your courage and your fists? Oh, you'll hear jokes aplenty at your expense wherever you go. I'm not pretending you won't. Those men riding with me will torment you till you're ready to crack their skulls open, but if you hit harder, ride longer, and fight with more courage than any of them, those knights will come to call you *brother* and run any man through with their swords if they hear him say one mocking word about you.'

And Raffe had needed no other words to persuade him.

The two of them had stayed sitting side by side under the vast arch of stars. Gerard talked of the manor of Gastmere and his own beloved parents. His father had left him in charge when he rode off to the Holy Wars with King Richard. Gerard had been desperate to ride with his father, but his father would not hear of it. It was his duty to stay and look after his mother and the manor.

Besides, as his father confided when they were alone, 'I would not have your poor mother lose a son and husband in the same battle, if it should come to it, and it likely would, for I should be so distracted by marking your progress in the fight, I would surely fail to protect myself.'

'So why do you ride to the Holy Land now?' Raffe asked. 'Your mother, is she dead?'

Gerard shook his head, then hesitated. 'There is a woman in our village. I was . . . fond of her once. She has a gift of second sight. She told me that my father would soon find himself in mortal danger. His thoughts would turn to me and he would desperately need my help.'

'You trust this woman?' Raffe asked him.

Gerard stared up at the bright stars for a long time without answering. 'Did you know that men call the stars by different names? Some look at the same sky, but see quite different shapes and creatures in it? I thought once that the names I knew were the true names of the stars, but if all men have different names for the same objects, how shall we know which of them is their real name? Do you suppose the stars have names that only they know?'

He turned and fiercely grasped Raffe's arm. 'My father needs me and I have to go to him. I could never forgive myself if I discovered that I might have saved him, but I did not. If there is any chance I can help him, I must do it, do you see?'

Raffe nodded, but in truth he didn't see at all. At seventeen he could not imagine feeling such love or loyalty for any man, certainly not for his own father. But now, after all these years, he finally understood what a man will do for love.

In the end, it had all been in vain. Gerard had arrived at Acre too late to save his father, but that night, that gloriously starry night, it seemed impossible to those two young men that they could ever fail. He and Gerard had sat together under the olive trees. The darkness throbbed with the rasping of the cicadas. The warm air rose from the earth around them, anointing them with scented oils of wild thyme and summer. And all the while they sat there, they talked and talked of nothing and everything, till weariness overcame them and they slept like infants cradled upon the moon-washed earth.

The Crusaders left the next morning, Raffe riding upon a mule until a better mount could be bought for him. Raffe's father had managed, if not exactly a blessing, at least a mumbled, *Take care of yourself, boy*. Raffe had not looked back as they trotted away; there would be nothing to see. His mother was already inside her house, trying to repair the devastation the unruly knights had brought to her home. When she and Raffe had said their curt goodbyes to each other, her eyes had been as dry and lifeless as the sun-scorched grass. She had finished weeping over the chickens. They were just bones in her stock pot now. What was the point of any more tears?

A shrill whistle startled Raffe out of his reverie, and he saw the black smudge of a low craft sculling towards him across the river. He rose and almost fell over as his legs were seized by a cramp. He jiggled them, trying to shake the feeling back into them. God curse the English weather.

The marsh-boy had borrowed a longer craft than his own light coracle, and despite the chill night his fingers were sweaty as he passed Raffe the rope. His passenger had evidently not helped him to scull the boat. But as Raffe grasped the priest's cold hand to pull him ashore, he realized that he would have been more a hindrance than help, for such soft delicate little fingers as these would have blistered before he'd made half a dozen strokes.

'The boy says you've got me passage on a ship. Where is it?' The priest shivered, and glanced around him as if he really thought some great sea-going vessel would be moored up in the river.

Raffe ignored the question and addressed the boy. 'Hide the boat on the other side of the islet. I'll bring the priest back as soon as he's done and I'll make an owl's cry. When you hear it, bring the boat back.'

He handed the boy the basket of food, which the lad had been gazing at longingly from the moment he moored up.

'Try not to eat it all, the priest'll want some of it for the journey.'

The lad nodded, but Raffe had no great faith there'd be anything but crumbs left by the time they returned. He smiled and patted the boy's shoulder. He remembered what it felt like to be constantly hungry as a lad and didn't begrudge him a mouthful, though the priest undoubtedly would.

'This way, Father. And keep your hood pulled up; though your hair's grown long, it still has the faint shadow of a tonsure for those with eyes to see.'

He helped the priest up the bank and on to the track that led to the manor.

'But where is the ship?' the priest repeated, peering nervously at every tree and bush as if he expected them to be bristling with soldiers.

'When we are done here, we'll return to the boat and get you to the ship.'

The priest stopped dead. 'We must go now, at once, we might miss it.'

'I told you that you will not be going anywhere until you've anointed Gerard's body.'

Seeing the priest was again about to protest, Raffe seized the little man's arm and hurried him forward, growling in his ear, 'Without me, you'll not get to your ship, so unless you want to spend the winter hiding on the freezing marshes or lying chained in some sodden, stinking dungeon I suggest you come with me, and quietly at that.'

He felt the priest resisting every step as he hurried him along, but Raffe pulled him as easily as a child might drag a rag doll. At the manor gate he stopped and opened the wicket gate as silently as he could, peering in to see if the courtyard was empty. It was. He pulled the priest inside and hurried him across to the vaulted arches under the Great Hall.

Raffe had taken the precaution of finding a woman to

occupy the gatekeeper, promising to keep the watch for Walter in return for some invented favour he'd asked the gatekeeper to do for him. The woman was well past her prime, with straggly grey hair and a face ravaged by the pox, but Walter would not be looking at her face. The gatekeeper had gone off towards the village with a grin broad enough to split his wrinkled old face in two.

Walter in turn had assured Raffe that he could sleep soundly in the gatehouse, for the pair of hounds would bark loud enough to rouse him from his grave if any should approach the gate. And so they would have done, had Raffe not slipped them each a tasty piece of mutton with a pelt of poppy paste in each one. Now the only sounds which came from the hounds were deep and drooling snores.

Raffe led the priest to the back of the undercroft and lifted up the trapdoor and then the grid which covered the prisoner hole. As soon as the wooden trapdoor was raised, a stench rose up from the hole which was enough to make even a battle-hardened warrior retch. The priest drew the neck of his hood over his mouth and nose.

'I've unsealed the wall and opened the coffin ready for you,' Raffe informed him.

The priest shuddered in disgust. 'I can smell that. But it was unnecessary.'

The little man glanced uneasily round the dark and silent courtyard, his nose twitching like a frightened mouse that fears danger from all quarters.

'I'll say the prayers for the dead, but we must make haste,' he said, crossing himself rapidly as he knelt down.

But his callused knees had scarcely touched the flags when Raffe seized him by the arm and hauled him up again.

'What do you think I opened the coffin for?' Raffe whispered. 'Go down and give him the unction of God.'

The priest's jaw went as slack as a hanged man's. 'No! No! Holy unction is for the sick. If he were newly dead and the spirit might yet be lingering near the body, it is permitted.

But that man has been dead for months, you admitted as much yourself, and even if you hadn't, my nose would testify to the fact. Besides, unction is only permitted once confession has been heard and the sacrament of penance given, or, if a man is too ill to confess, that the priest is assured he has at least undertaken an act of sorrow for his sins.'

'Gerard lived in constant horror of his sins. Never did a man feel so much sorrow for what he had done.'

'That's all very well for you to say,' the priest protested, 'but how am I to know that?' Then he added petulantly, 'In any case, it is far too late to anoint a corpse that long dead and . . . and besides, I have no holy oil left.'

Raffe was gripped by such a rage that it was all he could do to stop himself wringing that scrawny, lying throat.

'Give me your scrip,' he ordered.

The man instinctively clutched tightly at the small leather bag that hung from his belt, but the look of fury on Raffe's face was so terrifying that when Raffe held out his great hand, the priest, with trembling fingers, unbuckled his belt as meekly as a bride disrobing for her husband. Raffe reached inside and pulled out a tiny flask of finely wrought silver, inscribed with an image of the crucifixion. He opened it and sniffed, holding the open flask in his hand.

'A miracle, is it not, Father? God has filled your flask with oil while you lay sleeping.'

'But that is all I have,' the priest wailed. 'And if I should come across the sick and dying, what would I have to anoint them with? It's too late for your friend, but surely you would not condemn other souls to torment? Suppose it was your wife or child . . .' He gulped, plainly realizing too late that mention of wife or child to a man such as Raffe was like jabbing a stick at a roaring bear.

'Don't give me that,' Raffe snarled. 'You have no more concern for the souls of others than a dog has for its fleas. You just want to make sure you have oil enough to anoint yourself before death. Thought of a sea voyage scares you, does it, or worse, burning up with fever in one of King John's filthy cells?'

Raffe took a step nearer the prisoner hole. He held the flask above it.

'Anoint him properly and you will have some drops left for yourself. Or I shall do it by pouring the whole flask into his coffin.'

'No, please!' the priest whispered frantically. 'God in heaven, don't! I'll do it. I'll do it!'

Raffe closed the flask and placed it back in the shaking hands of the priest, who grasped it, pressing it tightly to his lips and kissing it fervently.

'You'd better get on with it then,' Raffe urged. 'Ship sails with the tide and waits for no man.'

The little man fumbled hopelessly as he put the flask back in his scrip, rebuckled it about his waist and set one foot on the rung of the ladder. He paused, casting one more beseeching glance up at Raffe, but his expression was as implacable as granite. Slowly the priest descended into the stench of hell.

Raffe crouched on the edge of the hole, holding the lantern down inside. The priest stood in the damp earth, peering into the hole in the side of the wall in which the exposed coffin lay. His body shuddered convulsively as he retched and whimpered like a wounded dog.

He lifted his pale face to Raffe. 'There's . . . nothing to anoint. Just bones and bits of putrefying flesh and . . . and most of it is already melted to liquid. I can't touch him.' Tears ran down the man's face. 'Please, please, don't make me do this,' he begged.

'If he has bones you can tell where his lips were, his private parts, his hands,' Raffe said with a coldness he didn't feel.

It was taking every drop of self-control he had not to burst out screaming and sobbing at the sight of the foul, stinking abomination that had taken the place of his dearest friend's face.

'Do it, Father. Do it now or by God, I shall close these bars and leave you down there to rot until you look just like him.'

The priest bowed his head. Then, as a palsied man struggles to move a deadened limb, he stretched out his shaking hand into the darkness of the coffin. His fingers coated in the precious drops of holy oil, he made the three-times-five crosses – three for the Trinity, five for the senses – anointing eyes, ears, nostrils, lips, hands, feet and genitals, or at least the places on the rotting flesh where these organs which cause a man to sin had once existed.

'I anoint . . . I anoint thee with . . . holy oil in the name of the Trinity that thou mayest be saved for ever and ever.'

Raffe bowed his head, crossing himself, and so fervently did he pray that he almost missed the sound of the footsteps crossing the courtyard. But a man who has watched through many a long night waiting for that slight intake of breath that the assassin makes before he sticks the dagger in your back or slices his knife across your throat, can never again give himself over to prayer or sleep or even love-making without his sixth sense remaining ever watchful.

Quicker than an arrow flies from a bow, Raffe had withdrawn the lantern and closed the trapdoor over the prisoner hole. Below him, he heard a shriek of fear from the priest. Raffe stood astride the wooden door in the hope that his voice would carry downwards as well as across the courtyard.

'Who goes there?' he challenged as loudly as he could.

He prayed that the priest would have the sense to stay still and would not in his panic lose his wits so far as to cry out.

'What are you doing skulking in the shadows, gelding?'

Devil's arse! It was Hugh. The last man Raffe wanted to see that night.

Raffe strode as rapidly as he could into the courtyard to draw Hugh away from any sound the priest might be making down there, trapped in the darkness with the rotting corpse.

'Doing my rounds as a steward should, making sure that no one is helping themselves to the stores. And you, what keeps you awake at this late hour – can't find a woman to warm your bed?'

By the scowl on Hugh's face he knew he'd hit the mark.

'A bed-warmer is all the use you can put a woman to, isn't it, gelding?'

Raffe noticed with some satisfaction that Hugh was limping. The rumour among the sniggering servants was that he'd been thrown from his horse earlier in a hunt that day. His fall and the fact that the hunt had failed to kill a single boar had made him even more foul than usual.

Hugh nodded in the direction of the gatehouse. 'One of my brother's men, Raoul, has not returned from Norwich. I intend to rouse that bone-idle gatekeeper to learn if Raoul has sent word about his delay.'

So they didn't yet know about Raoul. Raffe muttered a rapid prayer of thanks for that. But he had to prevent Hugh from going to the gatehouse. If Hugh found the gatekeeper absent it wouldn't just be Walter who suffered; sooner or later Hugh would be bound to discover who had sent Walter away and his suspicions would be thoroughly aroused.

But Raffe was careful to betray nothing of his anxiety on his face. 'If a message had come, word would have been sent to you straight away.'

'Walter would have sent a servant with a message, but since you never bother to school them in their duties, no doubt the numbskull would have forgotten what he was about before he was half-way across the yard. There's not enough wit between the whole pack of servants in this manor to animate a single slug.'

He made to turn in the direction of the gatehouse, but Raffe blocked his way.

'I wouldn't go into the gatehouse if I were you. Walter's stricken with a fever. It might be nothing more than a touch of marsh ague, but if it's a contagion then it could spread. We won't know how serious it is till morning. In the meantime, I told him to go to his bed and I'd take his watch.'

Walter and his woman would be sow-drunk by now, and with luck he'd have a raging hangover by morning and would look sick enough to convince anyone he'd spent the night with a fever.

Hugh rocked on the balls of his feet, half of him plainly determined to see for himself, the other not wanting to go anywhere near a sick man for his own safety.

Finally caution won out. 'Bring me word at once, no matter what the hour, if there is word from Raoul. I trust you can get that much right at least.'

Hugh gestured towards the gate. 'Well, go on, gelding. If you're keeping watch, do it. Lie down and keep watch with the other hounds. At least for once you know your place. I always said it was among the curs.'

Raffe had to force himself to keep silent, though it almost cost a tooth for he was clenching his jaw so hard, but he meekly walked across to the gate and sat down by the brazier, warming his hands.

Hugh stood watching, then, apparently satisfied, he climbed the steps up to the Great Hall. An unnerving silence descended on the dark courtyard. It was so quiet Raffe could hear the leaves rustling on the trees outside, but still he dared not move to release the priest from his tomb. A flicker of movement at one of the darkened upper casements told him Hugh was still watching him. Raffe prayed that the priest would not think himself abandoned, and start hollering and banging to be let out. Raffe wrapped his cloak tightly around himself and let his head gradually droop forward on to his chest as if he was dozing.

There he remained for as long as he dared. Finally he let his eyes flick up to the windows without moving his head. He could not see anyone standing there. Please God, Hugh had grown tired of watching and had at last retired to his bed. Raffe feigned a yawn, stretched and stood up, ambling round the courtyard as if he was merely checking all was well. Once he reached the arches under the Great Hall, where he could no longer be seen, he hurried to the prisoner hole and pulled up the trapdoor; the stench rolled out like a dense cloud of fog.

'Father,' he whispered. 'I've come to take you to the ship.'

There was no reply. Raffe lay on his belly and hung the lantern down as low as he could. The feeble light showed a crumpled figure lying at the bottom of the pit. His eyes were closed and he was not stirring. Sweet Holy Virgin, was he dead, suffocated?

As rapidly as he could, Raffe descended the ladder. There was scarcely room at the bottom for him to stand without treading on the prone form of the priest. Raffe bit his lip hard to stop himself from gagging and carefully avoided looking into the black hole in which the open coffin lay. Awkwardly he bent down and shook the priest, but there was no response. He pushed his hand inside the man's shirt and with enormous relief discovered a faint heartbeat, though the man's skin was fish-cold.

Raffe dragged the limp body upwards and crouched down so that he could hoist it across his shoulders. It wasn't easy mounting a ladder in such a confined space with the dead weight of a man on his shoulders and he repeatedly felt the priest's head bump and graze against the stone wall. They were almost at the top when the rung beneath his foot splintered under their combined weight and Raffe felt himself plunging sideways.

The ladder twisted, almost throwing Raffe off, but for once the narrow space proved his salvation. His shoulder crashed hard against the wall, but the ladder was prevented from falling any further.

Raffe balanced there, trying to get his breath, but the ominous creaking of the wood reminded him that the staves would not bear his weight for long. With a supreme effort he managed to push the priest's body up through the hole so that the weight balanced on the rim. Then, kicking against the ladder, he heaved himself up beside the man.

Raffe's limbs trembled with the effort, but fearful that the sounds might have aroused sleeping servants, he had no choice but to heave the priest's body back over his shoulder and stagger as fast as he could to the gate. He abandoned caution for speed; if Hugh was watching now Raffe couldn't bluff his way out of this one. His only hope was to reach the boat before Hugh could rouse his men and get to the gate.

At the bank of the river he sank to his knees, thankfully dropping the body to the ground. He gave the owl call to summon the boy. At first there was no answer, then he called again and this time a peewit cry answered. Almost at once he saw the dark smudge of the boat emerging from the lee of the islet.

'What happened?' the boy asked fearfully, catching sight of the body on the grass. 'Is he dead?'

'He lives. He's just fainted,' Raffe assured him.

'Fainted?' The boy prodded the body cautiously with his bare toe, as if he'd never heard of such a thing before, for the marsh-dwellers are a hardy lot and not given to swooning like milk-sop priests.

Raffe unceremoniously heaved the priest into the boat. Trying to find something with which to revive the man, Raffe reached for the basket of food he'd left with the boy. All that remained was the flagon of wine, and then only because the lad was unused to it and couldn't abide the taste, as he told Raffe, wrinkling up his nose. Between them, they managed to pour a little wine down the priest's throat, which at least made him open his eyes, though it nearly choked him.

Raffe glanced behind him towards the manor. All was quiet save for the rushing water of the river, no sounds of pursuit. Yet with Hugh on the prowl, Raffe dared not be found absent from the gate.

'I can't come with you, lad. You'll have to take him alone to the meeting place. There's an old jetty downstream of here by the Fisher's Inn. There'll be a boat waiting there with two men in it. Give them this as a sign.' Into the boy's grubby palm Raffe tipped the token Talbot had entrusted to him. 'And this,' he said handing the boy a small purse, 'is payment for the men who wait for you downstream. They'll know what to do. Can you scull him there yourself? It's not far.'

'Course I can,' the boy replied with disdain, 'but what about him? He's moon-mazed, he is.'

The priest lay curled up on the bottom of the boat, staring unblinkingly up at the sky, his teeth chattering with shock and cold. He was muttering to himself over and over, *Sed libera nos – deliver us*! Though it seemed he could remember no more of the prayer.

The boy eyed him warily. 'Suppose he attacks me or tries to jump from the boat? There was a man on our isle once got mazed by the boggarts and ran out into the mire though he'd lived on the marsh all his life and knew the mire would swallow him.'

'Just get him to the men. If he stirs, give him the rest of the wine. That'll calm him.'

The boy still looked doubtful, but he finally nodded and, taking a firm grip of his scull as if he meant to crack the priest across the head with it at the first sign of trouble, he steered the boat out into the centre of the river. In only a few strokes the boat had slid into the darkness and was gone.

Three Days before the New Moon, August 1211

Bracken — When bracken is grown to its full height, if it be cut across near the base, marks will be found on the stem. Some mortals believe these to be the letters signifying Christ, others the Devil's hoof print, and some find therein the initials of those they are to marry. At Midsummer the root of the bracken may be dug up, carved into the likeness of a hand and baked till it shrivels. Mortals call it *Dead man's hand* and use it to ward off the power of witches and demons.

The seeds from the bracken will enable the gatherer to summon any living creature, beast or human, from the earth, air or water. The seeds also render the gatherer invisible if he should swallow them or place them in his shoe. A parcel of seed plaited into a horse's mane will make horse and rider invisible to evil spirits on the road or to thieves who lie in wait for the traveller.

But the seeds are not easily gathered. It must be done just before the midnight hour on Midsummer's Eve. The gatherer must place a cloth of white linen or a pewter dish beneath the frond. It is dangerous to touch the frond at this hour with his bare hand, so he must bend it with a forked hazel twig so that the seed shall fall upon the cloth or dish. But bracken is well guarded by spirits and demons who do not desire that mortals should gain such power. They will torment the gatherer as he tries to collect the seed, pinching and striking him, and appearing in such a terrible aspect that some mortals have died of fright. And many return home to find the seed they gathered in the cloth has vanished.

The Mandrake's Herbal

The Cat

Gytha wandered back towards the bothy, her wicker basket full of nettles, wild onions and sorrel. Two fat trout lay nestled under the cool of the leaves. She had coaxed those from the stream with nothing but her fingers for a hook and her cunning as the bait. She could have caught more, but she knew that if you took more than you needed for that day, the river would not let you take from her again. In the same way, she was careful always to eat from the tail to the head lest she make the fish turn away from her, and careful to collect up every tiny bone and return them to the stream, so that the fish might be reborn. That was the way of it. Learn the laws of the forest, marsh and stream, learn the ways of the beast, fowl and fish, and food would always come to you.

Gytha scuffed her bare feet in the warm, crumbling leaf litter, and breathed in the hot summer breeze, fragranced with the rich fruit of decaying leaves and the bitter tang of the white-headed cow parsley. Beech, oak and elm stretched out their long limbs above her as she paddled through the drops of green light filtering through the sun-soaked canopy.

She would be sorry to leave this forest when the time came to move, but they would have to leave soon anyway. They would need to find warmer shelter and build up food stores before winter. For she knew from experience how quickly the warm, sultry days could turn to rain and killing cold. Still, perhaps they would be back in their own cottage before then. Madron seemed sure that before the year was dead, Yadua would have finished her work. Gytha wasn't convinced. She had been born into the waiting. It was the only state she had ever known, and she couldn't imagine what would replace it.

Madron was sitting outside the bothy where Gytha had

left her, nestled comfortably among the gnarled roots of an ancient oak, like a tattered old crow on its nest. Her twisted hands were turning the heap of yellowed bones in her lap, but her sightless eyes were already turned in Gytha's direction as her daughter emerged from the trees.

'Yadua has been fed,' she announced triumphantly as Gytha came into the clearing. She licked her wrinkled lips, as if she herself had tasted the red milk.

'And?' Gytha asked. She did not doubt the truth of what the old woman said for a moment. There was and always had been a bond, stronger than mother and child, between Yadua and Madron. Even now, when the mandrake was miles away, Madron could always tell when it stirred to life, perhaps because of the way she had acquired it. But Gytha could tell by the excitement in the old woman's voice that this time there was something more.

Madron pronounced her words slowly, as if she didn't want to part with them too soon. 'I scattered the bones and when the spirits led me to pluck one, I found a butterfly had settled on it and would not be dislodged.'

'A butterfly . . . on a dry bone? That means there's been a death.'

The old woman nodded in satisfaction.

Gytha laid her basket down and hurried forward. She knelt in front of her mother, staring at the bones in the old woman's lap.

'Which . . . which bone was it, can you remember?'

The old woman snorted. 'I'm blind, not doting. I know my bones.'

She folded her lips tight and turned her face away. Gytha knew that expression of old: it meant that Madron would refuse to tell her any more until she had been appeased. Angry with herself and the stubborn old besom in equal measure, Gytha returned to the basket and set about cleaning the fish without another word. Two could play that game.

Madron sniffed. 'Fish for dinner?'

'For *my* dinner.'

The old woman cocked her head on one side. 'You wouldn't let me starve.'

'Wouldn't I?'

'I could put a hex on you that you'd never undo,' the old woman raged. 'I could bring a cooked fish alive in your throat even as you swallow it to choke you to death. You still don't know the half of what I know, girl, and you never will. You don't have the skill or patience to master it. Haven't had to learn it to survive, not like me, and that's your trouble.'

'Do your worst!' Gytha stuck the tip of her knife into the trout's belly and sliced it open savagely. 'But just you think on this: if I'm dead, who's going to catch your next fish or rabbit, or even fetch you a bite of nettles?'

Neither spoke for a long time. Then Madron said grudgingly, 'It were the bone of a dog.'

It was on the tip of Gytha's tongue to ask if the old woman was sure, but she knew Madron would not make a mistake, not with her bones. She sighed in disappointment.

'Nothing to wail about, girl,' Madron said. 'You must give it time. The shadow of the fox is running, just like you said, hard on the heels of the bairn. She is doing well, our little Elena. She is calling them to her one by one, though she doesn't know it. Like flies to a corpse they will be drawn to her. Be patient. Can't rush the stretching of a new bow, else it will snap and all that work'll be wasted. Tonight you must pluck another thorn from the apple. Then we wait and watch.'

Gytha poured a little water into her wooden bowl, and dropped the bloody fish guts into it, watching as they wriggled like eels in the swirling water before settling.

Once, Gerard had sat cross-legged opposite her, staring into the bowl with such concentration that anyone watching might think he knew how to read the entrails. He didn't. He relied on her, trusted her. And she had never betrayed him. She had simply told him the truth. That's what he asked for, that's what she'd given.

'Your father is walking into mortal danger. He wants you to help him. He needs you.'

She had given her lover what all men wanted; she had revealed to him the future, knowing that he would not be able to resist acting upon that knowledge, and in doing so he would damn himself. Men always did. They couldn't help it. And no power in heaven or earth could punish him for the hurt he had done to her, as effectively as that single gift. Tell a man his future and he will destroy his own soul. It was the consummation, the pinnacle, the perfection of vengeance.

She pauses at the foot of the narrow stone spiral staircase. It is dark, so dark she cannot even see her own hand, let alone the hand of another who might be creeping towards her. The clash of swords, the clatter of metal on stone, the shouts and screams of dying men echo from the vaulted ceiling and down the long narrow passages, the sound is twisted, distorted. It might be above her; it might be below her; it might be in her head.

She cranes her neck trying to peer up the stairs. The flicker of a pale yellow light, fragile as a moth's wing, glows high above her, but she cannot see the source. A candle on the wall? A lantern in a man's hand? These staircases were built to be defended. A right-handed man could strike down on anyone trying to fight his way up the stairs, but his opponent's blows would be impeded by the wall. A man must learn to strike with both hands, if he wants to survive.

She waits, listening. Is someone also waiting out of sight on those stairs, listening for the sound of her footsteps? She hears breathing, but it is so cold here, entombed in these thick walls, that it might be the sound of her own breath rasping. Is this the place where she will die, struck down in this darkness, her blood pouring out on to these icy stones?

She tries to fight down her terror. She can wait no longer. She must move. She transfers her blade to her left hand and eases herself slowly up the steps, bracing herself against the wall in case someone should lunge down at her. The light gathers in strength as she walks towards it, but still she cannot see where it is coming from. Cautiously she winds her way up and up, until the light bursts full upon her.

She is staring into a tiny open chamber, not much bigger than a recess in the wall. A man in monk's robes kneels with his back to her. In front of him is a table on which stands a carved and painted figure of the Virgin Mary holding the infant Jesus in her arms. The child's hands are outstretched as if begging to be plucked from his mother's grasp. Three slender candles burn around the base of the figure. Encircled by their trembling flames, the painted scarlet mouth of the Virgin smiles as if she knows what is about to happen, and it amuses her.

The monk lifts his head like a hound scenting the breeze. He seems to realize he is not alone. He scrambles up, turning towards her with a look of terror. She puts her finger to her lips, warning him not to cry out. She takes a pace backwards down the stairs. She means to leave him unharmed. She will not hurt him, not a holy monk. But the terrified monk seizes the heavy wooden statue in both hands. Holding it over his head, he charges towards her with a shriek. The sleeves of his robes fall back and she sees the muscles bulging in his arms, bracing themselves to strike.

She knows she must protect herself. She knows she must strike first, but he is a monk. She cannot harm a man in holy orders. The grinning face of the Virgin hurtles down towards her head. Instinct takes over. She thrusts her blade up towards the monk, meaning only to warn him to stay his hand. But even as she does so she sees a shadow looming up behind him. The monk's arms freeze in the act of striking. He arches backwards with an agonized cry as the point of a sword emerges from his chest. He falls to his knees, pitching forward straight on to her blade. The Virgin and Child fly from his hand and shatter against the cold stone wall. As he falls, the draught of his robes instantly extinguishes the flames of the three candles, as if the devil himself has snuffed them out.

She is standing in utter darkness. She can see nothing. But she feels hot liquid on her hands, and she knows the holy blood of a monk is dripping from her fingers on to the sacred stones.

Elena woke with a cry and sat bolt upright, breathing so rapidly that she felt as if she'd been running. The blood pounded in her temples. Her body was slippery with sweat and the cover of the thin straw pallet was as wet as if she had thrown water over it. It took a few minutes for her to calm herself and try to rid her mind of the images in her head.

The heat inside the sleeping chamber was suffocating. She hadn't been able to get cool all day. Now that the sun had begun to dip behind the buildings and the shadows were lengthening, it would have been cooler to sit in the garden, but she hardly dared leave the sleeping chamber any more. She was terrified that the bailiff and his men would return and walk in on her as she sat outside, before she had time to prepare herself. She knew that if the bailiff asked her anything she would give herself away in a word.

Luce had dyed her hair and eyebrows with a paste containing walnut juice to darken them. Ma's orders. It was a pity, Ma had told her with a sigh, for men liked copper-heads and would pay more. Elena couldn't get used to the sight of herself with black hair. It made her face look paler than ever and she felt as if she was staring back at a stranger whenever she glimpsed herself in one of the silver mirrors the girls shared. She wondered if Athan would even recognize her, much less think her pretty now.

The door opened and Luce stuck her head round it, searching the beds. 'Here, Holly, I need you.'

'A man?' Elena's stomach lurched.

'No need to look like a calf that's seen the butcher's knife. The man's not for you, it's a boy he wants. Come on, hurry up. Ma will kill me if the boy isn't ready.'

Elena scarcely had time to pull her shoes on before Luce was tugging her out of the door and towards one of the upstairs chambers.

'It's Finch,' Luce grumbled. 'He won't get dressed. And he won't let me dress him neither. If I try to touch him he goes rigid and starts shrieking. If I fetch Ma or Talbot they'll take a switch to him, but he trusts you. I thought you could persuade him.'

'You're dressing Finch for this man?' Elena grabbed her arm. 'No, not him, please, Luce. He's so little. You can't make him do it. Send one of the other boys.'

'Ma's orders. She's chosen Finch.' She smiled ruefully. 'You know how it is, Holly. He has to work, same as the rest of us.'

Luce marched along a passage with Elena scuttling behind her. Then, opening a heavy wooden door, she pulled Elena inside.

In the centre of the room was a huge wooden bed curved up high at either end. A wooden cupboard leaned drunkenly against one wall and against the other was a long table on which stood a flagon and goblets, together with platters of spitted duck, hare and heron and a glistening haunch of venison. Crowning the table was a roasted hog's head with savage fangs, its face blackened with grease and soot to resemble the coarse dark coat it wore when alive.

The walls of the chamber were painted with scenes of hunting. Bulls were being slaughtered with spears. Bears pawed wildly at the arrows sticking out of them, and men and women dressed in skins cowered from the swords that were hacking at them. Each of the triumphant hunters was naked, their muscles taut as they ran towards their victims, their scarlet mouths wide with the cries of battle.

Even as Elena stepped forward, she was aware of a strong animal stench filling the room, overpowering the smell of the roasted meat. With a shudder she remembered the creatures in the cellar. The stench was not nearly as strong or rank in here, but there was no mistaking some creature was or had been in the room.

In the same instant as the thought struck her, Elena heard a deep snarling. Before she could locate where it was coming from, she glimpsed a movement as something hurtled towards her from behind the bed. She flattened herself against the wall as the creature sprang up, only to be dragged back in mid-air by the chain around its neck. It fell with a heavy crash on the floor before scrambling to its feet, glowering and panting. The creature was black as the Devil's hounds, with short, close fur and eyes ringed with yellow. It looked for all the world like a cat, but that was impossible, for it was the size of a wolfhound. The muscles on its shoulders rippled under the fur. After a moment or two it slunk back behind the bed.

'What is that?' Elena whispered, her heart still pounding from the shock.

Luce wrinkled her nose. 'Ma calls it her witch's cat. But if that's a cat, the mice that brute hunts must be the size of bloody badgers. It's all right though, the beast can't get free. That chain would hold a charging boar, as I keep trying to tell *him*.'

She gestured to the corner of the room furthest away from the cat, and for the first time Elena realized there was someone else in the room. Finch sat in the far corner of the chamber, his legs drawn up to his chin and his head buried in his arms.

'He's got to get dressed in that. Ma's orders.'

She pointed to the floor where a long drape of dark fur lay crumpled. The hair was dense and short, and it looked as if it had been made from the skins of numerous rats sewn together.

Elena crept across the room with her back pressed against the wall to where the little boy sat, and squatted beside him, stroking his hair. She kept a nervous eye on the bed, but the creature remained crouched behind it, though she could hear the rasp of its hot breath as it panted.

'Are you scared, Finch?' Elena asked, her own voice none too steady. 'Is that why you won't get dressed?'

Finch nodded, but didn't raise his head.

Luce put her hands on her hips. 'I keep telling him, if he's not ready when the man comes, Ma'll more than likely feed him to that beast herself.'

Elena glared at her. 'That isn't helping! Course he's scared. Anyone would be with that thing in the room.' She turned back to Finch, coaxing him softly. 'But Luce is right, the cat's on such a stout chain that not even a dragon could break it.

And besides, look at all that meat on the table. The man couldn't eat all that, that's for the cat, that is. That's what it can smell, not you.'

As if it understood the word *meat*, the great cat snarled from behind the bed, and the little boy cringed still further into the corner. He stared desperately up at Elena, his face blotchy with tears.

'But what's the man going to do with the . . . cat? Maybe he'll let it go.'

'He won't,' Elena said soothingly. 'He'd be too afeared the creature would turn on him. And besides, Ma wouldn't let him, she'd not want that thing roaming round scaring all her customers away.'

'But why's it here then?' Finch persisted.

Elena glanced at Luce, who shrugged. 'Gets some men excited,' she said.

Elena wasn't sure she even understood that herself, though by now, listening to the giggling tales of the other girls, she had learned a great deal about what excited men. Very little of it made sense to her, but she knew that a giant cat was by no means the strangest.

With her thumb, Elena rubbed away the tears on Finch's softly rounded cheeks. 'The big cat can't reach you. It's just as safe as when it's in one of Ma's cages. And you're not afeared of those caged beasts, are you? Remember, you told me it was safe to walk by them. Please, Finch, you know you have to do what Ma says. We all do. If you just let me help you dress, everything will be all right, I promise.'

It took a lot more coaxing and pleading before Finch finally allowed Elena to strip the clothes from his thin little body and pull the fur over his head so it hung from him like a little tunic. He stood still as she dressed him, his arms as limp as a rag doll, his head bowed, as if he knew there was no point in putting up any kind of fight. Elena saw the old dead look creep into his eyes and knew he was trying to shut her out, to shut out everything and close himself off until it was over. She knew that, because she had done the same thing that night in the pit at the manor, when she thought they were going to hang her. Sometimes, when the body is chained and cannot escape, the only thing you can do to save yourself is to let your mind fly away instead.

They had just finished when the big cat began to growl in a deep, throaty rasp, and a few moments later Elena heard the sound of heavy footsteps approaching the room.

The door opened, but this time the big cat didn't spring up. It walked as far as it could on its short chain to the side of the bed and stood there, its ears pricked and tail held high.

Ma entered, followed by a dark-haired man.

'Is the boy . . . ?' she began, then broke off as she caught sight of Elena kneeling beside the child. Her eyes flashed in alarm. 'Luce, I thought I said you were to get him ready.'

'I couldn't, Ma. He'd only get dressed for her.'

'Disobedient brat, is he?' the man said, taking a step forward. 'All the better, Mistress Margot, I'll take great pleasure in schooling him.'

'He doesn't need schooling,' Elena snapped. 'He was afraid, that's all. That beast's enough to scare anyone.'

'That's quite enough,' Ma said quickly. 'Off you go now.'

Elena turned towards the door, but the man stepped in front of her, barring her way. He seemed oddly familiar to Elena. His features were well fashioned and his hair was almost as black as the great cat's, but it was his eyes she remembered, grey and cold as a November sky.

He seemed to know her too. He was staring at her as if he couldn't quite place her. 'What's your name, girl?'

'Holly,' she murmured. Then suddenly she realized who he was. Before she could control herself a look of fear flashed across her face. She tried to compose herself, but the man was staring even harder at her.

'I'm sure we've —'

Ma Margot clapped her hands briskly. 'Out, girls, quickly now, I'm sure this fine gentleman is impatient to get on with his fun, he doesn't want you two chattering on, ruining his evening.'

She shooed the girls towards the door.

'Now, sir, you'll find everything you need in that cupboard and if there's anything else you desire, I'll have Luce stand at the end of the passage and you can call her to fetch it.' Ma wagged a stumpy finger at little Finch. 'You do exactly what this gentleman tells you or you'll have me to answer to.'

The last thing Elena glimpsed was the child's terrified face as he watched the man cross to the bed.

At the end of the passage, Ma grabbed Luce and thrust her against the wall with a force that made the girl cry out.

'You stay there, all night if needs be, case he wants anything – that'll teach you to disobey my instructions. When he's ready to leave you take him straight to the door. Don't let him go wandering around. And if he asks about Holly here, you tell him that she used to work in the market in Norwich till she came here. You got that?'

'Yes, Ma.' Luce nodded earnestly, rubbing her bruised shoulder.

Ma led Elena downstairs and outside, pulling her well away from the staircase to the chambers before stopping again. 'You should never have gone in there. I couldn't refuse a man like him. It would have made him think we'd got something to hide. But if you and Luce had done what I said, he would never have seen you. You know who he is, I suppose?'

Elena was trembling. 'I think he might be . . . Lord Osborn's brother.'

'Yes, Hugh of Roxham. Talbot recognized him at once. Now Hugh knows he's seen you before, but it's plain he's not sure where. How often have you met him?'

'I . . . I saw him in the Great Hall the first evening Osborn came to the manor, but only at a distance and he never spoke to me. I didn't think he'd even noticed me for there was a crowd of servants.' Elena gnawed at her knuckle. 'Do you think he's come here looking for me?'

'He's not asked about a runaway, and even if he has some-how discovered Raoul came here the night he died, he can't know you were the girl who pleasured Raoul . . . or murdered him,' she added with a glower. 'There's no reason to think he was looking for anything more than pleasure, and where else would any gentleman come for that but here? Ma Margot's is known far and wide as the best. So if we all stick to the same story, we can convince him he's seen you on the streets in Norwich, that's why you look familiar. It's as well we dyed your hair. You've not told Finch anything about yourself, have you, like where you come from?' Ma grasped Elena's hand, digging her long nails into the flesh. 'You'd best tell me now if you have.'

Elena winced, but shook her head. Ma searched her face for a long time, then grunted and dropped her hand. 'Go on, get yourself to bed and be sure to keep out of sight till Luce tells you he's gone.'

But Elena didn't move. 'Ma, what's Hugh going to do to little Finch?'

'What he does is no concern of yours,' Ma snapped. 'But you'd best pray that he gets so much pleasure from it that it puts any thoughts of you right out of his head.'

'But he's not going to hurt the boy, is he? He's so very small.'

Ma frowned and Elena shrank back, thinking she was about to lash out. But when Ma spoke there was an unusual gentleness in her voice.

'A little, that's inevitable, but I warned him not to go too far.'

She looked up at Elena, a pained but savage expression in her yellow-green eyes.

'All things pass, my darling, that's what you've got to hold on to. In just a few short years Finch will be a young man. He'll be able to do what he likes then to old men and women too who'll be only too willing to make fools of themselves and lick the ground he walks on just for a smile or a tender caress from a beautiful young man. It'll be them suffering then, not him. Trust me, one day you'll feel sorry for them.'

'But that won't wipe out what happened to him,' Elena said. 'He'll remember it.'

'Oh yes,' Ma said with grim smile, 'he will always remember, I'll see to that, and one day he will make them pay dearly for what their kind did to him. That's when he'll know he has beaten them all, and I can promise you he will enjoy that moment better than the finest banquet ever set before a king. Survive, my darling, that's all you have to do, just survive, and if you can, then time will give your revenge.'

Raffe, peering impatiently out of the casement in Lady Anne's chamber, finally saw her emerge from the stables and cross the courtyard below him. She looked weary, hardly surprising after her long journey. She'd been away almost two weeks at her cousin's home and every day Raffe had grown more anxious for her return. He glanced over the yard towards the gate. Osborn had sent a messenger ahead to announce his return from court that very afternoon. Raffe prayed fervently he wouldn't arrive until he'd had time to talk to Anne.

He followed her painfully slow progress across the yard. With gracious nods she acknowledged the hasty bobs and bows of servants as they hurried across the yard with fruit and herbs for the kitchen or armfuls of linen for the washing tubs.

Then the door of the Great Hall opened and Hilda, Lady Anne's sour-faced old maid, bustled down the steps, her hands flapping frantically skywards like a clipped-winged goose. Hilda's bellyache must have seemed like the answer to a prayer for Anne, who was plainly craving a week or two of peace. She couldn't travel with a maid who was rushing to the privy several times an hour. So Hilda had been forced to remain behind, moaning and fretting in her mistress's chamber. Raffe knew that Hilda was now reciting all the insults, both real and imagined, she had suffered in her ladyship's absence. But Lady Anne was merely nodding absently at Hilda's prattling, plainly not listening to a word.

Raffe ranged up and down the wooden floor, praying Anne would retire first to her chamber and not stay to eat in the Hall. He needed to get her alone. After an agonizing wait, he finally heard Hilda's shrill bleating approaching the chamber and knew Anne must be with her.

'. . . and Lord Osborn's manservants show me no respect. Why, the other day that one with the missing finger had the audacity to tell me, *me*, that I should fetch . . .'

The door opened and both women entered, looking startled to find Raffe waiting for them.

Raffe bowed stiffly. 'Welcome home, m'lady.'

Anne grimaced. '*Home*, is that what I should call it? I fear it feels less and less like my home each time I return.'

She limped towards a chair, sinking wearily into it. Her face was grey with fatigue and even the effort of pulling off her riding gloves seemed to exhaust her.

Raffe swiftly poured a goblet of wine and handed it to her.

'M'lady, I must speak with you . . . alone,' he added, pointedly staring at Hilda.

Anne waved a dismissive hand at him. 'If these are more complaints about Osborn's retinue, they will have to wait. I am too weary to hear them now. Besides, you know there is nothing I can do to make Osborn's servants curb their behaviour. By order of King John, Osborn is the master here now. You'd best try appealing to him, if you think it will do any good.'

Raffe inclined his head. 'I am sorry, m'lady, but this can't wait. It's not a matter concerning Osborn. In fact it is imperative I speak with you before he returns.'

Hilda, her eyes now aglow with intrigue, crouched down to unlace Anne's boots, and gazed up eagerly at Raffe, as much as to say, I'm listening.

'You'd better speak then,' Anne said with heavy resignation.

Raffe swiftly knelt down and, elbowing Hilda out of the way, began untying Anne's laces himself.

'It is a delicate matter, m'lady . . . if you would be so good as to dismiss your maid.'

Hilda turned on him, spitting like a cat whose tail has been trodden on. 'Her ladyship has only just returned and I have to help her out of her soiled clothes and dress her. Are you proposing to do that? Anyway, as she said, she's far too exhausted to talk to anyone just now. And I won't have you making her ill. Whatever you have to say will just have to wait. I'm sure it can't be *that* important.'

Anne closed her eyes and sighed. 'Hilda, be so good as to tell the kitchens I will take a warm posset in my chamber. When Osborn returns, tell him I have taken a chill on the road and will not be joining him in the Great Hall this evening.'

'But m'lady . . .' Hilda protested.

'Please, Hilda, go quickly, for I fear I shall be ill if I don't eat at once.'

Hilda's indignation at being excluded was forgotten in her concern for Lady Anne's health and, convinced that only a warm posset would save her dear mistress from certain death, she sped from the room without another word.

Anne leaned forward and grasped Raffe's shoulder as he knelt before her. 'Make haste then, Raffaele, if it really is important.'

Raffe glanced at the heavy oak door to check it was fastened, then back at Anne.

'While you were away, m'lady, a boy came with a message for you. He brought a sign. It was the pilgrim badge of St Katherine, her wheel.'

Anne's eyes opened wide in alarm. 'Did he . . . did he speak of me?'

'He said the message was for you alone, but if Osborn had caught him –'

'But he didn't?' Anne asked in alarm. 'The boy is safe?'

'He is safe.'

'I must get word to tell him I am returned.' Anne half rose

from her chair as if she was going to dash out through the gates.

Raffe took a deep breath. He wasn't sure how she was going to respond to having her private messages intercepted.

'I convinced the boy to give me the message.'

'He was given strict instructions to tell no one, *no one*, except me,' Anne blazed. Despite her exhaustion her eyes flashed with the old fire that had once made even her husband quail. 'And you had no right to intercept a private message for me. Just because you were my son's friend does not give you leave to –'

Raffe's temper snapped. 'It's as well I did, otherwise that poor priest would still be shivering out there on the marshes. Did you expect him to starve until you returned?'

'A priest?' Anne was all concern now. 'What's happened to him? Who was he?'

'The Bishop of Ely's chaplain. He was hiding out on the marshes in fear of his life. I arranged his passage to France. He'll be safe ashore by now, or nearly. But the question is, m'lady, why did he send word to you? What game of madness are you playing? Don't you realize there are some who would count it treason to aid those fleeing from the king? Osborn is one of John's most loyal men. If he had the slightest suspicion of what you are about, he wouldn't hesitate to hand you over to the king. And I have reason to believe that treason is already suspected here.'

Anne winced. For several minutes she said nothing. Then finally she reached towards him and clasped one of his hands in both of hers.

'I am no traitor, Raffaele, but I must do this, don't you see? There are priests and innocent people being hunted down by John's men. If I can help to save them, help God's faithful servants reach safety, then Christ and the Holy Virgin will surely have mercy on my son's soul. It is my penance for Gerard, do you see? The only one I can make for him. I failed my child in his life. I must not fail him in his death.'

Her expression was that of an earnest little girl pleading for a parent to make everything all right. Had she been of lowly birth, Raffe might have taken her in his arms and hugged her simply to comfort her, so lost and desperate did she sound, but he could not embrace the Lady Anne.

'M'lady,' he said gently, 'before the priest left for France he came here to the manor and anointed the body of your son for death.'

Tears of joy sprang into her eyes and she gripped his fingers hard. 'Tell me it is the truth. Swear it is so. You would not lie to me about that, would you?'

'It is the truth, I swear,' Raffe said solemnly. He tried to meet her gaze steadily, but he couldn't. He could feel her eyes boring into him, trying to read his face. Raffe knew he could more easily withstand the torturer's knife than the pain of her stare. But what in all truth could he tell her?

The priest had begun to anoint her son, but would God bless such a sacrament when it had been forced from his servant by threats? Raffe could not be sure that extreme unction had even been completed, for the priest could hardly have been trusted to continue after Raffe had been forced to slam down the lid of the pit. Even if he hadn't fainted straight away, he was more likely to have cursed Gerard than blessed him.

Raffe silently cursed himself. What had he been thinking of? The priest was right, what good would it do anointing a corpse so much decayed? And yet, the bones of the saints still had power to heal, didn't they? Even though the bones were dry and crumbling to dust, people still kissed them and begged them for a blessing.

But Gerard was no saint. No perfume of sanctity wafted from his tomb. A priest would no doubt tell him that the unnaturally rapid decay was proof that he had died in mortal sin. And the rotting remains that lay in that box, the putrid liquid, the foul stench, that was not Gerard; it was not the man he loved and called friend.

As if she could read his thoughts, Anne whispered, 'My son, how did he look? Did he seem at peace?'

Raffe frowned, trying desperately to frame an answer that would not hurt her more. He nodded without meeting her gaze.

'Thank you,' she whispered, but Raffe wasn't sure if she was thanking him for his reassurance or for offering her the gentle lie.

'That girl, Elena, who carries my son's sin, is she safe . . . have you heard news of her?'

'I believe she is safe . . . for now,' Raffe added. He could hardly tell her that Elena might not remain so once Osborn returned, without revealing where she was.

Anne gave a weary smile. 'I am glad of it. I know that we did what had to be done to save my son's soul from torment, but still I cannot help feeling guilty that we deceived an innocent girl. I would not wish to see her come to any harm.'

Raffe winced. What would Anne think if she knew that Elena, whom they had both risked their liberty to protect from Osborn, might after all be a cold-blooded murderess?

Shouts and bellows rose from the courtyard below, followed at once by the clatter of hooves and barking of dogs. Osborn had returned. Raffe struggled to his feet.

'I should not be found talking to you alone. Osborn might suspect us of plotting against him. But m'lady, promise me this, you must not get involved in giving any more aid to the king's enemies. It's too dangerous, especially with Osborn here. Neither your birth nor your sex would spare you if you were charged with treason. John has not even shown mercy to his own kinsmen, and in truth it seems that the more noble they are born the more cruelty he devises for them. Promise me you will do no more.'

But Raffe never heard her reply, if indeed she made one, for Osborn was yelling his name as he ascended the staircase to the Great Hall. In a couple of strides Raffe had crossed the room and was out of the door. As it closed behind him, Lady Anne pressed a hand to her mouth and began to weep.

Elena had lain awake long into the night. She could not stop thinking about Finch. She had never before worried about what a customer was doing to any of the boys or women. On the contrary, ever since she had arrived, her only prayer had been, *Let them do it to the others, but not to me. Holy Virgin, don't let them do it to me.* And always there was that great unknotting of her stomach when she knew the last customer had left and no one would send for her that night.

She was growing accustomed to the pattern of night noises now. First came the sound of women coaxing the men across the courtyard to the rooms, the odd giggle and squeal as men already in the mood for fun would pinch a backside or try to snatch a kiss. Then would follow several hours of muffled laughter, shrieks and moans from the chambers, giving way again to voices and footsteps recrossing the yard: the men's words now slurred with drink or fatigue; the girls' giggling now more forced; the final pinches, slaps and kisses. And then, as each of the women bade farewell to the last of her customers for the night, the door of the sleeping chamber would open and close repeatedly as the women and boys drifted in, yawning, falling asleep almost as soon as they lay down on the rustling straw pallets. Finally a great safe blanket of darkness would settle down upon the brothel and the torture of waiting would be ended for another night. Usually Elena would sigh with relief and curl up into sleep, pausing only to pray that God would keep her little son and her beloved Athan safe, and that she would see them again soon. *Tomorrow, let Athan come for me tomorrow*, she'd whisper fervently.

But tonight Elena lay awake in the suffocating heat listening to the snuffles, snores and groans of the sleepers and the occasional distant barking of a hound somewhere in the town. Finch had not returned. His small, fragile face floated before her eyes. She was haunted by that look of fear and abandonment he had cast at her as she'd walked out of that room, leaving him alone with Hugh and that monstrous cat.

But Finch wasn't the only thing keeping her awake. Luce was absent from the sleeping chamber too. If she was still on watch, that must mean that Hugh was still somewhere here in the brothel. Maybe he too was lying awake at this moment or sipping his wine, trying to remember where he'd last seen the whore in that chamber. It was the sort of thing that people nagged at in their minds. It was the kind of recollection that came suddenly in the middle of the night.

Even with her dyed hair, he might recall her face, an expression, a gesture. What if he'd already left and was even now on his way back here with the sheriff? Elena lay rigid, her stomach aching with fear. Despite the heat, she had not dared to undress. It made her feel less vulnerable to be clothed, and if they came for her, it would be easier to run and hide, or even break away from them at the door.

She found herself planning how she might escape. If they came while it was still dark, she could run down into the cellar where the animals were. She was sure none of the other girls knew the entrance, for if they did then she'd have surely heard them gossiping about the identity of the mutilated man in the cage.

But if they came in daylight, what then? Would Ma be able to hide her before they searched? Would Ma even want to hide her? She'd already threatened to hand her over if Elena didn't earn her keep, and she knew she had hardly done that.

Elena became aware of a movement in the darkness. Slowly and silently the door of the sleeping chamber was opening. Elena drew herself up and crouched tensely in the darkness. *Please let it be Finch*, she prayed.

The figure behind the upraised lantern was short enough to be Finch, but it wasn't. Ma held the lantern aloft, sweeping the soft light over the sleepers, most of whom barely stirred. When the yellow beam caught Elena crouching on her pallet,

Ma beckoned with a long pointed fingernail, the flame glinting in the ruby on her hand.

Panic tightened Elena's throat. Was this it? Was Ma going to hand her over to them? On shaking legs she picked her way through the sleeping women, her mind galloping ahead of her. If she pushed Ma over, she could run, but where to? Ma knew all about the cellar. Her only hope was to make a dash for it once she was outside the brothel.

Elena blundered towards the door. Ma caught her wrist and pulled her outside.

'You're trembling, my darling, I can feel it. Are you getting a fever?' She held the lantern up, peering suspiciously into Elena's face.

Elena shielded her eyes from the light and stared wildly round the courtyard. 'Have they come for me?'

Ma chuckled softly. 'Ah, so that's it. No, they've not come . . . yet. But I need your help with Finch. This way.'

She started off in the direction of the upper chamber, but Elena hung back.

'Come on, my darling. If you're afraid of running into Master Hugh, he's long gone, for now anyway.'

Ma thrust the lantern into Elena's hands as she heaved herself up the staircase, clinging to the rope which ran alongside. Although the steps were shallower than normal to accommodate Ma's shortened stride, still her progress was laborious. There was no sign of Luce. Ma thrust open the door of the chamber. She hung the lantern on a hook inside and with a jerk of her head motioned Elena to enter.

Elena edged cautiously through the door keeping close to the wall, expecting the cat to spring out at any moment, but there was no warning growl.

'The beast's safely back in its cage below,' Ma said.

It was hard to make out anything clearly in the dingy yellow light of the lantern, but Elena saw that the pallet on the bed had partly slipped off and there seemed to be dark stains on it, though what they were, she couldn't tell.

'Right, my darling, I'll send Talbot along with some water and clothes. You get him cleaned up and settled down. He'd best stay here the night and you with him for company. I'll get Talbot to fetch up some herbed wine with poppy juice in it. Get him to drink that if you can, it'll send him to sleep.'

Ma lifted the corner of the pallet. Finch sat under it in the tiny cave formed by the hanging pallet and the side of the bed. His knees were drawn up to his chin and he was rocking backwards and forwards. As the light hit him, he screwed his eyes shut and began to sing in a quavering high-pitched voice – *Lavender's green, diddle diddle, Lavender's blue.* He kept repeating the one line over and over, as if it was a prayer.

Elena moved closer, bending down. But the child kept his eyes so tightly shut that no chink of light could possibly penetrate them. He was half naked. The long grey rat's-skin cloth was shredded, and beneath, Elena could see great long livid welts, oozing blood, standing swollen and proud from his flesh. His arms and legs were also scored with them, and though she could not see his back she guessed it might be the same. Had he been flogged? She suddenly realized what the dark stains on the pallet were – they were bloodstains, Finch's blood.

Outraged, Elena sprang up and wheeled round to face Ma. 'You promised! You said he'd only hurt him a little. Is that what you call a little? You knew he was going to do this, didn't you? How much did he pay you to let him hurt Finch? How much?'

Without thinking what she was doing, she made to grab Ma and shake her, but the tiny woman was too quick and strong for her and in an instant had seized both Elena's wrists in an unbreakable grip.

'You little fool! Do you really think I wanted this? Apart from anything else, it will be weeks before this boy is fit to work again, and I'll have to feed and physic him all the while.'

Even though Ma's fingers were crushing her bones, the pain did not cool Elena's temper.

'Is that all you can think about – coins, money, jewels? He is just a little boy and he's been badly hurt and scared half to death. He's in pain. Don't you feel anything for him?'

'You think you know about pain or hurt?' Ma retorted savagely. 'I've seen more pain and known more hurt than any soldier on the battlefield. You haven't begun to understand what cruelties men can inflict, my darling, and women too; they're sometimes the worst. But do you really imagine it will help the boy if I sit and cry with him? Will that help him fight it the next time and the next?'

'You're not going to let Hugh near him again? You can't, please, Ma, you can't let him,' Elena begged.

Ma released her hands and stood shaking her head sadly, so that the jewelled pins in her shiny black hair glittered in the candlelight.

'My darling, do you think that if I tell that man I don't like what he's done to the boy, it will stop him doing it to someone else, to another child who has no protector?'

'You dare to call this protection?' Although Elena was rubbing her bruised wrists, her tone was still sharp with defiance and fury.

'If this had happened outside the stew, he probably would have gone on until he killed the boy.' She patted Elena's thigh. 'Tend to Finch,' she said wearily. 'You're the motherly sort. You can soothe him.'

At the door, Ma paused. 'Remember what I told you, my darling. If you survive you can always have your revenge. Trust me when I tell you that the man who did this will pay dearly for it, I can promise you that. He will pay.'

After Ma left, Talbot came lumbering in with a bowl of steaming water steeped with sage and thyme, cloths, and almond oil and honey to rub in the wounds, as well as a flask of wine. At the sight of the brawny gatekeeper, Finch retreated further under the pallet.

'You want me to get him out?' Talbot growled.

Elena spread her arms defensively in front of the boy.

'No, no, leave him to me. He'll come in his own time.' She added this more to reassure Finch that she would not force him than for Talbot's benefit.

The gatekeeper grunted and made for the door, rolling from side to side on his bandy legs. 'If there's aught else the little runt needs, you fetch me, you hear?' he said gruffly. 'Food, ale, anything he fancies. You just ask.'

Elena looked up, startled by this unexpected softness in the surly gatekeeper. 'You're a kind man, Talbot.'

Talbot looked. 'Aye, well, no lad deserves to be used like that. I tell you straight, you leave me alone in a dark alley with that bastard and I'd soon teach him what fear is. I'd have him squealing for his mother in less time than it takes for a priest to say a paternoster.' As if he already had Hugh standing in front of him, Talbot clenched his great fists. 'By the time I'd finished with him, he'd not be able to find his own prick to play with, much less someone else's. One of these days that bastard'll get what he deserves; I'll make sure of that.'

He closed the door behind him and Elena could hear his heavy footsteps retreating back down the stairs.

'Everyone's gone now, Finch,' she said softly. 'Come out and let me wash those cuts and put something on them to stop them hurting.'

But the child didn't stir. Elena tried again and again, coaxing him with wine and the promise that she would not hurt him, but still there was no movement. She refused to pull him out. Enough force had been used on Finch already. Finally, she retreated to the far side of the room and sat exhausted, propped against one of the walls, at a loss to know what to do next.

What on earth had Hugh done to the child? She'd been long enough in the stew to know what certain men usually wanted from small boys, but those marks, how had he inflicted those and what else had he done?

From under the pallet, she heard that faint, high-pitched singing again.

Lavender's green, diddle diddle, Lavender's blue.
Lavender's green, diddle diddle, Lavender's blue.

It was a thin, strange little voice that didn't sound like Finch or any child she knew, more like the mewing of an animal in distress. Softly Elena joined in.

You must love me, diddle diddle, 'cause I love you,
Call up your maids, diddle diddle, set them to work.
Some to make hay, diddle diddle, some to the rock.
Let the birds sing, diddle diddle, let the lambs play,
We shall be safe, diddle diddle, deep in the hay.

Without warning the child erupted from under the pallet and flew across the room at her, shrieking and pummelling her in the chest with his small fists. The attack was so unexpected that Elena instinctively turned into the wall, covering her face as the boy punched, kicked and tore at her in a frenzy.

'You promised,' he screamed. 'You said that if I got dressed everything would be all right. You said the cat wouldn't hurt me, you said . . . you said it couldn't get me. You lied, just like all of the rest. I hate you! I hate you!'

He crumpled on to the ground, exhausted, and lay there sobbing.

Elena hesitated, fearful of another assault, but finally she reached out a hand and gently stroked Finch's curls. He flinched, drawing away from her and twisting himself into an even tighter ball.

'Go away. Leave me alone. I hate you.'

Tears filled Elena's eyes. 'I didn't know he would hurt you, I swear I didn't. I'm sorry, so sorry.'

But what the boy said didn't make sense. She couldn't imagine the cat allowing itself to be mastered by any man it didn't know. Surely not even someone as arrogant as Hugh would be so foolish as to unleash such a beast when it could just as easily have turned on him.

'I don't understand, Finch. Did he let the cat off the chain?'
The boy, still lying on the floor, shook his head.

Elena stared again at the long open cuts on his arms. She had been clawed by her mother's tabby cat a few times when playing with it as a child and recognized the parallel marks, though nothing as frightful as the marks on the boy. The boy's flesh had been ripped open, yet deep though the cuts were, surely a beast of that size would have ripped his arm off, not merely torn the skin. And his face was unmarked.

She reached out again and stroked the little head once more. 'Finch, please tell me what he did. You say he didn't let the cat off the chain, then how did it hurt you?'

He raised his head and stared at her, his face was blotched from crying and his nose was running. His breath came in thick, hiccupping sobs.

'The man, he was the cat . . . he pulled off his shirt and tied a pelt around his waist. He was muttering. *You will feel the strength*, over and over. His eyes went strange . . . like he was staring at something that wasn't there. Then . . . then he started changing, turning into a beast, 'cept it wasn't a beast like those ones.' He gestured to the paintings on the walls. 'He was . . . he was a werecat. He could stand like a man, but he wasn't a man, he was a huge cat with great long claws. And he wasn't chained, he leapt at me. He had hair on his hands, thick hair, and his eyes were deep and mad like demons'. He . . . caught me and I couldn't get away. I couldn't get away . . .' Finch broke off in a shuddering moan of fear.

Elena, shaking as much as the boy, drew the child to her and folded him in her arms, burying his face in her shoulder. He didn't resist, but clung to her, sobbing and trembling. They sat together like that for a long time, before the boy's breathing finally calmed. At last he let her wash him, wincing in pain as the cloth touched the cuts, but making no sound. She rubbed almond oil and honey in the cuts to soothe them and help them heal, then coaxed him to drink the poppy-laced wine.

She pulled the pallet off the bed and dragged it into the far corner. Then they both lay down on it, she with her body curled protectively round the boy's, he holding tight to her arm wrapped across his small chest.

She could feel him relaxing as the wine and poppy syrup took hold.

Just as she thought he was asleep, he murmured, 'The werecat was asking about you.'

Elena's body recoiled as if she had been struck. 'What . . . what did he ask?' she said, trying to keep the fear from her voice.

'Your name,' Finch murmured drowsily. 'I told him it were Holly. I had to tell him, he made me.' He started to shake again and Elena stroked his head. 'Of course you had to, it doesn't matter. But did he say anything else? Did he say anything about me?'

She could feel the child drooping in her arms, but she needed him to stay awake and answer her.

'Think, Finch, I know it's hard, but please, it's important, what else did he say about me?'

There was such a long silence that Elena was sure Finch was sleeping, then he muttered. 'Said next time . . . he was going to take you.'

3rd Day after the New Moon, September 1211

Marigold – called also the *Jackanapes-on-horseback*, *Summer's bride* or *Husbandman's dyall* for the flowers follow the sun faithfully. For this reason maids weave it into their bridal garlands to keep their husbands constant. And if any maid would make a lover faithful, she should dig up the earth from his footprint and put it in a pot and therein plant her marigold seeds.

The flowers are eaten in possets and puddings. The flower-head rubbed on a sting will soothe the pain. The seeds crushed into white wine will cure or ward off agues and all manner of fevers. Mixed with hog's grease and turpentine, and rubbed upon the breast, it succours the heart in a fever.

If a mortal gazes into the flower at dawn it shall preserve him from contagion all day, and if he smells the flower, it shall banish the evil humours from him. Eaten before all other food is taken, it will cure the melancholy spirits and shall comfort those who sorrow.

Mortals regard the marigold as a symbol of cruelty in love, and of pain. And mortals must have pain, as a fish must have water. For mortals it is not enough that others should inflict it upon them, but they strive to inflict it on themselves.

The Mandrake's Herbal

Foul Wind from France

'Hugh, for God's sake stop exciting those brutes,' Osborn snapped irritably. 'Or I'll have them banished to kennels with the rest of the hounds.' He pulled the glass ball that magnified the light of the candle closer and bent his head once more over the rolls of parchment and ledgers scattered on the table before him.

Hugh was sprawled in the casement seat of the solar, feeding choice pieces of roasted meat to his two favourite hounds. They were drooling and yapping excitedly as he held the juicy morsel high up out of their reach. When he finally tossed the piece of meat the length of the solar the hounds bounded after it, skidding on the silk rugs and leaping to catch it before it fell. The loser came racing back to Hugh, his claws clattering on the wooden floor, and sat there hopefully gazing up at him again.

For a moment Hugh considered defying his brother, but one glance at Osborn's face told him his brother was in such a foul mood that if crossed, he'd probably order Hugh's dogs to be butchered and fed to the rest of the pack. Hugh laid the pewter dish of meat, bread and gravy down on the floor and watched the two dogs lick it clean.

He wandered across to the table and selected a fat mutton chop. God's blood, he craved meat. He could never seem to get enough of it these days. Thank heaven, the churches were closed. You were still supposed to abstain from meat on Fridays and the dozens of Holy Days in the year, but with no priest to wag his finger, Hugh didn't even make a pretence at obeying this rule. He licked the grease from his fingers. Time enough to do penance for that when the priests returned, and when they did, it would take a cathedral full of them a whole month to hear his confession.

For a start there was what he'd done with that boy in the whorehouse. It had disgusted and excited him at the same time. He had never felt so alive, so powerful. He had never desired a boy before, and the thought of it revolted him, even though he ached to repeat it. Even the hunt, which once had excited him, now seemed dull and insipid, like drinking milk-whey after a good rich wine. He gritted his teeth, trying to suppress the stirrings in his groin which the mere memory of that night aroused.

With a deliberate effort at concentration, he strolled across to Osborn and flicked one of the scrolls of parchment. 'This from King John? I saw the messenger arrive. Is it about Raoul's murder?'

His brother shook his head irritably. 'John wants money, a loan, he says, for the building and equipping of a warship. He's asking all his loyal lords to finance the building of new ships to increase the fleet. But where am I to get this kind of money? Half the merchants from Europe have ceased coming to England to buy wool, because of the Interdict. The Church tells them it's forbidden for good Christians to trade with those who are excommunicated; besides, they don't want to get on the wrong side of Philip. The prices of wool have dropped so much I can hardly give it away.'

'Then refuse John the loan,' Hugh said casually, spearing another chop.

Osborn slammed his fist down on to the table. 'How can I refuse the king after he granted me this manor?' He glowered at Hugh. 'You always were a complete numbskull in these matters. It's as well I was born the elder. You'd have lost all our father's lands and property within the year if you'd had charge of them, and probably your head too.' He raked his fingers through his beard. 'I'll just have to borrow from the Jews. No doubt they'll demand extortionate interest.'

'But the Jews are the king's property,' Hugh reminded him. 'He decides what interest they should charge. In fact I doubt you could lift any juicy piecrust anywhere in this land without finding John's thumb in it somewhere.'

Osborn eyes narrowed. 'Guard your tongue, little brother. If the king got to hear those words, you would lose it.'

Hugh waved the chop-bone at the room. 'There's no one to hear us and I am not such a *numbskull*, brother, as to speak it outside. Anyway, what surety is the king offering for this loan?'

'He promises to grant me, and the others who support him in this, wealthy estates taken from the rebel barons, when he defeats Philip,' Osborn said morosely.

'*If* he defeats Philip! You hoped for such things before when you hunted down the rebels for John after he captured the castle of Montauban, and all you managed to persuade John to give you for your trouble was this piss-poor manor. You should have demanded more. Our father would have done.'

Osborn threw back his chair and leapt up. Without warning, he struck Hugh hard across his cheek with the back of his hand.

Hugh reeled back, grunting in pain, and his hand reached for his dagger before he even realized what he was doing. It was only with supreme effort that he stopped himself drawing it. He turned away, breathing hard and seething with fury.

After a moment he felt a hand grasp his shoulder. 'Forgive me, little brother. I am weary. I should not . . .'

You should not have done what, brother? Hugh thought savagely. Hit me? Treated me like a child and fool for years? Kept me penniless like a base-born villein?

Hugh painted a smile on his face and turned back to Osborn with a respectful incline of his head. 'I'm the one who should ask forgiveness of you, brother. I spoke foolishly. As you say, I am a numbskull.'

It took every grain of self-control he could muster to utter those words in anything approaching a civil tone. But Osborn did not appear to hear the crackle of ice in his voice and merely nodded as if he thought all was mended between them.

Fearful of letting his rage explode, Hugh rapidly searched for a diversion. 'I'm surprised that John made no mention of Raoul.'

Osborn sank down again at the table, without looking at him. 'I have not told him yet.' He held up a hand as if to forestall a protest. 'I thought it wisest not to do so until Raoul's killer has been apprehended. John sent Raoul here to look for a traitor, and His Majesty might take it ill if one of his men came to harm while under my protection. Besides, John has too many cares just now to burden him with another. Time enough to tell him once I've got Raoul's killer by the heels. I'll go to Norwich myself and kick that feckless sheriff into action.'

Hugh felt as if God and all the saints of heaven were beaming down on him. The band of fur around his waist seemed to tighten and throb against his skin, even as he felt that shudder of pleasure rising between his legs.

'No, brother, no, you have enough to concern you over this matter of raising the money for John. Let me go to Norwich. As you say, I am useless when it comes to tending to estate matters. But I can be of service to you in Norwich. Let me go.' He watched Osborn's face eagerly, willing him to agree.

Osborn hesitated. 'There is something you should know. Raoul was in Norwich not on John's service, but mine. I'd heard that my runaway villein had taken refuge there. I sent Raoul to see if he could find her. This traitor, whoever he is, may have seized the opportunity to follow him and killed him for fear of discovery, or else someone killed him to stop him finding the girl. But either way, little brother, I caution you to take great care.'

Hugh smiled. 'Have no fear on my part. Unlike Raoul, I know how to defend myself, and I swear I will return not only with his killer, but with your runaway villein too. I won't rest until I have tracked that bitch down and run her back here tied to a horse's tail, as a gift to you.'

Hugh accepted his elder brother's warm embrace as if all had indeed been forgiven between them. But beneath his smile, his rage throbbed as fiercely as his cheek. The blow was neither forgiven nor forgotten. He swore he'd make his brother regret this latest insult in a long line of humiliations he'd suffered at his hands. Before the year was out he'd make Osborn remember each and every one of them.

A twist of mean, broken little cottages surrounded the Fisher's Inn. The ramshackle wooden buildings were threaded along a narrow strip of dry land squeezed between the dark river and the black, sucking marshes. The inhabitants of the cottages didn't earn enough between them to keep an alewife dry shod, never mind provide the business an inn needed to flourish. But despite its isolation, flourish it did, as far as anything except leeches and midges could thrive in that lonely place. It was its very remoteness that was attractive to a certain type of customer. Lost travellers, eel men, wildfowlers and the boatmen, sedge collectors and reed-gatherers all had reason to be grateful for its location when going about their damp and lonely tasks in the daylight hours. But there were others who sought it out by night, when dark corners and concealed nooks gave welcome shelter to those who had no wish for their faces to be seen.

Although the inn stood out plainly enough in the daytime, Raffe always marvelled how at night the wooden building seemed to melt into the darkness. The reeds blurred its outline and so faint were the lights burning inside that no glimmer escaped its shadows, even through the cracks of weather-beaten shutters.

Raffe lifted the latch on the heavy door and sidled in. As usual, he gagged as he took his first breath in the cloying, fishy stink of the smoke that rose from the burning seabirds, which were skewered on to the wall spikes in place of candles. In the dim oily light, he could make out the vague outlines of men sitting in twos and threes around the tables, heard the muttered conversations, but could no more recognize a face than see his own feet in the shadows.

A square, brawny woman deposited a flagon and two leather beakers on a table before waddling across to Raffe. Pulling his head down towards hers, she planted a generous kiss on his smooth cheek.

'Thought you'd left us,' she said reprovingly. 'You grown tired of my eel pie?'

'How could anyone grow tired of a taste of heaven?' Raffe said, throwing his arm around her plump shoulders and squeezing her.

The woman laughed, a deep, honest belly chuckle that set her pendulous breasts quivering. Raffe loved her for that.

'He's over there, your friend,' she murmured. 'Been waiting a good long while.'

Raffe nodded his thanks and crossed to the table set into a dark alcove, sliding on to the narrow bench. Even in the dirty mustard light he could recognize Talbot's broken nose and thickened ears.

Talbot looked up from the rim of his beaker and grunted. By way of greeting he pushed the half-empty flagon of ale towards Raffe. Raffe waited until the serving woman had set a large portion of eel pie in front of him and retreated out of earshot. He hadn't asked for food, no one ever needed to here. In the Fisher's Inn you ate and drank whatever was put in front of you and you paid for it too. The marsh and river were far too close for arguments, and the innkeeper was a burly man who had beaten his own father to death when he was only fourteen, so rumour had it, for taking a whip to him once too often. Opinion was divided on whether the boy or the father deserved what they suffered at each other's hands, but still no one in those parts would have dreamed of reporting the killing. And since the innkeeper's father lay rotting somewhere at the bottom of the deep, sucking bog, he wasn't in a position to complain.

Raffe leaned over the table towards Talbot. 'You sent word it was important. What's happened? They haven't arrested Elena, have they?'

'Nay, she's safe enough for now. But there's another matter needs attending to.'

He took a long, slow draught from his beaker. Raffe's heartbeat began to slow. All the way here, he'd been so afraid Talbot was bringing terrible news of Elena, but if she was still safe, then nothing else seemed of much import.

Osborn had not gone chasing off to Norwich as soon as he had returned, as Raffe had feared. In truth he'd seemed curiously unmoved by Raoul's murder, preoccupied with other concerns. And with every day that passed, it seemed less likely that the sheriff's men would discover the murderer at all.

Talbot set down his beaker and wiped his mouth on the back on his hand. 'I've had word that package you sent by ship arrived safely.'

'That's good,' Raffe said absently, still preoccupied by the thought of Elena and Raoul.

'Though if I'd known who he was, I'd have charged him double.'

Raffe grinned. He might have known that Talbot would find out somehow that the man was a priest. To be honest, if it had just been the priest's life at stake, Raffe wouldn't have much cared whether he reached France or not, but there was always the danger that if he was captured he might start talking. Raffe knew that they'd merely have to show that little runt the hot irons for the priest to start spilling every name in his head, even proclaiming the Blessed Virgin Mary a co-conspirator if he thought it would spare him pain.

'Maybe not as good as you think,' Talbot said. 'I get the feeling for some reason he took against you, the ungrateful bastard. Thing is,' Talbot leaned in closer, dropping his voice even lower, 'there's another package to be delivered and our friend insists he wants you to take charge of it personally.'

Raffe frowned. 'Speak plainer, man.'

Talbot glanced around the shadowy room. Everyone appeared deeply engrossed in their own muted conversations; all the same, he was taking no chances. He tapped Raffe on the arm and gestured with his head towards the door. Raffe rose and, slipping a more than generous payment for the scarcely touched eel pie to the serving woman, he left the inn and wandered out beyond the cottages to a small, open wooden shelter where the fowlers stored their nets and wicker tunnels for driving the ducks. The air was sharp after the fug of the inn, and even the stench of rotting vegetation and mud smelled clean compared to the fishy stench of the burning seabirds.

Raffe perched on an upturned keg in the darkness, listening to the gurgle of the black waters and the rustling of the reeds. Then he heard soft footsteps behind him. Talbot slipped into the shelter and squatted close to Raffe, facing in the opposite direction, so that he could watch the door of the inn.

'You wanted me to speak plain,' Talbot said, keeping his voice so low that Raffe had to lean in to hear him. 'Word from the priest is that a messenger from France needs safe passage for a meeting at Norwich.'

'With whom?' Raffe asked.

Talbot shrugged. 'Not likely to give us names, is he? But if this envoy is on France's business you can safely wager it won't be John's friends he wants to meet.'

'I'll not do it!' Raffe burst out angrily.

Talbot gripped his arm. 'Keep your voice down,' he whispered.

He glanced anxiously about him, but Raffe was too angry to stay silent though he did lower his voice.

'Much as I'd gladly see that devil John hanging from the highest gallows in the land, I'll not betray my country to the French. You think I want Philip on the throne? This is England and I'd no more see it under France's heel than I would be slave to the Saracens.'

'But it isn't your country, is it?' Talbot said quietly. 'Your mam wasn't squatting on English soil when she gave birth to you, nor her dam, nor hers afore that. What allegiance can a man have for any land save the one that drank his mother's blood when he was born?'

The truth of what he said hit Raffe like an unexpected blow from a fist. For so many years, even before he set foot on it, he had thought of this land as his own. It was Gerard's home and he had pledged life and limb to Gerard, and therefore to his lord's land and lineage. All through those years as they'd travelled and fought for King Richard, then John, the men had sat around the camp fires in the evening talking of home, of their favourite inns and serving wenches, of familiar hunting forests and grey stone manors, the trees they had climbed and the meadows in the shires where they had played as boys.

And Raffe had almost come to believe that their memories were his own. Like them, he too spoke longingly of the comforts of home. And the home he meant was England. He belonged here. It was the only place where he had ever been allowed to think he belonged. And any idea that others might still consider him a foreigner had long since vanished from his head. Talbot's challenge stung him as smartly as a splinter driven under his fingernail.

'I took an oath to Gerard and I am still bound by that. He would never betray his country, any more than I can betray him.'

'Aye, well, there's the problem, see?' Talbot muttered.

'No, I don't see,' Raffe said coldly.

'Word is that if the envoy doesn't complete his mission safely, other messages can be sent from France to Osborn or even the king himself, explaining how you and others he could name have helped those fleeing from John.' Talbot spat disgustedly into the darkness. 'I always knew priests were devious bastards, but you'd have thought at least they'd not turn on those who've helped 'em.'

Raffe felt the blood drain from his face. He knew exactly why the priest would be willing to see him hanged or worse. The little weasel had plainly not forgotten, much less forgiven, being trapped with Gerard's corpse. Raffe had little doubt the priest would carry out his threat. What was to prevent him?

But Raffe didn't have to stay and wait for John's men to

come for him. Talbot had arranged passage on a ship for the priest – why couldn't he arrange it for Raffe? Not to France, of course, nor any of the lands where John still held sway, but there were other countries. He could go anywhere, just walk away from this. What was to keep him here?

Talbot suddenly gripped Raffe's shoulder. 'Priest said there were others who'd helped. What did he mean? Who did you talk about?'

Even though it was too dark to read the gatekeeper's expression, Raffe could feel the powerful fingers digging into him, and knew exactly what he was asking.

'Upon my life, I swear he knows nothing of you.'

'Then who?' Talbot demanded.

Raffe tried to think. 'I suppose the marsh-boy who delivered him to the boatmen, and the boatmen themselves . . . but he'll not know their names.'

'You sure there was no one else?' Talbot growled. 'He said others he could *name*.'

Raffe suddenly knew with sickening clarity who the priest meant. When he was in hiding, the priest had sent the boy to find not him but the Lady Anne. The priest had to know her identity, and that was why he was so certain his threat would work. If Raffe fled, she would be left behind to face the wrath of Osborn and John.

There was no way out of this. Raffe couldn't smuggle Anne out of the country in secret. Such a flight would mean travelling at night, climbing on to ships in the dark, even hiding in the bilges until they were safely clear of the coast. A young woman might have managed it, but not her, even if she consented to do it. He'd seen how exhausted the journey from her cousin's home had left her; she would never survive a voyage as a fugitive. And if she did, what would become of her in a foreign land? He could take any menial job to put food in his belly, living rough in the open if he had to, he'd done it before, but he couldn't expect a woman of noble birth to end her days in some peasant's hut in a foreign field.

He could sense Talbot studying him, waiting for a reply, but he was not going to give him the name he was looking for.

'Even if I do what they ask, what's to stop the priest betraying us . . . me anyway?'

Talbot shifted his weight, 'Nowt,' he said bluntly. 'But you'd have information to trade, once you find out who it is the envoy has come to see. If it's that bastard Hugh, then you'd have your proof and could name him without needing to drag Elena into this. You'd be able to buy your way out of a deal of trouble, maybe buy a pardon for the lass too, with a traitor's name to parley with. It's a gamble, to be sure, but seems to me you've a simple choice: cast your dice or accept a certainty – a *dead* certainty.'

Raffe knew Talbot would give anything to see Hugh tried as a traitor. He'd always wanted to get even with him ever since the man had tried to hang him at Acre. All the same, he had a point. If he could prove Hugh a traitor without Elena having to repeat what she'd overheard, he'd not only keep her alive, she might be able to return to Gastmere.

The inn door opened and Talbot drew back into the shadows. 'I'd best be on my way. Word is ship's to weigh anchor seaward side of the isle of Yarmouth. They learned their lesson with the *Santa Katarina*, so they'll not risk running the ship into Breydon Water. Too easy to get trapped there. But Yarmouth's a free port, so there's none of John's men stationed in it, leastways not officially. I'll get word to you when ship's been sighted.'

'But what . . .' Raffe began, then realized he was speaking to the empty air. Talbot had vanished.

Raffe sat on the keg, staring out over the whispering marshes. The black bogs seemed to suck all the light from the stars and moon. The stinking, bottomless mud gurgled continuously like the stomach of a great beast digesting its prey. Here and there unearthly shrieks rang out from the tall reeds, but he knew of old that there was no living soul out there, only the tormented restless spirits who wandered the marshes.

But it isn't your country, is it? What did it matter if he betrayed England? What did it really matter? He owed this land no loyalty. It was Gerard's home, not his. Talbot had said he had a choice, a simple choice, he'd called it: betray Gerard's beloved country to the French or let Gerard's own mother be taken and executed as a traitor.

Once, as a little boy, he had knelt in the great abbey church and fervently prayed before the hot, bright candles for the life of his father. Now in the darkness he sank again to his knees among the stinking fishing nets and prayed once more with all his soul.

Gerard, forgive me. Forgive me for what I am about to do.

✝

10th Day after the New Moon, September 1211

Mice – are particularly efficacious when stewed, roasted, baked or fried, to strengthen sickly children, cure them of colds, fits, the pox and fevers, or prevent them from wetting the bed. If a mortal has a persistent cough, let him hang a bag of live mice about his neck and the cough will travel to the mice. When they are all dead the patient will be cured.

Mouse teeth are often worn as charms. Ailing cattle may be given water in which teeth or bones of mice have been laid. When the milk teeth of a child fall out they must be placed in a mouse hole so that the child's new teeth will be as small, white and sharp as a mouse's.

If a mouse squeaks in the chamber of one who is sick, the person will die. Likewise, if a mouse should run across a living person, he is doomed, for the spirits of man often appear in the likeness of a mouse. If the mouse should be red, the spirit is pure, but if black the spirit is steeped in sin.

If a mortal sleeps, a mouse may be seen running from his open mouth, and that is his spirit which leaves the body to travel through the dream world. But take heed, if you should move that man from his place while he sleeps, or wake him before his mouse-spirit has returned, that man will wake, but it will be as if he is dead, unable to talk to the living. He will wander senseless like a corpse and after some days or months he will die.

The Mandrake's Herbal

The Freedom of the Lark

Talbot grasped Raffe's arm and led him through the door to Ma's staircase. But instead of mounting the stairs, Talbot opened a small door tucked in behind them. In all the years he had been coming here, Raffe had never noticed the door before. In the dark recess of the stairwell, it was nigh on invisible.

Talbot led the way into a tiny cell. A shaft of early morning light streamed in through a slit in the stones, high up on the wall, revealing the low, narrow bed and a banded wooden chest which occupied most of the narrow space. From the clothes strewn across the bed, Raffe guessed this must be where Talbot himself slept, close enough to the main door to reach it quickly should he be summoned in the night.

Talbot turned to face Raffe. 'It's well you've come, saves me a journey. The ship carrying your cargo has been sighted off the coast. *Dragon's Breath*, she's called. They reckon she'll put in at Yarmouth tomorrow on the evening tide. Her crew'll not be allowed ashore till the day after her cargo's been inspected and tolls have been paid. You'd best meet them then.'

'But if they inspect the cargo . . .' Raffe protested.

Talbot waved his hand dismissively. 'Yarmouth folk aren't interested in men, only goods they can tax. They'll not look twice at the passengers, not unless John's men get wind of it, of course.'

At the mention of the king, anger welled up in Raffe again. 'I won't do it. I won't meet this man. I can't give aid to England's enemies.'

Talbot's fist shot out and grabbed the front of his tabard. 'You bloody will, you old bullock. That priest meant what he said about spilling all. He's nothing to lose and a great deal of favour and money to gain. You might not have told him about my role in this, but there's no knowing what he might have learned on board the ship. Besides, I want Hugh's head on a pike, and this French Skegg might just be able to give us the proof we need to see him die as a traitor. If not . . .' His eyes flicked up to the beams above and he lowered his voice to a whisper, 'no matter what her upstairs says, I'll use that lass of yours to nail him, even it does see her hanged for Raoul's murder into the bargain.'

Talbot wasn't a man to make idle threats. Raffe's friendship with him went deep, but was it as deep as Talbot's hatred of Hugh? Besides, Talbot's warning was sufficient to remind him of what else lay at stake if the priest chose to talk. The one name he could be certain the priest did know, besides his own, was Lady Anne's, and he couldn't risk him uttering that. Raffe nodded weakly.

Talbot let go of his tabard and gave him a friendly punch on the arm. 'That's more like it. Now, give the boatman this.'

He grabbed Raffe's hand and tipped a small tin emblem of St Katherine into Raffe's palm, just like the one the priest had sent to Lady Anne.

'He'll ask you where the cargo comes from. You're to tell him Spinolarei in Bruges. He's expecting that answer and he'll know you're the right man and not one of John's spies.'

Raffe was aware that Bruges, eager to keep the lucrative trade with England, was known to favour England against France, so no suspicions would be aroused should anyone chance to overhear the remark.

'You got money?' Talbot asked. 'The man's been paid already but he'll expect more. They always do, the greedy bastards.'

'And you do it for love, I suppose,' Raffe said sourly.

Talbot grinned, but was instantly serious again. 'Be there, Raffe, for all our sakes, especially that lass of yours. I'd hate to see her pretty little neck stretching on a rope.'

*

Elena cautiously opened the door and eased herself into the small chamber. Master Raffaele was standing at the casement, staring up at the white clouds drifting across the brothel garden. The bright morning light washed his face, rubbing away, just for a moment or two, the wrinkles and sagging fat around his jaw.

Catching sight of him in profile, Elena glimpsed the ghost of the beauty that had once made her mother see an angel in him, but then, just as rapidly, it vanished, leaving behind only the wreck of flesh, the awkward, ungainly proportions of the too long limbs and the massive buttocks. Elena gave a little shudder.

'Master Raffaele . . .' She shuffled uneasily, not knowing whether he had heard her. Had he finally come to take her away? Why wouldn't he look at her? She meant to wait for him to speak, she really did, but the silence in that room was too much to bear.

'My Athan, is he well? Have you seen him? And my mam —'

'They told me about Raoul,' Raffaele cut in.

'I didn't do it, I swear.' Sweat burst out on Elena's forehead. 'I couldn't have . . .'

'But Talbot says you knew how he had died before you were told. That's not easily explained away. Elena, tell me the truth. For once in your life trust me. If Raoul hurt you, if he . . . if he forced himself on you, I wouldn't blame you for killing him. It would be natural that you wanted him dead, honourable even, but I must know the truth.'

Elena's hands were clenched so tightly it hurt. She didn't want to talk about it, especially to him, but she knew Raffaele would go on questioning her until she did.

'I hated him for what he did. I hated him touching me. He was revolting. I felt sick. And if I could have killed him then to stop him, I would have, believe me, I would have done it gladly, but I couldn't. He was too strong.'

She swallowed the hard lump that had risen in her throat, trying to think how to explain it so that Raffaele would understand.

'Afterwards . . . after he'd gone I fell asleep. I dreamed I'd killed him, but it was only a dream, just a dream. I couldn't have done it. I've thought about it over and over again. I don't remember walking through the streets. It must have been a dream.'

'Like the dream you had about your son?' Raffaele snapped. 'Curious, isn't it, how you dream and deaths always follow? There are those who might say that is worse than murder; they might call it witchcraft.'

Elena gaped at his back. He couldn't be saying this. 'But my son isn't dead. I told you . . . I told you that Gytha took my son. I thought you believed me. That's why you helped me, wasn't it, because you knew I was innocent?'

'I don't know what I believe any more!'

Raffaele gripped the edge of the casement so hard that Elena thought he was going to tear it apart with his bare hands. For several moments he stood there, his head bowed, his knuckles white. Then he seemed to regain control of himself.

'You shouldn't speak about your dreams to anyone,' he said quietly. 'If Ma or the other women think they are harbouring a witch, they will not keep you here.'

'But I don't want them to keep me here,' Elena said. 'It isn't safe.'

For the first time since she'd entered the room, he turned to face her, staring at her as if she was a stranger. Elena realized it was the first time he'd seen her dyed hair. Her hand slid up, pulling her cap further down over her coiled plaits, but she couldn't hide her eyebrows. Luce had insisted on dyeing those too, saying her pale auburn ones were in too marked contrast to her dark hair.

'Your hair, what happened to your beautiful hair?' Raffaele said, aghast.

'Luce dyed it. Ma insisted in case the sheriff's men came back.'

Raffe continued to stare at her, then he seemed to remember where he was. 'Talbot tells me that no one has returned here again to enquire about the murder. That's good. That means they don't link Raoul's death with you.'

'But what about Hugh?' Elena said. 'He saw me. He didn't seem to remember who I was, but he said he thought I looked familiar. And he asked Finch about me. I can't stay here now. What if he returns?'

Shock and fear flashed across Raffe's face. He grasped her shoulders, staring down into her eyes so fiercely that she was forced to lower her gaze.

'What's this about Hugh? He was here? When . . . when was he here?'

'More than a week ago . . . two maybe.'

'Was he here looking for you?'

'I don't think so,' Elena said. 'He was here to . . . use a little boy. He just happened to see me. But what if he remembers where he saw me before? You have to take me away.'

Raffaele stepped back from her, running his hand distractedly through his thick grizzled hair. 'I will . . . I will, I give you my word, but not yet. There's something I must do, and until that's finished, I can't be with you to look after you. This is the only safe place I can leave you.'

'But it isn't safe!' Elena wailed. 'What if he comes back?'

Raffaele was pacing the floor, gnawing on the edge of his thumb.

'Hugh only saw you fleetingly when he was at the manor, one of dozens of servants. He wasn't there when you were accused. Everyone in the manor knows that villein escaped the gallows. There won't be a man in Osborn's retinue who doesn't know he'd pay a fortune to capture you, but even so, Hugh won't be able to link a face to a name. Even if he was the man who you overheard talking about the *Santa Katarina*, you said yourself he didn't see your face.'

Elena lurched violently, grabbing hold of the edge of a table, trying to keep herself from falling.

'Hugh! You think Hugh was the man I heard in Lady Anne's chamber? But . . . but I don't understand. That night when I told you, you said it was one of Osborn's servants.'

Raffaele shook his head impatiently. 'I know that's what I said, because I couldn't imagine who else it could be. You told me the man you overheard had fought in the Holy Land, but even then it didn't occur to me it could be Hugh. Hugh's a cold-blooded bastard, but I couldn't believe that even he could be so base as to betray his own king and country. And I wouldn't have believed it, unless I'd seen him with my own eyes, skulking among the trees, watching for the *Santa Katarina*. He was expecting that ship. He must have been the man you heard in the chamber, how else could he have known about it? And why would he have been trying to conceal himself, if he wasn't afraid of being caught by the king's men?'

'Then you have to take me away from here before he comes back, you have to . . . if he knows it was me who heard him, he'll kill me!'

'I can't!' Raffaele snapped. Then he took a deep breath. His voice was heavy with weariness. 'Hugh can't be certain you heard anything. In fact he must believe by now that you didn't. I've taken great care not to tell anyone what I suspect, in case he realizes what you overheard. Hugh's bound to have heard that Osborn's missing villein is a red-head, and if he glimpsed your red curls that night outside the chamber, he may well have made the connection. But . . .' Raffaele held up a warning hand seeing that she was about to protest again, 'but don't you see that means he's looking for a red-head? That's all he knows of you, and you're not that woman any more.'

Raffaele crossed over to her and slipped off her cap. He pulled the pins from one of the braids and let it fall. Then, with an almost childlike curiosity, he ran his fingers down it, unravelling the braid, letting the long dark hair fall in soft waves across his palm. Elena, her thoughts still occupied with her fear of Hugh, was too bemused to move. Raffaele gently rubbed the locks of her hair between his thumb and forefinger, then his gaze lifted to her face and, bending his head close to her, his lips parted and she felt his hot breath on her mouth. She stiffened, flinching away.

Raffe instantly straightened up, letting her hair fall. He turned abruptly back to the casement, but not before Elena glimpsed the dark flush on his cheeks.

'It is your eyes,' he said in a strangely broken voice. He cleared his throat. 'Luce has done her work well with your hair, and the colour of your brows changes the shape of your face, but still anyone would know your eyes. Though you need have no fears about that where Hugh is concerned, I doubt he's ever noticed a woman's eyes.'

Elena, thrown entirely by his abrupt change of tone, could only stare at him.

Raffaele crossed to the door and opened it. 'If Hugh returns, just stay out of sight,' he said without looking back at her.

Seeing him stride away snapped Elena out of her immobility. She ran after him, catching his arm. 'Please, Master Raffaele, please take me with you. I could stay in an inn or find work as a maid in the town. You said no one would recognize me.'

He looked down at the little fingers grasping his sleeve and for a moment she almost thought he was going to agree, then he seized her wrist and roughly thrust her back into the chamber.

'I told you, you will stay here! Do you think I'm Athan or some frog-witted plough-boy who's nothing better to do than dance attendance on you and your selfish little wants? I saved you from the rope, what more do you expect of me? And not one word more about your dreams, do you understand? Better you confess you put a knife in a man's back with your own hand than that you killed him by witchcraft. It is dangerous, can't you see that, you stupid little fool? And I won't be there to save your wretched neck next time.'

The door crashed shut behind him and Elena stood there,

massaging her wrist. Tears filled her eyes, tears of fear, rage and anger, but above all misery. For she suddenly realized that the only person in the world she really trusted, the only person who had believed in her innocence, had just walked away from her. Until that moment she had never understood so completely how it was possible to feel such utter loneliness and desolation surrounded by so many people.

Raffe bounded up the stairs to Ma Margot's chamber two at a time. He knocked on the heavy oak door, but didn't bother waiting for an answer before he burst in. The chamber was empty. The shutters, as always, were tightly shut and only a single candle burned on the wall behind the serpent chair. A hooded sparrowhawk perched on a block of wood on the table. The bird flapped its wings angrily as the draught from the open door ruffled its downy breast feathers. Raffe instinctively reached out a finger to stroke it, soothing it with murmurs of reassurance, but a vicious peck from the curved beak made him withdraw his finger with a curse, and he sucked it, trying to stem the flow of blood.

A low chuckle made Raffe jerk round. Ma was standing in front of the curtain.

'She's been taught to defend herself even when she is hooded. Haven't you, my angel?'

Raffe's temper reboiled with the throbbing of his finger. 'What's this I hear about Hugh coming here? Talbot didn't tell me that.'

Ma shook her head warningly, then twitched back the curtain. Luce was standing behind it, her shift clutched in front of her, but otherwise as naked as the day she was born. She was panting slightly. Her face was flushed and her eyes danced brightly in the candlelight. Ma smiled up at her and jerked her head towards the door. With a wink at Raffe, Luce slid as lithely as an otter from the room.

Ma mounted the steps to her own serpent's chair.

'Sit, Master Raffe, you're making the bird nervous. Now

come, you know we never discuss our customers. Not, that is, unless they wind up dead at your friend's hands.'

'Elena didn't kill Raoul!'

But even as Raffe said it he knew he sounded like a man who was lashing out from uncertainty. He couldn't even convince himself of the truth of that. This was the second time in a few months Elena had been accused of murder. Was that just unlucky? Both times he'd so desperately wanted to believe that she was innocent, but then once he'd thought she was a virgin and all that time she'd been sneaking off behind his back to trysts with that lout Athan, even when she swore to him she was not going to see a man.

Part of him had dreaded seeing Elena again and yet he couldn't keep away. He hadn't been able to bring himself to look at her at first, because he knew that Raoul had had the pleasure of her. He had wanted to punish her, make her the whore she was, but now that it had happened, he was terrified of seeing that look of hardness in her eyes, that loss of innocence that had still remained even after Athan had bedded her. He wanted to seize her and shake her until she told him every single filthy thing that she and Raoul had done together. He wanted to know in each minute detail how she had looked when Raoul had touched her, what she had said, what she'd thought, what she felt.

Yet Raffe knew that if Elena had told him, he would have pressed his fingers to his ears and run away screaming. He had tried to convince himself that nothing she had done with Raoul would have been done willingly. Yet there was a worm that burrowed into his head, a worm of jealousy and doubt that made him lash himself over and over again with the thought that she might have surrendered herself to Raoul as willingly as she had once done to Athan. Even the smallest whimper of pleasure, the tiniest thrust towards Raoul's body would have been an act of betrayal.

And yes, Elena could have given herself entirely to Raoul and still have murdered him. He'd known women in the Holy

Land, fragile, delicate beauties who could whisper words of undying love and press their soft lips to a man's mouth. And then, as they fondled his manhood with one hand, with the other they'd pushed a knife between his ribs, as coldly as any battled-hardened soldier. Women could be far more ruthless than men when they had made up their minds to kill.

Raffe's face was burning, and he was suddenly aware that Ma was watching him with that usual knowing smile of hers. He was seized with the desire to wring her filthy neck, but instead he contented himself with trying to wound her pride.

'I thought you always said that not even a tick from a dog could crawl in or out of here without you or Talbot knowing about it. Are you telling me a simple girl managed to escape and get herself back in here and murder someone without you seeing her? You're getting old, Ma, losing your touch. Eyesight failing? Nodding off at your window?'

But if he hoped to needle her, he should have known better. She merely raised her thick black brows, like a schoolmaster warning an errant pupil.

'Talbot and I were attending to other things. The girl could easily have slipped out through the door. And there are other ways out of here,' Ma said. 'I found her in the cellar with that boy Finch; who knows what else she or that little brat has discovered. Too inquisitive for their own good, the pair of them. Besides, there's some that have the power to send out their spirits to do mischief while their bodies lie sleeping, even when they are locked in a gaol.'

But Raffe wasn't listening. 'The cellar, you found her in the cellar, what has she seen there?'

The ghost of a smile slid across Ma's mouth. 'My pets, *all* my pets.'

A chill ran through Raffe's frame. 'You told her about the man?'

Ma pulled the ruby pin from her hair and spun it idly in her fingers so that sparks of blood seemed to fly from it around the room. 'Told her? Now just what could I tell her, Master Raffe?'

Raffe tried to resist staring at the whirling ruby lights. He struggled to pull his thoughts together. Think! Hugh, that's what mattered now.

'Why did Hugh come here?'

Ma laughed again. 'Why does any man come here? He has needs, desires he can't satiate anywhere else, well, not without a deal of questions being asked. I dare say even he can't do as he pleases with his servant boys without raising a few objections. And, you know, men are curiously shy about having the whole world know the exact depths of those stinking mires in which their desires frolic.'

'Does Hugh know Raoul came here too?'

'According to Talbot's informants at the Adam and Eve, Raoul didn't know of this place until he arrived in Norwich, so he won't have told anyone in the manor where he was going, and Talbot saw to it that the bailiff made no report of it to the sheriff.'

Raffe frowned. He sensed Ma knew something, something she had no intention of telling him. That night Hugh had almost caught the priest anointing Gerard's body, Hugh had claimed to have been waiting for Raoul to return from Norwich. Raffe had been so preoccupied that he hadn't even considered why Hugh was so anxiously waiting until now. If Hugh feared that Raoul had discovered his treachery, or was about to do so, might he not have sent someone to follow Raoul and silence him? Had he been waiting in fact not for Raoul's return, but for news that the deed was done? And now Hugh had come here. Ma had said it was for pleasure, but what if he had realized that Elena had overheard his plotting in the manor? Having got rid of Raoul, he would certainly not hesitate to murder her too to keep his secret.

Raffe moistened his dry lips with his tongue. 'I must move Elena to a safer place. If Hugh has been here once, he is very likely to return, and even with her dyed hair, he will surely remember her eventually.'

Ma's brows arched for the second time that evening. 'And

if she's caught and tells them where she's been hiding and where she met Raoul? I don't think so, my darling. I want her here where I can make quite sure she doesn't get the chance to open her mouth. Besides, she's hardly paid for her keep and my trouble. And think of all the effort we've put into protecting her.'

'You can trust her not to talk, I swear, and I will pay what is owed for her keep,'

Ma's lips curled in a humourless smile. 'Anyone can be made to talk. And unless you've suddenly come into a fortune, my darling, I rather fancy you'll find that paying me and whoever you next ask to shelter the girl will leave you with a debt you cannot possible repay. And not everyone is as patient as I am when they are asked to wait for their money. Tongues grow slack when bellies are empty, and the price on the girl's head as a double murderer will weigh heavier than a crown. There are those unscrupulous rogues who could find themselves sorely tempted, Master Raffe, and we wouldn't want to put temptation in their way, now, would we?'

Raffe was about to open his mouth to reply when Ma stopped him with a wave of her hand.

'Before you make up your mind, let's ask my angel, shall we?'

She reached for a small wooden box on the table. Ma's tastes usually ran to objects that were jewelled and elaborately carved, but this box was plain save for the carving of a single eye framed by a triangle in the centre. The eye had been inlaid with ivory, with a glistening pupil of blackest jet.

Ma gently slipped the hood from the sparrowhawk's head, and the bird shook out its feathers, staring around the room, its bright yellow eyes searching for something. With the bird's hooked beak inches from his face, and his finger still smarting, Raffe could not help but slide his chair back a little, and Ma laughed.

'She'll not harm you, unless you touch her.'

Ma flicked open the box and pulled out a handful of strips of parchment which she fanned out in her hand. Then she spread the other hand, the heavy rings flashing in front of the bird.

'Tell me, Master Raffe, what can all men feel, but none can hold? What is so strong it can destroy a forest with a single blow and yet is small enough to creep through the smallest chink?'

'The wind, of course,' Raffe said more sharply than he meant to, because he couldn't anticipate what she was going to do. 'Every child knows that riddle.'

'But how easily we forget what we learned as children, my darling. As you say, it is the wind, and it is the wind which carries this bird to the heavens. Every word men utter of truth and lies, knowledge and ignorance is borne on the wind, but only a creature of the wind may catch them.'

She held out the fan of strips towards the bird. Rapidly it leaned forward and pulled one, two, three strips from her hand and dropped them on the table as if it was plucking feathers from its prey. Ma laid the strips in a neat row, then reached for something in the shadows. It was a tiny wicker cage. She opened the door wide.

If the skylark had only stayed in its cage, it would have been safe, it would have lived. Whether the foolish creature didn't see the sparrowhawk, or whether it just made a wild, brave dash for freedom, thinking, if indeed it thought at all, that soaring upwards would save it, who can tell? But the skylark didn't even reach the topmost beam in the room. Raffe felt the hawk's wingtip brush his face as it shot past him and heard it land with a thud on the floor, the tiny bird dead between its claws.

Ma didn't even turn her head to look, but stared instead at the symbols on the three strips of parchment the bird had pulled from her hand.

'The wind carries treachery, Master Raffaele. But whether you are the betrayer or the betrayed, you alone know.'

Raffe rose, flinging the chair back. He strode from the room and thundered down the stairs. He didn't know what he had hoped to achieve in that chamber or what he had thought he would learn. He had meant to tell Ma not to admit Hugh again, but he knew that even had he begged her on bended knee she would do precisely what it pleased her to do. How much did Ma know about the message from France? Was that demonstration with the bird meant as a threat not to remove Elena or a warning of something else?

Without even thinking what he was doing, he hurried across the courtyard to the room where the boys entertained. It was deserted, as he expected it to be, since the noon bell had not yet sounded from the churches in the city.

He made his way to the back of the room and found the low doorway. He peered at it, looking for a latch, but the thick boards were smooth. It had been five years or more since he'd last forced himself to come here. How had Ma opened the door then? Surely there had been a latch? He tried to visualize Ma standing in front of him at this door. She'd stood on tiptoe, reaching up for something. He remembered that. Was it a hidden key?

Raffe groped back and forth along the door until he felt a small hole. It came back to him now. She'd used a knife. He withdrew his own knife from his belt and slid the point inside until it hit metal. Wriggling the blade, he managed to slide it under the metal bar and felt the latch rise on the other side. He pushed the door and it swung open.

It was as well that he'd had to bend double and almost crawl through the doorway, otherwise he would have surely cracked his head open on the stone archway on the other side, but once under it, he could just about stand upright at the top of the stairs. The stench of animal piss, rotting meat and dampness hit him with the force of a siege engine, making his eyes sting and water. Surely it hadn't been this foul before? He groped his way down, sliding his hand along the dripping walls until, half-way down, he reached the torch burning on the wall and removed it from the bracket.

As he passed each cage, the animals snarled or growled,

some shrinking back from the blazing torch, others hurling themselves at the bars, their sharp teeth glistening in the flames. How many times had they beaten themselves on those bars over the long days and nights that stretched together to form interminable years? And yet they had still not learned that the iron would not yield. Was it impotent rage or unshakeable hope that made them do it, Raffe wondered, or perhaps making humans flinch just amused them.

He threaded his way past the animals, keeping to the middle of the passageway so as not to brush against any of the cages. He knew what such beasts were capable of. Behind him he could hear the rasp of hot, fetid breath and the click of sharp claws on iron as the beasts restlessly prowled up and down in their straw. The heavy animal odours of fur and dung filled his nostrils and burned the back of his throat. He closed his eyes, wondering just how long it would take a man to get used to these smells and sounds and know it for his home.

Opening his eyes again, Raffe edged forward until the light from the torch fell on the last cage. Its occupant was awake, sitting up, no doubt roused by the disturbance of the beasts and the flames moving towards him. He stared at Raffe, blinking in the sudden light. His expression revealed no recognition, only curiosity. He lifted his arm, brushing the wild hair back from his eyes with his stump, and tilted his face up. He shuffled forward on his knees, dragging the twisted remains of his legs behind him, holding out his mutilated arms as if he was begging, though Raffe noticed he didn't extend them through the bars, as if afraid that someone might hurt him. The bars were as much his protection as his cage.

Raffe crouched down until he was on a level with the man. 'You know me?' he asked softly.

The man blinked his startlingly blue eyes, holding out his arms again, this time more insistently, but with no sign of recognition in his face. Raffe cursed himself that he hadn't brought food. Then he remembered the leather bottle he always carried at his waist. He felt for it. He'd drunk most of the contents on the journey here, but there was a little wine left. He took out the wooden stopper and held the mouth of the bottle through the bars. For a while the man in the cage simply stared at it as if he had forgotten what the object was.

'Drink,' Raffe urged.

Slowly the man shuffled forward again, finally putting his lips to the bottle. Raffe tilted it and the liquid ran down, making the man choke and cough, but when Raffe tried to ease the flow, he grasped it with both stumps, pulling it towards him and sucking and sucking until finally convinced there was not a drop more left inside, then he it let go.

Raffe squatted down on the damp flags of the cellar opposite the cage. For a long time the two men stared at each other.

'Do you remember me?' Raffe asked again, searching for the merest flicker of recognition, but the man's face was expressionless. He offered nothing.

A man had looked at him like that once before, when he was just a boy. Raffe could remember it even now, his father standing there framed in the great doorway of the abbey church, the sun burning so fiercely behind him that the hills were bleached white in the light. Raffe had looked back as the priest led him away down the long aisle of the church. His father was just standing there motionless, his broad hat in his hand, his face tanned to the colour of the soil, but there had been no expression at all in his eyes. Nothing. He'd watched his son being led away, as unmoved as the ancient olive trees on their farm. Relieved, maybe, that he need not work so hard now; proud, perhaps, of what his son would achieve? Who knows, Raffe certainly didn't, for his father had never seen the need for words.

Raffe turned his face away from the man in the cage, kneeling on the cold flags.

'Talbot told me that this is not my country. So why should I care who sits on the throne of England? John is not my king. I owe him nothing. I am betraying nothing. All that matters, all any man can be expected to do, is to protect the ones he loves. I have to save them.'

Raffe stood up and began to pace back and forward, as restless as the caged beasts.

'Anne and Elena, they are both part of Gerard. As long as Elena still carries what he did in her soul, there is hope for Gerard in the next life. But I don't know how to protect them. I don't know what to do. If I take Elena from here, I might be taking her to her death. In here she is safe. She is alive.'

He turned to face the man in the cage whose blue eyes stared out at him fixedly from the grime-blackened face.

'I had to make that choice once before, and I need to know if I was wrong, if I made the wrong choice. This may be the last time I can come to you. What I did, what I am about to do, I do only for love. You cannot ask any man to harm what he has given his very soul to protect.'

Raffe gripped the bars of the cage, shaking them violently, as if he could wrest an answer from the man who crouched in the straw.

'You have to forgive me. You have to give me absolution. There is no one else left who can . . . speak to me, damn you, just speak! Just one word, one sign even, that's all I ask, just one!'

But the man in the cage didn't move. The torchlight flickered as twin flames in the great black pupils of his eyes, but he didn't take his gaze from Raffe's face. All around him the animals prowled restlessly up and down, their paws rustling through the straw, their claws clicking against the iron bars, and somewhere in the far distance came the hollow dripping of water, like a giant heartbeat, falling ceaselessly down into the gaping black hole in the floor.

Raffe picked up the torch and threaded his way back up between the beasts' cages. They too stared at him as the flame passed them, and they watched him as the darkness ebbed back behind him. Raffe felt their glowing eyes on his spine, but he did not turn around. As he mounted the steps, the darkness obliterated any trace of his presence as the tide washes footsteps from the sand.

But it wasn't until the very last ghost of light had vanished from the cellar that the man in the cage finally whispered, 'I do forgive you, Raffaele, because I know you will never forgive yourself.'

But only the great black cat heard him utter a word.

The Day of the Full Moon, September 1211

Seagulls – To kill a gull is to murder a man, for gulls that hover restlessly over the waves are the souls of drowned men. A gull which flies unerringly in a straight line follows a corpse that drifts beneath the waves. It is the unquiet spirit of that mortal, which cannot abandon the body that once was its home.

When sailors or fishermen die they are transformed into gulls, for the wind and the waves have captured their souls and they cannot leave the sea. The mortals took from the sea while they lived and now in their death they must pay for what they took. It is a devil's bargain.

If a gull should strike the casement of a house, a member of that household out at sea is in mortal peril.

When seagulls fly inland, a storm is brewing out at sea. But if they fly out to sea or rest upon the sand of the shore, the weather is set to be fair.

Mortals fear to look a seagull in the eye, for if they do the gull will know them and remember them. And should that mortal then ever venture to swim in the sea or fall from a ship into the waves, they will be at the mercy of that gull. It will peck out their eyes and leave them blinded and helpless to their fate.

For like the sea itself, gulls show no mercy to mortals who are foolish enough to venture into their kingdom.

The Mandrake's Herbal

The Sea Is Coming

Raffe stepped from the boat on to the island that was Yarmouth. He slid a coin into the palm of the boatman, who appraised it carefully before hiding it among his clothes. Shivering in the grey dawn light, he picked his way along the slippery wooden jetty that jutted out into Breydon Water, where the three great rivers surged into the salt water of the estuary. The gravel beneath Raffe's feet sparkled with silver fish scales. They were everywhere, dried and blowing in the wind, heaping in tiny transparent drifts like snow against the buildings.

He made for the Rows stretched out on either side of him, a hundred or so alleys running parallel to one another down to the open sea. He chose one at random and edged down it; the passage was so narrow that in places he could have touched the walls on either side. An open sewer ran down the middle, like the vein on the back of a shrimp, but the sharp salt breeze funnelling through it mercifully blew away much of the stench of excrement and rotting food, leaving only the overpowering smell of fish which clung to the tarred wood of the buildings like a second skin.

Many of the dwellings also served as shops or workshops, their goods spilling out into the narrow street to make space for the day's work in the tiny rooms. Dotted between the tiny wooden houses were small courtyards where he glimpsed women cooking over open fires, weaving creels or pounding linen in their wash tubs. Their fingers never once paused in their labour, nor did their tongues cease from chattering to their neighbours, but their sharp eyes missed nothing. Raffe kept a firm hand on his purse as he was jostled backwards and forwards, for ports were notorious for the rogues they attracted.

He breathed easier when he finally burst from the end of the Row and found himself on the seashore. There was no less activity here. Everywhere as far as the eye could see along the sand, men were busy making or repairing boats, or striding past with baskets of fish, or unloading bales, kegs and boxes on the precarious wooden jetties that jutted out into the waves. And beyond them in the grey sea, the great sailing ships rolled at anchor, while tiny shoreboats plied back and forth among them like shoals of sardines among whales.

Raffe tramped half the length of the beach looking for the *Dragon's Breath*, but it was impossible to pick out one vessel among all the ships out there. He enquired of a few of the men, but each shook his head, too many boats coming and going.

'Toll house.' One fisherman jerked his head towards the far end of the shore. 'They keep tallies of all ships, so as they can collect the toll.'

Raffe found the wooden building easily enough, but finding someone to speak to was another matter. He made his way up the outside steps to a square room, crammed with small tables and crowded with merchants and ships' captains shouting and waving rolls of parchments heavy with wax seals. Eventually, Raffe managed to force his way through the throng and by sheer dint of grabbing hold of a man bodily, managed to get his attention.

'Can you tell me if the *Dragon's Breath* has put in here?'

The harassed-looking clerk gave a squeak of laughter at the sound of Raffe's high-pitched voice, but quickly straightened his face and wearily gestured towards a great stack of parchments on his table, rolling his eyes. Raffe slipped a silver coin into his palm.

'Came in yesterday,' he muttered. 'Dealt with her myself. Wine, spices mostly, some timber, not good quality. Ivory, five bales of furs, wolf and bear, no sable and –'

'Where's her shoreboat?' Raffe interrupted impatiently. The clerk huffled a little, clearly insulted that his feat of memory was not being given the admiration it deserved. His hand slid again over the table, but Raffe was not about to part with another coin. He'd not forgotten or forgiven that laughter.

He leaned across the table, pushing his face into the clerk's. 'I said, where is it?'

The clerk glowered at him, but seeing that Raffe wasn't going to move away, he gestured back in the direction he'd come. 'Crew'll be in the Silver Treasure, up Shrieking Row.'

It took Raffe a while to find the Row for the names were known only to the local townsfolk. Finally one old fishwife grudgingly directed him to Shrieking Row and, once there, Raffe quickly spotted the Silver Treasure by the carved herring above the door, together with the few twigs of a dried bush that proclaimed it as an alehouse.

It was still early morning, so most men were hard at their labours, but those who had no pressing business to attend to sat in the small yard to the side of the house, pouring ale down their throats from blackened leather beakers as if they hadn't slaked their thirst for a week. From the stench of them, Raffe took them to be fishermen. He ignored them and peered into the tiny room beside the courtyard. Three men sat on benches around a narrow table, talking in low voices and evidently haggling over some deal. The only other furniture in the room was a rickety ladder leading through a trapdoor to the attic above.

As Raffe slid in through the open doorway, blocking out the light, the men looked up sharply and, just as swiftly, a hand covered some object lying on the table and swept it from sight, but not before Raffe had glimpsed the wine-red flash of a ruby.

'I'm looking for the crew of the *Dragon's Breath*.'

'You have business with them?' one of the men asked in a thick Spanish accent.

'I've come to take delivery of some cargo.'

The man's mouth shrugged, as if to say he would need a good deal more than that before he revealed anything.

The sunken-cheeked alewife came in from the yard, rubbing

her hands on a filthy old scrap of ship's sail tied around her waist to protect her skirts. 'More ale, masters?'

All three heads swivelled in Raffe's direction. He knew what was required of him.

'Bring a large flagon and another beaker.'

'As you please,' the woman said without the flicker of a smile. Raffe wondered if any emotion ever crossed her sallow face. All the life and colour in her eyes seemed to have been bleached out by sun and sea, leaving them with only the faintest tinge of faded blue, like watered-down milk.

One of the men slid his buttocks a few inches down the bench and Raffe took that as an invitation to join them at the rough table which was blackened with old tar, having been assembled from bits of old ships' timbers and driftwood.

After the alewife had slopped a brimming flagon of ale down between them and drifted back outside, Raffe poured the ale into the men's beakers and tried again.

'The cargo I've to collect is a live one.'

They regarded him steadily, their faces tanned almost to the colour of the beakers, betraying nothing. Raffe wondered if they could even understand him.

He delved into his scrip and laid a tin emblem of St Katherine's wheel on the rough table.

All three men regarded it for some time in silence, then the leader picked it up and returned it to Raffe. 'This cargo, where does it come from?'

'Spinolarei in Bruges.' It was what Talbot had told him to say, though Raffe doubted his visitor had ever set foot on that particular quayside.

The sailor nodded.

'Can you take me out to him?' Raffe asked, taking this nod to be the only sign of acknowledgement he was going to get.

'No, no!' the sailor said with unexpected vehemence. Then he seemed to realize some kind of explanation was called for. 'Captain does not want strangers on ship. But I fetch him. You have money?'

Raffe pulled out a leather purse and unfastened the draw-string, tipping the contents into his hand.

The sailor spat contemptuously on to the floor.

'Not enough. We have others to pay. Much expense. I need more.'

Raffe had expected they would, but none the less he made a show of arguing that was all he would pay, until finally, seeing that the sailor would not budge, he reached under his shirt and pulled out the gold ring which dangled from a leather thong about his neck. Without removing the thong he leaned forward so that the sailor could examine the intricate gold knot that held in place a single lustrous pearl beneath. It had been Gerard's ring and his father's before that. It was on this ring, the hour Gerard died, that Raffe had sworn his oath that he would not let him carry his sins to the grave.

On the day that Lady Anne had drawn it from the hand of her dead son and given it to him, Raffe had believed that he would never part with it, but now . . . now he could not bear to keep it. He knew it for what it was: tainted, bloody, like the withered hand of a thief. And if it would buy Lady Anne's protection and keep the priest from betraying her, then giving it away would be an act of cleansing, an absolution for what he done. He could almost convince himself that the ring had been given into his hands for this very purpose.

The sailor peered at the finely wrought design. Then he beckoned, indicating that Raffe should hand it over.

'No, no, my friend, I am not that stupid. You bring the cargo, then I pay you.'

The sailor glowered at him, then bent his head to his companions, muttering softly. But even had they shouted their conversation across the room, it would scarcely have mattered, for Raffe couldn't understand them.

Finally the man straightened up. 'We take the ring now. Then you give us the purse when we bring your cargo.'

Raffe hesitated. He could see that they were not the kind of men who would be prepared to leave with nothing, and the ring was easier to identify than coins if they tried to double-cross him.

Raffe pulled the leather thong over his neck. The sailor swiftly examined the ring once more. Clearly he had learned not to trust any man. Then he looped the thong over his own head, dropping the ring down inside his shirt even as he strode to the door.

'Tonight I bring him here. But I do not wait. You are here, good. If not, your cargo it sinks to the bottom of the sea, you understand?' He returned a few paces to Raffe, staring him in the face. 'Tonight you give me the purse, no argument. You try to cheat me, and the crabs they have a good breakfast.'

The sailor spat on the palm of his hand and extended it to Raffe. He did likewise and they shook, their fingers gripping each other's with equal force. The transaction was sealed and there was no going back on it.

She gingerly pushes open the door of the courtyard, alert for an ambush. The sun is burning down, bleaching the stones a dazzling white, and for a moment she is blinded, unable to see anything. Then she hears the sound of fast, rapid breathing. Three girls are crouching in the corner of the tiny yard, pressed into a sliver of dark shadow, their arms wrapped around one another, their heads buried into one another's chests, so that they seem to be a single ball of limbs. Flies crawl everywhere in thick black waves, over the weeds as dry as parchment, over the dusty ewers, over the backs of the girls. As they hear the sound of footsteps behind them one of the girls begins to whimper, but they do not move.

Elena is thirsty and running with sweat. She is weary to the bone. She just wants to get this over with, get it finished. She strides to the corner and grabs an arm at random, trying to prise the little knot of bodies apart. But the others cling to their sister with surprising strength, considering how skeletally thin they are. Elena is almost afraid that if she pulls too hard, the bone of this slender arm will snap off in her fist. But pull she must. She seizes the girl round the waist and drags her out. The two remaining sisters snap together, clinging to one another more fiercely than before.

The girl struggles, but soon her arms are bound behind her. She stands sobbing and helpless. She is trying to mumble something. Is it a plea for mercy or a fervent prayer? Elena cannot tell. But whatever she is saying is repeatedly broken each time a new scream echoes through the street outside. Some screams continue on and on, like the wind howling. Others are cut abruptly short, severed in mid-cry. Although Elena longs for the screams to stop, her heart jolts with pain each time they do.

Elena has pulled a second sister out from the corner and is tying her wrists. This one does not even try to resist. She is numb, her eyes glazed and lifeless as if she is already dead.

But as Elena binds the two sisters together, one behind the other, the third girl suddenly springs up from the corner. Before Elena can stop her she is running for the stone steps that lead up from the yard. Elena tries to make a grab for the hem of her skirts, but the cloth slips through her fingers. The young girl bounds up the stairs in her bare feet. At the top she turns and lifts her face up to the golden sunlight. Then she closes her eyes and jumps. She crashes down on to the flags of the courtyard, and lies there, her legs twisted at grotesque angles. A trickle of scarlet blood runs from her head, and meanders slowly over the white stones. The flies are already crawling towards her.

But the fall was not high enough. She is still alive, still twitching. Her bones are broken, but her brown eyes are wide open and crazed with pain. Her two sisters stare at her aghast, then as one they begin to scream. She looks at them, her mouth opening wordlessly, her eyes pleading desperately for help. They struggle to cross to her, but they are tethered and cannot even reach out their hands to hold hers.

Elena watches the tears running down their faces. It shouldn't matter. She shouldn't care. She's seen the tears on hundreds of faces today, young and old. The sisters' fate will be the same as all the others'. Minutes, hours, what difference can it make in the end? By the time the sun sets today they will see nothing, feel nothing any more. For what seems like eternity she stares at the flies swarming over the trickle of blood. Then she crosses swiftly to the girl on the ground and cups her left hand over the pleading brown eyes. With her right hand she pulls out her dagger and plunges it into the girl's heart.

*

The clouds had been building all day, and now great purple walls of them were towering over the lead-grey sea. The wind was howling and white waves charged towards the land, rearing up and crashing down on to the shore, sucking up great mouthfuls of sand to be spewed out again as the tide rose higher and higher up the beach. The gulls had long since deserted the island of Yarmouth and fled inland, shrieking doom like witches in the sky.

Men were dragging the smaller craft out of the water and pulling them as far up the shore as they could. Others were sculling the bigger boats which could not be beached out into the deeper water. Once the boats were safely anchored and the ropes tethered to the shore to ensure they couldn't twist side-on in the wind, the men dived into the waves, hauling themselves by the mooring ropes back to the beach.

The wind funnelled between the Rows, moaning like the damned in hell, and sending the dried silver fish scales whirling in the air, stinging the faces of the men as they hurried back to their homes. Fish oil lamps began to flicker in the upper rooms and the tiny wooden houses hunkered down and braced themselves for what the night might bring.

Raffe trudged back to the Silver Treasure. The wind was too sharp now for anyone to be loitering in the yard and the brazier had been extinguished. The little ale room too was empty save for a solitary old man with red-rimmed eyes, who sat hunched in the corner over his leather beaker.

He raised his watery eyes as Raffe struggled to close the door against the wind.

'Dead are coming,' the old man pronounced solemnly.

Raffe nodded without understanding. The door opened and the alewife brought in a small flagon and a beaker. She banged them down in front of Raffe and waited, hand on hip, for the coin. Her face was as expressionless as before. She crossed to the old man to refill his empty beaker.

'Last one, then it's home with you. Your daughter'll be wanting to bar the door afore the wind takes it.'

'Where's he going?' the old man asked. They both turned to stare at Raffe from their hollow, sea-bleached eyes.

The woman shrugged. 'He's to wait,' she said, as if she knew all about Raffe's business.

Outside the skies darkened and the wind rattled any loose pieces of wood or reed-thatch it could find, like a naughty child testing to see if it could be yanked off. Raffe walked over to the door. He opened it a crack, holding it tightly against the wind. The Row was deserted. Here and there in the dim pools of yellow light cast by the oil lamps in the casements he could see small pieces of gravel being hurled up the alley by the wind, and in the far distance at the end of the Row, he glimpsed flashes of white foam on the tar-dark water.

Raffe was torn with indecision. Part of him was sure they would not come tonight. Surely no one would want to commit their lives to a little craft in these seas? Yet he dared not leave, for he had little doubt they were capable of carrying out their threat if they came and he wasn't waiting.

Forcing the door closed again, he slumped back down on the bench. The old man drained the last of his ale and hopped to the door, leaning heavily on a crutch.

'Be sure and give the sea back her dues, afore she comes to take them,' he muttered.

The door had scarcely shut behind him again when it flew open with bang. The sailor from the *Dragon's Breath* stood in the doorway, wiping his spray-wetted face on his sleeve and peering into the dimly lit room. He saw Raffe and grunted, pushing a man in through the door in front of him.

'Your cargo,' the sailor said, without any greeting. 'My purse.' He held out his open hand. The skin on his palm was thicker than the hide on a man's heel, but across it and between the fingers were deep raw cracks from the cold and the salt which would never heal, not until he settled ashore. And that was not likely to be anytime soon, for when a man's got salt water in his blood and a sea wind in his lungs, neither wife nor land can keep him from the waves.

Raffe ignored the outstretched hand and regarded the newcomer. He was short and slight, made to seem smaller by the muscular sailor standing beside him. His cloak was still pulled tightly around him and his face had a sallow, greenish tinge of one who is about to vomit. He swayed slightly on his feet. Then, stumbling towards a bench, he sank on to it.

The sailor was still holding out his hand, but Raffe gestured impatiently for him to wait. The Frenchman was leaning on the table, holding his head as though it would roll off his neck if he didn't hold it in place. He had a clerk's hand with thin fingers and swollen knuckles, as if he'd spent many hours writing in the cold, but his left hand was twisted and scaly like a bird's claw, though he could plainly use it to grasp, albeit clumsily.

'How do I know this is the man?' Raffe demanded, still regarding the Frenchman.

Without raising his head the man opened his tunic; the badge of St Katherine was pinned inside.

The sailor clapped a heavy hand on Raffe's shoulder and spun him round. 'You give me the purse now! Storm is coming.'

To lend weight to his words, there was a roar and a clatter as a violent gust of wind dashed a handful of gravel against the wooden wall of the alehouse. Raffe slid the purse across to the sailor. He opened it, counting the coins, then he slipped it into his shirt. At the door he turned, grinning, showing a large gap in the front teeth, and gestured towards the hunched man.

'He thinks he escapes the sea. He don't like her. But the sea, she still wants to play with him. Women are like that, no? When you tire of them, that's when they want to make love to you.'

As the sailor struggled to close the door, the alewife ducked in under his arm, carrying a small sacking bundle. She set it on the table and unwrapped it, displaying some coarse dark bread and two small cooked herring.

'We can't stay to eat,' Raffe explained. 'We have to leave straight away to get to the mainland. I have a boat waiting.'

The woman ignored him and crossed to the door and, lifting

a stout beam of wood, set it in the iron brackets across the door to brace it shut.

Raffe started forward. 'No, you don't understand, we have to leave.'

The woman turned to him, her hands on her hips, her body square in the doorway.

'There'll be no man willing to take you ashore tonight, tide's running in fast against the rivers. That wind'll push it hard in, but rivers'll only be pushed so far, then they'll come roaring back. You'd best stay here tonight, less you want to play with the sea, like the sailor said.'

She climbed the rickety ladder to the upper chamber and, moments later, two long thick pallets tumbled through the trapdoor and fell in a heap on the floor below. The woman leaned forward and squinted down at Raffe through the hatch.

'Mind you don't open that door again tonight till it's light, no matter who begs to come in. There's some foreigners would cut your throat just for a parcel of herring heads.'

She glowered at them both, as if she suspected the pair of them were in league with a band of murderers. Then she heaved the ladder upwards till it disappeared through the hole in the ceiling and the trapdoor fell down with a loud clatter. Raffe heard a beam of wood being drawn over the trap to brace it firmly shut.

Raffe cursed under his breath. All he wanted was to get this Frenchman to Norwich and off his hands as quickly as possible. He'd arranged to lodge the man in the north of the city among the tanners, who could be counted upon to keep their own counsel, for they loathed the sheriff as much as he despised them. And the knowledge that this part of the city was just about the most unpleasant and noxious a place as you could lodge any man was, for Raffe, an added bonus. But he knew there would be no way off the island tonight, not in this wind. And if he was forced to spend the night with this spy, the isle of Yarmouth was the best refuge they could hope to find themselves in if they wanted to avoid John's men.

Two years or so back, King John had made Yarmouth a Charter town, not from a sudden rush of generosity, of course, but as a way of raising more gold for his coffers, for the townspeople had to pay him fifty-five pounds a year for the privilege, far more than he could shake out of them in taxes. But it meant they administered the king's justice now and collected the tolls, so officially there were none of John's officers here. Raffe was certain, of course, that John would have men in the town who were paid to send regular reports to him, for he'd trust no one in Yarmouth, not with all the foreign ships coming to trade. But if John's men had found out about this Frenchman, they could no more get a message off the island tonight than Raffe could. So as long as the storm raged they were safe. After that, all he could do was pray.

Raffe arranged the pallets on either side of the banked-down fire and lay down on one fully clothed. It crackled as he shifted his weight. It was a sailor's pallet, fashioned from bits of old sailcloth patched together and stuffed with feathers. The cloth had been repeatedly rubbed with wax and tallow to waterproof it. Twine was bound around each corner to form handholds, so it could be used as a float if the ship floundered.

The Frenchman, whose face was now a little less pale, swivelled round on his bench to face Raffe.

'What are you doing? Why are we not leaving?'

'You heard the alewife; no boat will put to sea this night. There is no other way off the island. We have to stay until morning.'

The stranger had turned pale again. 'I cannot stay here. I must get to Norwich. If your soldiers find me . . .'

Raffe propped himself up on his elbow, seething with resentment against this snivelling little wretch. The slightness of the man's build might have fitted him to a cloistered life, but he had a restlessness about him that would never be contained in a monastery. His gaze was constantly flicking round the room, never meeting your eyes for quite long enough.

He looked every inch like one of the scavengers who swarmed around great men, scrawny, hungry, feral cats waiting their chance to dart in and snatch a piece of wealth and glory.

'Be grateful for the storm,' Raffe said sourly. 'At least you won't be looking over your shoulder tonight. Neither John's men nor any other will be prowling the island on a night like this. It'll be a different story when you get to Norwich. You'll have to sleep with a knife in your hand there, that's if you dare risk sleeping at all.'

Raffe had no intention of making the man feel at ease. If he could add to his discomfort, he would.

'*If* we reach Norwich,' the man said. 'The Frenchmen on the *Santa Katarina*, they did not, I think.'

Raffe's head jerked up. 'What do you know of that ship?'

The Frenchman shrugged. 'That an ambush was waiting for her. It is rumoured there was a man on board called Faramond. He was well known in France for his services to Philip. You know of him?' The man kept his voice low, glancing up at the trapdoor.

'I know of nothing save that every passenger was lost,' Raffe said.

But Raffe knew the name of Faramond only too well. Elena had repeated it when she had spoken of the conversation she'd overheard in the manor. It was this Faramond Hugh had come to meet the night the *Santa Katarina* burned. That louse Hugh had fought for John once, and been rewarded well for it too, but he thought nothing of betraying him to the French.

There was silence for a moment, then the Frenchman persisted, 'You are sure Faramond did not make land?'

'Tell me about him,' Raffe said. 'Friend of yours, was he?'

'I did not have the pleasure of meeting him myself, though he was known to me. But if he was betrayed, how am I to know I will not be also? These boatmen you hired, you trust them? They are loyal to our cause?'

'I don't work for your cause!' Raffe blazed. 'I am doing this only because I must. As for the boatmen, they're loyal to gold. And that's the only loyalty you can count on in most men these days.'

'And what of these men I am sent to meet?' the Frenchman asked quietly.

'I told you, I know no one,' Raffe said.

It was all he could do to stop himself adding that if he did, they would already be in irons. But he was supposed to be helping this little piece of French shit. Lady Anne's life and his own depended on delivering him safely to Norwich. Raffe had to disguise his loathing for another few hours at least.

Raffe glanced over at the little Frenchman. 'I don't even know your name. What would you have me call you – *spy*?' In spite of his resolve Raffe couldn't help himself loading the word with the disgust he felt.

The bench creaked as the Frenchman shifted his weight. 'Martin,' he said without any sign that he had taken offence at the word.

Raffe hesitated. Could he ask this Frenchman directly if he was coming to meet Hugh? If he admitted to it, then it would be the proof Raffe needed that Hugh really was the traitor. But if Hugh found out Raffe was asking about him, before Raffe was able to act on the information, he could easily turn the tables on him. No one would take the word of a man like Raffe over that of a nobleman. Besides, Hugh had already been to the brothel once; what if he did remember where he'd seen Elena before and realized she was the girl who had been listening outside that room the night he talked of Faramond? One word that he was suspected might be all it would take to convince Hugh that Elena was a threat to his life and had to be silenced. Raffe couldn't risk that.

The Frenchman's gaze darted once more round the room as if he was trying to memorize all the doors and windows in case of attack. Finally, ignoring the empty pallet, he drew his legs up on to the bench and settled himself in the corner, prepared to sit out the night. He made no attempt to extinguish the oil lamp, so finally Raffe was forced to rise once more and blow it out, leaving only the faint ruby-red glow of the damped-down fire to give any shape to the tiny room.

Outside the little alehouse in Yarmouth, the thunder of the sea grew louder. The narrow Row funnelled the sound from the beach, so that it seemed as if the waves were breaking against the little house itself. The wind dashed sand and stone against its wooden walls, shaking the shutters like a child in a tantrum demanding to be allowed in. Still hunched in the corner of the bench, Martin didn't stir. Raffe, pulling his cloak more tightly around himself, finally drifted into a restless sleep.

He wasn't sure how long he'd slept, but he was jerked awake by something crashing against the wooden wall of the house. The roar of the wind and waves seemed even louder than before, but Raffe could have sworn he heard something else outside, a high-pitched cry, like the shrieking of gulls. But gulls didn't fly at night.

The room was in complete darkness. Even the glow of the fire had vanished. Raffe reached out his hand to adjust the cloak that covered him, and stifled a cry as he felt an icy wetness beneath his fingers. He tried to struggle up from the pallet and promptly slipped sideways with a splash. The floor was awash with water. It wasn't deep, just two or three inches at the most, but it had trickled into the fire pit, extinguishing the embers. He could smell the wet, acrid smoke.

Raffe splashed through the freezing water, cursing vehemently as he blundered into the table and scraped his shins against a bench. He groped along the wall until he felt the edge of the casement and unfastened the shutter of the tiny square window. The wind almost tore the thick wood from his hand. At first he couldn't make sense of what he saw. The ground outside was writhing as if the earth itself was unravelling. Then something black reared up, crashing into white foam inches from his face. The Row was deep in water, waves were being driven up the street, between the houses. The sea was surging in.

Almost blinded by the stinging spray, Raffe struggled to close the shutter, but as he fought with the wind, he became aware of something else. There were figures moving along the Row in the black water. It was so dark that it was hard to make out what they were, but he saw a hand pale against the oily water, a face half turned towards him made blurry by his watering eyes. Fishermen trying to reach their homes? Men trying to rescue the stranded? Raffe didn't know, but it was madness to be out there in this storm. How any man could stand against that surge was beyond his understanding.

He finally managed to slam the shutter against the wind. He groped for one of the benches and swung himself on to it, pulling up his legs as the Frenchman had done. His soaking feet were numb with cold. The water didn't seem to be rising too quickly. The heavy tarred door was doing its job well, but water was seeping in from somewhere, probably up through the floor itself, or else oozing through cracks between the tarred planks of the walls.

The timbers of the house creaked and groaned as the waves surged past it. Raffe found himself wondering how much it could withstand. If it started to collapse, it would go very quickly. They'd be crushed by the timbers. Would it be safer to be outside with those men? Were they fleeing collapsed homes? The walls trembled as the wind beat itself against them, shrieking with frustration and fury, as if the demons in hell were hurling themselves at the house.

Then he heard it, a fist beating on the thick wooden door. The sound was muffled, but there was no mistaking someone was knocking.

'Let me in. For pity's sake, let me in!'

The anguish in the voice was so terrible that Raffe found himself swinging his legs down before he remembered the alewife's instruction not to open the door to anyone. He pulled his legs up again.

The hammering came again. 'Let me in! Merciful heaven, I'm drowning. I'm drowning!'

Raffe tried to ignore it. There were other voices out there, raised above the wind, all begging and whimpering. He knew they were struggling in that freezing water, clinging on to anything they could grasp, desperate not to be dragged back into the raging sea.

'Let me in. I've been betrayed. You must let me in. They tried to kill me.'

Raffe glanced up at the ceiling. Was the alewife lying awake up there listening to the cries? Could she hear them above the wind?

The voice outside rose higher, shrieking desperately to make itself heard. 'Have mercy on me. I'm so cold, so very cold. I cannot bear it. For pity's sake, don't leave me out here in the dark.'

The fist hammered frantically against the door. The man outside was sobbing, screaming. Raffe could stand it no longer. He struggled to his feet, splashing across the room, and with numb hands tried to trace where the bracing beam was positioned in its brackets. He began to wriggle it loose, and had almost succeeded when he felt an ice-cold hand grasp his.

'No, no!' Martin shrieked at him. 'What are you doing? You must not open it.'

Raffe shrugged the hand off. 'Can't you hear him? A man is in trouble out there. We can't leave him to die.'

'Who? Who would be wandering abroad on such a night? I can hear nothing except the wind and water. If you open that door, the water will pour in and we will all drown, maybe even the house will fall.'

The voice outside rose again in a shriek for help, the pleas so tormented that Raffe felt as if a fist was twisting his guts.

'Can't you hear that?' Raffe shouted. He pushed Martin aside and began again to wrestle with the beam.

'It is just the storm you can hear,' Martin said. 'Things banging in the wind.'

Raffe could not believe that Martin was pretending not to

hear the man pleading for his life outside. That snivelling little wretch was such a coward, he was willing to let a man drown just inches away from where he stood and do nothing. Raffe fought with the beam and almost had it clear when a fist hit him so hard in the diaphragm that he doubled up, gasping and struggling to draw breath. He sank to his knees in the water, his hands clenching and unclenching, and he tried desperately to force air into his lungs, then finally, with a burst of effort that felt like an explosion inside him, he drew breath. He knelt there in the icy water wheezing painfully as he heard Martin forcing the beam back into place.

Raffe was still on all fours in the water gasping for breath when he felt Martin's legs against his thigh and the cold, sharp prick of a dagger in his back.

'Reach slowly and give me your knife,' Martin ordered.

Raffe reluctantly did as he was told. In his younger days, he could have disarmed the man in a trice, but he had a feeling that Martin, for all his weasel build, knew how to defend himself better than most.

'Now you will sit over there on that bench. And if you go near to the door again, I will kill you.'

The man's tone was suddenly cold and hard. There was a calm resolve in it which left Raffe in little doubt that he meant it.

They sat there opposite each other on the benches until daybreak, listening to the storm rampaging through the streets. Neither spoke again. The voice outside finally fell silent and the howling of the wind now seemed hollow and empty as if all life had vanished from the world.

Towards dawn, the storm died down and, despite the cold and his wet clothes, Raffe must have drifted off into some kind of sleep for he woke to the sound of the ladder creaking as the alewife descended into the room. A pale, milky light filled the room. The shutter stood open and Martin was peering out into the Row.

'The water, it has gone,' he said, turning to the alewife.

'Aye, well, it would. Sea goes back to its bed right enough, soon as the wind dies down.' She heaved the beam from the door and flung it open. Without even bothering to look out, she picked up a birch besom and began sweeping vigorously, shooing the black muddy water along the floor towards the open door.

'You'll be off then.' It was more a statement than a question.

She reminded Raffe of his own mother. She could never wait for the men to leave the house each morning. She regarded men and children as something to be shaken out with the dust, beaten out, if needs be.

Martin extended Raffe's knife to him, offering the hilt with his clawed hand. There was no embarrassment or apology, merely the curt return of it as you might hand over an object someone had accidentally dropped.

Raffe took the knife and at the same time grabbed Martin's arm with his other hand, pulling the little Frenchman in towards him.

'You try that again,' Raffe snarled, 'and you'll find my knife in your ribs instead of in your hand.'

'I hope,' Martin said levelly, 'that it will not be necessary to *try that again.*'

The alewife's besom nudged pointedly round their feet, compelling them to move towards the door and then leap swiftly out of it, as she swept a wave of filthy water towards them.

Outside, the small courtyard was a wreck. Although most of the water had indeed drained down the sloping Rows back into the sea, puddles still filled the smallest hollow. The tables and benches in the yard were smashed again into the pieces of driftwood from which they had been crafted, and lay in a heap against the far wall covered in wet sand. Barrels were stranded on their sides, bound fast in bright green seaweed. Dead fish stared up glassy-eyed from the sand or flopped desperately in the brackish puddles. Starfish, still twitching the tip of an arm, were strewn among lumps of tar, pieces of rope, broken flagons and a single rosy apple.

A movement drew Raffe's attention and as he watched, a large crab crawled out sideways from under a tangled piece of net and scuttled for safety towards the wood pile, holding a piece of something white in its raised claw. Now that the crab had drawn his attention, Raffe could see that there was something large and pale buried under the old net. He couldn't make out what it was. Mostly from idle curiosity he bent down and tried to disentangle the net, which had been so long in the sea it was covered with slime and goose barnacle shells. But the net was caught fast. As he pulled, something flopped out of the tangle on to the wet sand. It was the tattered sleeve of a garment, bleached of any colour, but it was not that which made Raffe drop the net hastily. Poking out from the end of the sleeve were the bones of a hand.

It took a whole breath before Raffe realized he was staring at a human corpse, or rather the upper half of one. Whoever the poor bastard was, he had been in the sea for a long time. Most of the face was eaten away and what little flesh remained clinging to the bones of his hands and chest was feathery and bone-white. A cluster of black winkles had adhered themselves to one of the rib bones and purple bladderwrack dangled from the bones of his neck.

There was a cry behind him and Raffe turned to see the alewife standing in the doorway, her birch besom fallen to the ground and both hands pressed across her mouth. A neighbour passing in the Row heard the cry and rushed over to her.

'Whatever is it?' the neighbour cooed soothingly, then, following the wild stare of the alewife, she gasped. She crossed herself several times before throwing her arms around the alewife. She tried to pull her inside, but the stricken woman wouldn't budge.

'It's my man, my Peter.'

The neighbour pressed her own hand over the alewife's mouth.

'Hush now, would you drown your own husband? There's

been no word his ship's come to any harm. He'll be walking in that door bold as you like one of these days. And you'll be giving him a right mithering afore he's even got his boots off.'

But the alewife shook her head. 'I knew he was gone that day the cormorant sat on the roof of our house from dawn to dusk. They always come to warn that a ship's foundered. It knew Peter was lost. It knew and came to tell me.'

The neighbour tried to pull her inside again. 'They found another corpse this morning. I've seen that one and that's not your Peter either. Dead always come back from the sea in their own time. But not your Peter, sweeting. Your Peter's not dead.'

The alewife shook her head. 'I know it's him come back to me. I heard him last night in the storm begging for me to let him in. Said he was cold, so cold. You heard him, didn't you, master, you heard my dead husband knocking at the door?'

She raised her head and looked straight at Raffe, though her pale eyes had no sight in them, only an endless streaming tide.

Two Days after the Full Moon, September 1211

Apples – If fruit and flower appear on the same branch it is an omen of death. For the Celts believe that in Paradise the hills are covered with apple trees that bear fruit and flowers together.

When plucking the fruit, some apples must always be left on the tree for the faerie folk and the spirits of the grove.

On Twelfth Night, all in the village must assemble at dusk bringing with them their iron pots and tools and choose one apple tree to stand for all. And to that tree all present must drink its health in cider and pour cider over the roots and hang bread soaked in cider in the branches. The lowest twigs are dipped in cider and men must bow down three times and rise staggering as if they bear a heavy sack of apples on their backs. Then must all the villagers bang their iron tools together to make as much noise as they can, to awaken the spirits of the tree, so that they will stir the trees to life and bring a good harvest.

Apples cure melancholia and eating an apple at midnight on All Hallows Eve will guard against colds for a year. At Samhain each unwed mortal standing around the fire whirls an apple on a piece of string. Whoever's apple falls first shall be married within the year, but the one whose apple falls last shall die unwed. If a maid would know if her lover is true, she should lay apple pips around the fire; if the pips burst with a pop her lover is faithful, but if they shrivel and burn silently her lover is deceiving her.

The Mandrake's Herbal

St Michael's Day

Lanterns were being hung all around the brothel garden, though it was not yet noon. Garlands of late flowers were being sprinkled hourly with cold water from the well to keep them fresh, but their perfume was fighting a losing battle against the spices and herbs of the pastries, honeyed fruits, roasting geese, baked meats and syllabubs, which were being stirred, basted and dressed in the kitchens. Low tables had been set ready beside the seats and turf banks, and later, as it grew dark, they would be groaning with food and wine.

Ma had hired extra cooks for the day, for the older women were needed to strew fresh herbs among the rushes, drape cloths artfully over the dark corners to give an illusion of privacy where there was none, and above all to help the girls dress. It was the glorious feast of Michaelmas and Ma Margot was determined not to be outdone in her celebrations. She stood back, hands on hips, gazing up with satisfaction at the centrepiece she had commissioned for her garden. It was a wooden life-sized statue of a standing naked woman with angel wings. One hand was cupped invitingly around her plump painted breast and the other pressed coyly between her open legs.

Even Elena found it impossible not to be caught up in the merriment of the women around her. She had been busy all morning hanging fruits from the trees and bushes where any might pluck them. Red cherries hung in bunches from the birch tree, apricots grew from rose bushes and dozens of rosy apples ripened on the willow tree in the very centre of the garden, as was only fitting in such a garden of delights.

Luce beamed at her as she passed her with an armful of newly aired clothes, blood-red for the devils and diaphanous white gowns made to resemble angels' raiment with tiny wings fashioned from real swans' feathers.

'You chosen what you're wearing tonight, Holly?'

Elena's stomach lurched. A cloud had passed over the sun. 'But I'm not . . . entertaining.'

Luce gave her the sort of half-puzzled, half-amused look that adults reserve for small children who've said something ridiculous.

'Course you are. Every woman and boy will be at the festivities, even the older women join in. You wait, tonight there'll be more men in here than weevils in a sack of grain. They come from miles around. A few girls get bedded, but mostly it's just flirting, dancing and getting drunk, like any regular saint's day.

'Ma reckons it brings in the new customers, specially the young lads too shy to come aknocking on the door. Lets them see there's nothing to be afeared of. They can pick a girl that takes their fancy, have a quick fumble and a few kisses. It whets their appetite, see, and that's not the only thing it wets, if you get my drift.' Luce giggled. 'They'll go home with only one thing on their minds – when can they come back and give it to her properly? She knows her business, does Ma.'

'But Ma said I was only to serve the special customers.'

'Everyone's special tonight, besides, like I say, you don't have to do anything except flirt. You can do that, can't you? And if one of them tries to go a bit too far and you don't fancy it, just give him a playful slap or tell him you're going to fetch some wine and then go and talk to someone else. Mind you, you want to be careful, that can make some of them keener than if you let them have their grope and get it over with.'

Seeing the anxious expression on Elena's face, she added, 'Look, just keep pouring the wine and cider down them; a few glasses of that and they'll not be able to get it up, much less find where to put it if they do. You ever watched a drunk try to get his finger in a latch-hole? Come on, choose your costume soon else the best ones will be gone.'

Luce swept off towards the sleeping quarters where, judging by the giggles inside, the girls were already waiting to claim their gowns.

Elena picked up a bunch of grapes and wandered over to the turf seat to find a place to hang them. It wouldn't be so bad, would it, if it was only what Luce had said? After all, at the feast days back in the village, that's what they'd all done, danced and flirted a little. Wasn't that where she'd first noticed how handsome Athan was, when she saw him with a group of lads at the feast, and observed how every time she'd glanced in his direction, he seemed to be looking at her?

Luce said they came from miles around. Suppose, just suppose Athan was to come here tonight. He might if Master Raffaele had told him where she was. It would be his chance to see her without risk of betraying her hiding place. Elena hugged herself in delight.

Then just as suddenly she was seized by fear as another thought struck her. If Athan knew where she was then he knew she was in a brothel. She had grown so used to living in this place, she had forgotten how it would appear to Athan and his mother, Joan, even to her own mother. Athan would think she was a common whore, that she'd given herself to other men. He'd be disgusted. What if he came and told her he despised her, and that he never wanted to see her again? She couldn't bear that. She couldn't let him find her here.

'Will he come tonight?' a small voice whispered beside her. Looking down, she saw Finch squatting behind the turf seat. For a moment she thought he meant Athan, then she saw the misery etched in his face.

The boy tugged at her skirts. 'The werecat? Holly, will he come back for me?'

It was on her lips to say no, to reassure and soothe the child, but she stopped herself. Once before she had told him everything would be all right, but it had been far from all right, and she knew Finch had been hurt much more by that false promise from her than by anything Hugh had done to him. The slashes on his arms were healing well, but the scars would remain as long as he lived.

She stroked the pale golden curls. 'I don't know, Finch, I don't know if he will come, but there will be lots of people here. Everyone will be together in the garden. You won't be alone.'

'He could still take me to a room,' Finch said in a dead voice.

Elena knew that was true. Whatever Ma's plans, if any man dangled enough money in front of her, he would be able to buy whatever he wanted, she was sure of that.

Finch stared anxiously about him to see if they could be overheard, then he wriggled closer, staring up at her with a look of fierce determination.

'I'm gonna run away today.'

Elena shook her head. 'You can't, Finch, you'd never get past Talbot.'

'I know a different way out. I found it. In the cellars, there's another tunnel. Leads to a gate. It's a way out of here. Talbot doesn't watch that one. He thinks no one knows about it, 'cause it's hidden. But . . . but I can't open it myself. I know how to, I've seen Talbot do it, but I can't do it by myself. You could help me though. We could do it together, then we could both run away. You want to leave here too, don't you?'

Elena crouched down and looked into the child's face. 'We can't, Finch, it's too dangerous. You don't understand, there are people looking for me. I can't leave here. Besides, where would we go? How would we live?'

'I'm strong, I can work. Look!' Finch clenched his small fist, lifting his thin little arm to try to make the muscles bulge. 'I can earn money for us both and we could sleep in a barn. You remember, Holly. *We shall be safe, diddle diddle, deep in the hay.*'

He smiled up at her with the unshakeable confidence of a child, his eyes bright with excitement for the very first time she had known him.

She felt her own heart leap upwards. Why not? Why couldn't they just go? She didn't have to wait for Master Raffaele, why should she? He'd made it very plain that he had more import-ant matters to attend to than her. Who knew when he'd come back, if he ever did? He probably had no intention of taking her away from this place. He had not protected her from Raoul. He'd allowed Ma to put her to work as a whore. Maybe, maybe Ma had even paid Raffaele for her. He certainly wasn't going to protect her from Hugh. *Stay out of his way* – those were the only words of comfort he'd offered. Only she could save herself now.

No one would recognize her with her dyed hair, besides which they'd probably long forgotten about the runaway serf. No one would be looking for a woman travelling with a boy. There were other towns, other cities. They could go anywhere.

Elena seized the boy's hands. 'Finch, are you sure about this? Are you sure the gate really leads to the outside, not just to another cellar?'

Finch's eyes were sparkling. 'I saw it. I looked out through the bars and saw a great river right outside. I could . . . I could nearly touch it.'

His eager little grin only made him look smaller and more vulnerable. Could she really look after them both? She had worked ever since she could toddle, but she'd never in her life had to seek work. As a villein, she had merely done what others told her to do. She wasn't even sure how to go about finding a master or mistress. What if they started asking questions, demanding the parchment to prove that she was a free woman?

Did the boy understand what he might be facing out there? Winter would soon be here and if they couldn't find shelter they'd starve or freeze to death in some stinking alley like the other beggars. But at least if they ran, Finch would have a chance. She knew only too well what it was like to spend your days waiting in fear and dread. If Finch had been her son, she wouldn't hesitate.

Elena looked down at the boy. 'If we do run away, we won't be able to stay in Norwich. They'll come looking for us. Do you understand that? We'll have to walk, maybe a very long way, for days, weeks even.'

She realized that she had no idea what might lie beyond Norwich, nor even in which direction she should go. Not back to Gastmere, that was certain, even her dyed hair would not disguise her there. Gastmere lay down-river of Norwich, so they must walk upstream. But what lay upstream, another town, a marsh, a lake? She didn't know.

Elena bit her lip. 'We might not be able to find food for days. And we'll be hungry and cold, but we'll have to keep moving no matter how tired we are or how many blisters we have on our feet. Are you sure you can do that?'

The light in Finch's eyes had not dimmed for an instant. 'I can, I can! I promise. Afore my uncle gave me to Talbot, I was hungry all the time and cold too, for I slept with the dogs. But I never cried. I promise I won't ever cry, even if I'm starving. Please, Holly, please let's go now, afore the werecat comes,' he begged, tugging on her hand.

'No, we can't go yet. Talbot or Ma might look for us, or go to the cellars to feed the animals. We'll have to wait until this evening, until everyone is busy, then we won't be missed. And we'll have all night to walk in the dark with less chance of anyone seeing us.'

'But what if the werecat comes afore we get away?'

'Ma won't let anyone in here until it's dark, not tonight.' Seeing the child's face crumple, she said quickly, 'You get whatever clothes and food you can, tie them in a bundle and hide them near the cellar door. But be careful no one sees you. Then tonight, once the feast has started, I'll meet you . . .' she stared around the garden trying to find a suitable place, 'over there.' She pointed to a large bush closest to the court-yard wall. 'Keep moving around, but keep watching that bush. I'll go there when I think it's safe. I'll nod to you. When you see my signal you creep along to the boys' chamber and make sure it's empty. If it is, go and hide in there till I come. Can you do that?'

Finch nodded eagerly and in a fit of joy suddenly hugged her, so fiercely that Elena thought he would never let her go.

The moon rose bright and fat, clad only in a few wisps of cloud. The evening star pierced the indigo sky, but few gazed upwards to see it as one by one the lanterns were lit in the brothel garden, misting the trees with soft yellow pools of light. The naked wooden angel now pissed wine that sprayed out in a graceful arc from between her spread legs whenever someone pressed her lusciously rounded breast. The older women bustled out from the kitchens, piling the tables with platters of food, but there were none of your dainty dishes and pewter goblets at this feast.

Flagons of mead, wine, ale and cider graced the little tables, surrounded by all manner of curious little vessels a man might wish to drink from: a polished goat's horn, a leather cup fashioned as a woman's shoe, or a breast-shaped pot from which he could suck his chosen libation through a hole in the rosy nipple.

There were other plump round breasts formed from curd tarts with cherry nipples, which nuzzled alongside goose-filled pastries shaped like men's cocks which squirted thick rich gravy into the mouths of the biters. Custards were moulded into buttocks, with rosehip jelly syrups dribbling between their fat cheeks. Breads were baked into curvaceous torsos. Brawn became shapely legs and arms, whilst rosewater pudding was moulded into sweet red lips. Pike in galentyne was formed into a female belly, with strands of green samphire dripping with melted butter artistically arranged as her pubic hair. In short, every part of the human anatomy that a man could desire was fashioned in sweet or savoury, salt or sour to whet his appetite.

As soon as a good crowd of men were gathered, the crowning glory of the feast was borne in to a loud rattle of drums from the musicians who at once struck up a lively tune. Not for these gentlemen a cooked duck artfully disguised as a living peacock. No, a man could see exactly what meats he was being offered here. A giant penis had been created by stuffing larks inside a boned chicken, the chicken in a goose, the goose in a heron. At one end, on either side of the long thick sausage of meat, two sheep's stomachs had been packed with mutton, beef and pork until they were as round and taut as the rising moon. And, in honour of the Archangel Michael whose feast it was, two goose wings were attached on either side as if the whole creation was in flight.

The four women who bore in the flying genitals on a great wooden board swooped and swerved in a mocking dance, wafting the tip past the girls with cries of 'You think you can stretch to this one, Annie?' 'Now this'll give you something to get your teeth into, girl.' The men roared their appreciation.

All over the garden, men and youths were lounging in twos or threes. Girls were sprawled across their laps, feeding them meats and pastries from their own fair fingers, dripping with juice or sauces, which the men sucked at like infants at their mother's knee. A few men and women were dancing to the bawdy songs of the musicians, while others joined in the choruses, bellowing like bulls near cows in heat, with much enthusiasm but precious little melody.

A few couples had already retreated behind the gauze hangings, clearly wanting privacy for their passions. But the customers, unlike the brothel girls, were oblivious to the fact that the artfully placed lanterns threw every twist and turn of their antics as giant shadows on to the walls, much to the amusement and delight of those watching the play.

Elena tried to keep to the corners of the garden as much as possible, and whenever a man did try to catch hold of her, she slipped away on the pretext, as Luce had advised, of fetching him a drink or some food, but never returning. She gazed anxiously round for Finch. She saw the other boys who were plainly enjoying the feast, stuffing themselves with food or sitting on men's knees, letting themselves be fondled while sipping wine from the men's own goblets. But of Finch there was no sign.

She was so preoccupied with searching for him that she didn't notice Luce heading purposefully in her direction until it was too late. Luce was leading a young man by the hand who could have been scarcely more than thirteen or fourteen summers. To Elena, a woman at sixteen, he was a mere boy.

'Here we are then,' Luce said in a motherly tone, thrusting the blushing youth at Elena. 'This is Holly, she'll take care of you.'

Seeing that Elena was about to make some excuse, Luce leaned forward and hissed, 'You best take this one. Ma's watching you and if you don't take him, she's liable to fix you up with someone herself. Besides, this one'll do no more than stare, poor lamb. He's not a clue what it's for, except to piss with, and I doubt he's even learned to do that straight yet.'

The lamb in question must have heard her, for he blushed even more furiously and chewed his knuckle. Elena glanced across the garden. On a high gilded chair placed against one wall Ma was following the proceedings with the intensity of a hunting hawk. With a flick of her jewelled fingers, she motioned girls towards the shy, the elderly or the ugly who were gazing at the more fortunate men and their giggling lovers with hungry expressions.

Ma's black hair gleamed with a dozen gold pins, each inlaid with emerald-green glass that glinted in the candlelight so that it seemed as if a dozen eyes blinked out of the dark nest. She wore a long, viper-green cloak trimmed with sable which, though greasy and a little worn, still looked lustrous in the flattering light of the lantern. It must once have been made for a lady of normal height and Ma had arranged it around herself so that it covered her legs and fell to the floor. Thus enthroned, anyone who did not know her would think her the height of any other woman.

Ma's head was turned towards Elena. At this distance she could not be sure Ma was watching her, but she could take no chances. Elena forced a smile and asked the young lad if it was his first time here.

He nodded, staring at her chest, though Elena couldn't decide if that was lust or that he was merely too shy to look her in the face.

'My brother brought me. Said it was high time I . . . my brother's had hundreds of girls,' he finished lamely. He gave a jerk of his head over to where three gangling young men were all but hidden under the buxom girls who sat on their laps, nuzzling their faces.

'I'm sure he hasn't had as many as he boasts,' Elena said. She led the youth to a pallet placed under one of the trees that she had earlier decorated with fruit and plucked a few grapes from the bunch. Sitting beside him, she tried to feed him the grapes one at a time as she'd seen the other women do, but whereas other men would have lain back and made a sensuous game of it, the lad hunched forward, allowing her to stuff the grapes into his mouth, with no more pleasure than a fretful infant allowing a mother to spoon gruel into him.

'You . . . you can touch me, if you want,' Elena said reluctantly, but knowing she must do something.

She gazed around, searching the garden for Finch. Where was he? They must go soon. They needed as many hours of darkness as they could get to put distance between them and Norwich. What if they couldn't find a way out of the town? She knew some towns had gates. They hadn't passed through a gate when they'd entered, but that was because they'd come by boat. Could you simply march out of the city? She realized she had no clear idea of where they were in Norwich, only a hazy recollection of walking through a maze of streets to get here. Finch said the tunnel in the cellar came out near a river. If they followed the river, it must lead –

'Where?'

She was startled by the voice. 'Where what?'

'You said I could touch you,' the young lad said. 'Where should I . . .'

Elena stared at him blankly. Finally in desperation she muttered, 'Why don't you kiss me instead?'

He threw himself at her, pressing his lips tightly against hers. He began to move his mouth in a vague chewing action. His hot, sweaty hands grabbed at her neck as he tried clumsily to pull her tighter.

Staring over his shoulder, Elena suddenly froze. A man was sauntering across the garden towards Ma Margot. She was certain she knew the walk, but as he passed by one of the trees, the full light of the lantern shone on his face. It was Hugh.

The lad had given up his attempt at kissing and had tentatively slid a hand on to her kirtle over her breast, but Elena was too scared even to register this. She watched in horror as Hugh reached Ma's throne where, as if she really was a queen, he made a bow and pressed her hand to his lips. If this was mockery, Ma evidently didn't treat it as such, for she rewarded him with a smile and sent a girl scurrying for a goblet of wine and a plate of pastries.

It was evident that whatever she had intended when she said Hugh would pay dearly for what he had done to Finch, she wasn't going to let it interfere with business. From the way she leaned towards him as she fed him one of the prick-shaped pastries, slipping it into his mouth with her own taloned fingers, you might have thought he had never laid a hand on Finch. No doubt, Elena thought bitterly, what Ma meant was that she would simply double or treble the price, because Hugh had damaged her goods, but she'd still let him use her boys as he pleased.

Finch! Any moment Hugh might ask for him. Elena pushed the lad's hand away.

'Stay there,' she said, trying to sound as casual as possible. 'I'll fetch you some good strong wine to relax you, then I'll . . . we'll do things that will make your brother so jealous, he'll never laugh at you again.'

The boy beamed at her, and tried to lounge back nonchalantly on the pallet, but without success. Elena hurried to the bush she had pointed out to Finch earlier that day. She gazed desperately around for him, nodding in case he could see her. But there was still no sign of him. She could only pray he'd seen her and had already gone to the boys' chamber.

She waited as long as she dared, then when Ma was bending forward to say something to Hugh, she slipped back behind the bush and through the gate which divided the courtyard from the garden, edging along the wall towards the boys' chamber. There was no one in the courtyard. The sounds of the music mingling with laughter and chatter which rose up from the garden only seemed to heighten the stillness of the courtyard. The lanterns dangling from the topmost branches of the trees in the garden threw soft pools of light on to the flinty cobbles. Elena edged around the light as a man might avoid quicksand.

She had almost reached the door when she saw someone else enter the courtyard by the gate. Footsteps hurried across. Elena froze, suddenly realizing that she could not offer any explanation as to why she was standing in front of the boys' chamber. She started back towards the gate at a run and collided with Luce coming towards her.

'Hey, steady there.' Luce grabbed Elena's arm to stop herself slipping on the cobbles. 'You seen Finch? Ma wants him, but I reckon the lad's hiding somewhere, doesn't want to be found.'

Elena shook her head, unable to trust herself to speak.

Luce groaned. 'There'll be hell to pay if I can't find him. Ma won't want any of her guests disappointed tonight, specially him. That gentleman's not the type to go quietly if he can't get what he wants, and Ma doesn't need a bear roaring through the beehives, not tonight. I'd best see if Finch is in the boys' chamber.'

This time it was Elena who caught her arm. 'No, don't waste your time. He's not in there. I was looking for him too and I checked there. You know Finch, he's always hungry. Why don't you check the kitchens? He's probably hanging round the cooks. I'll look in the sleeping quarters.'

'Kitchens, yes, you're right. With that pretty little face of his, he could wheedle food from the king's own plate. Those cooks are probably stuffing him like a capon.'

She turned to go, then looked back at Elena. 'I know you feel sorry for the lad, Holly, but if you find him, you'd best take him to Ma straight away, even if he begs you not to. It'll be worse for him in the long run if he makes a fool out of her. She doesn't take kindly to that. You've not seen Ma in a rage and you'd best pray to every saint in heaven, and the Devil too, that you never do.'

Elena waited until Luce was out of sight, then ran back to the boys' chamber and slipped inside. It was as dark as a grave, for the boys were not expected to entertain in there tonight and not even the fire had been lit in the pit. She groped her way forward, using the partitions between the stalls as her guide. When she judged herself almost at the back of the room, she called out softly, 'Finch, Finch, are you there? It's me, El . . . Holly.'

Almost at once she felt a small cold hand slip into hers.

'Where have you been? I've waited ages and ages. I thought you weren't coming.'

'I'm here now.' She squeezed the little fingers gently. 'Can you find the door in the dark?'

'Course I can.' He sounded more confident than she'd ever heard him, just like any cocky little village boy. She felt his body taut beside her, but knew from his tone and the urgent tugging of his hand that his tension came from excitement, not fear. She guessed he hadn't seen Hugh arrive. He didn't know they were looking for him.

She swallowed hard. 'We must hurry, Finch, there isn't much time.'

They found the burning torch half-way down the cellar steps as before and Elena lifted it out of its bracket. Although she knew exactly what to expect now, still that raw stench of savage beasts made her stomach contract. She dreaded passing them. Would Finch be able to walk past that great cat after what had happened? But he didn't turn towards the cages. Instead he tugged her towards the side of the stairs and the open hole in the floor with its hollow drip, drip of water.

'Careful,' Finch warned.

He pulled her back against the wet slimy wall as they inched around it. The slippery flags beneath Elena's feet sloped at a perilous angle towards the great black hole. Finally they reached the back of the staircase. Finch darted forward and grabbed at something. Elena held up the burning torch and saw a thick piece of sacking hanging against the wall. Finch held it aside and at once a new smell of mud and rotting fish billowed towards them on an icy current of air. In front of them was a tunnel, sloping downwards away from the cellar. Like the other, it curved round, so that Elena couldn't see the end.

'Down there, that's the river and the gate,' Finch whispered.

Elena suddenly remembered the blazing torch in her hands. Once they reached the end of the tunnel anyone on the river or the bank would see its flame for miles in the darkness.

'Finch, we have to put the torch back. If Talbot comes and finds it missing he'll guess someone is down here.'

Elena knew she should be the one to replace the torch in its bracket on the stairs, but she couldn't go back there, not if it meant returning here in the dark. She was terrified that one false step and she would fall into that hole. Without a light, how could she even see where it was?

Finch hesitated, but only for a minute. 'You stay here. I can find my way in the dark. Done it hundreds of times.' But his voice was trembling.

She wanted to stop him. She knew that she should, but she couldn't. She let him take the torch from her hands.

'You'll stay here, Holly, won't you?' he begged her. 'You promise you won't go without me? You'll wait for me?'

As the boy slipped under the sacking, Elena stood rigid in a darkness so thick that it seemed to suck the very air from her mouth. She pressed herself against the dripping wall. She was back in that pit, next to Gerard's coffin, chained by the neck, screaming and screaming and yet knowing that not a sound was escaping from her lips. Again she heard the grating of the trapdoor opening and Raffaele's voice calling to her, Raffaele's hand bringing her light and freedom. What would he say when he found her gone? He had told her time and again to trust him, and everything which had gone wrong in her life had been because she hadn't gone to him, hadn't trusted him.

Elena tried to force the memories down, to silence Raffaele's voice in her head. Above her, even now, Luce was searching for Finch, Talbot too probably, and maybe others. Hugh would be growing impatient. It would only be a matter of time before Ma sent Talbot to search the cellars. Elena shivered. It was so cold down here. Where was Finch? Suppose he'd fallen into that hole or was standing in the darkness, too frightened to move? What if he couldn't find the entrance to the tunnel? She would have to go out there. She'd have to find him.

Elena felt a cold waft of air on her skin as the sacking curtain moved.

'Holly, Holly, where are you?' Finch sounded terrified.

'Here, I'm here.' She thrust out her hand, feeling round until she touched something warm. Finch seized her hand, then threw his arms about her waist, pressing his face into her belly in a frantic hug.

'I heard someone calling for me up there,' he whispered. 'Are they looking for me?'

'Come on,' Elena urged. 'Quickly!'

Moving her hand along the slimy wall, they edged down the passage. Several times they both slipped on the wet stones beneath their feet, but they managed to steady each other. At last, as they came round the curve of the tunnel, Elena felt a breeze on her face and saw before them the thick iron bars of a gate glinting in a shaft of moonlight.

On the other side of the iron grid, three steps led down to the water's edge. Stretching out in front of them was the broad river; black and oily in the silver light, it twisted and writhed as it rushed past them. Moored along either bank were the dark humps of boats. Here and there the red glow of a small brazier on a boat's deck, or the yellow smudge of a lantern hanging from a mast or prow, showed that their owners were spending the night on board, but most of the little craft rocked at their moorings, black and silent. On the far side of the broad river more fires burned outside a small cluster of wooden shacks, but beyond that was darkness.

Finch pointed to a rope hanging from the roof of the tunnel. 'See, you have to pull that and the gate comes up, but it goes down as soon as you stop pulling.'

Elena grasped the thick rope and tugged. It took all her strength to make the grid swing upwards just the span of her hand, but as soon as she slackened her grip, it fell back into place with a crash that echoed through the tunnel. She and Finch both froze, holding their breath, but they heard nothing except the rushing water.

Elena looked around, her heart thumping in her chest. Time was running out. There had to be a way to keep the gate open. She searched both sides around her. Then she saw a metal bar, jutting out high up on the wall. When the gate was raised fully, it should be possible to loop the rope over the bar and hold it open, but they'd never be able to close it behind them. They'd have to pray that no one came down here for hours.

'Finch, listen to me. As soon as I lift the gate, you get under it and scramble up the bank beside the steps.'

'But you're coming with me. You promised.'

'I will, I will, but you have to go first. Go as soon as I tell you. Are you ready?'

Finch nodded. Elena planted her feet wide and grabbed the rope in both hands. She heaved. The heavy iron gate lifted a few inches. She pulled harder, the rough fibres of the rope biting into her hands. The gate lifted a little higher.

Then she heard it, faintly but unmistakably, a man's voice calling from somewhere behind her.

'Finch! Answer me, you little brat! Finch!'

Finch heard it too and turned. In the moonlight she could see his eyes wide with terror.

She heaved on the rope with all her strength and the gate rose just another few inches. 'Now, Finch, now! Crawl under. Go on quickly. I can't hold it.'

Finch hesitated, then as the voice above them called again, he dropped to his knees and slithered under the gap. It took all Elena's remaining strength not to let the gate fall with a crash; she eased it down as slowly as she could, but even so iron fell back on to stone with a dreadful clang.

Finch threw himself against the closed gate with a wail. 'Holly, Holly, open it! Open it! You can do it.'

Behind her, Elena heard Talbot's voice again, nearer this time. 'Finch, you'd best come out now, lad, or Ma'll flay the hide from your back and worse. Come on, lad, no use hiding, you know I'll find you.'

Finch cringed, but he still thrust his arm through the bars, trying to touch Elena.

'Please, Holly, please,' he begged. 'Open the gate. Let me back. I'm scared. I don't want to be out here. Let me back in, please.'

Elena crossed to the gate and took his cold little hands in hers.

'I can't, Finch. I can't. That man, that werecat has come back. You have to go. It's not safe for you here.' She reached through the bars, stroking his mop of soft curls.

'Listen to me, Finch. You have to be a brave boy. You must get on to the bank and follow the river. Keep walking all night, and when daylight comes find a place to hide and sleep. Then walk again when it gets dark. Walk until you are a long way from here. When you reach another village or town, then you can look for work. But, whatever you do, don't trust the boatmen. Don't let them see you. Too many of them come here. They might recognize you or Ma might ask them to find you.'

'But Holly, how are you going to escape?'

'Don't worry about me. I'll find a way out, you see if I don't.'

Talbot was bellowing again, fury in his voice. The caged beasts were snarling and hurling themselves at their bars, disturbed by his shouting.

She pulled her hands away. 'Go, Finch, go quickly! Talbot is coming.'

The boy stood motionless, his little fists gripping the bars. His face was ghost white in the moonlight, and silver tears were running down his cheeks.

Elena softly began to sing.

Lavender's green, diddle diddle, Lavender's blue.
You must love me, diddle diddle, 'cause I love you.

'Remember, Finch, always remember.'

As she resolutely turned away, her throat tight with tears, she thought she heard a soft echo behind her, a tremulous, broken little voice that might almost have been the sobbing of the river.

Let the birds sing, diddle diddle, let the lambs play,
We shall be safe, diddle diddle, deep in the hay.

She did not turn round.

Elena groped her way back up the slope as quickly as she could. She was desperate to reach the cellar before Talbot could come down the passage. She had to stall him long enough for Finch to get clear. She only prayed that the boy had the sense to run and was not still standing there. 'Blessed Virgin, look after him, keep him safe.'

It seemed much longer going up that tunnel than going down. She began to fear that she had taken a wrong turn, but there was no turn. She dragged her hand along the wall, feeling her way. The other she stretched out in front of her, to feel for the sacking curtain. She could still hear Talbot. He wasn't calling now, but cursing and muttering as he poked among the cages. The animals snarled, hurling themselves at their cages to drive away his unsettling light and defend their own tiny territory.

Something brushed lightly over her hand, and she almost yelled out until she realized it was the piece of sacking. She slid from behind it, keeping herself pressed against the wall as she edged round in the darkness. Talbot must be at the far end of the other passage for there was no light from the torch, unless he had given up and left.

Without warning, her shoe, slippery from the mud in the tunnel, shot out from under her and she crashed back against the wall, sliding down it. She scrabbled to find a footing, but there was nothing, nothing beneath her feet. She was sliding down the slope of the floor. She was falling into the hole. She thrashed wildly, trying to find something to hold on to, but her cold hands encountered only the smooth wet flagstones. She screamed, her legs kicking into the black empty space.

Light suddenly blinded her and even as she blinked her eyes, she felt a rough hand grab her wrist and yank her up so hard she cried out again, this time in pain. But with her other hand she managed to grasp a booted ankle and she hauled herself into a sitting position. Still holding on to the thick, sturdy legs, she clung there, shaking with terror.

Talbot hauled her to her feet.

'Another inch and you'd have been dead, lass,' Talbot said gruffly. He pushed his misshapen nose close to hers. 'So, what you doing skulking down here?'

She could smell his hot, sour breath, but tried not to turn her face away. 'I . . . I was hiding. I didn't want to . . . entertain the men.'

'Is that so?'

He held the blazing torch up so close to her head that she was afraid he was going to burn her. She still had her back to the hole and dared not wrench herself away in case she fell again. He peered behind her at the corner of the stairs. 'I reckon Ma's right, you have found a way out of here.'

It was on the tip of her tongue to deny it, but then she saw it was useless. 'I did find a gate, but I couldn't open it. It's too heavy.'

He stared at her for several moments and his eyes narrowed. Then he lowered the torch. 'You seen that boy, Finch?'

Elena swallowed. 'He was heading towards the kitchens last time I saw him.' She knew Luce would have already checked there, but at least it was the opposite direction to the cellar.

'Aye, well, he's not there now,' Talbot growled. 'That bastard'll not be kept waiting much longer. Ma'll feed us to the beasts if we don't find the brat soon.'

Elena left Talbot continuing to search the cellar. She knew he would check the gate and she prayed with all her strength that Finch would have had the courage to run before Talbot went down that passage.

Elena raced back to the sleeping chamber. She only had one thought in mind. She had to buy enough time for Finch to get far enough away. If they discovered he was not here, and Talbot mentioned finding Elena in the cellar, it wouldn't take Ma a fingersnap to realize what had happened and send Talbot to search the river bank for him. Elena had to divert them.

She stripped off her own muddy kirtle and dashed cold water on her face and arms. She looked wildly around. An angel's gown still lay across one of the pallets. It was old and slightly torn, which was why the other women had rejected it. She pulled it on. It had been made for a woman twice her weight and height. The front hung loose in a low sweep, exposing most of her breasts.

She dared not delay, but ran out and across the garden. To her alarm she saw Talbot making his way across to Ma from the other side. She had to reach Ma first. She was half-way across when the young lad she'd abandoned stepped out in front of her, eyeing her new costume with a mixture of undisguised drooling and the kind of acute embarrassment that he might feel if his mother caught him with his hand up a woman's skirt.

'Are you . . . did you get some wine?' he finished lamely, evidently not having given up hope, even after all this time, that she would keep her promise.

'I'll be back,' she said, pushing past him, feeling desperately sorry for him as she heard the snorts of laughter and jeers from the boy's brother and his friends. But she could do nothing for the lad, except hope that one of the other girls would take pity on him.

She reached Ma just before Talbot. Hugh was sitting in a carved chair beside her. Ma was evidently trying to keep him occupied by talking, but he had long since given up any pretence of politely listening. His jaw was set hard, and he seemed only a breath away from venting his fury at being kept waiting.

Ma's yellow-green eyes widened in alarm as Elena, grabbing a flagon from the nearest table, gave a low curtsy.

'May I refill your goblet, sir?' Without waiting to be asked, she bent forward, deliberately letting the front of her gown fall open inches from his face. She'd no idea if this would please him, but she'd seen the other girls do it often enough to know it seemed to excite most men.

She straightened up. She could see at once that Hugh was not as easily witched as the village lads, but all the same she had caught his attention. He was eyeing her with the same puzzled curiosity as that night when she dressed Finch. Ma must have seen the look too for as Talbot approached, she quietly signalled to him to stay back.

'Well, now. If it isn't the feisty little black-haired maid . . . Holly. Isn't that what the lad called you? If I remember rightly you challenged me. Told me I was frightening the boy.'

Elena swallowed hard. 'He was afraid, sir.'

'And you? Are you afraid of me? I think you are not, or you wouldn't come marching up to me, flaunting yourself.'

He ran his fingers lightly over her breasts and Elena gave an involuntary shudder, flinching away. She recovered herself, but she knew Hugh had felt it.

His mouth curled in a slow smile. 'Or could it be that you enjoy a little fear? You get a thrill out of poking the stick in the lion's cage to rile it, see if it's really as dangerous as they say.'

He stood up so abruptly that Elena almost spilt the flagon of wine over them both. He inclined his head towards Ma Margot.

'I've changed my mind, mistress. Forget the boy. What's the pleasure in the hunt, if the quarry cowers in a corner waiting for the spear? A she-bear who turns and fights is far more challenging. There's good sport to be had in bringing her down.'

'You, man,' he called to Talbot, who still hovered in the corner. Hugh tossed a small bag of coins at him. 'Take us to a room and see to it we are not disturbed.'

Even before Hugh had flung her into the chamber, Elena knew instinctively that all the arts of seduction that Luce and the other women had explained to her would only anger him: the playful words, the slow teasing strip, the slide on to his knee and soft caresses would have no effect on him.

Elena was terrified, but she knew the one thing she must not do was show it. She had to keep him occupied long enough for Finch to get away. She had to stand up to Hugh, that was what he wanted, and if she was to get out of here alive, she must give him what he wanted. Wasn't that the one thing Ma had taught her, give them what they want and survive? Nothing else matters but to survive.

Hugh stood on the other side of the chamber watching her, his arms folded. Between them was a bed that almost filled the chamber. It had been carved to look like a boat, with a high dragon prow. Ropes hung from its sides and sacks of raw wool were piled in a heap inside, layered so deep that you could dive in head first and come to no harm. The whole chamber smelled of sheep's fat and damp wool, like Athan always did when he returned from the shearing in Gastmere. Elena tried to swallow the hard lump rising in her throat.

Hugh prowled around her, looking at her from every

angle. 'You know, I'm sure I've seen you before. I was certain the other night, but I just can't place . . .'

'I used to work in the market place in Norwich,' Elena said quickly, falling back on the lie Ma had invented.

'So that other wench said, but I am not in the habit of buying either fish or women in market places. I have servants to fetch the one and I would not dream of soiling myself on the other.'

He pulled off his shirt. A band of sleek black fur was fastened around his waist. He stroked it and for a moment his expression became glazed as if he was listening to something in the far distance. The pupils of his eyes dilated so wide they looked like huge black holes in his skull. He slid a long knife from his belt and fingered the blade.

'Now, suppose you tell me the truth, or shall we make a game of it? A game that I think I shall rather enjoy, although I can't promise that you will.'

✝

Early Morning after the 2nd Night of the Full Moon, September 1211

Pearl – A pearl denotes a tear. It is for grieving and mourning, and thus a pearl ring must never be given as a wedding gift. Yet, above all, it is an emblem of female beauty, of chastity, of sex, of the moon, and of the sea-born goddesses.

It grows in beauty like a mortal woman if it is worn against her skin, for it feeds upon her heat, grows lustrous on her passion.

Mortals believe that at certain times the oyster shell opens itself to the sky and drops of heavenly dew fall into it and impregnate the virgin oyster and from this union 'twixt the earthly and the divine are pearls conceived. In like manner, so they say, the virgin womb of Mary conceived the Holy Child. Thus the pearl brings fertility, for it is conceived of water and the moon, and is wombed within a shell as it grows.

But if a thunderstorm should rage, the oyster closes its shell and scuttles away in fear, and the pearl is aborted and drowns.

The Mandrake's Tale

The Bridge of Sleep

She is standing in a large, empty hall. It is night and the room seems to extend far back into the darkness as if it has no walls. The floor is cold under foot, but smooth, very smooth, almost as if she is walking on glass. There is something in her hand, heavy, but weighted evenly as she balances it in her fingers. She is breathing hard. Her blood pounds in her ears, like a drip echoing in a deep well. She is shaking with anger, a blind fury. She knows not at whom the rage is directed. She only knows she wants to rip, to tear, to smash, and yet she had already done that, but it isn't enough, not nearly enough.

She senses a movement in the darkness ahead of her. Someone is coming towards her. She raises her arm to defend herself. She hears a cry.

'Not here, I beg you. Do not desecrate this holy place with my blood. I am not worthy.'

A shaft of moonlight falls upon the disembodied head of an old man. His pate shines in the light and his beard flows in a silver cascade from his hollow cheeks. She draws back with a gasp, crossing herself as the head floats towards her out of the darkness. Then, as it comes closer, she sees the outline of a body hung in simple black robes.

The monk holds up his hands, as if in surrender. 'I will come with you outside. You may do what you wish with me there. I will not resist you. But I beg you, do not spill my blood in here, not here. I have cared for this place all my life, I could not bear to think my death had violated what I have always striven to keep holy.'

A cloud drifts in front of the moon, and the light slowly dims. The old man moves towards her, then passes her as if to lead her outside. He shuffles ahead of her up the smooth marble floor. Then, without warning, he stumbles and falls, sprawling across something lying in his path. Painfully he pushes himself into a kneeling position, rocking backwards on his heels. He moans softly, crossing himself again and again. 'God have mercy. Mea culpa, mea culpa . . .'

She walks towards him, her footsteps echoing. He glances up, his arm raised to shield his head as if he thinks she is going to strike him. Then, as she stands there staring at the bundle on the ground, he turns on her, his voice raised in anger and grief.

'What have you done? God have mercy on you, what sacrilege have you committed in this holy place?'

She kneels beside the old monk. A body lies on the cold, hard floor. She can distinguish little in the dark, except that the body isn't moving. As she bends to peer closer the moon emerges from behind the clouds again and a beam of cold silver light illuminates the figure.

A man is lying on his back, a pool of blood darkening on the white floor at his side. But she can see no wound on his body. Her gaze travels up over his neck and thence to his face. Two dark holes mark where his eyes should have been. Tears of blood, black in the moonlight, trickle down from the corners of the empty sockets. His face has been slashed across, not once nor twice but almost a dozen times, as a furious child might scribble out a drawing he wants to obliterate.

Still kneeling beside her, the old monk raises his face to heaven; his arms crossed tightly over his chest, he rocks back and forth in a frenzy of grief and outrage, muttering and wailing to himself in Latin.

She stretches out her right hand to make the sign of the cross over the corpse. Only then does she see what she had been grasping so tightly in her fingers. It is a knife and the blade is dripping with blood.

Elena stirred as acrid fumes burned her nostrils. Something wet and cold trickled down her forehead. She lashed out blindly and heard a woman's voice cursing as something clattered to the floor.

'She's not dead at any rate.'

Elena forced her eyelids open, wincing in the light of the lantern that hung over her. Ma was kneeling beside her on the boat-bed, dabbing at her head with a vinegar-soaked cloth.

Elena tried to focus her eyes, but the green emerald flashes in Ma's dark hair seemed to be darting back and forth like angry bees. Her tongue felt bruised and swollen. Her jaws ached.

'Hugh!'

She fought to sit up, but Ma pushed her back. 'He's gone, girl. Let me look at you. Are you hurt?'

Elena felt the throbbing bruise on her temple and another on her jaw. One had been from Hugh's fist, the second where her head bounced off the wooden frame of the boat-bed.

Ma slid her hands under the sheepskin that covered Elena's belly and ran her fingers down the length of her body, probing at the bones. Elena suddenly realized that she was naked.

'Few cuts and bruises, girl, but nothing that won't heal. You're lucky he hit you.'

'Lucky?' Elena whimpered.

'He fancied he'd killed you. Not that he was too worried about that. "Who cares if there's one less whore in the world?" he said. "There's always plenty more." But there was no point carrying on after you were dead. No pleasure for him in that.'

Elena remembered very little. Terror and pain had driven much of it from her head.

'Thing is, girl, did he remember who you were?' Talbot's voice broke in, and Elena was suddenly aware of him standing behind the lantern light. She struggled to cover her breasts, wincing as she moved.

'I don't . . . I can't . . .'

She saw a sudden image of Hugh coming at her with the knife, pinning her against the wall by her throat. She'd fought like a rat, convinced he was going to stab her. She'd squeezed her eyes shut as the deadly point came slowly nearer and nearer to her face, then the knife plunged down on to the neck of her gown, slicing through the fabric like a fishmonger cutting through the belly of a fish. The blade caught her skin beneath the gown, leaving a thin red seam running down between her breasts and over her belly to her groin, as the dress fell away from her. Beads of scarlet blood oozed from the vertical cut.

Hugh looked down at her naked body and grinned.

'What have we here, little Holly? It seems you're not a

raven-haired maid after all. The bush never lies.' He roared with laughter. 'Oh, I see it now – Hollybush! I like it. But why would you try to disguise the fire, I wonder? Unless . . .'

'Well?' Ma demanded. 'Talbot asked you a question, my darling. Did Hugh remember who you were? Did you tell him?'

They were both watching her, waiting for an answer.

'I think, he may . . . he didn't say, but . . . he saw my . . . hair . . . below.' She passed a vague hand over her groin.

Ma whipped up the corner of the sheepskin and peered closer. 'Devil's arse,' she cursed. 'I told Luce to make sure she dyed everything. How could she have been so stupid? I'll swing for that girl.'

Elena tried to struggle up on to one elbow. 'No, no, it wasn't her fault. She wanted to, but I wouldn't let her. I was embarrassed and I didn't think anyone would see.'

'Embarrassed is better than hanged, my darling,' Ma said. 'And what possessed you to throw yourself in his path tonight? Him of all people! Why didn't you stay out of his way?'

'To give Finch time to escape,' Talbot growled. 'I've searched high and low and there's no sign of the lad. And I found this one in the cellar just before she came over to Hugh. She must have opened the gate for the lad and then she tried to cover for him.'

'I didn't,' Elena cried. 'I don't know where Finch is. He's probably just hiding in one of the rooms. You know how small he can make himself when he wants to.'

Ma's hand shot out and slapped Elena so hard across her face that she almost passed out again. Her cheek burned like fire where Ma's long fingernails had raked her skin.

'You're nothing but trouble. Have been since the day the Bullock brought you here. I suppose you think you've done the boy a kindness. Don't you realize Finch has no more idea how to fend for himself out there than a blind kitten? He grew up on the Isle of Ely. His mam died in childbirth, so his father had him reared by one of those wet nurses, takes in half a dozen children at a time and none of them get enough milk. Most of them die before they're a year old. God alone knows how this brat survived. Where do you think he's going to find work, a scrap like him? Without apprentice fees or even good strong muscle, who's going to take him in? I tell you, if any do, it won't be to put him to an honest job. If that boy doesn't die starving in a ditch, he'll die on the gallows for thieving, for that's the only occupation any master will be able to put him to.'

Tears slid down Elena's cheeks. Not just for Finch, but for her own aching body, the throbbing bruises, the smarting cuts. She couldn't bear any more tonight. She hastily rubbed the tears away, but not before Ma had seen them.

'It's too late you wailing now, my darling. You may as well have strangled the boy yourself with your own two hands, and spared him the misery of waiting.'

'I didn't help him escape,' Elena protested miserably, but she knew that neither of them believed her.

'Go on, get you to bed. There's still a few hours left before daylight. In the meantime, I suppose it's me and Talbot'll have to think how to get out of this mess.'

Elena, clutching the sheepskin around her, limped out of the chamber. The garden was deserted now, all the lanterns extinguished. In the sleeping chamber, no one stirred as she softly opened the door and slipped under her own covers. She lay awake in the darkness. Every inch of her ached and burned. She longed desperately for sleep, but it wouldn't come.

She hated Hugh. She loathed him more than she had ever known possible. A white-hot fire raged through her. If it hadn't been for him, Finch would not have wanted to run. And now, now he knew about her too. He hadn't made the connection yet, of that she was sure, but he'd go on thinking about her red hair, and why she'd tried to disguise it. He'd realize who she was in the end. And unless he really did believe he'd killed her tonight, as soon as he discovered the truth, he would return.

And where was poor little Finch now? Ma said she and Talbot would sort the mess. Did that mean they would go looking for him? She had to know if the boy had got away safely. She had to know what would happen to him. Suppose Ma was right and she had sent Finch to his death. She couldn't bear to believe that. He must be safe, he must!

Almost without thinking, she slid her hand under her pallet and felt for the little hard bundle. She unwrapped it, her fingers tracing the outline of the withered limbs, the head, the body. She spat on her finger.

That foul animal had forced her mouth open, held her jaws apart with the hilt of his knife, as he pushed himself between her lips. She almost vomited again as the scalding memory welled up inside her. When he'd finished she'd retched until there was nothing left in her stomach. That's why he'd hit her, cracking her head against the wooden bed. She could still taste him and taste her own blood where the dagger hilt had dug into her mouth. She smeared her blood-stained spittle on the mandrake and wrapped the little body again, pushing it back beneath the pallet, then she curled herself up in a little ball and tried to dream of Finch.

Hugh leaned over the wall of the bridge, gazing down into the river below. A pale dawn light was just creeping along the edge of the sky and gilding the filthy water below with flecks of gold. The faint glow of a dying lantern revealed the outline of two watchmen hunched against some hurdles at the far end of the bridge. Bishop's Bridge formed one of the entrances to Norwich by day, but at night the bridge was closed and supposedly guarded. Not this night though, for these two watchmen were snoring like pigs in mud. Hugh was torn between a desire to kick them awake or curl up beside them and sleep. His body felt drained, as if every drop of blood had been sucked from it, but his mind was racing.

He felt for the band of fur beneath his shirt, and smiled. That cunning woman had bestowed her gift on the right man. He was going to obtain everything he desired and deserved. And unlike his brother, he knew how to use power.

It had been so easy to find this runaway of Osborn's. She'd practically crawled into his lap as if she'd been drawn to him. Not that it was the first time a girl had done that. Some women just couldn't help playing with fire; they wanted to be burned. It would be rather annoying if she was dead. He would have enjoyed watching what Osborn would do to her. But he'd call back to the stew later and find out if she lived. If she did, he could find some place in town to keep her safely locked up until he was ready to return to Gastmere. Either way he had no intention of leaving Norwich yet. He had pressing business of his own to pursue.

It had been a blow to learn that fool Raoul had come to Norwich on Osborn's bidding to find the girl. He'd been so sure that Raoul had come here because he'd found out something about the traitor, something that Hugh could use to his advantage. Hugh was still convinced that Raffaele was involved in this treachery somewhere and he was determined to find some proof of it, even if it was only for the pleasure of watching the gelding begging for mercy at the hands of the torturers. But if Hugh could catch Raffaele along with the other men who were helping the French, he'd have something to offer John. He'd not make the same mistake as Osborn, waiting on empty promises of future lands. He'd insist on having his reward now – their heads for a wealthy estate. It was a fair bargain.

The prize had almost been within his grasp before when he'd learned about the *Santa Katarina* from the marsh-man he'd caught stealing. But even after a thorough beating the man had told him little except that the ship was smuggling Frenchmen, and the wretch couldn't or wouldn't tell him the names of those who were helping the French. Try as he might, Hugh had been unable to find out any more.

So in the end he had to settle for sending an anonymous warning to the garrison. That way, he thought, he could take the credit if the French were captured, but not look a fool if the tale proved to be false. He'd expected the garrison to station John's soldiers on land and seize the Frenchmen when they came ashore. He'd even gone to the bay to watch events unfold, certain that whoever was helping the French would be waiting to meet the ship and he could lead the soldiers to them.

But John's men had ruined everything in their bungled attempt to take the ship itself. With the boat in flames there was nothing even to prove the French had ever been aboard. And for all he knew, the snivelling little thief had invented the tale just to try to save his skin. The whole business had proved worthless to Hugh, but now, if he could discover who had murdered that idiot Raoul, it might yet lead him to the nest of traitors, the perfect gift for a king.

Finding this runaway girl seemed like an omen. Surely, as the cunning woman had prophesied, his star was in its ascendancy? He would find the traitors where that fool Raoul had failed. He would earn the king's gratitude and the lands he wanted. Why not all of his brother's lands too, wouldn't that be the crowning glory? Yes, Hugh rather thought he would insist on that little detail into the bargain.

God's bones, but he was weary. That wretched girl had taken it out of him, and Ma had been plying him with far too much strong wine all that time he'd been waiting for the boy. Now the drink was catching up with him and his head was muzzy and heavy. He leaned more heavily on the wall of the bridge, resting his head on his hands, trying to summon the energy to stagger back to the inn where he was staying.

Hugh was just about to pull himself upright when a movement on the river bank below caught his eye. A tiny, fair-haired boy was darting along the narrow track. Hugh would not have given him a second glance had the boy not been crouching low and peering fearfully at the boats moored along the river, trying to slip past them unnoticed. There was something familiar about the child. Hugh squinted down at the little figure.

'Finch, is that you, boy? I've been looking for you. Don't think you can get away from me.'

Finch jerked and spun round to see the man he most feared in all the world standing on the bridge above him. The child was paralysed with horror. He was shaking so violently that he couldn't seem to walk, much less run. He began to whimper helplessly. But even as he stood there staring up, he saw a terrible spasm of shock and agony burst across Hugh's face. He saw Hugh's hands gripping the top of the wall as he arched backwards with a groan. Then the man fell, his head crashing against the stone wall as he crumpled on to his knees. The terrified child didn't wait to see more; he turned and ran as if all the cats of hell were at his heels.

Hugh lay in a spreading pool of his own blood. The first stab wound in his back had killed him, so he never felt the knife slashing at him again and again just to make certain he could never wake in this world. Some might say that was a pity, for he deserved to feel every one of those cuts. His attacker certainly thought so.

The watchmen who found him, when they finally woke as the bright dawn light disturbed their infant slumbers, stared in horror at the corpse and shuddered to think how close they had come to having their own throats cut. For surely only a madman could have done this. They briefly contemplated trying to heave the body off the bridge in the hopes that he would be found further down river and nowhere near where they were supposed to be keeping watch. But one glance at the boatmen cooking their breakfasts on the little crafts below convinced them that not even the most dull-witted river man could fail to notice a blood-soaked corpse hurtling down past their ears and falling with a great splash into the water. The watchmen stared miserably at each other. There was nothing for it but to raise the hue and cry, and pray for a miracle to save them from the punishment that would surely follow. They didn't need the powers of a mandrake to tell them this was not going to be a good day.

A grinning demon with the face of a pig and the ears of a bat swung upside down, peering down at Elena. Something furry rubbed itself against her cheek and as she fought to move her head, a wolf with bared teeth lunged out at her. She screamed, trying to raise her arms to shield her face, but they were as heavy as marble and she couldn't move them. She heard a slow, heavy tread somewhere behind her and then two bulging frog's eyes blinked slowly at her. A long red tongue flicked out, and from a very long way off she heard the boom of a voice, but she couldn't make out the words. She thrashed wildly, trying to wriggle away, but she couldn't move. She seemed to be caught in a web.

The frog spoke again. 'Lie still, my darling. It's for your own good. You were raving when Talbot brought you home.'

Slowly, as if a mist was dissolving in her mind, Elena began to recognize fragments of where she was. She was lying on a bed of furs. She had been here before in the room of the grotesques. It was Ma Margot's chamber, the one with the spy mask to see out into the entrance hall. She had no idea if it was day or night, for the room was windowless, and only the light from a single candle flickered across the carved monsters that peered down at her. She tried to sit up, and only then did she realize why she couldn't move her arms. She was bound wrist and ankles by soft leather straps to the corners of the bed.

Something loomed towards her out of the fog in her head.

'Brought me home,' she repeated. Her words sounded slurred. Her tongue was swollen and dry.

Home, Ma had said home, but this wasn't her home. Where was home? She felt as if she was a crazy old woman wandering the streets, knowing the place had to be found, but not knowing where to look. Ma pulled up a low stool. An image flashed into Elena's head of a milkmaid seated beside cows, except that surely the maid hadn't sat on a stool mounted on the back of a carved kneeling angel.

Ma slowly pulled the jewelled pins from her hair and laid them one at a time on the fur-covered bed. Elena shrank back as far as her bonds would allow, trying to twist away, but

Ma took no notice. Freed from its pins, Ma's hair uncoiled by itself in a thick rope slithering down over her shoulders, to curl itself up again in her lap. It was as black as polished jet. From a tiny silver flask that hung at her waist, Ma tipped a few drops of a musky-smelling oil into her palm and smoothed it down the length of her hair. She pulled out a comb, fashioned from an ancient yellowed bone.

'You know what this is?' Ma didn't wait for an answer. 'It's the comb they used to anoint the ancient kings and queens of this land when they were crowned. Always remember that gold and silver are but as worthless as bird grit, unless you have the power to control others.'

She began to comb the oil through her thick hair, fanning it out like great black wings on either side of her head. Only then did Elena notice that the centre of her scalp was completely bald, as if she had been tonsured.

Without any change in tone, Ma said, 'Talbot found you near the church of St Helen. It's lucky for you that he discovered you before the sheriff started the search. Only minutes before, mind, for the soldiers were already rushing down that road towards the bridge as he was carrying you home.'

Ma began to twist her hair, round and round, tighter and tighter.

'They say he died instantly, a stab in the back between the ribs right up into the heart. It was well aimed, my darling.'

'Who . . . who died?'

The oily gleaming hair was tightly coiled up on top of Ma's head once more. She began to pierce it with her pins, slowly, one at a time, with a practised hand that required no mirror to guide it.

'Hugh, my darling, but you know that. It was your hand guided the knife.'

Elena started up but the leather straps pulled her back. 'No, no, I didn't, I swear. I couldn't have . . .'

'You wanted him dead,' Ma said calmly.

'But I couldn't have done it. How could I have got outside?'

'But you *were* outside. Talbot found you. And the gate in the cellar was open.'

'But I didn't open it. It was too heavy. I could only raise it a little way when Finch . . .'

She stopped, seeing the hard, cold smile spread across Ma's face. 'So you lied. You did help Finch escape and now you want me to believe that you didn't murder Hugh.'

'All right . . . I did help Finch. But I couldn't raise the gate enough to loop the rope around the bar. If I'd been able to, I would have gone with him. I wouldn't have stayed here for one single hour longer than I had to. Maybe I would have starved out there, like you say Finch will. But I wouldn't have cared, anything . . . anything would have been better than being a filthy common whore!'

Ma's hand moved so fast that Elena only caught the blaze of the jewel on the pin as it flashed before her eyes. The pin stabbed right through her ear lobe, fastening her to the bed. She squealed in pain, struggling desperately against her bonds.

Ma regarded her with interest, as a small boy might watch a beetle he has impaled on a thorn.

'A priest once told me, my darling – yes, I've entertained many priests in my time – that in the days of the ancient Israelites, if a slave was offered his freedom but wanted to stay a slave, his ear was pierced as a sign. No girl in this stew is a whore, my darling, unless she chooses to be one. Every woman here sells what talents she has, and that makes her an artist, a merchant of goods. She does no more or less than a scribe, a musician, or a trader in holy relics. Only a woman who lets a man take her because she is afraid of him, or of making her own way in the world, makes herself a slave and a whore. More whores have graced the noble marriage beds of Europe than ever worked in brothels.'

Elena was whimpering with pain, but with her hands bound she could not pull the pin out. Ma picked up the last pin from the bed and ran the sharp point lightly across Elena's face. Elena screwed up her eyes, sick with dread, but she couldn't even turn her head away for the pin ripped at her earlobe.

'So you went out last night,' Ma said softly. 'What do you remember? Tell me.'

'I had . . . a dream, but that's all it was, a dream.'

'Ah yes, another dream, my darling. And in this dream you killed Hugh.'

'No, no,' Elena protested. 'In my dream a man was dead. But I don't know who it was . . . his face, it was . . . I was holding a knife, but I didn't stab him. You have to believe me.'

'I told you, my darling, the first night you came here, that I don't have to believe anything. And the undeniable fact is Hugh is dead. You wanted him dead. You were found outside in the streets. You remember seeing him dead and you remember holding the knife.'

'But I couldn't have got out, Ma. I couldn't lift the gate. It's too heavy.' Elena was almost sobbing. Her ear was burning, and her head throbbing. She remembered nothing clearly enough to make sense of it.

Ma reached over and slowly pulled the pin from Elena's ear. Elena gritted her teeth against the pain, feeling the warm trickle of blood run down her skin and pool wetly behind her neck.

Ma wiped the scarlet blood from the pin on her gown and slid it back into the coils of her black hair.

'I knew a woman once. Beasts pulling a wagon were spooked and broke into a gallop, the wagon toppled over and fell on her little son, pinning him by his legs. He was screaming, and before any of the neighbours could reach him, his mother had got hold of the wagon and lifted it off her son. Not even a man could do that by himself.

'Fear and hate can lend a woman strength greater even than a blacksmith. You had a reason enough to hate. I saw it in your face the night he finished with Finch and again when he took you. I'd not condemn any woman for taking a knife to a man who deserves it. In fact I'd admire her spirit. But this is serious, my darling. Osborn will turn this town upside down looking for his brother's killer. Too many men saw Hugh at the brothel just hours before. There will be some who'll be too ashamed to admit where they were and so will keep silent, but others will not care if it be known where they went, especially if a heavy purse is dangled in front of their eyes.

'Talbot and I can talk our way out of this, but we can't have Osborn questioning you. One of my whores, already a fugitive from justice, has killed two noblemen. If they ever discover you killed them, they'll accuse Talbot and me of luring them here, maybe even paying you to do it. We'll all hang together and I've no desire to get my neck stretched. I can't risk you being caught and questioned. You'll have to stay down here, hidden. The girls already believe you've run off, and will say so if asked, but you'll have to remain here and stay quiet. Talbot's fetched your things.'

She nodded to the corner where Elena could dimly make out her small bundle.

Elena nodded. 'I swear I'll stay hidden. But please, don't make me stay like this. Please untie me and I promise I won't make a sound or try to get out.'

Ma hesitated. She glanced over at the mask on the wall which was her eyes into the guest hall. She crossed over, climbed the steps in front of it and, after briefly glancing out, she swung the wooden shutter across it and latched it.

Then she returned to the bed. Standing at the end, her short stubby arms wrapped across her ample breasts, she frowned at Elena.

'I'll release you, but you stay quiet and keep away from that.' She pointed to the shutter. 'You make a single sound, or open that shutter, or make any attempt to leave this room, and I will cage you with the other wild beasts. You'll be in good company, for they are man killers too.'

Four Days after the Full Moon, October 1211

Hare – It is unlucky if a hare crosses the path of a mortal, and if he is setting out on a journey or to take to the seas in a boat, he must turn back and not venture forth that day. If a pregnant woman should chance to see a hare, her child will be born with a harelip. If a man dreams of a hare it is a certain sign his enemies are plotting against him. The name of the creature is never uttered on a ship for fear of raising a storm and if an enemy wishes to curse a ship, he will hide on board a hare's foot and then that ship shall surely founder.

But a hare's right foot if worn or kept on the person will ward off the aches of age in the limbs or the cramps.

If a lover deserts a maid and she dies of grief, she will be turned into a white hare. Witches can, at will, turn themselves into hares, and in this form they will sit upon a cow's back and milk her dry, and likewise they will dry the milk of sheep, and in the form of a hare do great mischief on the farm. A witch-hare may only be killed with a silver knife or silver arrowhead, and if a hare is wounded then escapes, mortals search the village to find a woman who is similarly injured and then they know her for the witch.

But once, long ago, when the old gods ruled the land, the hare was honoured and no mortal man could harm her or eat of her flesh, for she signified the return of spring and was sacred to the goddess Eastre.

As with mandrakes, those women with gifts that men cannot control, men fashion into witches and demons, that they might destroy them.

The Mandrake's Herbal

The Devil's Bargain

Down in Ma's hidden chamber, Elena heard the bell tolling in the guest hall and moved closer to the hollow mask on the wall. She dared not open the shutter which covered the mask for she guessed the light from the candle in Ma's chamber would shine out of the eyes of the mask and give her away. And she was too afraid of being left in the dark to extinguish the candle.

Elena had not been permitted to leave the chamber since Ma had hidden her here. She could only count the passing of the hours by the guest hall bell. She knew it must be evening when the bell in the guest hall began to toll repeatedly as the customers arrived and then later she would hear the great door opening and closing as one by one they left. But as far as she could tell it was morning now, too early for customers. Was it the sheriff's men? Her heart began to race.

So she pressed her ear against the wooden shutter, but she could hear little except Talbot's deep growl. No words of any visitor, which meant there was only one of them, she thought. If there were a group of men in the guest hall, she would surely hear them. The sheriff wouldn't come alone.

The trapdoor grated above Elena's head. She tripped and almost sprawled headlong in her effort to get back on to the bed before Ma descended the ladder. But there was no creaking of the ladder.

Instead, Ma put her head through the hatch. 'Come here, my darling.'

Elena crept over to the foot of the ladder. Ma's face peered down at her, as distorted as one of the grotesques on the wall.

'Hurry up, my darling, you have a visitor.'

Slowly, still trembling, Elena mounted the steps and emerged in Ma's chamber. Talbot was standing in the doorway.

'Best show her visitor up here,' Ma said. 'We can't have Holly seen below.'

Talbot grunted and moved off down the stairs.

'Is it Master Raffaele?' Elena asked. Ma must have got word to him that she was no longer safe here. This time he surely would take her away. He must, no matter what he'd said before. Her heart gave a little judder of excitement and fear.

'Not Master Raffaele, but someone from your village.' Ma glanced up at her curiously. 'Someone you haven't seen for a long time.'

Despite the dark hollows that fear and sleeplessness had carved around Elena's eyes, they suddenly shone so radiantly that you would have sworn someone had lit a candle behind them.

'Athan! It's Athan, my husband. I knew he'd come in the end. I knew Raffaele would tell him where I was.'

But her delight was suddenly tinged with fear. In her joy at the prospect of seeing him, she had almost forgotten her dread of him finding her in this place. But if he'd come here asking for her that surely must mean he wanted her back. She heard footsteps on the staircase and it took every grain of willpower she possessed to stop her feet from running down the steps to meet him.

Talbot entered the room first and stepped aside. The smile of joy on Elena's face dissolved instantly as a tall, slim figure stepped out from behind him. The woman threw back her hood. Ma was right. It was someone she had not seen for a very long time and someone she had never thought to see again.

Gytha, the cunning woman, stood in Ma's chambers, gazing round the small shuttered room with a look of admiration and amusement, her eyes darting from the petrified forest of wax to the serpent throne. She ran her fingers lightly across the carved snakes, which almost seemed to ripple and purr under her touch.

'So the spirits speak to the dwarf too.'

Talbot was staring at the dark-haired woman, his jaw hanging as slack as a pimple-faced youth's. As if Gytha could read his thoughts, she turned swiftly round to face him, her cold, slate-blue eyes regarding him with an unblinking stare. He hastily averted his gaze and backed out of the chamber, surreptitiously spitting on his two forefingers like some old crone warding off a hex.

Elena, numb with shock, looked round for Ma, but she had vanished.

Gytha glanced at Elena's hair. 'A good disguise, though I'd still have known you, lass.'

Shock gave way to fury and Elena suddenly sprang to life. Not caring who might hear her, she screamed, 'Where's my baby? What you have done with my son?'

Gytha regarded her with amused tolerance. 'Don't fret yourself. He's well enough and safe . . . for now at any rate. I promised you he would be.'

'Where is he?' Elena demanded again. 'Where did you take him? Why did you disappear like that? They accused me of murdering my baby. I told them I'd given my bairn to you to keep him safe, but they couldn't find you anywhere and they wouldn't believe me. They tried to hang me.'

'You look very much alive to me,' Gytha answered calmly.

'Only because . . .' Elena stopped herself just in time.

She didn't know how much Gytha knew of Raffaele's part in her escape, and yet surely only Raffaele could have told Gytha where she was hiding? Who else knew?

'How did you find me? Who told you where I was?'

Gytha let her fingers trail across the box with the carved eye on Ma's desk. She paused, her hand hovering above it like a falcon hunting.

'The spirits told us. Madron and I, we've been watching you, lass. Her with her bones, me I see things clearer in my bowl, but no matter, the spirits tell us the same things. We've performed some powerful charms for you, and see,' she touched Elena's cheek, 'you're thriving like a cow on fresh pasture.'

Elena flinched away. 'But then you knew! You knew what I was accused of and still you didn't come back and speak for me.'

'There was no need, lass. The danger passed.'

Up to that moment, Elena had been too bemused and angered by Gytha's unexpected visit to think through what this now meant. She had been expecting Raffaele to take her away from this place, but it suddenly occurred to her there was no need. If Gytha simply gave her back her son, she could go home and prove that she had been innocent all along. True, she was still a runaway villein, but surely if they could see she had been falsely accused then all would be well. Only Ma and Talbot knew she'd killed Raoul and Hugh and they wouldn't tell anyone. As Ma said, they'd be putting themselves in danger if they did.

Athan would be overjoyed to see them both and filled with remorse at not having believed her. She could already feel his arms about her; smell the familiar, comforting warm-hay scent of his neck; hear him say he would do anything to make it up to her. And that bright, multi-coloured dream drove all other thoughts from Elena's head. She was a drunkard who laughs at the pretty dancing flames without realizing that it is her own house that is burning.

She beamed at Gytha. 'Now that you've come, I can take my son back home to Athan. I don't have to hide here any more.'

Gytha frowned. 'Athan, but . . .' A curious look came over her face. 'So,' she breathed softly, 'so Madron was right, this will make it easier.'

'What?' Elena demanded. Then, receiving no answer, she said eagerly, 'When can I see my little son? Is he here in Norwich? Is he grown? I've longed so much to hold him again.'

Gytha's eyes flicked round each of the chairs in the room, then, drawing up a footstool, she squatted on that instead, as if she was back in her own cottage. She motioned Elena to sit, and without thinking, Elena hunkered down on the wooden floor. It seemed natural now that Gytha was here.

'Don't fret over your bairn, lass, you'll see him soon enough. But you made a promise, remember? A debt. You must needs pay it afore you can see your son.'

'You mean money for the child's keep?' Elena said. 'I can get that. How much does the wet nurse want?' She was sure Raffaele would give it to her.

Gytha gave a grunt of laughter. 'Not for the bairn, for Yadua. You bought her from me, remember, so you could learn what the night-hag would show you in your dreams. I told you Yadua can't be got with coins or jewels, only for the same payment for which she was bought. I warned you that some day I would ask you for a small service. And you swore you would do it.' Gytha had leaned forward, and now her cold, hard eyes were boring into Elena's so intensely that Elena felt her skin prickle. 'That day has come, lass. Time to pay what you owe.'

Without knowing what she was afraid of, Elena's stomach shrank into a knot. 'What is it . . . what do you want me to do?'

Gytha cupped her hands together like a bowl, and stared down into them. Whether it was the angle at which she held them to the candles, or something more, Elena couldn't be certain, but it seemed to her that an ice-blue light was flickering in the hollow of Gytha's palms as if she held a tiny imp imprisoned there.

'Let me tell how Yadua was bought, lass, the price that was paid for her. Then you'll understand what you must do.'

Gytha's gaze flickered briefly up to Elena's face before returning to the dancing flame in her hands.

'Many years before I was born, a poor man called Warren came to visit a healer in the city of Lincoln in the dead of night. This woman's name was Gunilda. Warren told her his little daughter had been cruelly raped by a Norman knight, but being a poor man, he could get no justice for his child who lived in constant terror that the man might return and attack her again. He begged Gunilda for a poison to kill this knight, so his daughter might recover her wits. Gunilda felt pity for him, for she had a daughter of much the same age, and seeing how distraught he was, she agreed to give him the poison, and in exchange he gave her the priceless treasure of a mandrake.

'But the man had lied. He had no daughter, nor any bairn to his name then. He was himself a wealthy knight and wanted the poison to murder his innocent wife, so that he could marry his pregnant mistress. But when his wife lay in her coffin, the foul deed was discovered. Warren swore that Gunilda had visited his wife and poisoned her while he was away from home. Gunilda was tried by ordeal and found guilty. She was strangled and her body burned in front of her little daughter. Before she died, Gunilda cursed Warren and all his descendants.'

Elena was staring in bewilderment at Gytha. The story shocked and saddened her. After her own trial, she could feel only too well the despair of the woman at not being believed, the cruel and bitter injustice of it. But she couldn't understand why Gytha was telling her this.

Gytha opened her palms. The bright blue-white flame darted upwards and vanished, leaving only a curling tongue of silver smoke in the form of a running fox. Gytha cocked her head on one side, watching Elena.

'You want to know what this has to do with you, don't you, lass? Before you bought Yadua, this story was nothing to you. But now it is your story. You belong to it, as it belongs to you. Before she was executed Gunilda gave the mandrake Warren had given her to her own little daughter. And now you own that very mandrake, because, you see, Gunilda's little daughter is my mother, my own Madron. And she was forced to stand alone in the square in front of the great cathedral and watch her Madron burned to ash. The priests wanted to make sure that Gunilda was utterly destroyed both in this world and the next. For without a body, the priests say she cannot be resurrected at the world's end. They wanted to obliterate any trace of her, any memory. She was nothing to them and they would make sure that nothing of her would remain.

'And in due course, Warren's mistress, now his new bride, was brought to bed of a boy, a precious son. Now that bairn is grown to a man. And you know that man, lass, you know him only too well. It was he who ordered you to be hanged. Warren's son is Osborn of Roxham.'

'Osborn!' Elena's eyes opened wide. For a moment all words fled from her. Then she whispered, 'It makes sense that a man as cold as Osborn should have such an evil father. Your poor grandam, and your mam too, she must hate that family.'

Gytha's mouth twitched in a flicker of a smile. 'More than you could ever know. But many have cause to hate him, especially you.'

Elena felt suddenly chilled. She had touched the mandrake that this dead woman had held in her own hands, perhaps even lying in a dungeon the night before her execution, as Elena had lain in hers. She felt as if the dead woman's hands were grasping hers and would not let go, but were dragging her back down into the earth.

Elena drew in a deep, shuddering breath. 'You said you wanted me to do something for you, but you still haven't told me what it is. When I get back to the village I could –'

'This will not wait till you return to the village, lass,' Gytha said. 'Yadua was bought with my grandam's life, a life taken by murder. I warned you that as the mandrake was bought, so she must be paid for. Warren's first-born son is coming here to Norwich to hunt for his brother's killer. And you must kill him. That is how you will pay for Yadua. She was bought with blood, and only in blood can you pay the price for her.'

Elena sprang to her feet, her eyes wide in horror. 'No, I can't! I can't kill Osborn. I'll give you back the mandrake. I'll fetch it at once and you can take it. I don't want it.'

She tried to push past Gytha to reach the curtain which

concealed the trapdoor. But Gytha reached out a long bony arm and barred her way.

'I can't take her back, lass. She belongs to you. She has proved that, for she has been your fetch. If she had not truly been yours, she could never have shown you the dreams. You swore on spirit bones that you would pay the price for her. You gave your oath.'

'But I didn't know you meant this,' Elena pleaded. 'I can't kill anyone. I wouldn't know how. Osborn is a man, a knight, how could I possibly kill someone like him?'

Gytha smiled. 'But the dwarf tells me you have already killed Raoul and Hugh. Have you forgotten so soon why Osborn is coming here, to find his brother's murderer? To find you!'

'But I can't have. I only dreamed –'

'Yadua cannot lie. You saw yourself doing it and you have certain proof that you did it, for both men are dead. You killed them, and you know full well you would have murdered your son also, had you not begged me to take him to safety. If Osborn discovers his runaway serf has murdered his own brother, a man of noble blood, he will not just hang you; he will have you executed for treason. You will burn to death and you will taste such agony as you have not even imagined. You will scream to die, but they will not let you. It is you or Osborn. It's only a matter of time before he discovers the truth.'

Elena was pacing the room frantically, almost dashing herself against the walls in a frantic attempt to escape Gytha's words.

'No, no! It isn't true. I didn't kill Hugh or Raoul. They will find the real killer. God won't let me die for something I didn't do. He protects the innocent. That's why I was able to escape from the manor, because God knew I was innocent.'

'My grandam was innocent and God did not protect her,' Gytha said savagely. 'Once Osborn discovers you here, that will be all the *truth* he needs.' She rose, towering over Elena. 'Listen to me. You can deny it to others, but you know in your heart you have already killed twice. Osborn is an old man compared to Hugh. You can do it again easily enough. You are strong. Think about how he tried to hang you, without a second thought.'

'But I wasn't hanged. He was angry. Maybe . . . maybe in the morning he would have shown me mercy. Perhaps he just meant to frighten me to test whether I was telling the truth. And if I can show him my son, prove to him that I didn't kill him, then he will believe I am telling the truth about Raoul and Hugh too.'

Gytha clamped her hands on either side of Elena's face, forcing her to look up at her. 'You think Osborn would have shown you mercy, do you, lass? Like the mercy he showed Athan, when he discovered you'd escaped?'

A cold bubble of fear shot upwards through Elena's spine. 'What . . . what did he do to Athan?'

Gytha's face was impassive.

'What?' said Elena, frantically. This time it was she who was trying to force Gytha to look at her. 'Tell me, what did he do? Did he beat him? Fine him? What?'

'Osborn hanged him,' Gytha said quietly.

'No.' Elena's legs gave way beneath her and she crumpled to the floor. 'No, no, he can't have. Athan is at home waiting for me. I know he is. Raffaele would have told me . . . he would have told me. Athan can't be . . . dead. He can't . . .'

Gytha crouched down. 'Osborn hanged him in place of you, because he thought Athan had helped you to escape. He was your lover, after all. Athan denied it, but Osborn wouldn't listen. Do you still think he will listen to you, lass? Osborn murdered Athan, an innocent man. Can you really tell me you don't want to kill that devil for what he did?'

Elena's teeth were chattering uncontrollably, but she was too shocked to cry. She still couldn't take it in. It had been so long since she'd seen Athan. All this time she'd been imagining what he was doing each day, who he was with. Every morning she'd looked up at the little square of sunshine or rain or cloud above the courtyard, thinking that soon that cloud would drift across

Athan, or that rain would fall on him. It had almost been a way of touching him. She'd pictured him scrubbing the sweat from his face with a twist of hay, or sitting at the fireside plugging his leaking boots with wisps of sheep's wool, or shovelling down his pottage as if he'd been starved for a week. She could see him turning towards her with a bashful grin as she called out his name. In her head he was still doing all these things, and being told he was dead couldn't stop her seeing him alive.

Elena didn't even notice that Gytha had crossed the room and was standing by the door.

'Kill him, lass, and the debt will be paid. You'll have your son safe. But if you fail, remember what Madron told you that day you came to me. Yadua has other powers, powers she can turn against those who do not pay the price for her. Fulfil my grandmother's curse and destroy Warren's son, else by the power of Yadua, her curse will fall upon your own son. And that I swear. Ka!'

Elena didn't know how long she crouched there on the floor of Ma's chamber. At times her thoughts flashed so quickly through her head, she couldn't make sense of them, then they were drifting down around her like the seeds from a dandelion, blowing away when she tried to grasp them. Athan was dead . . . no, he was still waiting for her. All these months she had been praying for him, thinking about him, so he couldn't be dead . . . he was lying in the cold earth, decaying, his flesh was rotting, his cornflower-blue eyes eaten away . . . No, no they couldn't be because she'd seen them laughing at her as she ran towards him.

It was easier to imagine her own baby dead, because she'd seen that in her head, but not Athan. She'd seen the other men dead too, and now Gytha wanted her to kill Osborn. She could picture him too in her head, bored, impatient, ordering her hanging as if he was ordering a cook to wring a chicken's neck. A huge man, a powerful man, who could knock a soldier down with a sideways glance.

'You made your mind up, my darling?'

Ma was sitting on the serpent's throne, peering down at her. A dozen ruby eyes stared out unblinking from her crow-black hair.

'She speaks sense, that friend of yours. There'll be no convincing Osborn his brother was killed by the dog-fighters. It's him or you, my darling.'

Elena stumbled to her feet. They were so numb from where she'd been kneeling that she almost tumbled into Ma's arms.

'But I can't. I can't kill a man. I couldn't kill anything.'

'But you have. You can't cod me. When you're in your right mind you're as soft as rabbit fur. But if you hate something enough, you can kill as ruthlessly as any soldier. Think about how much you hated Hugh for what he did to you and Finch. You loathed him. You thought he deserved to die, and you saw to it he did. You made sure Hugh could do to no other lad what he'd done to Finch. And Finch wasn't even your flesh and blood.'

'But I don't remember doing it.' Elena collapsed on to her knees again, her head pressed against Ma's legs.

Ma gently stroked her hair. 'That's a good thing, my darling, the best way,' she murmured. 'Means when your blood is up, you're not yourself and you've the strength of ten. If you can kill one brother so easily, why not the other? You going to let Osborn live after what he did to your Athan? Are you going to sit back and wait for him to do the same to you? And what of your little one, if Osborn has you executed, who's going to take care of him? Do you want him to grow up like Finch to live in a place like this, where other Hughs will use your son as he did that boy? Because there's one thing I'd wager this brothel against, my darling, that friend of yours is never going to tell you where she's hidden your baby till she knows for certain Osborn's dead.'

The wall inside Elena which had held firm for so many months finally burst apart and she howled in grief and fear.

*

Elena woke to the sound of murmuring voices. At first she thought she was back in the girls' sleeping chamber, but then she realized that she was lying on a fur. She wasn't down in the chamber beneath the trapdoor though. A faint light was filtering in from behind a heavy drape in front of her and she knew that she must be behind the curtain in Ma's upper chamber. The last thing she remembered was Ma giving her a beaker of heavy wine that for all its sweetness still had a curious bitter aftertaste. She licked her parched lips; she could still taste it now. Her head throbbed and she knew it had been laced with poppy syrup. She must have fallen asleep at once.

She lay where Ma had placed her, unable to summon the will to move. She felt dismembered, as if her limbs were no longer joined to her body but had been dropped carelessly beside her. Thoughts swam in and out of her head, but they didn't stay. *Gytha had been here. Athan was dead. Her baby was alive. Osborn . . . what was it about Osborn?*

The voices behind the curtain floated towards her, joining the darting shoal of words in her head. A chair scraped against the floorboards.

'She'll never do it, not Osborn,' a man's voice said. 'She's too afraid of him.'

'She will, if she's frightened enough of the consequences if she doesn't.' That was Ma's voice. 'There's her child to think of. That cunning woman threatened to curse the boy. Make no mistake, that's no idle threat. I've seen the mandrake that girl's got in her bundle. Felt it. It's real, trust me, that's no bryony root. I've known some powerful charms in my time, but the mandrake's stronger than all of them put together. Most spells only have power in this life, but a mandrake's born at the same instant a man dies. That means its curse can follow you through the gates of death itself and into the life beyond. I'd not go against it, not for a whole kingdom and every lusty man in it.'

'You could throw the lass out,' Talbot growled. 'She'd take the curse with her and then we'd be done with it. She rides an ill wind, that one.'

'Maybe it's you I ought to throw out,' Ma snapped. 'Those fights of yours have knocked the wits clean out of you, if indeed you ever had any. Hugh's dead. You got the revenge that you wanted for him trying to hang you, so now you think we've no further use for the girl. Don't you understand, we need the girl to kill Osborn? That cunning woman was right, any commoner arrested for Hugh's murder will more than likely be charged with treason for killing nobility. You given half a thought to what that will mean for us? If Osborn thinks that one of my girls murdered his brother, you think he's not going to hold me responsible? And if he comes for me, then you'll hang too, my darling. I'll make quite sure of that.'

There was a violent scraping back of a chair as if someone had sprung to their feet.

'You try to take me down, you old witch, and I'll take your eyes out long afore the hangman gets his hands on that scrawny chicken's neck of yours.'

If Ma was impressed by the threat, she did not betray it. Her voice was as unruffled as ever. 'If Osborn dies it'll be up to Raffe, as Osborn's steward, and the sheriff to make report of it to the king. Neither of them is exactly going to shed any tears over Osborn, are they? And the Bullock's going to make damn sure that no one suspects the girl. If they have to find a pigeon to truss up for hangman they need look no further than that Frenchman Raffe brought to Norwich. He can be blamed for anything, especially murder. John won't need any persuading that the French have a hand in this. From what I've heard, if a bean gives him the bellyache he swears it was a French one.'

'But if the lass fails?' Talbot protested.

'She can't. She's got the mandrake. By rights that girl should be dead a dozen times over, but she has a charmed life. She just needs convincing that she's killed before. But you'll have to help her,' Ma continued. 'You needn't scowl like that, my darling; I'm not asking you to kill him. The racket you'd make doing it, we may as well put up a tent and charge the crowd a penny to watch. Subtlety was never your strong point and this one must be dispatched quietly. But we need to make it easy for the girl. You'll have to keep a watch on Osborn when he arrives here, you and that gang of street urchins of yours, for I'm certain that cunning woman is right, he will come to Norwich. And when he does, we need to find a way to get him alone for long enough for the girl to do her work. You can surely manage that much at least.'

Talbot growled. 'If you ask me, it'd be easier to stuff the pair of them down that hole in the cellar, Osborn and the girl, save ourselves a deal of bother. I should never have hauled her out of there, but that's me, too tender-hearted for me own good.'

Six Days after the Full Moon, October 1211

Cabbage – will strengthen the sight of those whose eyes are weak and ease the pain of those with gout. The juice of the cabbage in wine will aid those bitten by vipers. If the leaves are boiled in honey and eaten, they may relieve a hoarseness of the throat and help those who are falling into a consumption.

Mortals who would know their future must pull up the whole plant with their left hand upon the midnight hour. The quantity of soil that clings to the roots shall be the measure of their future wealth.

When the cabbage is harvested, a cross must be cut in the stalk that remains in the ground, so that it shall be protected from the Devil and bring forth new shoots. Likewise, a cross must be cut in the stalk of the plant before it is cooked, so that evil spirits may not hide among the folds of the leaves and so be swallowed by the eater and take possession of him.

For it is the nature of evil to hide where mortals least think to find it.

The Mandrake's Herbal

The Ring

Another roar and a crash echoed out of the Great Hall and the servants in the courtyard glanced uneasily at one another. They moved hurriedly about their tasks, hardly daring to speak to one another, except for hastily whispered news of the latest outburst of Osborn's temper. Few dared to linger in the courtyard, still less in the Great Hall, unless they were forced to. Scullions and pages drew lots with straws to select the unfortunate lad who would next answer a summons for wine or meat, for those that did thought themselves lucky if they escaped with only the dish tipped over their heads or the flagon cracked across their skulls. Even Osborn's own men found excuses to be attending to their horses or falcons.

Osborn had been in a seething rage ever since he had learned of Hugh's murder the evening before. But if he had shed any tears over his brother's death, no one had seen them.

A messenger from Norwich had arrived just as the sun was setting. He had ridden swiftly ahead of the trundling ox-wagon which conveyed the lead coffin, to prepare Osborn and the manor for the sad burden they were shortly to receive. The messenger, though young, was well accustomed to being the bearer of unwelcome tidings and had delivered the news in what he thought to be suitably gravid and sympathetic tones. In his experience, after initial disbelief, whilst the women of a household would shriek, sob or even swoon, a grieving brother or father would usually bow his head in sorrow, or mutter a prayer, or just sit in shock and silence.

But Osborn did none of these things. Instead he sprang up and with a great bellow of rage had thrown over the heavy oak table, so that it crashed down from the dais. Only the messenger's adroit leap backwards had prevented the table edge from severing his toes. Osborn strode towards him and, grabbing the front of his tunic, demanded how, when and above all by *whom* this outrage had been committed. The quaking messenger could answer the first two questions easily enough, but as to the third, as he explained, no one had any idea, though the sheriff was even now looking for the culprit and would not rest until . . . But Osborn did not wait to find out when the sheriff would rest. He flung the messenger aside and, calling for his horse, rode out to meet the ox-wagon as it rumbled its slow, melancholy pace towards the manor.

The messenger started to run after Osborn. He had been given firm instructions to ask for the cost of transporting the body and the coffin, for lead coffins did not come cheap, and the sheriff was in no mind to dip into his own coffers. But even the hapless messenger could see that Osborn's wrath was more to be feared than the sheriff's. In the end Raffe took pity on the young man and paid him from the manor chests, though he did not add in the hefty bribe that the sheriff had hoped for to sweeten the long hours he would have to spend trying to find the killer.

The coffin, still sealed, now lay in the undercroft of the manor. In due course, when frost hardened the roads, it would be transported back to Hugh's birthplace in the south of England, but the tracks were sodden and muddy after the storm, and would become more so as autumn rolled on. This was no time to be transporting such a heavy load, and in any case Osborn had only one concern just now, to lay hands on Hugh's murderer and personally see to it that the wretch suffered all the agonies of hell, before he was dispatched there for eternity.

Osborn intended to set out for Norwich as soon as he could make ready. He had made it abundantly plain he had no faith in the sheriff being able to find a rabbit in a warren, never mind a murderer. So he would take charge of the search himself.

Grooms had been dispatched to check that the horses' shoes were firm and their feet sound. Scullions and maids were stuffing parcels of food and wine into the horse-packs, fumbling clumsily with the straps in their haste to have the tasks done and be safely out of sight before Osborn appeared. They glanced anxiously at Raffe as he ascended the steps of the Great Hall, but he waved them back to work, trying to reassure them. He knew there would be a collective sigh of relief from the whole manor as soon as Osborn's retinue clattered out of sight, but it would be nothing compared to the relief he'd feel.

He took a deep breath and pushed open the heavy door, a young maid almost butting him in the stomach as she raced from the Great Hall, tears filling her eyes and with dark red finger marks on her pale cheek. A pewter beaker came flying towards the girl's head, which Raffe deftly caught before it could hit her. One of Osborn's men, evidently the hurler of the beaker, scowled at Raffe. Osborn was venting his rage on his retinue and they were taking their humiliation out on the servants. The servants were yelling at the underservants and so it would continue down the chain to the lowliest little scullion whose only relief for his misery would be to find some tree to kick. Raffe suddenly thought again of that night when Gerard had found him punching the olive tree, and smiled.

'Think it funny, do you?' Osborn's man said. 'You'll not be laughing for long. He wants you.' The man jerked his thumb towards the private chambers.

Raffe tried to keep his face expressionless as he pushed through the curtain that hung over the entrance to the room. Osborn was pacing up and down, while around him small travelling chests lay open and his manservant scurried between them, packing linen, Osborn's favourite goblet and even packets of herbs and flasks of cordials. Osborn plainly trusted no one and was even taking his own cook with him as well as his pantler, for fear of poison.

Osborn wheeled round to face Raffe.

'You took your time. Now listen well, Master Raffaele, you will see to it that my brother's coffin has a constant guard on it day and night. I've heard of thieves making off with the lead coffins that lie above ground to sell for their value, and dumping the bodies in ditches.'

'Only those coffins left to lie outside the sealed church doors because of the Interdict,' Raffe said. 'No one would dare to –'

'They dared to murder him, a nobleman,' Osborn thundered. 'Why would they not dare to desecrate his body? You will do as I say. And if I see so much as a mark on it when I return, that shows someone has tried to tamper with it, I'll personally mark your hide so deep you'll carry it to your own grave, do you understand?'

'It will be guarded,' Raffe said grimly.

'If I have not returned before the next Quarter Day, you will see to the collecting of the rents and dues and you will bring them to me in Norwich as soon as you have them. There will be people to pay. Some men require a good deal of persuasion to loosen their tongues and unfortunately sometimes that must take the form of gold. Besides, I know that sheriff of theirs. Even with my boot up his arse, he'll not bother to do his duty thoroughly unless his palm is well greased.'

Thinking of the messenger's comments the night before, Raffe couldn't help thinking it would take a barrel load of grease to cover the sheriff's greedy palm.

'How long will you be away, m'lord?' Raffe asked the question with uncustomary deference for he knew the whole manor would ask him just as soon as Osborn had gone. They would all be praying it would be weeks or even months, though miracles like that were seldom granted.

'I'll be away just as long as it takes me to find my brother's killer, so stay alert, Master Raffaele, because I shall be riding back here when you least expect it.'

He grasped Raffe's shoulder, his cold grey eyes boring deep into Raffe's own. 'If I discover even the flimsiest shred of proof that someone close to this manor had a hand in Hugh's death, that man will find himself begging and screaming for death long, *long* before it is granted to him.'

Raffe met his gaze calmly. 'Your brother had a talent for making enemies. You'll not lack for suspects in Norwich. Any man who ever had the misfortune to exchange a word with Hugh will have had good reason to have killed him.'

Raffe heard the horrified gasp from Osborn's manservant, but he did not brace himself for a blow. Hugh would have lashed out instantly and viciously, but Osborn's revenge was always planned and something he liked to savour.

His eyes as he stared into Raffe's own were as hard as granite pebbles.

'My brother was watching you, that much he confided in me. There was something about you he didn't trust, something he was on the point of proving, and when I find out what it was, I give you my oath, Master Raffaele, you will wish your head was even now rotting on a Saracen's spike, rather than that you had lived to fall foul of me.'

'Perhaps,' Raffe said levelly, 'you should have been watching your brother.'

'What do you mean by that?' Osborn demanded.

Raffe hesitated. 'I simply meant, m'lord, that had your brother been better guarded, he might not have been murdered.'

Raffe was certain in his own mind that Hugh was a traitor. But it would be impossible to prove without revealing what Elena had overheard, and even if he tried, Osborn would never listen to him, not in the mood he was in now. His brother's treachery was something Osborn would have to discover for himself.

The two men continued to stare at each other, neither willing to break his gaze first, but the manservant was unable to bear the tension. He hurried forward to assure his lord the travelling chests were now prepared. And Osborn at once snapped into action, bellowing for his retinue to prepare to leave at once, whether or not they were ready.

Raffe stood at the gate, watching the horses thunder out of sight around the bend, their hocks already splattered with mud.

Walter, the old gatekeeper, watched the last hoof disappear, then spat copiously on the track.

'They ride like that in this mud and one of them beasts is going to break its leg and its rider's neck.'

'Let's hope it's Lord Osborn's neck,' a boy's voice muttered behind Raffe, but he did not turn round to admonish the lad. He was certain every servant in the manor was making the same wish, as he certainly was.

He clapped Walter on the back. 'What say you to some mulled ale? I think we can all breathe easy now, at least for a week, but you'd best tether one of the hounds near Hugh's coffin, just to stop anyone going near it. It's not that I think anyone might come in here to steal the lead, but I'm not so certain they wouldn't take the body. A corpse with a heart as poisonous as that would be a fair prize to those who dabble in the black arts.'

'Aye, if I knew the man who'd killed the bastard, I'd embrace him and name him my own son, that I would. But God have mercy on the man who did drive that dagger in, whoever he was, for if Osborn finds the poor devil, it's certain he'll show him none.'

Walter shivered and, with a last look down the track just to reassure himself Osborn was really gone, stomped off towards the kitchens in search of his ale.

Raffe was about to follow him when he heard a long, low whistle. He spun round and saw the unmistakable outline of Talbot's bowed legs next to a clump of birch on the far side of the track.

He hurried across and, without pausing in his stride, drew Talbot behind the trees and towards the edge of the deep ditch. Only a few dead leaves still clung to the branches, which hardly afforded them cover, but at least they were out of earshot.

'What are you doing here?' Raffe demanded. 'Why didn't you send a message to meet you after dark?'

'No time to wait,' Talbot muttered. 'So he's left for Norwich?'

'Osborn? Yes, he means to find his brother's killer.' Raffe's eyes narrowed. 'Do you know something about it?'

'More than something. It was Holly, your girl . . . Elena. She did it . . . she killed Hugh,' he added, seeing Raffe's look of incomprehension.

'Elena? No! Why are you saying this?' Raffe yelled. 'It was madness even to think she might have killed Raoul, but Hugh, never!'

'Keep your voice down.' Talbot cast an anxious look towards the manor gate, but the servants were too busy celebrating Osborn's departure to be hanging round it.

'You know fine rightly she did kill Raoul. She'll tell you herself she remembers throttling him. And if she could murder him, why not Hugh 'n' all? Hugh recognized her. That's why she did it. Ma's got her hidden in her own chambers. The other women think she's run off. Thing is,' Talbot continued, 'Hugh came to Ma's Michaelmas feast. Everyone saw him there and saw him go to one of the chambers with Holly. Our girls'll say nothing, they know better than that, but there were dozens of men and lads from the town there that night. It'll not be long before one of 'em comes forward and tells Osborn where his brother was a few hours afore he died.'

Raffe was so stunned he could hardly breathe. There was no question that Hugh deserved to die. He would have willingly killed Hugh himself if he could, but to think of Elena committing cold-blooded murder, not once but twice, maybe even three times . . . In his mind he could still see her standing there on the manor steps looking up at him, her eyes wide with innocence. He felt himself torn between the horror of what she had become and the desperate need to protect her even now.

He grasped Talbot's sleeve, panic rising in his voice. 'We need to get her away, now, before Osborn starts searching.'

'Like I say, Ma's got her well hidden and all the girls will be able to put their hands on the Holy Cross and swear that she's gone for good, for that's what they believe. Safest thing is for you to leave her where she is. You try moving her while Osborn's turning the town arse over tit and you'll both be caught. Anyway, it's not the girl I've come about. No sense fretting over a fox among the lambs, when there's a wolf on the prowl. And this wolf is a savage one.'

Talbot fiddled inside his clothes and pulled out a leather pouch. He clumsily tried to get his great hand inside and after much scrabbling and grunting, he finally pulled out an object on a broken leather thong and held it up. It gleamed in the watery sunshine. He thrust it towards Raffe. 'Recognize this?'

Raffe, distracted by thoughts of Elena, barely glanced at it.

'Look at it, Bullock!'

Raffe stared down. There was no mistaking it. There were not two like it in the world. It was the gold ring set with the pearl. The same ring he'd given the sailor who had delivered the French spy.

Talbot was watching his face. 'I'm right, aren't I, that it's yours?'

Raffe nodded. He'd have known every twist of that gold knot even in the dark.

'How did you come by it?'

'The alewife you spent the night with in Yarmouth. She recognized it.'

'The sailor came back?' Raffe asked.

That was not surprising. Probably he tried to trade the ring in her alehouse. It was the kind of place where such clandestine deals were done, but the alewife didn't seem wealthy enough to buy it, and even if she had, why would she return it to Raffe?

Talbot dropped the ring into Raffe's palm. 'The night after the storm they found a corpse.'

'I was there,' Raffe told him. 'The poor woman was sure it was her dead husband, but it was too far decayed for anyone to be certain who it was.'

He shuddered. That voice pleading and begging outside

the door to be let in still rang in his head. Was it really the ghost of her husband or his revenant corpse?

Talbot grunted. 'That corpse wasn't her husband. When they laid him out they found he'd a silver amulet on a chain still hanging about the bones of his neck. There was a sliver of bone in it. Someone recognized the signs on the amulet. St Jude or St Julian, or some such. But the thing is, it was far too costly for the likes of her husband. There was another corpse washed up that same night though. Only this one wasn't decayed, it was fresh as an oyster. When the alewife heard of it she insisted on seeing it, in case she recognized it, though everyone said he wasn't a Yarmouth man. It was on that corpse they found your ring.'

Raffe looked down at the band of gold in his hand. 'It must have been the sailor. He must have tried to row back to his ship in that storm and drowned.'

Talbot shook his head. 'This man was no sailor and he wasn't drowned neither. He'd been knifed. The alewife spotted that ring clutched in his hand as if he'd grabbed it in a struggle and the thong had snapped.'

'Maybe the sailor went off to another inn after he delivered the Frenchman to me and got into a brawl.'

'Could be.' Talbot chewed on the words. 'But there was something else they found on the man, a token, the emblem of St Katherine.'

Raffe suddenly felt a cold chill run through him.

Talbot squinted up at Raffe. 'This man they delivered to you, what did he look like?'

'Small, scrawny . . . I might have taken him for a monk if he'd had a tonsure. Strong though. He'd been taught to fight,' Raffe added ruefully, remembering the well-aimed punch. 'And he had a withered hand. Not useless, a good grip, but I'd say the bones had been broken years ago and not healed straight.'

Talbot gravely shook his head. 'I found a lad who'd served on the *Dragon's Breath*. Cut loose at Yarmouth. Didn't want to go back, leastways not on that ship. He said there was only one passenger on board. But he'd no withered hand; the boy would have mentioned that. And this man was plump, gut-stuffed. Sailors made jokes about his whale-belly, said if the ship sank they'd all climb aboard and float ashore. The man they found stabbed in Yarmouth was exactly as the boy described.'

Raffe's face had blanched. 'Then the man I delivered to Norwich?'

'Is one of John's men, I reckon. Either someone else was expecting the Frenchman or maybe your sailor realized what was happening and saw a way to make money from both sides and the middle at the same time. Reported his suspicions when the ship laid anchor. We knew John would be keeping watch on Yarmouth now it's a free port. Whoever he told more than likely paid your sailor to kill the Frenchman on the evening of the storm, once he was safely off the ship, and then John's man took his place.'

'God's teeth!' Raffe pressed his fists against his head. 'I'm a fucking, bloody fool. That's why the sailor came back alone without his companions. Why wasn't I more careful? I should have checked more, asked more questions. If Martin is John's man all he has to do now is to follow the trail until he discovers every person involved, then try to catch us all in the net.'

'Unless he's silenced,' Talbot said. 'You know him. You'll have to find him. And you'd best do it quick, afore he gets word to the king. If he discovers you come from the manor, he'll more than likely warn Osborn, first chance he gets. You'd best see to it that he doesn't get that chance.'

Hilda stood squarely in the door of the Lady Anne's chamber, blocking the way.

'She's resting, poor soul. Scarcely closed her eyes all night, with that man shouting and raving about his brother's murder till the early hours. She was that exhausted after returning from her cousin. I've never seen her look so wan. I know her cousin is in poor health, but she shouldn't keep expecting Lady Anne to make that journey to sit with her. She must have tiring maids enough of her own could keep her company. It'll kill my poor mistress, you see if it doesn't.'

Lady Anne had returned from visiting her sick cousin only an hour or so before the messenger from Norwich had arrived and had straight away retired to her chamber, but when Osborn had returned with the body, he had been in such a rage that he was unable to rest or sleep and had made quite certain that no one else in the manor could either. He had not kept silent vigil over his brother's body, as might have been expected, but instead had raged and bellowed his curses against God, the Devil and Hugh's murderer long into the night, as he furiously gulped down goblet after goblet of wine, until finally the effects of the drink overcame even his fury and he staggered to bed.

For once, Raffe almost felt sorry for Hilda, for her eyes were as red-rimmed as the rest of the servants' and she looked as if she was about to fall asleep on her feet. He resisted the urge to thrust her bodily aside, and tried to reason with her.

'I know the Lady Anne is tired. But I must speak with her. I wouldn't disturb her if it were not so urgent. Trust me, Hilda, this is something she must know now and she will not thank you for keeping me from her.' Seeing Hilda's mouth draw tighter than a miser's purse string, he added, 'Lady Anne could be in danger.'

Hilda's hand flew to her mouth in alarm. Raffe knew that this was the one argument he could use that would win the sour old woman over. Whatever her faults, she would have offered her body to a shipload of bloodthirsty Saracens if she thought it would save her mistress.

Hilda nodded and hastened into the chamber. Raffe heard her murmuring to Lady Anne, then she returned and beckoned Raffe in. Lady Anne was sitting in a high-backed chair wrapped in a rabbit-fur robe, her head resting wearily in her hand.

'Hilda, can you wait outside the chamber and make sure none loiter where they can overhear us?' Raffe asked.

Hilda looked to Lady Anne for an answer. She nodded and Hilda reluctantly shuffled outside. Anne was utterly exhausted. The dark carved wooden chair only made her appear even more pale and fragile. Raffe wanted to scoop her up, put her back in her bed and bid her sleep, but he knew he couldn't. He glanced at the door. Hilda would keep away the servants better than any guard dog, but she would be straining to hear herself. While he knew she'd cut out her own tongue rather than willingly betray her mistress, nevertheless she was a gossip and as nervous as a newly trapped songbird. Raffe could not trust her not to let something slip in a fit of panic.

'Please, m'lady, if we could take the casement seat . . . .' It was the furthest from the doorway. He offered his arm and she took it, leaning on it heavily enough to suggest that for once she really needed support. The drawn yellow skin, the dark dry hollows under her eyes, suggested she had spent many a sleepless night watching over her cousin. Raffe could see why Hilda was so concerned.

As soon as Anne was seated, she motioned impatiently that Raffe should sit with her. She gazed down into the court-yard below, where a few of the servants stood in twos and threes talking earnestly about the night's events, making little pretence at working. Rumour of Hugh's murder must have already reached the villagers, for Raffe could see a few of them sidling in through the gates to find out if it was true.

'What is it, Raffaele?' Anne said wearily, without turning her head. 'Another priest in trouble?'

Raffe cleared his throat. 'Worse, I'm afraid. The priest who asked for your help, the one I helped to escape to France, sent a message demanding that I assist a French envoy to reach Norwich. He threatened to betray us both if I didn't.'

Anne turned sharply. 'But he wouldn't have done so, I'm sure, not a man of God. He must only have meant to frighten you to secure your help.'

'Perhaps, but I could take no chances. I couldn't risk your safety.' Raffe knew only too well the priest had meant every word, but he didn't want to hurt her by explaining exactly what had happened that night in the prisoner hole.

Anne's lips trembled and she reached out her hand, briefly clasping it over Raffe's. 'My son chose his friends well.'

'Not so well, it seems. I did as I was asked and conveyed what I thought was the envoy to Norwich, but I've just learned that I was deceived. The real envoy was murdered and the man I took to Norwich was an impostor, one of John's men. I believe he means to discover all the envoy's contacts and when he does he will surely report them to John. If he learns that I am steward at this manor, he may discover that you have given aid to the priests. Indeed, he may have already known about both of us, before I even met him. If he does, you can be sure he will tell Osborn, for he knows he's the king's man.'

Raffe had expected Anne to display some sign of alarm at the news, but her face was expressionless. He had to make her understand the danger.

'Even as we speak, Osborn is already on the road to Norwich. I intend to leave within the hour to try to find this spy of John's before he learns that Osborn is in Norwich and has a chance to reach him. But I had to warn you before I left. I think it would be wise for you to return to your cousin at once. I will send word if all is well and it's safe for you to return to the manor; if not, we may need to try to get you out of England.'

Anne was gazing out of the window again, as though Raffe was discussing the price of wheat. If she'd understood what he had said, her face showed nothing of it.

'He doesn't care, does he?' she said, without taking her gaze from the courtyard below. 'I thought that if there was one person in the world Osborn would grieve for, it would be his brother. I thought he would at least feel something resembling pain at his passing, but all he cares about is the insult and affront to his house and name.'

'I . . . I believe that grief sometimes shows itself in anger,' Raffe said, completely bemused by Anne's lack of reaction to what he'd thought would be alarming news. 'Osborn is a knight. He's fought many battles in the Holy Land and in France, seen many men die. A man like that doesn't display his feelings in tears, but in action.'

'And ordered the death of many men too,' Anne said, her hands clenching tight.

'That also. But m'lady, do you understand what I said, your freedom, your life could be in danger, you must –'

'I know what I must do!' She turned her face to him. Her eyes, though still tired, were bright with anger. Two spots of red appeared on her thin cheeks. 'Do you think Osborn feels anything? Do you think he cares that his brother was struck down without being granted one moment in which he could utter a prayer, or say a word of contrition or confession? He was sent straight from this life with every one of his sins hanging from his neck, dragging him straight down to hell where he belongs.'

Raffe was stunned by the bitterness in her voice, the fury he could see blazing on her face. He knew she disliked Osborn and Hugh, what woman wouldn't, having barbarians like them occupying her home and threatening her, but he had never heard her speak with such hatred for any man. He hadn't known her capable of it.

Anne searched his eyes. 'I know what Osborn did, Raffe.'

'M'lady?'

'He told me that day after he threatened to imprison me in the hole. The day Elena ran away. I confronted him that night over the hanging of poor Athan. I told him that he could threaten to do what he liked to me, but that I would not stand for innocent people being murdered. I said that I knew John had granted him the manor, but that I would appeal to the king myself, tell him what Osborn was doing and ask for justice. Osborn laughed.'

Raffe grimaced. He knew only too well how Osborn would

react to such a challenge. He was amazed that the man had merely laughed at her. He would have expected Osborn to punish her cruelly for daring to threaten him. He would have been vengeful enough if a man had done so, never mind a woman.

Anne pressed her fingers to her temples, massaging them. Raffe could see she was in pain, but he had to be sure she would leave the manor before he could set off for Norwich, and every moment that passed only increased the danger.

'M'lady, you must make ready to leave. I'll call Hilda to pack for you.' He rose and was walking away when Anne's voice halted him.

'Osborn laughed and then he said, "Do you think your precious son was so noble and pure? Do you think he didn't murder the innocent? Your son was drenched in blood, innocent blood, *holy* blood, and you think the death of one villein equates to that? You could do penance for a thousand years, mistress, and you would not wipe one day off your son's punishment. He is screaming in hell now and nothing you can do will release him. Look to your own house, mistress, before you dare to criticize mine."'

Raffe was staring at her in horror. But Anne gazed fixedly in front of her as if she could still see Osborn talking to her.

'He told me then, Raffe. He told me what you and my son had done four years ago in Gascony. Was that the evil my son spoke of on his deathbed? Was that the sin you feared he would carry to the next world?'

She turned her head to look at Raffe, searching his eyes.

'Tell me,' she ordered.

Raffe's face was frozen with misery. 'No, no, please don't ask that of me. I can't. I don't . . . Gerard never wanted you to know. I don't want you to remember him like that. He was a good man, a great man.'

'I have heard it already from Osborn. I must hear the truth of it from you. I need to know. He was my son.'

Raffe found himself sinking to the floor, his back pressed

against the wall, his eyes tightly closed. He had to tell her now. Whatever version she had heard from Osborn would be vile distortion. He couldn't let her believe that. All the same, it was several minutes before Raffe could bring himself to speak.

'We served under Osborn twice. The first was at the siege of Acre where Gerard's father was slain.'

'I know that both my husband and my son killed many infidels,' Anne said, 'but the Pope himself declared that whatever was done by those who fought under the Holy Cross was forgiven even before the act was committed. But tell of the second time with Osborn, tell me of Montauban.'

'Please, m'lady,' Raffe begged miserably.

Anne's eyes flashed in her pale face. 'Tell me!'

'The second time . . . was when King John tried to retake Aquitaine. We landed at La Rochelle and John led the march to the castle of Montauban, close to the rivers of the Garonne and Dordogne. John vowed he would take the castle back from the rebels, but he could not afford a long siege. He brought up every siege engine he had to batter the castle, and finally he succeeded in taking it. But some of the rebels managed to slip away as the castle was stormed. John sent out the order they were to be found at all costs. The nobles were to be held for ransom and those who had little value were to be mutilated and hanged. Osborn was determined to seek favour with John by capturing his rebels. He discovered that some had claimed sanctuary in a nearby Cluniac monastery.

'Osborn ordered Gerard to lead the men in and search for them. Gerard protested that the law of sanctuary could not be violated. It was against all the rules of warfare and of the Holy Church, but Osborn told him that if he didn't persuade the rebels to give themselves up, then he would burn the place down and all the monks in it.

'You have to know that Gerard reasoned with the monks for hours, trying to persuade them to hand over the rebels, but they swore there were no traitors amongst them. He reported this to Osborn but he refused to believe it. He told

Gerard to take his men and search the place, holy or not, or he would destroy it stone by stone and burn the monks alive.

'Gerard knew the monks wouldn't simply open the doors and let him walk in, so he waited until it was dark. There was only one man on watch. The monks, I believe, thought no one would dare to violate their sanctuary. After all, such a thing was strictly forbidden. Gerard tried to disable the watchman and take him prisoner. But the fear that what he was doing was evil in the sight of God made him clumsy and the man began to yell. Gerard had to kill him. He had no choice.

'Once inside, all of us scattered to search for the rebels, but there were so many chambers, staircases and passages in that maze of a building we could have searched for days while they simply moved the rebels from one part to the next, behind our backs. Some of Osborn's men, fearing we'd never find them, began looting the monastery's treasures, no doubt thinking that if they returned with gold and silver, Osborn would be mollified. Gerard attempted to call them to order, but they wouldn't listen. The monks tried to stop them taking the holy objects, fighting broke out, and Gerard . . . we lost control of the men.

'We discovered some of the rebels hiding in a crypt beneath the chapel, disguised as monks, but they refused to surrender, knowing full well what John would do to them. We were all fighting then, in the chapel and cloisters. It was dark . . . chaos. What few candles remained burning in the stone passages showed nothing clearly except shapes lunging this way and that. It was impossible to tell rebel from monk amid all the yelling and clashing of swords. Then finally the screaming stopped.

'All the rebels were dead and many of the monks. Osborn's men retreated with all the treasure they could carry to compensate for the loss of ransom for the prisoners. I couldn't find Gerard. I was searching frantically for him among the dead and wounded. I began to fear the worst, but then at last I found him. He was sitting on the floor of the monastery church cradling an elderly monk in his arms. There was a dead man lying at their feet. Gerard's hands were wet with blood. He was begging over and over again for the old monk to forgive him, but the monk . . . I don't know . . . maybe he was too close to death to hear him. But he said nothing.

'Then we saw a red glow through the open door and smelt the stench of smoke. Osborn had set fire to the monastery, maybe to cover up the slaughter and the looting or perhaps just for his own amusement. I don't know. I tried to drag Gerard out of the church, but he refused to leave the old monk. He just kept on begging him to forgive him, as if he couldn't move until the old man had given him a sign.

'The roof was already alight. It was only a matter of time before it came crashing down. In the end, I picked the old monk up and carried him across my arms. We battled down the aisle of the church through smoke and falling wood, stumbling over the overturned altars and broken statues to reach the door. It was open, but there was a line of Osborn's men standing there, swords in hand ready to slay any who tried to escape. When they recognized us, they lowered their swords, all except one man, Hugh.

'He ordered me to toss the monk back inside the burning building. I tried to push past him, I tried . . . but my arms were full. Hugh raised his sword. As if he sensed what was coming, the old monk opened his eyes and stared up at him. He cursed us, he cursed every one of us who had violated the House of God, then he tried to pray. But Hugh wouldn't let him finish. Gerard yelled out, but it was too late. Hugh brought his sword down across the man's neck as his head lolled back over my arm and struck the monk's head from his body. The blood spurted up into my face like scalding metal, I was half blinded and stumbled to my knees, still clutching the body of the corpse. I could hear the severed head bouncing down the stone steps, then, as Osborn's men saw it rolling towards them, they began to laugh. Behind us, there was a thunderous rumble and the roof of the monastery collapsed into the crackling flames.'

Raffe was shaking. He found himself with his hands over

his ears trying to block out the sounds of the screaming men, of sword severing bone, the violent laughter and the roar of the flames. He forced his hands down, pressing them between his drawn-up knees to stop them trembling.

Anne had covered her face with her hands. Her shoulders were heaving, but she made no sound. For a long time neither of them spoke. Then Anne said softly, 'And my son never made confession of it.'

'He couldn't bring himself even to speak of it. It tormented his sleep, that I know. Many a night I heard him cry out and saw him wake drenched in sweat. Sometimes he was too afraid to sleep, and then he would drink, drink far more than any man should, but that only sent him to sleep and back into his nightmares again. Who could he make confession to? Who would hear any of us? What priest in England would have understood and absolved us from the murder of holy monks in the very House of God? Even King Henry could not make penance enough for the murder of Thomas à Becket at Canterbury, and he was but one man slain, and the king's hand did not wield the sword.'

'No,' Anne said fiercely. 'But it was the king who gave the order and God will hold him more guilty than ever the knights who struck the blows.'

She swung herself around on the casement seat and her face was flushed and her jaw set hard. 'I am glad you told me of Hugh's part in this. I had thought to make Osborn suffer by taking away those he cared for, by sending them to hell before they had a chance to confess their sins, but now I see the murder of Hugh had its own justice.'

Raffe was still too troubled by his own memories to respond, but finally he managed to pull himself together and clamber to his feet.

'You must leave here this afternoon, m'lady. I have to go to Norwich, I must find John's spy before it's too late and more innocent men are slain. Promise me you will leave here before this day is out.'

Anne nodded. 'I've heard what you said and I will go. I have friends who will take me in. You're a good man, Raffaele, a loyal friend to my son and now to me. If you would do me one last service, buy me a little time to get away and I shall always be in your debt.'

'I will do all in my power, m'lady, and if it please God I find the man in time before he reaches Osborn or the king, you will be able to return here soon. I'll get word to you wherever you are.'

He bowed with a formality he had not used for a long time, and was half-way across the chamber before some thought in the back of his mind made him freeze in mid-stride. He turned back to Anne. She was still sitting where he'd left her.

'You said *you* had thought to make Osborn suffer?'

She stared up at him. The anger which had animated her face had drained away and she looked now as lifeless as a wooden mask.

'Yes, yes . . .' She drew a deep breath. 'You have confessed to me, so it is only fair that I should confess to you. Besides, I may not live long enough to find a priest to absolve me.

'You see, my cousin . . . she is not sick, at least, please God she is not, for the truth is I haven't seen her these many months. I have instead been to Norwich and there I sent first Raoul and then Hugh to God's judgment. Raoul, because I knew he was spying for John and it was only a matter of time before he discovered I was helping the priests. But you may ask why I next chose Hugh and not Osborn.

'Death would have spared Osborn the punishment he deserved. I want him to suffer in this life before he suffers in the next. I don't want him to escape that. I need him to know how it feels to go on living when the person you love with all your soul is suffering the torments of the fires for eternity, and you can do nothing to help them, not even place so much as a single drop of cooling water upon their burning tongues. I wanted him to live with that. I wanted him to know that before he dies, for surely that is the only torment that hell itself cannot inflict upon the damned.'

Her eyes were bright with tears now, but she would not let them fall.

'I confess I had thought it would be harder to murder a man. Men always say how tough and brave you must be. But then I thought about what Osborn had done to my beloved son, how he had corrupted and damned Gerard's soul. And how Osborn even now . . . *even now* has no remorse and laughs as if it were one of his greatest victories. Believe me, Raffaele, when you hate that much, it is not hard to kill a man at all.'

7th Day after the Full Moon, October 1211

Ash – Its wood is so tough that mortals fashion spear shafts from it. They plant it about their dwellings to protect them from the evil eye. If a man's cattle are diseased he should wall mice or shrews up in the holes of living ash trees, which mortals call the Shrew-Ash, and as the mice weaken and die, so shall the disease die out among the cattle.

If a mortal should suffer sores in his ear, he must boil ash keys in his own urine and therein soak black wool, and press the wool into his ear. A child passed through a split in an ash tree will be cured of bow legs or swellings of the groin. Many ash trees are adorned with the locks of children's hair, which if offered to the tree will cure that child of their cough. Honey made from ash blossom is smeared on the lips of newborn babes, or else they are given the sap which oozes from a burning ash twig, to protect them.

Mothers cradle their infants in ash wood to guard them from foul spirits. Witches use it for their brooms, so that they shall never fall into water and be drowned. Ash wood in a boat will keep it from sinking.

The female ash tree, *sheder*, will counter the curses of warlocks, and the male ash, *heder*, will work against the hexes of witches. For the ash is a sacred tree and the three weird sisters of fate – past, present and future – water the ash so that it will never die.

And, at the roots of the ash tree lie three wells – remembrance, rebirth and destruction. And the deepest well of them all is destruction.

The Mandrake's Herbal

Osborn, Son of Warren

'I have the clothes ready for you,' Ma said. 'Hurry now, it'll soon be time, and Osborn's not the kind of man to idly pick his nose and wait.'

She tugged impatiently at Elena's shift and indicated the kirtle and hooded cloak which lay on the table.

'I can't, Ma. I can't,' Elena wailed. 'Please don't make me.'

She'd had nothing else to think about these past three days except Osborn. Even when sheer exhaustion drove her to sleep, his face floated in front of her, with its cold, indifferent expression as if she was nothing more than a hog or a sheep he was inspecting at market, and worth even less. She could still hear the impatience in his voice as he pronounced her sentence, itching to have the business done with and ride out with his hawks. He'd dropped the words carelessly into the air, as a rich man might toss a coin to a beggar to stop him whining, although Osborn would sooner kick a beggar out of his path than give him charity.

And every hour of every day, she'd tried to imagine Osborn's face when he sentenced Athan to be hanged. Had it worn that same bored expression, or was it filled with anger because she had defied him and not waited meekly for the rope as he had instructed? Was that rage in his voice when he condemned Athan to death, or cold cruelty?

And how had gentle, bewildered Athan gone to the gallows? She imagined him standing there, his head lifted inviting the noose, bravely defiant. What were his last thoughts of her? Bitterness that he'd been punished for her, or was he glad to die for her? She knew in her heart it was not the latter. For his face, too, haunted her nights, the horror and disgust she'd seen in his eyes that night he'd thought she'd murdered his son.

And yet . . . and yet she still could not believe Athan was really dead. He was still there, still walking down that familiar track on the way to the fields. If Athan was gone, then it seemed the whole of her life before this place had merely been a child's game of make-believe. The village, the manor, her childhood and Athan had existed only in her dreams.

Ma pushed her roughly down on a low stool and pulled the kirtle over her head. Then she fastened an old woollen cloak about her shoulders, which smelt of cinnamon.

'Come on, my darling, there isn't much time. Now, listen carefully. Talbot'll take you to a part of the city they call Mancroft. There's an inn on Briggs Street between Sheep Market and Horse Market. The chamber on the upper floor at the back has its own separate entrance up the outside stairs. Osborn will be waiting there. He's expecting a woman alone, so he'll not be on his guard. He thinks you've got information about his brother.'

She opened a small wooden box on her table and lifted out a small silver amulet in the shape of a hand. Across the palm four curious shapes had been engraved. Elena supposed they were letters though they looked strange to her eyes, but since she couldn't even read her own name, they made no sense to her. Ma stood behind her and fastened the leather thong around her neck.

'Now, my darling, make sure anyone who sees you near the inn, either entering or leaving it, can see this.'

Elena looked down at it, puzzled. 'Why?'

'It's an amulet belonging to the Hebrews. Most of the Jews of the city live in Mancroft; if they see you wearing this they'll think you're one of them and you'll pass unnoticed, and if anyone does remember seeing you after the body is discovered, then they'll be looking for a Jewess.'

Elena shivered. 'Ma, please listen to me. I can't kill him. I know I can't.'

Ma clucked impatiently. 'You can and you will. You've done it twice already. Remember what that cunning woman said – the curse will fall on your son if you don't do what she asks. And if it does, everything you did to protect him – sending him away, your lover's death, you having to hide here – all that will have been for nothing.'

Ma crossed to her box again and this time drew out a long pointed dagger. She crossed the room and laid it in Elena's lap. Taking her right hand, Ma crushed Elena's fingers around the hilt.

'If he's facing you, just draw close to him. Pull the dagger from beneath your cloak and make one swift thrust there and upwards.' She touched the place on Elena's ribs. 'This blade is so slender and sharp, it'll be like poking a hole in jellied brawn. If he turns his back on you, it's even easier. You killed his brother that way, so you know what to do.'

Ma slid the dagger into a pocket already sewn inside the cloak just where the wearer could easily pull it out. Elena wondered briefly why such a pocket had been made in a woman's cloak, but the thought was lost in the sudden wave of nausea which engulfed her, as she thought of the blade piercing living flesh and jellied brawn spilling out. Ma pulled her to her feet, and she stood swaying, trying to choke back the sickness.

Ma gripped her hands tightly. 'Remember, my darling, Osborn murdered your husband. He sat and watched him dancing on a rope, choking and fighting for every breath, until his tongue swelled up in his mouth and his face turned black and still he struggled. Osborn did that. Osborn deserves to die. Athan's last prayer was to see his murder avenged. Athan died for you, my darling, so you must see to it that his killer is punished. If the innocent are slain, they walk the earth in torment without rest or peace, till their own murderer lies dead. Unless you kill Osborn, your poor husband will never rest in his grave. If you ever loved Athan, you will do this one last thing for him, so that he can be at peace.'

Ma's yellow-green eyes bored into Elena's own. The ruby pins winked at her in the candlelight and the viper's tongues trembled, tasting the air. It seemed to Elena that every eye in the world was turned upon her, waiting for her to do this for Athan and her son. They needed her. She could not fail them.

Ma seized Elena's arm and hurried her down the stairs to where Talbot was waiting. Almost before she knew it, Elena was outside on the street. The shock of the cold night jolted her into a realization of where she was. The sharp wind from the river buffeted her skirts and pressed the hard metal of the dagger against her thigh. She tried to turn back for the door, but Talbot locked her arm through his and set off at a good pace towards the centre of the town. His rolling gait made it hard to keep in step with him, but he held her close, keeping a grip on her arm that was so tight she feared her bones would snap if she tried to wrest them loose.

A draggle of men and women hurried up the street. Some lit their way through the darkened streets with horn lanterns, but a few held blazing torches that guttered wildly in the breeze, forcing those coming the other way to flatten themselves against the shuttered wooden shopfronts to avoid being singed. Most hurried about their business without giving Talbot or Elena a second glance. It was too cold a night to want to stay outside longer than they had to. But Elena couldn't understand why they didn't all stop and stare at her. She felt every person in the city must know what she was about to do, and with each step she took, the dagger thumped against her leg like the heavy tolling of the funeral bell.

The air was heavy with the sweet smoke of the peat fires. Dozens of supper pots bubbled away in the houses, filling the night with the fragrance of beans, boiled mutton, salt pork, burnt goatweed, bitter sorrel and sour ale. The savoury smoke mingled with the piss and dung of human, dog, goose and swine, mixed up with rotting vegetables and the fly-blown offal floating in the gutters.

Elena had grown so accustomed to the odours of the brothel, the sweat, the musky oils and suppurations of sex, that the city stench was as alien to her as a forest to a lapdog.

Talbot said he had found her outside on the street the night of Hugh's murder, but she didn't remember any of this.

They hurried through the alleys of the leather workers, and for a while the smell of new leather, hemp and beeswax feebly nudged their way through the other stenches. Unused to walking in the city streets, Elena continually slipped on the rotting rushes thrown out of the houses and felt the crunch of oyster shells beneath her feet.

Eventually the pair emerged into a broad, straight road, wide enough for carts and wagons to pass along it.

'We're in Mancroft,' Talbot announced, drawing her into the shadow behind some steps. 'Open your cloak, lass, so as they can see the silver hand. But keep your hood pulled well over your head and if you pass anyone, keep your face down. See, that way only the silver will catch the light of any lantern and that's what they'll remember.

'Now, you carry on down this street, then the first street you come to on the right, you go up there. The inn's towards the far end, but you'll not miss it. Look for the carved mermaid with a dried bush tied to its tail, that's it. Go into the courtyard round the back, and you'll see wooden steps. Chamber's at the top.'

'Aren't you coming with me?' Elena asked in alarm.

Talbot rubbed the bristles on his chin; Elena could hear them rasping against his rough hand. 'You're supposed to pass as one of the Hebrews. Their women don't walk with Christian men and no one's ever likely to mistake me for a Jew. For one thing, their men don't cut their beards. Go on now, and you do it soon as you get in there, very first chance you get, afore you lose your nerve.'

The brief moment of resolve Elena had felt in Ma's chamber had long since evaporated.

'I can't, Talbot. I'll fail, I know I will. I'm not strong enough. You could do it, please . . . please,' she begged. 'You've killed men before.'

'Aye, and so have you.' Talbot put a hand on her shoulder.

'It's got to be you that does it. That cunning woman said it was for the mandrake. If I do it, it'll not lift the curse.'

He bent his head close to hers. His hot breath smelled of raw onions. He pinched her cheek and there was almost a note of sympathy in his voice.

'You seen the other girls, the way they sidle up to a man and run their hand over his shoulder. Then they open their lips just a little and make to kiss him. Girl does that to a man and all his defences leave him. That's what you got to do to Osborn. Then, just as he bends forward to kiss you, you stick the dagger in and run straight for the door.

'Now, go on. Sooner you do it, sooner it'll be over and the safer we'll all be. Remember, lass, if he finds out you killed his brother, he'll not show you any mercy. He'll do things to you you can't even imagine, terrible cruel things. If you want to live, he has to die now, tonight, afore he's the one that's coming for you.'

He pushed her out into the street. Turning, she could just make out his dark outline standing in the shadows watching her, but only because she knew he was there. She shivered and walked slowly up the street.

The leet of Mancroft appeared to be no different from the rest of the town. The shutters on the shops were fastened for the night and the market squares were empty save for dogs and cats scavenging among the bones and rubbish that clogged the open ditches. A few men passed her, and she remembered to lower her face, pulling her hood down. Most of the men were clean-shaven, but she could not help glancing curiously at those with long beards, though unlike the Christian men, the Jews averted their eyes from her.

She turned right as Talbot instructed. The street was much narrower here. The doors and shutters of the houses were tightly fastened and only the faintest chink of candlelight glowed through knot-holes here or there. The street seemed even darker than the thin ribbon of blue-black sky above. She felt trapped, caged like a beast driven into a tunnel. A black shadow was rolling up the street behind her like a huge wave, obliterating every spark of light. She began to run, not knowing what she was running from except that she knew she had to reach the end of the street before it touched her.

She had burst out from between the houses and had run into the wide open market square before she could force herself to stop. She doubled forward, panting, grasping her side as a sharp cramp seized her. An old man hurried up to her, his wispy grey beard rising and falling in the wind as if it breathed on its own. He glanced at her neck, and she realized he was looking at the silver amulet.

'Has someone hurt you, my daughter?' His eyes showed concern, but there was weariness in his voice as if it was a question he had been forced to ask many times.

She shook her head.

He frowned. 'Let me take you to your home. A young woman should not be walking alone at night. We are not safe in the streets of our own town any more.'

He peered at her more closely. 'Perhaps I know your family? Your father's name, what is it?'

She turned and hurried back the way she had come.

'Your amulet, daughter,' she heard the old man call behind her, 'you should cover it on the streets. The goyim, they will see it.'

As soon as she re-entered the street, she heard the music. It must have been playing when she ran past, but only now was she conscious of it spilling out into the street with a babble of laughter and noise. She glanced up. A carved wooden figure swayed above her in the wind. A lantern had been hung so as to illuminate the mermaid, but the shadows it cast only served to make the creature more fearsome. Her tail and body were covered all over in green scales, even her menacing, pendulous breasts. Each of the wild tangled locks of her hair ended in the head of a writhing sea serpent. But it was her face that was most hideous with its black, hollowed-out eyes like a corpse's left for the crows to pick at, and lips drawn back in a terrible smile to reveal rows of needle-sharp teeth.

Elena could hardly tear her gaze away, but finally she edged away from the mermaid and into a courtyard behind the inn. A narrow flight of wooden steps rose from among a clutter of small shacks and lean-tos. Elena glanced upwards to the narrow walkway above. A thin arrow of candlelight shafted through the shutter of the single chamber beyond. He was already there, waiting for her.

Elena drew back as a girl emerged from behind the inn. She crossed the courtyard, two empty flagons trailing in her hands, and disappeared inside one of the wooden huts. She emerged a few moments later, balancing the brimming flagons on her hips, in the way a woman might carry young children, as she crossed back to the inn. As soon as she disappeared through the door, Elena ran for the stairs, knowing that once she had served her customers the girl might well return to fetch more ale.

Elena made her way softly up the steep wooden steps, trying not to let them creak. Her heart was drumming in her temples and her legs were trembling so much she had to cling to the rail to hold herself upright. She should have used the mandrake. If she had seen herself do it, then she would know that she could, but she'd been too afraid to use it. With Raoul and Hugh, she hadn't known that she would see herself killing them, but she couldn't bring herself to use the mandrake, knowing what she would see and then have to live through it all again. Besides, she'd tried to convince herself that this moment would never actually come. She was sure she would wake and once again find that this was only a dream.

Outside the low door of the chamber she paused, listening. Below and far away music and raucous laughter trickled out from the inn, but from behind this door was only a chilling silence. She felt for the dagger, grasping the hilt firmly. *You've killed two men. You've killed Osborn's brother and that was easy. You can do this. You're already a murderer, so what does one more death matter? Think of your son. Think of Athan dangling from a rope. Think of what Osborn will do to you.* She raised her left hand and knocked.

Raffe picked his way across the rickety wooden bridge, pausing for a moment to stare down at the dark water racing under the supports. Beyond the river was a little cluster of houses, and scattered between them the ruby glow of a dozen cooking fires. The tanners' homes and workshops were built well away from the castle so that the wealthier inhabitants of Norwich didn't have to endure the gut-heaving stench. Even a blind and deaf man would have no trouble at all finding the tanners' cottages; all he had to do was follow the stink of fermenting dog dung and rancid fat.

And it was for this very reason that Raffe had found lodgings in this quarter for Martin, or whatever his real name was, for few people, save the tanners themselves, ventured here unless they had pressing business. Any of John's men on the lookout for French spies would hang around the inns in the centre of the city, watching for those who were asking too many questions or seemed not to know the streets, but who would think of looking among the hovels of the tanners?

Around each of the tiny one-roomed cottages lay large open courtyards. The flames of the cooking fires in the pits guttered in the darkness. Women waved the stinging smoke from their eyes as they bent to stir their supper pots, while their half-naked children played perilous games of hide-and-seek between the great vats of lime and soaking hides.

Raffe counted the courtyards as he walked, *one, two, three, then turn left, two more then.* . . . He stopped so abruptly he almost lurched backwards into the wooden hut behind him. For a moment, he thought he must have taken a wrong turn, but then he recognized the solitary apple tree in the yard. A length of rope still girdled the trunk where the owner's great lolloping hound had been tethered.

But there was no fire glowing in this yard. No tallow rushes burning in the cottage window. The door swung open, leaning drunkenly sideways, one of the leather hinges torn away. The vats were overturned, their deadly soup of fat and lime leaving a huge glowing white stain on the mud of the yard. Skins had been chopped from their frames and trampled into the mud, and the stretching frames themselves had been hacked to kindling. Not a single pot or stick of furniture that was able to be smashed or broken had been left upright or intact.

Seeing the light of a fire in the nearby yard, Raffe hurried across. A woman was ladling a watery pottage into a wooden bowl. She caught sight of Raffe and, dropping the ladle, hurried inside yelling. At once two burly youths emerged, jamming themselves in the narrow doorway as they both struggled to get through it at the same time.

They advanced on Raffe, one holding a long iron rod, the other a hefty wooden paddle. Raffe raised his hands to show he was not reaching for any weapon, but he stood his ground.

'What d'you want?' growled the youth holding the iron bar.

Raffe, still keeping his hands where they could see them, nodded to the wrecked courtyard. 'I came looking for a friend, but the cottage is empty.'

'Friend, is it? Which friend?'

Raffe took a gamble. 'The tanner's wife. She is kin to my . . .'

He fumbled in his mind for a non-blood relation, but the young man didn't wait for him to finish.

'She's got a lot of kin all of a sudden.'

'What happened here?' Raffe asked. 'Was there an accident?'

The youth took another menacing step towards him. 'Weren't no accident. Soldiers from the castle came just afore dawn. First we knew of it was the hound barking and the sounds of them smashing their way through the door. Giles was roaring and Margery screaming fit to cut through stone.'

Raffe's heart was hammering in his chest so loudly he thought the two men must surely hear it. 'Did they arrest them?'

'Course they bloody did. What else would they have come for?'

'Old Giles, he didn't go quietly though,' his brother added. 'Those shits killed his dog just to stop it howling. When old Giles saw that, he went mad. Gave out a few bloody noses and black eyes afore one of the bastards cracked him over the head and dragged him off. Then Margery went for the soldier with her iron skillet like the old warrior queen herself, but it didn't do no good. In the end they managed to get her on the ground and tied her hands good and tight, but she was still trying to kick them as they led her off.'

The lad's eyes had lost their suspicious glare and were alight with the excitement of a good fight which would lose nothing in the telling around the fire for years to come.

'Course all the tanners came running, trying to help, but we couldn't get anywhere near, for there was a ring of those arse-lickers round the yard holding us off with their pikes. We could have taken them easily enough just with our bare hands, but they said any man that tried to interfere would be arrested too . . . for *treason.*' His voice dropped to an awed whisper as he pronounced the word.

There was a question Raffe badly needed to ask, but he had no idea how to do so without arousing their suspicion even further. The tanners would sooner die than denounce one of their own, but they wouldn't think twice about reporting Raffe to the sheriff, especially if they thought it might help Giles and his wife. Raffe was still trying to decide how to phrase the question when it was answered for him.

The brother holding the iron bar had still not lowered it, and now he lifted it a little higher.

'Soldiers weren't alone. I saw that little runt standing off at the far end of the lane. I reckon it was him who brought the king's men here and pointed out Giles's cottage, 'cause they went straight to it. No one from the castle would know which was Giles's yard unless it were shown to them. And what's more, he didn't run off when he saw what was happening. He stood there bold as a stag in rut, watching like he was enjoying it. He knew fine rightly he was in no danger of being taken himself.'

The lad's eyes narrowed. 'This man, he only came here to stay with Giles a few days ago. None of us had ever clapped eyes on him afore, but Margery said he was her kin. And now there's another of you claiming kinship. Anyone would think she'd come into a fortune.'

'This man,' Raffe asked cautiously, 'had he a withered hand?'

The two brothers nodded slowly and, glancing at each other, took another step towards Raffe.

'I came here to warn Margery that they were in danger. This man . . . he was only pretending to be kin . . . Margery had not seen her real relative before, so she'd only his word.'

'Pity you didn't get here sooner,' the younger of the two said sympathetically.

But his older brother lifted his chin. 'Aye, but that doesn't explain why he should want to pass himself off as family. They'd not got a spare penny to bless themselves with. And why would this man want to have poor old Giles arrested? He's no traitor, just trying to earn an honest living same as the rest of us. Why him? You tell me that!'

He jabbed at Raffe with the iron bar, not hard enough to hurt him, just to leave him in no doubt he was prepared to inflict some serious injuries if Raffe didn't furnish him with satisfactory answers.

Raffe rapidly considered his options. If he drew his knife he could probably take one or both of them, for he guessed for all their muscle they would be clumsy and slow in a fight. But he couldn't afford to get into a fight. He needed to get away fast. He swallowed, gambling that something near the truth would sound more convincing.

'This relative of Margery's, the real one, he's a priest. He's disappeared. The man with the withered hand poses as a runaway priest, so he can denounce any who give shelter to them.'

The two brothers again exchanged glances, as if they were a single man divided in two and could not think or act without the other.

The older brother's brows furrowed so deeply they met in the middle.

'I've lived aside Margery all my life and I've never heard her mention a priest in the family. Anyway, how do you know so much about this man? What's your business with him?'

'I haven't got time to stand here answering your questions,' Raffe snapped, hoping that a display of anger might deflect the youths. 'There may be others in danger. I have to warn them, before there are more arrests.'

He didn't wait for the brothers' reaction, but turned and strode rapidly away, praying that they would not follow him. As soon as he had turned the corner, he broke into a run and then, slipping into a darkened courtyard, he ducked down behind a stinking vat and listened.

He heard footsteps running up the track towards him. More than just the two brothers, they'd obviously roused others to give chase. Raffe crouched in darkness, his heart thumping, but not just because of the tanners. Martin was moving far more quickly than he'd anticipated. The arrest of Giles and his wife meant that the sheriff must know of Martin's real identity and mission. A messenger would even now be on his way to King John, who would send more men to help round up the traitors. And Raffe had no doubt at all that Martin, and probably the sheriff too, was already searching for him.

There would be no safe place for Raffe now in England. He'd have to leave the country at once, go abroad where John couldn't touch him. He could do nothing more for Lady Anne. Please God, her friends would help her, but he dared not go back to find her, even if he knew where she was. Besides, if he was caught with her he would put her in more danger. And there was still a chance that her part in this was not known. As for the murderers of Raoul and Hugh, all he could do was to pray that no one came forward who had recognized Anne near the Adam and Eve.

But there was one person Raffe could not leave in England.

He had sworn he would return for her. The poor child still foolishly believed that she had killed Raoul and Hugh. He should have known that she could never have done that. And she still believed against all hope that one day she could go home to her village and to Athan. She didn't know that Athan was dead, worse still that he, Raffe, had stood by and allowed Athan to hang when it should have been him dangling there.

He would make amends to her for that. He would take her away, back to Italy, and spend the rest of his life working to make her happy again, to help her forget all she had suffered and all she had lost. They were bound together with bonds stronger than ever tied a husband and wife. For Gerard was in her, and through her he could still hold on to the one man who mattered to him above all others. Nothing, nothing had ever defiled her innocence and purity, and he would give his life to ensure it never would.

If Osborn had come to the door and opened it, as Elena was expecting, all might have been over in a breath. But he didn't. Afterwards, Elena couldn't imagine why she'd thought he would. Unlike her, a man of his rank was not used to opening his own doors.

She knocked and heard him call, 'Enter!'

That deep, harsh voice slashed away the last remaining strand of confidence she clung to. She would have fled at that moment, had he not called out again. 'Come in, damn you. I haven't got all night.'

Perversely, it was that very element of command that generations of lords and villeins had instilled in her to obey which made her right hand drop from the hilt of the dagger and fumble for the latch on the door. She raised it without being able to stop herself.

Osborn was sitting on a bench on the opposite side of the small chamber, his back resting against the wattle and daub wall, and his drawn sword across his knees. He was alone, but was clearly taking no chances.

'Close the door, woman.'

Elena, trembling, did as she was bid, and turned back to him. The only light came from a single lantern hung by the door, but it was just enough to illuminate a long, narrow chamber with a great mound of hay heaped against one end. At the other end several thin straw pallets were piled against the wall, together with a heap of stained blankets and sheepskins which had seen much use. But beyond the bench which Osborn occupied, there was no other furniture.

'What are you standing there gaping for?' Osborn said. 'I was told you have information for me concerning my brother. Let's hear it.'

Elena opened her mouth, but no words emerged. This wasn't the way it was supposed to happen. Talbot had told her that Osborn was expecting information, but it hadn't even occurred to her to plan what she might say. All her thoughts had been on striking the blow.

'I . . . I . . . shall I fetch you some wine, master, if we are to talk?'

'I don't want wine, girl. I want information. Tell me what it is you know.'

When she still made no answer, he sighed impatiently. 'I know what will loosen your tongue.' He picked up a small leather bag from the bench beside him and fished out a small gold coin. 'That's what all you Jews want, isn't it, gold? Give you people anything that glitters and suddenly you remember everything. A miracle, isn't it?'

For a moment Elena couldn't think what he was talking about, then she remembered the amulet Ma had fastened around her neck. Perhaps he recognized it, or he had been told to expect a Hebrew woman.

He must have mistaken her expression, for he added. 'Don't worry, you shall have your gold, and more besides, if what you have to tell me discovers my brother's murderer. Here!'

He tossed the coin towards her, but her hand had once again reached for the hilt of the dagger inside her cloak and she made no attempt to catch the coin. It fell with a clink on to the boards.

'Pick it up, girl, go on, grovel for it.'

She bent, trying to feel around for the coin without taking her eyes off Osborn, but it had rolled away and she couldn't find it.

Osborn was watching her curiously. 'Have we met before? I can't recall speaking to any of your faith in Norwich, though I've run my sword through plenty of them in the Holy Land.'

Elena turned away, trying to hide her face on the pretext of searching for the coin.

'Leave that,' Osborn ordered impatiently. 'You can search for it later. Tell me why you've dragged me from my warm fireside to this beggar's hovel. And I'm warning you, girl, if you've been wasting my time, you will pay dearly for it.'

Elena didn't rise, still trying to keep her face concealed in the shadow of her hood.

'I'm . . . I am afraid if I tell, the murderer –'

'I'll see you come to no harm,' Osborn broke in impatiently. 'Just give me his name and I promise you he'll be in the dungeons of the castle by daybreak.'

'But . . .'

'Speak, girl! Believe me, I am more to be feared than any murderer. If you don't tell me what you know I will take you to the castle myself this very hour. And I can assure you, there are men there who know how to persuade a stone to speak.'

A voice was pounding in Elena's head. *Do it! Do it now before it's too late. You've killed two men before, this time it should be easy . . . like poking a hole in jellied brawn.*

But Osborn was still sitting on the bench facing her, his drawn sword across his knee.

I've killed two men before. I can do it. I can do it!

Talbot's voice growled through all the others clamouring in her head – *You've seen the other girls, the way they sidle up to a man, run their hand over his shoulder and make to kiss him.* If Luce had been here, she would have sauntered across to Osborn and sat in his lap, distracting him with promises of what she could do. Luce wouldn't have had to think twice. Elena had seen her do it. No man had ever brushed her off. It looked so easy, just a winsome smile, a hand caressing his hair, stroking his face and the man would melt like lard in the fire.

Elena didn't give herself time to plan how to do it. She rose and stumbled across the room until she was close enough to touch Osborn's legs with her own. She leaned over him and ran her fingers through his wiry grey hair. She tried to imitate the playful, seductive tones she'd heard Luce use.

'You're a very handsome man.'

Osborn gaped at her in amazement. She quickly bent forward and pressed her lips to his forehead, running her fingers softly over the back of his neck. He pulled his head away.

'God's Blood, what are you doing, girl? I didn't come here to whore. I came here to learn about my brother's killer.'

'But . . . but I can't resist you,' she stammered unconvincingly, trying again to kiss his face. He pushed her away, then stared at her.

'I do know you! Of all the brazen tricks. You're my runaway villein, the girl that listens at doors. The moment Lady Anne told me you worked as her maid, I realized it was you I'd seen running away. So you've come here thinking to blackmail me, have you? You think I will pay you to keep silent about what you heard. Do you really imagine the king is going to take the word of a runaway villein, a baby killer, over that of a loyal, trusted lord of England? I'll make you wish you'd hung on my gallows before I've finished . . .'

He tried to struggle to his feet, but she was standing too close to him. His sword slid to the floor with a clatter. He bent forward to recover it and as he did so, she pulled the dagger from the pocket in her cloak and stabbed it as hard as she could into his back.

Osborn yelled in shock and agony, slumping to his knees on the wooden boards. He groped behind him, trying to grasp the dagger hilt that was still sticking out from his flesh. At the same time his other hand grabbed Elena's skirts and held on.

She struggled to pull her skirt free, but his grip was too tight. Seizing a handful of his hair, she yanked his head back as hard as she could. It was enough to make his grip slacken momentarily. She managed to free her skirts and ran to the door. She fumbled desperately with the latch, but her hands were slippery with his blood.

Osborn finally managed to grasp the dagger hilt. With a groan of pain, he wrenched it out and lumbered to his feet, her dagger gripped in his hand. He lunged at her, but just as he did so, the latch gave and the door swung open. She tumbled out, half falling down the stairs in her blind panic to get away.

As Elena fled across the courtyard, Osborn was shouting for help and staggering down the steps. The serving wench was crossing the yard with two flagons in her hand. She stopped in mid-stride, staring up in alarm at Osborn, who was still clutching the bloody knife. Elena crashed into her, sending the girl reeling backwards, her flagons smashing on the cobbles. Above the sound of music and laughter pouring out from the inn, Elena could hear Osborn bellowing at her to stop. But she didn't wait to see him reach the bottom of the stairs. She fled into the night.

Raffe yanked at the bell rope and hammered furiously on the door of the brothel. The small shutter opened and a face peered out through the stout metal grill. The face did not belong to Talbot, but to the woman they called Luce.

'Someone's certainly got a fire in his breeches tonight,' she scolded. 'You worried it'll fall limp afore you hit the target?' Then her face broke into her usual generous smile. 'Why, if it isn't the Bul . . . Master Raffaele,' she hastily corrected herself.

Raffe had never bothered to use a false name at the stew. What would be the point? When you stand out so much from the crowd, any attempt at disguise is useless. Luce unfastened the door and swung it wide before closing it behind him. He followed her into the guest hall where, as usual, platters of meats and flagons of wine and ale stood ready for the customers, for as Ma was fond of saying, 'A man needs good red meat if he's to hold his end up.'

Luce turned and winked, arching her back so as to push her plump breasts forward in the manner that had become second nature to her.

'What's your pleasure this evening, Master Raffe? Name the girl you fancy and I'll see if she's free to serve you.' She ran her strawberry-red tongue slowly over her upper lip. It was a gesture as habitual to her as a serving maid's curtsy.

'I need to see Talbot, it's urgent.'

She laughed. 'He will be flattered. He doesn't get many customers asking for his services.'

Then, seeing the strained expression on Raffe's face, she seemed to realize this was no joking matter. She dropped her seductive tone and became in the instant serious.

'Talbot's not here, Master Raffe. That's why Ma set me to mind the door, but she said he'd not be long.'

She'd scarcely got the words out before there was a series of raps on the wooden door.

'That'll be Talbot now,' she said. 'I know his knock, never uses the bell, he doesn't.'

She ran to answer the summons as Raffe paced impatiently up and down the long chamber. Talbot started as he saw him. Luce looked from one man to the other, a puzzled frown wrinkling her forehead.

'Go on back to your quarters now, Luce, there's a good girl,' Talbot ordered, still not taking his eyes off Raffe.

'Might have known it,' she said lightly. 'Do what a man asks and then . . .' Her voice faltered in the tension of the hall.

Talbot picked up half a pie and a flagon of wine at random and thrust them at Luce. 'Here, take them.'

Luce beamed at the unexpected treat.

'But no one's to know Master Raffe is here, you under-stand, my girl?'

'Course I do. Like Ma always says, act like a rose – smell sweet, open your petals and stay dumb. Oh, and scratch them bloody if they try to pluck you without paying.'

'Get!' Talbot jerked his head towards the door and Luce didn't wait to be told twice.

As soon as the door had closed behind her, Raffe turned to Talbot. 'John's spy . . . it's too late. The couple he was stay-ing with have been arrested, taken to the castle. The bastard led the soldiers straight to them, which means word will already be on the way to John.'

Talbot turned sharply, accidentally catching a platter with his arm and sending it clattering to the floor. 'God's thunder-ing fart, what possessed you to come here? If they've set a man to tail you . . .'

'They haven't!' Raffe said with a certainty he didn't feel. 'I looped back several times and kept watch to see if any were trailing me. Besides, Martin doesn't know I'm back in Norwich. If he's discovered who I am by now, he'll be expect-ing to find me at the manor. They'll have sent men there to arrest me and I plan to be well away from here by the time they find they've been dispatched on a fool's errand.

'I'm leaving tonight and I'm taking Elena with me. If Osborn learns Hugh came here the evening he was killed, he'll personally search this place from top to bottom, and even with her dyed hair, he'll recognize Elena at once. Hugh wouldn't condescend to notice anyone beneath his rank, but Osborn misses nothing. I have to get her away before he comes. So where is she? In Ma's chamber?'

Talbot grimaced. 'The girl's not here.'

'Don't lie to me, Talbot. I know Ma wants her money's worth, but even she must see that Elena's no good to her now. She can't risk keeping her here. Osborn will arrest Ma and you too, if he learns that you've been hiding a fugitive.'

'I doubt that he'll be in a position to, my darling.'

Raffe spun on his heel to find Ma standing in the doorway behind him.

She advanced a few steps into the room. 'Osborn won't arrest us, because Elena is seeing to that as we speak.'

Raffe stared from Ma to Talbot and back again. 'I . . . I don't understand. What do you mean – *seeing to that*?'

'She's gone to kill him,' Ma said in the same calm tone in which she might have announced that Elena had gone to fetch a pail of water.

Raffe felt as if he'd been punched in the stomach. He was certain he must have misheard her.

'The cunning woman from your village came here to see Elena,' Ma said.

'Gytha?'

'That's the one. Apparently, some months ago back in the village, Gytha gave Elena a mandrake and now she's come looking for payment. Evidently there's bad blood between Osborn's family and hers. Osborn's father falsely accused Gytha's grandmother of poisoning his wife, then had her executed. Not unreasonably, she cursed him and his descendants. Now Gytha wants Elena to kill Osborn to avenge her grandmother.' Ma smiled. 'You needn't look so horrified, my darling, Elena will do it all right. After all, she's killed two men before. She's the strength and resolve of a dozen men when her blood is up.'

'But she hasn't killed anyone!' Raffe put his head in his hands and groaned. 'I've proof that she didn't murder Raoul or Hugh. She's no more capable of killing a man than a sparrow is of killing a hawk. You've sent a girl . . . a child . . . after a battle-hardened knight. At the very least, he'll recognize her. What the hell have you done, you malicious old hag?'

He lunged at Ma, but Talbot stepped between them. His great fist slammed into Raffe's jaw. Raffe staggered backwards, crashing into one of the benches, and fell, sprawling across it.

His head reeling from the blow, he was only dimly aware of the clanging of the bell. Ma hurried across the room.

'Get him upstairs to my chamber, Talbot, and keep him quiet. Knock him out cold if you have to.'

As she pulled some steps into place so that she could peer out of the grid in the door, Talbot heaved Raffe to his feet. And Raffe, feeling the floor tilting alarmingly beneath his feet, allowed himself to be half dragged towards the staircase to Ma's room.

Elena let go of the bell rope and pounded on the door. It seemed as if she had been standing there for a lifetime before the shutter finally opened and Ma's face peered out.

'Ma, please, please let me in,' she begged.

'I'm coming.' The firmness in Ma's voice sounded strangely comforting.

Elena pressed herself against the door in an agony of waiting as she heard Ma loosening the bar and clambering down off the steps. When the door finally swung open she almost fell over the tiny woman in her haste to get inside. Her teeth were chattering uncontrollably. Her legs suddenly refused to move and she knew that if she attempted even a single step she would fall over. She stood swaying in the room, her arms wrapped tightly round herself.

Ma pulled at her hand. Her fingers felt scalding hot against Elena's icy skin.

Elena's breath came in shallow, jerky little gulps. 'Why couldn't I kill him, Ma? Why couldn't I? I killed Raoul and Hugh. But he wouldn't die. I thought . . . if I just . . . pushed the dagger in, it would be over. There was blood, but . . . but he pulled the dagger out and came after me . . . Why couldn't I kill him, Ma? Why was it so easy with the others? They died like they were supposed to but he wouldn't . . . he just kept coming . . .'

'So he's wounded?' Ma gnawed at her lip. 'Did he recognize you?'

Elena jerked her head in the semblance of a nod.

Ma took a deep breath. 'Raffe's right, we have to get you both away from here, tonight.'

'Master Raffaele. Is he . . . ?'

'He's here, my darling, come to take you away. Now, you go and sit with him awhile, get your breath back, you'll be needing it. Talbot and I've got work to do.'

Without even being aware of how she got there, Elena found herself sitting in Ma's chamber clutching a beaker of wine in her trembling fingers. Raffaele was sitting on a stool at her feet. She had allowed him to wash Osborn's blood gently from her hands in a bowl of water. She'd stared in uncomprehending wonder as the water turned pink, then scarlet. The candle flames danced, and she thought she was back in a cottage in Gastmere watching Gytha's blood falling drop by drop, swirling around and around. She shivered. She couldn't seem to get warm.

Raffaele reached out and touched the bruise where Hugh had struck her, as tenderly as any father might. His eyes were so gentle and kind, searching for hers and gazing into them as if he could see everything inside her and did not judge her.

She wasn't even aware that she was talking. But somehow all of the events of that evening spilled out of her as if she was a fractured pot and couldn't hold anything in.

Why couldn't I kill him? Why didn't he die? She was drowning in a thousand terrors: that Osborn would come looking for her; that she had failed Gytha; that her child would be cursed; that she would never find her son again; that Athan would never rest in his grave. And yet the only question that her mind could cling to was – why couldn't I kill him? Why? Why?

Raffaele took her frozen hands in his, chafing them to warm them. 'You couldn't kill him, Elena, because you don't know how. You've never killed anyone.'

'But Hugh and Raoul . . . I killed them. And they're dead.'

Raffaele looked earnestly into her face. 'But you didn't kill them. I know now who did, and you must trust me, it wasn't you. You only dreamt of their deaths, as you said all along.'

'But the mandrake . . . I used the mandrake to help me see the dreams clearer. And it was clear. I was in a church. There was a man lying on the floor, stabbed, and his face, his eyes had been put out. There was a monk too . . . he was begging me not to defile the holy place.'

Raffaele frowned. 'But Hugh wasn't stabbed in a church.'

'Then who was?' Elena said. 'Someone was. I saw them.'

An expression of horror slowly dawned in Raffaele's eyes. He drew his hands away and covered his face. He was moaning, and for a moment or two Elena thought he was crying. She lightly touched his bent head.

'Raffaele, the man I dreamed about. Did I kill him too? You know, don't you? You know who it was.'

For a few minutes he didn't answer her, then he began to speak, staring not at her but at his hands.

'I think what you saw, was not what *would* happen, but what *did* happen four years ago. Gerard and I . . . you must understand we had no choice . . . or perhaps we did. Can any man really blame another for making him do what he knows to be a crime against God? You didn't dream about what you would do, but what we had already done.'

'But I saw myself doing it,' Elena protested. 'I was there. I saw the knife in my own hands.'

Raffaele stared up at her, his face stricken with anguish. 'Do you remember the first day I brought you to the Lady Anne? She asked you to eat and drink from a chest. You remember that?'

Elena nodded. 'The day before her son died.'

'When you came into that chamber, Gerard was already dead. I'd put his body into the chest. The food was laid out for you on top of it and you ate from it. Bread and salt, as I asked you to.'

Elena's eyes had widened in fear. Her throat was closing up so tightly it was as if a hand was pressing its fingers tightly around her neck.

'But . . . to take bread and salt that has laid above a corpse, that means you take the dead person's sin upon you! You tricked me . . . you tricked me into becoming a sin-eater!'

She threw back the chair and frantically paced the chamber, wiping her hands up and down her kirtle as if the blood had seeped back over them again.

Raffaele struggled up too. 'I'm sorry. I'm so sorry, but I couldn't let Gerard die in mortal sin. I swore to him I would not. I owed him my freedom, my life, everything. He was like a brother to me, more than a brother.'

Elena turned to him, blazing with anger. 'But you let me carry his sin. How could you? If it was so terrible, how could you make me carry it?'

'I swear on my life, I truly believed it couldn't hurt you. You were a virgin, pure and untouched. You could not be hurt by it.' Raffaele's hands hung limply at his side like a helpless child's.

Elena stared at the wax dripping from the candle. 'A virgin, but . . . I wasn't. I'd slept with Athan for the first time the night before. That was the night . . . he got me with child. What have you done, Raffaele?' she screamed at him. 'What have you done to me and my baby and to Athan?'

'I didn't know. I swear I didn't know. You're the last person on this earth I would hurt. If I'd thought for one moment . . .'

'But you didn't think. You didn't. You let me carry it. You made me carry it. You made me a murderer.' Her head snapped up and she stared at him. 'My dream about my baby, hurting my baby, was that also what Gerard did?'

Raffaele lifted his head, bewilderment mingling with his pain. 'But there was no baby in the monastery at Montauban. I don't understand . . . tell me, tell me what you saw.'

'I was in a room, there was cloth hanging everywhere and baskets full of it. A store room, but round, not square. I could hear a babe crying. I was angry, so angry that they were hiding it from me. When I found it, I just wanted to kill it. I dashed it against the wall. Night after night, I dreamed I was killing that little bairn. I thought . . . I really believed that was what I was going to do to my own son. That's why I gave him to Gytha, to keep him safe, so that I couldn't hurt him.'

Raffaele sank back on to the stool. He was murmuring to himself, so softly that Elena could hardly make out the words.

'This cannot be. The Church promised us that if we took the Cross every sin we had committed before the Holy Wars and while we fought them would be instantly forgiven, wiped out as if they had never been. They promised. He was an infidel. An unbeliever. It was a holy slaying, a righteous act. The Church swore that we were forgiven.'

'What?' Elena demanded. 'Was there a baby? Did Gerard murder a baby? Tell me, I have to know. I have to know it wasn't me.'

Raffaele wrapped his arms over his head, then let them fall helplessly. 'Yes, there was a baby, many babies. But this one, this was not like the others. You have to understand . . . it was war. Men do things in war . . . things that they would never . . . good men . . .'

His face convulsed as if he was trying not to cry, and it took several moments before he could continue.

'Some months after Gerard's father set sail to fight under Richard in the Holy Land, Gytha came to Gerard and told him that the spirits had warned her that his father was in danger and was calling for his son to help him. Lady Anne pleaded with him not to go, but Gerard was adamant. He would not fail his father, he said.

'As soon as Gerard arrived, he sought out Osborn to whom his father owed allegiance, thinking to find him fighting under his command. Osborn told Gerard he was too late. His father was dead. The sappers had been tunnelling under the city walls to weaken them, Talbot was one of them, but the Saracens were burrowing out the other way, using the tunnels to attack under the cover of the Greek fire which the defenders were hurling from the city ramparts.

'Gerard's father had been close by the wall when one of

the Saracen raiding parties broke out from the tunnels under the cover of smoke. He was last seen fighting them off, but then he disappeared. That night they searched for his body, but they had little hope of finding it. Many corpses were so badly burned or crushed it was impossible to distinguish one man from another. Even the chevrons and emblems that distinguished knight from foot solider were burned or torn away. The best that could be done was to bury the remains of the dead in mass graves, but at least they had priests aplenty to say Masses for their souls.

'Gerard was grief-stricken by his father's death. He blamed himself for not having arrived sooner, but he vowed to finish what his father had begun and so we joined Richard's army.

'A few days after we arrived, Acre surrendered. Richard set tough terms. He vowed to spare the lives of all those in the city, if Saladin would give him two hundred thousand golden pieces and release the fifteen hundred Christian prisoners he held. As a pledge of faith, Richard let many of the ordinary men in the city depart in safety with their wives and children, but he kept two thousand of the more prominent men and their families hostage until Saladin should meet his demands.

'But Saladin refused to hand over the men and money on the appointed day. Some said he had already killed the Christian prisoners, others that he had sent word that he couldn't yet raise the full sum of money demanded, and was asking for more time. Who can tell which was the truth? I only know that these two great leaders could not come to terms, so Richard gave the order that every hostage in the city was to be slain.

'Gerard and I were mercifully spared the task of actually slaughtering the captives, instead we were sent to drive them out of the city, so that they could be executed in plain sight of Saladin's camp. We were ordered to go from house to house and drive them to the gates of the city. The men were bound and led out like slaves, the women and children left to walk behind or, if they refused, lashed together with ropes and dragged out. Beyond the walls we could hear the screams and wails as Richard's men herded them together. The men they dragged to their knees and struck off their heads; the women and children they ran through with swords and pikes.

'It was late in the afternoon when we came to a house on the far side of the city. We were exhausted, sodden with sweat and maddened by the flies that crawled over every stone in that city. A man ran out of the house and knelt before Gerard. He seemed to be trying to tell us his name was Ayaz. He had a cloth in his hands and he opened it up to show Gerard. He'd evidently bundled up anything of value he possessed – his wife's jewels, tiny silver cups, coins and other trinkets. He begged Gerard to take them all in exchange for their lives. Gerard refused, but Ayaz continued to plead. He laid the cloth at Gerard's feet, picking up handfuls of the gold and silver, trying to thrust them into Gerard's hand.

'Gerard was wearily pushing them away. Then suddenly he froze, staring at one of the objects in his hand.

' "My father's ring!" he cried. He held up a gold ring with a single pearl held in place by a knot of gold. "This is my father's ring. Where did you get it?"

'But the man couldn't understand him.

'Gerard pushed the ring in his face. "Where! Where!" he was shouting.

'Ayaz kept shaking his head in incomprehension, then finally he shrugged and drew his finger across his throat to show he had taken it from a dead man, a murdered man. I heard Gerard gasp and turned to look at him. An expression of horror and rage was spreading across his face. Gerard had realized that it was this very Saracen grovelling before him who had slain his beloved father; the father he had arrived too late to save.

'With a scream of grief and fury that seemed to rip heaven itself apart, Gerard lifted his sword, then stabbed it into the Saracen's heart. Ayaz dropped where he still knelt, a look of utter bewilderment on his face. Gerard, pausing only to draw out his blade, ran into the house. I followed hard on his heels. Ayaz's wife lay dead inside, a bloody knife in her hands. She had stabbed herself rather than be taken alive. Gerard was beside himself with rage. He ran from room to room searching everywhere. He was sure she had hidden her children and he was determined that not a single child of his father's murderer should remain alive to carry on that infidel's name.

'But though he searched every conceivable nook and chamber, he could not find another person in the house. Then he heard a baby crying. He followed the sound and eventually found the infant hidden in a basket under a pile of linen. I watched him pick the baby boy up by the feet. I shouted at him to stop, and he turned to face me, the infant dangling from his hands.

' "And let him grow up to slaughter other good Christian men?"

'His voice was harsh and bitter. I'd never heard him speak like that before, it was as if another man was speaking through his mouth. It wasn't him, I know it wasn't him. Then, as if he was killing a fish, he dashed the baby's head as hard as he could against the white wall.

'I was horrified. But I don't know why I should have been. We both knew the child would be slaughtered anyway by Richard's men outside the wall. You could say what Gerard did was more merciful, for at least the child died instantly. If it had been thrown into the mêlée outside, fallen beneath the bodies of terrified men and women, or been hacked at by the exhausted, frenzied stabbing of Richard's men, the infant might have taken hours to die in pain. But it was the shock of seeing Gerard, that good, noble, brave man, commit such an act that rocked the foundations of all that I knew and loved about him. It was an indelible stain which seemed to haunt him from the moment the deed was done.

'By nightfall every Saracen in the town was dead, save for the prostitutes. Some three thousand died that day, so they said. Gerard finally reported to Osborn that the town was cleared. He told him of the many bodies he'd found inside: men who'd poisoned their own children rather than leave them to the mercy of Richard's soldiers; girls who'd jumped to their own deaths, women with their babies in their arms who'd thrown themselves down wells rather than be taken alive.

'All this he told Osborn, and Osborn laughed . . . he just laughed . . . I've never been able to forgive him for that. It was at that moment I understood what a truly good man Gerard was. He cared about what he'd done. He remembered it. He condemned himself for it. But Osborn, with the murder of hundreds on his hands, had only laughed. He regretted not one moment of the pain he had caused, nor one drop of blood he had shed.

'That night the priests who travelled with Richard's army came round blessing the men and trying to cheer them, assuring them that all their sins had been washed away that day, and that they had done God's glorious work, for these pagan cattle were doomed to hell. They stood on any mound they could find and shouted the words of St Bernard of Clairvaux into the sweltering night – "The Christian glories in the death of a pagan, because thereby Christ himself is glorified."'

Raffaele was staring at the wall in Ma's chamber. He seemed to have forgotten where he was or that Elena was even there. She felt sick. She had been there. She had seen the girl hurl herself down into the courtyard. She had seen Gerard murder that innocent baby, just as Raffaele had watched it, except that Gerard's hands had become her hands. It was her own fingers that dripped red with that infant's blood.

She flinched as Raffaele suddenly began to speak again, distantly, as if he was explaining something to himself rather than to her.

'But I could never bring myself to tell Gerard the truth about what else I discovered in Ayaz's house. It would have destroyed him. And I couldn't add to his pain.

'You see, after he killed the baby, Gerard ran from the house. He was violently sick, but he didn't want any man to see him vomit in case they thought him a coward. I was about to leave too, when I noticed a low door that we had over-looked before. I discovered it led to some kind of chamber, shaped like a giant pot, with a channel running into it from the flat roof above. I took it to be some kind of cistern. In the winter rains, it would fill with water, but it was summer then and the siege had been a long one. Every drop of water was gone. But the cistern was not empty.

'There was a man inside. He lay curled up at the bottom, under a blanket. As I entered he cried out in alarm and I knew at once by his words he was a Christian prisoner. There was something familiar about his face and I guessed he was one of the soldiers I had met when we'd first arrived, though I couldn't recall his name. I scrambled into the cistern to help him up, telling him I would take him to safety at once, but to my astonishment, instead of being delighted to be rescued, he begged me to kill him.

'I was astounded. I told him the siege was over. Richard was the victor and he was safe, but still he pleaded with me to end his life. I couldn't understand it. He threw off the blanket and then I saw why he wanted me to grant him the mercy of death. His feet and hands had been lopped off. No man on God's earth would want to live out his days like that.

'He told me that he had a son and wife at home whom he adored. He couldn't bear to return home to them, unable to do the smallest task for himself, not able to feed himself or even clean the shit from his own backside. Better his son believed that his father died a noble death on the battlefield than that he lived on as a useless mockery of a man. How could he be a father to his son, or husband to his wife like this, he asked me, with tears streaming down his face. He was humiliated to weep in front of me, and he couldn't even wipe away his own tears.

'I felt as if all the breath had been sucked out of me, for as he spoke of his home, I knew at once where I had seen his face before, or rather, a younger version of it. I told him that his son, Gerard, was here in this city. That he had been in this very house not minutes before. But he begged me not to tell Gerard he was alive.

'And then . . . and then he asked me to do all in my power to protect Ayaz and his family. He told me how he had been captured by one of the raiding parties from the city and dragged back through the tunnels into Acre itself. The city leaders had mutilated their captives and left them to die. But that night Ayaz had found Gerard's father crawling among the dead and dying prisoners. He'd smuggled him home, tended to his wounds, fed him with what little they had, and sheltered him.

'You see, like many in the city, Ayaz's own father had fought in the last Holy War, not as a Saracen, but against them, as a Christian. Ayaz's father had been taken prisoner and forced to convert to the Muslim faith in exchange for his life. He had married a local Muslim woman, and their son Ayaz, like so many others in the city, now found himself fighting against his own Christian cousins. Ayaz had tried to save the life of Gerard's father out of honour and respect for his own father who had once been a Christian.'

Elena had hardly dared breathe in case she interrupted Raffaele's tale, but now she couldn't help blurting out the question, 'Did you do what the poor man asked? Did you kill Gerard's father?'

'I couldn't do it.'

The words were spoken so softly and with so much grief that despite her anger, Elena wanted to throw her arms about him and comfort him.

'I was a coward. I couldn't kill him, not once I knew who he was. I made arrangements for him to be brought back to England . . . I think . . . I hoped that in time, when he had learned to live with what he now was, he might want to see his son again.

'But the more I got to know Gerard, the more I realized what the knowledge would do to him . . . do to them both.

Gerard had slaughtered the man who'd saved his own father's life and, worse still, he had murdered Ayaz's only son, a helpless infant. Gerard couldn't have borne that knowledge. And if I had reunited them, then his father would also come to know what Gerard had done in his name. How could I add to the pain of either one of them? Weren't they suffering enough?'

Elena pressed her hands over her mouth to stop a scream escaping. 'That man . . . that poor man in the cage in Ma's cellar, that is Gerard's father!'

Raffaele raised his head and looked at her, his face distorted in misery. There was no need for him to say anything.

'How could you leave him like that in the cage?'

'What else could I do?' Raffaele sank his head in his hands. 'I had to keep him safe and hidden. I didn't have the money to pay for lodgings for him and someone to take care of him, not for all the years he might live. How was he to survive, by begging on the streets? Ma took him in when I didn't know where else to take him. She was grateful to me for saving the life of her brother Ta . . . a brother she had not seen since she was an infant. She agreed to take him. A life for a life, she said. And at least in here he is not forced to endure the contempt or pity of the world, for Ma pities no one.'

Elena couldn't look at him. She closed her eyes, trying to piece together all the fragments of her thoughts that lay shattered around her. The dreams had not been about her. She was never going to harm her baby. All that had happened, her arrest, Athan's death, what Raoul and Hugh had done to her and now tonight, attacking Osborn, none of this would have had happened, had it not been for a single dream, a dream which was not even her own, but one that Raffaele had forced on her.

'Why?' she screamed at Raffaele. 'Why did you choose me? You could have chosen anyone as the sin-eater – a beggar, a thief, a stranger, anyone. Why me? Why punish me? What had I ever done to hurt you?'

He stared at her. 'But don't you understand? It was never to be a punishment. I couldn't carry this alone. While Gerard lived we bore it together. It was our burden, but also our bond that made us closer than any blood brothers. Once he'd gone I couldn't give that to a stranger. This is my past, my memories, my whole self, and I wanted you to share it. You were the only person in the world I could give this to, because . . . because I love you.'

Elena froze in horror, staring at the pathetic wretch of a man in front of her. Tears were running down his sagging cheeks. He held his great hands out in a useless gesture of a child seeking comfort, and then let them drop as if he knew they would never be grasped.

The door banged open and Ma scurried into the chamber. Raffaele turned abruptly away, scrubbing the wetness from his face. Elena couldn't move. She could only continue to stare at him in utter disbelief.

Ma glanced from one to the other, sensing the atmosphere, but there was no time to pander to it. She snorted impatiently.

'On your feet, the pair of you. There's a boat waiting for you down river. He can't risk coming closer to the town for fear of being stopped and searched. I'll take you there myself. I need Talbot here in case the soldiers come. Hurry, it'll soon be dawn and we want you safely out of sight of Norwich by then. Here's your bundle, my darling. Now, give me that cloak and amulet, case any sees it.' She thrust a darker, shabbier cloak trimmed with grey rabbit's fur into Elena's arms. 'This'll keep you warm on the water.'

'Water?' Elena repeated dumbly.

'Haven't you told her yet?' Ma scolded Raffaele. 'What on earth have you two been talking about? Master Raffe's come to take you with him.'

Elena flung the cloak off, her eyes blazing with fury. 'Go with him? I can't go with him! I won't! You don't know what he's done.'

Ma just as firmly thrust the cloak back at Elena again. 'So you are going to stay here, are you? You've just attacked the most powerful man in these parts, wounded him and let him recognize you, and now you think you're going to sit and wait for him to find you? Well, you're not waiting here, my darling. You may not be fond of your own head, but I'm planning to keep mine on my shoulders for a good few years yet, if the Devil can spare me.'

'You needn't fret, I won't put you in danger,' Elena said, jerking her chin up defiantly. 'I'll leave this place, but I'll leave it alone. Not with him, never with him.'

'Brave words, my darling. And what exactly will you do alone? Even supposing you manage to evade capture with half the country looking for you and a wolf's bounty on your head, how do you imagine you're going to live? Begging, or whoring in the alleys of some filthy little town? You think the girls here are hard done by, but you wait until you're forced to service the stinking drunks and poxy rogues who can't afford a girl from a whorehouse. When they fuck you against a wall and give you a punch instead of a coin, when you have to spend what's left of the night sleeping hungry in a graveyard, then you'll understand what it really means to be alone.'

Ma's words were brutal, but they did what she intended them to do and slapped Elena into understanding the reality of her situation. For the moment she felt herself sinking in despair, but then she remembered what had been floating somewhere beneath the surface of her mind. She clutched at it desperately.

'We can tell them,' Elena said, 'tell them what Osborn did. Then they'll arrest him not me.'

Raffaele and Ma glanced at each other as if her wits were wandering.

Elena turned to Raffaele. 'Remember I told you what I overheard in the manor about a ship and the French? I know now who it was who was talking in the bedchamber.'

Raffaele said wearily, 'I already know. It was Hugh, but –'

'No, no, it wasn't. It was Osborn. I should have recognized his voice at the trial when my son . . . but I was too upset to even think of it.'

Raffaele stared at her. 'You're wrong. Osborn is the king's man. It was Hugh who was the traitor. After all these months, you couldn't possibly remember his voice.'

'I didn't,' Elena said. 'But tonight when he realized that I was his villein, he told me he knew I was the girl who he'd seen running away from the door. He thought I'd come to ask him for money to keep quiet about what I heard.'

Raffaele looked stunned. 'All this time I thought . . . but it was the wrong brother.'

Ma grunted. 'It would explain why Osborn was so keen to get Elena back.' She turned to Elena. 'But, my darling, I'm afraid this isn't going to help you. It only adds to the danger you're in. You've no proof except what Osborn told you and he'll deny it, but now he'll be more determined than ever to silence you for good.'

Raffaele's face was haggard and pale in the candlelight. 'Elena, please come with me. Let me try to atone for what I've done to you. I'll protect you and see that you want for nothing that a man can provide for a woman. I know that my body repulses you. I've always known that and, believe me, I understand how you feel better than you can ever imagine, for my body disgusts me too. But I swear on Gerard's soul I will not lay one finger on you. And if you should in time find a man who loves you, and whom you love, I promise I will let you go to him with a glad heart. I begged you before to trust me and I did not deserve that trust, but I shall. I swear it.'

Talbot poked his head round the door. 'If they don't go now, Ma, there'll be no going at all.'

Ma nodded. She didn't wait for Elena to reply, but thrust her bundle into her arms, pushing the girl firmly towards the door. Elena found herself hurrying down the stairs behind Raffaele without even knowing if she had agreed to go or not.

Outside, Ma grasped both their hands and with one on each side of her she hurried them through the silent streets. To any casual observer glimpsing their shapes in the darkness, Ma must have looked like a child walking between her parents.

The streets were completely deserted now. The inns and alehouses had emptied. Candles had been extinguished or long since burned away, and there was not a chink of light to be seen in any of the blind houses. A fine drizzle was falling, which clung to their faces in a wet mist of tiny beads, soaking their clothes. Elena shivered.

Raffe carried a lantern low down, so that they could pick their way across the open sewers and through the tight little lanes. A beggar, curled up in the entrance of a courtyard, groaned in his sleep as the light from the lantern brushed his eyes. He turned over, hugging himself tighter against the cold and rain. His sallow wrinkled flesh glistened wetly through the holes in his rags and his filthy bare toes scrunched into fists.

The three strange figures steadied one another over the slippery cobbles, the lantern casting a misty yellow halo around their feet, but their faces were hidden in the darkness. Elena glanced over Ma's head at the tall figure lumbering beside her. He kept his head and his shoulders hunched forward like a prisoner being marched to the gallows.

Elena still had no idea what she intended to do. She could not forgive what he had done to her. Yet, though she told herself she hated him, she understood the need to share your most terrible secrets with someone. Who could you allow to glimpse the dark creatures that prowl within you, except someone you truly love? And Raffaele did love her. She knew that. Deep down, she had always known it.

But he'd used her. Raped her in a way that was worse than anything Raoul or Hugh could have done, for such men can only touch the body, not the soul. He had made her guilty of crimes she had not and could never have committed. And yet the blood of that baby, and of those holy monks, was now on her soul and she would be punished for them for all eternity, as he would . . . as *they* would be together. The fear of that was so enormous that she could not even think about what it meant. If she allowed herself to dwell on the terror of that for one moment, she would run mad.

All she knew was that she wanted to be a hundred seas away from Raffaele. Yet she understood why he felt the loss of Gerard so intensely, because no one else could understand Raffaele's torments, no one else could see the horror of what he'd seen except Gerard and now her.

Even if she searched for the rest of her life, there could be no one she could share this with, for how could even the most devoted lover understand the images that were for ever in her head and the horror and revulsion that were in her heart, except the one man who also carried those things inside himself? She might hate Raffaele with every inch of her being, but they were one flesh. She could no more live alone with this than he could. It was more enduring than marriage; it was stronger than love, for sin would bind them together even beyond death. And for that very reason, Elena suddenly knew she had no choice but to go with Raffaele, because without him, she would have to carry this nightmare alone and that would be the most terrible sentence of all.

They had left the closely packed streets behind them and the land had opened out into the marshy ground that bordered the river. The wind was stronger here and rain slashed their chilled skin. Thick, knobbly trunks of pollarded willows stuck up from the boggy ground like giants' cudgels. And here and there the dark smudges of huts and bothies were dotted among the birch scrub.

Ma took the lantern from Raffaele and swept its beam across the wet grass, searching for something. She pointed to a peeled twig sticking upright from the ground. Her finger to her lips, she set off, following the trail. Elena trod carefully behind her, and Raffe brought up the rear. She could hear his boots squelching in the boggy ground, but she did not turn round. They were close to the river now.

Ma grabbed Elena's hand and pulled her down behind a low thicket of bushes. Raffaele crouched behind her. In front of them the great black river slid past; Elena could feel the chill of it, even colder than the rain. She glanced up, squinting against the falling drops; darkness still wrapped itself around the city, but a fiery red glow was running along the horizon. Dawn was beginning to break.

Ma covered her lantern with her cloak, then moved the cloth so that the light flashed towards the river several times in rapid succession. They waited, hearing nothing but the pattering of rain on their heads and the rushing of the water. Then out of the darkness came an answering flash. Slowly the tiny light drew closer, floating suspended above the river.

Ma turned, keeping her voice to a whisper. 'Soon as the boat lands you run for it, get in and keep low till you're well out of sight of the city. The men know where to take you. You can trust them. They're good customers of mine.'

As they watched, the outline of a small boat gathered out of the darkness as if it was forming from the shadows.

'Please, Elena,' Raffaele whispered, 'come with me.'

He extended his hand, white and glistening wet in the lamplight; it looked like the hand of a drowned man. Elena hesitated, then slowly, very slowly, her fingers edged towards his and she grasped his hand, feeling not the coldness of his skin but the answering clasp as his fingers gently but securely locked around hers.

The shrill *weet-a-weet* alarm call of the green sandpiper suddenly split the air. Elena turned and saw figures darting towards them across the ground, spread out and ducking low against the lightening horizon. The first rays of the watery sun caught the flash of metal in their hands.

'Devil's arse! It's the king's men,' Ma hissed.

Raffaele let go of Elena's hand and pushed her hard, so that she sprawled flat beneath the bushes. 'Hold her, Ma! Whatever you do, keep her safe.'

Like a crab, he scuttled forward on his hands and knees until he was far enough away from Ma and Elena, then he leapt up, running openly along the river bank, drawing John's men's attention away from them and the boat.

There was a cry as the soldiers spotted him. At once they

changed direction, running towards him as fast as the boggy ground would allow, weaving around the trees and shrubs. Their progress was slow for they repeatedly tumbled over as their feet stuck in soft ground, but they heaved one another out and continued to pursue their quarry. But soon the darkness had enveloped them all.

As the shouts grew distant, Ma seized Elena's arm.

'Move, my darling, quickly. No, don't stand up; they might have left men on watch. Crawl!'

Elena raised her head to look for the little boat on the river, but the men on board had extinguished their lantern as soon as they saw the soldiers and Ma had done the same. Now both she and Ma were creeping towards the bank on their hands and knees, Ma calling out softly to the boatmen. But there was no answer.

Elena, putting a hand down on the ground in the darkness, winced as a sharp thorn was pressed deep in her palm, but she didn't stop. They were almost at the water's edge. The wiry grass had given way to soft mud. She stared across the river. Dawn was just beginning to edge over the horizon, revealing the black outlines of distant craft, but there were no boats close by. From a long way off, the wind carried the soldiers' voices as they shouted instructions to one another.

Elena squeezed her eyes shut. *Holy and blessed Virgin Mother, in your mercy look after Raffaele. Keep him safe. Don't let them catch him. Please don't let them take him.*

Ma was cursing under her breath. Then she caught hold of Elena's arm and pulled her back.

'Rancid lumps of lard, the pair of them! Useless flea shit. You just wait till those boatmen dare to show their faces in my house again. I'll use their balls for crab bait.' Ma sighed. 'Still, I can't say that I blame them, they say the only people worth risking your life for are your own kin, and I'd not risk my life for any of mine.'

She glanced anxiously upriver from where the shouts of the soldiers drifted back to them.

'We need to get away from here, as fast as we can. Raffe's leading them off best he can. We should go in the opposite direction.'

'But we can't leave Raffaele.' Even as Elena spoke the words, they heard the clash of swords echoing across the marsh.

'Sounds as if the Bullock has his hands full . . . no, no!' Ma grabbed Elena as she started to run in the direction of the sound.

'There's nothing either of us can do to help him. We'd only make things worse. When Raffe makes his escape, he'll find his way back to you. Then we'll find another ship for the pair of you. But best thing now is to get you out of Norwich as quickly as we can, for Osborn will be tearing the town apart house by house looking for you. Come on, my darling. I'll walk with you till I've set you on the right road.'

Elena turned round one last time. She thought she glimpsed a group of people in the far distance, the first few rays of dawn flashing off metal, but she couldn't be sure, perhaps it was just water. She turned back and meekly trudged after Ma.

Raffe knew he could never outrun the soldiers. Sooner or later they would catch up with him; he just wanted to lead them far enough away from Elena and Ma so that they had a chance to escape.

The effort of stumbling over the soft, wet ground was tearing at his calf muscles and he already had a pain in his side, but he would not stop until they forced him to. Glancing back over his shoulder, he saw three of the soldiers were close. They were signalling to one another to spread out, obviously hoping to cut him off.

Raffe drove himself harder. Glancing now at the river, he wondered if he should jump in. He could swim well enough, but the river was swollen and fast. He'd never make it to the other bank, but he might be able to hide under the near bank, if he could find something to cling on to. He needed to find a place where the bank overhung . . . . He yelped as his foot stepped down into empty space.

With a splash of icy water that took his breath away, he found himself floundering on his back in soft mud. He'd fallen into one of the deep, narrow gullies that cut across the marsh into the river. Even in daylight, these gullies were hidden until you were on top of them. Raffe thrashed around in shallow water, trying in vain to get his feet under him in the slimy mud.

There were shouts and yells above, and immediately Raffe lay still, praying that what remained of the darkness would hide him. The voices seemed to be moving away. As slowly and silently as he could, he tried to right himself, but it was useless. The silky soft mud on the sides of the gully just came away in his hands. He gave up, and began to wriggle backwards, trying to edge towards the river. If he could drop down into it, and ease himself along under the bank, then, with God's help, he could hide there until they'd abandoned the search.

The narrow gully sloped gently downwards so that with only a small effort Raffe found himself sliding backwards towards the river. His fingers and toes were numb with cold, his body convulsed with shivering. He couldn't see where he was going, it was still too dark, but just another yard or so and he would be safe in the water.

He stifled a cry as his head connected with something hard and he felt himself being yanked upright by the back of his cloak into a sitting position.

'Thinking of leaving us, were you, traitor?'

A soldier was standing behind him in the gully. Raffe tried to grab his legs and pull them from under him, but before he could, hands reached down from the ground above to grasp his arms. Two men hauled Raffe upwards, dragging him over the edge of the gully and sending him sprawling, face down, across the wiry marsh grass. Raffe looked up. Six or seven men stared down at him.

The soldiers parted as a small, slight figure pushed through them. And Raffe found himself gazing up into the face of Martin, who grinned as broadly as if he was greeting an old friend.

'You look like that corpse we saw in Yarmouth. Or you soon will, Master Raffaele. I understand they have a very special death planned for you. High treason, that is the charge, I believe. Osborn himself is waiting to question you. He insists on doing it personally and from what he tells me he is much looking forward to it. There may unfortunately be a short delay before he can attend to you. So you'll have to amuse yourself listening to the screams of your fellow traitors in the castle dungeons. Osborn has unfortunately been wounded, did you know that? But thanks be to God, the blow glanced off a rib, so the physicians say he will recover well. He should be fit enough to attend to you personally in a week or so, though I fear he will still be in some pain when he questions you, which I am told by those who know him does not improve his temper.'

Raffe did not need to be told what Osborn would do. He had a healthy fear of the pain of torture, as much as any normal man, but it was not that which filled him with horror now. It was knowing that Osborn would be enjoying every twist of his muscles, would be studying his face for every spasm of agony, and watching him die with that same cold amusement with which he had watched Athan hanged. Above all, Raffe knew that Osborn's laughter would be the last sound on earth he would ever hear and it would pursue him into hell. Raffe had not gone through all this to become a prisoner of that man now.

Martin turned to the soldiers. 'Bring him and make sure he does not escape you. But treat him gently. Lord Osborn wants him unharmed and in a good state to talk.'

Raffe forced himself to go limp. He offered no resistance while two of the men pulled him to his knees, as though he had already accepted defeat. Then, just as his feet were firmly planted on the ground, he swung his great fist at the face of the nearest man, catching hold of the man's sword arm with his other hand. The soldier reeled backwards, crashing into the fellow beside him. It was only a momentary stagger, but it was enough to allow Raffe to grab his sword. Raffe held it out before him, sweeping the blade in a wide circle towards the other men.

Swift as a weasel, Martin slipped behind the soldiers. 'Disarm him, you fools, but don't kill him. Osborn wants him alive.'

It had been some time since Raffe had wielded a sword and this was not a good one. The balance was wrong and it was shorter than any he was accustomed to, but his long arms made up for that. He whirled around and lunged at one of the men in the circle. His opponent, taken off guard, stumbled backwards, but quickly recovered himself.

Raffe fought fast and furiously. He was used to fighting at close quarters and though it was still barely light, the flash of the rising sun on the whirling blades around him gave him warning enough to fend them off. He cut this way and that, beating them back with a manic fury born of desperation. One man reeled away with blood pouring from a slash on his face, another dropped his blade with a scream as Raffe's sword slashed down across his arm.

Raffe pushed forward until there was a gap in the circle of men just large enough for him to see the river glinting with shimmering gold lights as the sun caught it. With a roar he leapt through the circle towards it. He was within three strides of the water when he felt a white-hot pain slash into his back. He fell to his knees and tried to crawl forward, but his arms gave way beneath him and he crashed to the ground. He almost screamed in agony as hands seized him and roughly turned him over.

His back felt hot. For a moment or two he was grateful for the sudden comforting warmth, though he couldn't think what it was, until he realized it was his own blood pooling beneath him.

'You fuck-wits, I told you not to hurt him. Have you any

idea what you've done? Do you know what Osborn will do to you when he finds out?'

Martin was kneeling beside him, slapping his face, trying to make him open his eyes. But he was suddenly very tired now. All he wanted to do was sleep. It was becoming harder to breathe, as if someone was holding a wet cloth to his face. He couldn't feel his legs. He knew he was dying and he was glad of it. It is not granted to many men to choose the hour of their own death. Osborn would not get the satisfaction of watching him die.

Raffe gave a cry of agony and pressed his hands to his chest. He felt as if someone had put his fist inside his chest and was clenching his heart. His eyes squeezed shut as he fought with all his strength to fight down the pain. There was something else, something he must do. He must stay awake long enough. There was only one way he could make atonement now, only one way to protect those he had wronged. It was the living who mattered, not the dead. The living should not suffer for those who are beyond life.

He opened his eyes and looked up into Martin's face. 'My confession. I want . . . to confess,' he whispered.

Martin leaned closer, his face alive with excitement. 'That's it, you must confess for the sake of your soul. You are dying and must tell me the truth now. It's the last chance to save yourself from the fires of eternal damnation.'

'No time . . .'

'Give me names,' Martin urged. 'Just names, that's all you need to say. I will do the rest. Speak.'

'*Confiteor Deo omnipotenti* . . . I confess . . . before you and Almighty God, that I . . .'

Raffe stared up into the sky. It was growing darker. That wasn't right. It was morning, surely he had seen the dawn? He remembered the red glow like blood, a long, thin trail of blood running across the whole world.

Martin was shaking him. 'What did you do? What do you confess? Tell me!'

'I confess that I murdered . . . Raoul and Hugh. But you tell John this . . . it is Osborn of Roxham who is the traitor. He is working . . . for Philip of France . . . it was Osborn that . . . your French spy was to meet. As a dying man I swear by the Cross of the Crusaders that it is the truth. Tell John that . . . and tell Osborn on the scaffold . . . that he knows his brother's murderer. Tell him I did it for Gerard, for the monk and for a Saracen's child. Tell Osborn that as you execute him . . . let it be the last thing he hears . . . for I swear with my dying breath that I killed his brother, Hugh . . . I swear it on my immortal soul . . .'

New Moon,
October 1211

Bread – Mortals make a cross in the dough before it is set to rise, to redeem it from Satan and guard it from the evil eye. No loaf must be cut with a knife while another is baking in the oven, else the new loaf will spoil. If a loaf is placed upside down on a table, a ship will founder or the breadwinner of the household will fall sick. Likewise, it must always be cut from only one end, else the devil will fly over the house.

Whooping cough may be cured if a piece of bread is wrapped and buried in the earth for three days then eaten. A loaf baked on Good Friday and kept in the home will guard that house from fire and vermin, and all who dwell in it from evil spirits. A Good Friday loaf or hot cross bun, if dried and crumbled into water, will cure all fluxes of the bowel.

To take, unbidden, the last piece of bread from a platter will bring misfortune, but to eat the last slice if it is offered will bring wealth or a spouse to the one who receives it.

At the harvest of the grain, the spirit of the corn resides in the last sheaf cut. From this sheaf a loaf is baked in the form of a human figure or sheaf of wheat and borne to the harvest-home feast with great reverence. All who have taken part in the harvest will together break and eat of this loaf which is the body of the corn spirit, and so ensure that the spirit of the field is not lost and will return to bring a good harvest in the years that follow. For the spirits must always find a home in which to reside and if they are not welcomed in, they will enter at will and possess any creature they choose.

The Mandrake's Herbal

Yadua

The harsh honking of a flock of wild geese woke Elena with a start. She couldn't remember where she was at first. Wisps of the straw she was lying on were sticking to her face and arms. Her back felt unpleasantly damp and cold. She was lying on a narrow wooden hayloft looking down into the tiny room of a cottage. Stacked about her were fishing and fowling nets, wooden tools and sacks of beans, nuts and bulrush roots, with just a small space left on the boards where the children could sleep.

A cold light, pale as whey, was flowing in through the open door below her, and the smell of peat smoke and boiled fish told her that someone was already outside, cooking. She turned her head to see a little tow-headed boy of about three years asleep beside her, his thumb in his mouth, his pale eyelids trembling as he dreamed. Elena's back did feel very wet. She touched the damp place with her fingers and smelled them. The little boy had evidently peed on her in the night. But Elena only smiled fondly and eased herself gently from the straw, trying not to wake the child.

She pulled her kirtle on over her wet shift and, still plucking the straw from her hair, clambered down the few rungs of the wooden ladder and wandered outside. The river glittered in the pale morning sun, grumbling to itself like an elderly maid as it combed the dark green water weeds beneath into a fan of rippling hair.

A woman squatted on the ground, slicing through the fat black body of an eel and throwing the pieces into the simmering pot. She nodded at Elena, but didn't smile. Her two older children, who sat huddled together on the ground, regarded Elena with wide green eyes, but, just like their mother, their faces registered no expression. It was a chill morning. The blue smoke of the peat fire rose vertically into the primrose light and a white mist hovered over the bend in the river.

The woman handed Elena a steaming wooden bowl of eel meat and a piece of flat ravel bread, baked over the embers of the fire. Both were offered without comment. Finding nothing else to sit on, Elena knelt on the damp ground.

The woman and her children ate in silence. They drank the liquid from their bowls and used their fingers to scoop the lumps of eel and herbs into their mouths. Elena smiled as she saw the little girl surreptitiously slide the bitter stewed herbs on to the grass and only pop the pieces of eel into her mouth. The boy in contrast shovelled everything into his mouth with a ravenous appetite. Elena wondered how her own son fed. Was his belly filled this morning or was he crying with hunger?

The only thing that mattered in the world now was finding him. It would be pointless to ask Gytha where her son was, even if Elena knew where the cunning woman was living. For unless, miraculously, Osborn had died of his wound, then she had failed to kill him, and Gytha would never reveal where she had hidden her son. But Elena had to find him. Gunilda's ancient power lived on in her granddaughter Gytha. Kill the descendants of Warren or suffer the scream of the mandrake in this world and the next. Maybe, if Elena took her son far enough away, the curse would not be able to reach him. Everyone knew that if a cunning woman sent out her own spirit to harm her victim, that spirit had to return to her body before daybreak or else she'd die. How far could a spirit travel in one night?

Yet, knowing what she carried in her own soul, how could Elena risk seeking out her son? She bore an evil sickness, a deadly fever, which even an innocent kiss might transfer to the child.

As she and Ma had walked out of the city through the dawn light, Elena had confided to Ma all that Raffaele had confessed to her. There was no one else now that Elena could tell. Ma had listened, her head cocked to one side like a bright-eyed robin, and she did not once condemn Raffaele.

'Love is a greater madness than hate,' she'd said, shaking her head in wonder.

She squinted up at Elena. 'I'm not often mistaken about people, but I was wrong about you, my darling. I thought you were one of those women who couldn't survive in life without someone to take care of them. But you're not. You and I, we're more alike than you'd think. I told you a while back that only a woman who lets a man take her because she is afraid of him or of the world is a slave. And you are no slave. You don't need Raffe, you don't need anyone to lead you through this world. Find your son, my darling, and make your own life.'

'But Gerard's sin,' Elena said. 'I can't carry that alone. I can't bear it and don't know how to get rid of it. When the Interdict is over I can seek out a priest, but who knows when that will be and it may be too late then? I must find my son before Gytha harms him.'

Ma chewed her lip for a while as they walked on in silence, then her face brightened.

'We had this Hebrew man come to us regularly once a week, until the law declared it's now forbidden for a Christian to lie with a Jew. Then the poor man had to stop visiting us. A physician he was, with a belly as big as a pregnant sow, though of course the Jews don't eat the flesh of the hog. The girls adored him. Said he always tried to pleasure them before himself, and there's not many men who do that even in the marriage bed, let alone if they are paying for their pleasure. A kindly, gentle man, they said, and he made them laugh. The girls always love a man who can make them laugh.

'Anyway, after he had been coming regularly on the same day for several months, he missed a week. The next time he came I asked him if he'd been sick, but he said no. He told me that once a year the Jews set aside eight days they call the Days of Awe when they reflect on their sins and resolve to sin no more, so for that week he couldn't come for he was thinking of his sins.

' "And how do you rid yourself of your sins?" I asked him, for I know they don't have the mercy of Christ's death to atone for them.

'He said, "In the afternoon of the first day of the New Year we go to the river with a scrip full of crumbs. We recite our sins over the crumbs, then sprinkle them on the water, and the fish they come and eat them, then swim away out to sea, carrying our sins away with them." '

Ma smiled up at Elena. 'Maybe, my darling, you should make the fishes your sin-eaters.'

Ma had left her then on a lonely track that led through the forest. To her surprise, Elena found herself crying as she bent to hug the tiny little woman. Ma had pushed her away with her usual impatience.

'Off with you, my darling, and remember, keep well away from the main highways and the ports too, for Osborn will have a watch on those.'

For the briefest of moments Ma held Elena's hand between her own and pressed it gently.

'Remember one thing, my darling,' Ma said. 'You learn nothing by looking into the future. If you want to find your way home, if you want to find yourself, you have to look behind you. Unless you see the way you've come, how will you ever find your way back?'

She turned then, and waddled off along the track back towards Norwich. Elena watched her go, the ruby pins in her dark glossy hair winking in the morning sun. Then, just as she reached the bend, Ma turned and flapped her hand.

'Stop standing there, gawping like a cod-wit. You think I went to all this effort for you to get caught? Get going! Satan's arse, I swear you've been nothing but trouble ever since the day I clapped eyes on you.'

But Elena could have sworn those bulging yellow-green eyes were bright with tears.

The two children had finished their morning meal and wandered off. The woman was scraping the remains of her own bowl back into the iron cooking pot and damping down the fire with turfs to keep the embers hot until they were wanted again. Elena wiped out her bowl with a handful of grass and returned it to the woman. She picked up her pack ready to depart, pressing a coin from the purse Ma had given her into the woman's hand. The woman nodded gravely, but showed no reaction, neither pleasure nor disappointment. Life gave you what it gave you. Some days there was a fish on the line, sometimes there wasn't. There was little point in being happy or angry, it changed nothing.

Elena thanked her anyway for the night's lodging and was walking away when she saw the two children lying on the bank of the river. The boy was throwing small stones at something in the water and, more from idle curiosity than anything else, Elena drew closer to see what it was. A crude toy boat was stuck fast in the reeds just beyond the boy's reach and he was evidently trying to knock it free so that it could sail on or he could sink it. Either way he would lose it. The boat was little more than a long curved section of thick bark from a felled tree. Someone had stuck a twig in it and a scrap of sacking for a sail, and now it bobbed up and down as if impatient to be free and off.

'May I have the boat?' Elena said.

The two children turned and stared at her, unblinking.

'If I fetch it may I take it?' Elena persisted.

'S'mine!' the boy said, his eyes narrowing.

'But you're going to let it drift away down the river and then it'll be gone anyway.'

Elena could see from the way he thrust out his lower lip that because the child now knew she wanted it, he was determined not to let her have it. She was reluctant to part with any more of the precious coins from the purse Ma had slipped into her hand; besides, the crude boat was worth nothing. But she fumbled in her scrip and found a piece of dried mutton that Ma had placed there along with some bread and cheese.

She pulled off a long strip and held it out to the boy. 'For the boat?'

He grabbed it from her hand and ran off with it, trying to stuff the tough chewy strip into his mouth before his sister, who was clamouring for her share, could catch up with him.

Elena took off her shoes and hose and waded into the reeds. The water near the bank was not deep, mostly mud and weed, and she easily retrieved the fragile craft. Hastily drying her feet on her kirtle, she struggled back into her hose and shoes, and walked away, the cries of the quarrelling children fading behind her.

When she was out of sight of the cottage she stopped. She opened her pack and carefully unwrapped the mandrake. It lay there on its cloth, shrivelled and black, like the wizened hand of a saint that had once been brought to their village by the monks collecting alms. For a while she was afraid to touch it with her bare hand, in case she saw something more – another corpse, another nightmare, her own child dead. But she knew she must hold it for one last time. Touch it and give all Gerard's dreams back to it.

There would be no white milk this time, only red. She took her knife and sliced it across her finger, letting three drops fall on the mandrake's head. She didn't remember the words you were supposed to say to the priest when you asked for your sins to be taken from you. It had been too long since she had said them. But if blood could wash sins away, then her blood must do it now.

In the little boat she placed a piece of bread. That was right, wasn't it? That was what cleansed you of all sins, the body and blood, bread and wine, except her blood would be better than wine. Her sins were in her blood, and her spilled blood would carry them away.

She grasped the mandrake, feeling beneath her fingers the flutter of a heartbeat like a little sparrow, but as she held it, the flutter grew to a throb and she could feel its heart beating louder and stronger, its black blood running through its veins.

'Eat them. Drink them. Take them back!' she cried. 'Take all the dreams back from me. Carry them far out to sea and drown them in the waves. Let them lie at the bottom of the ocean for ever.'

She laid the mandrake in the little bark boat beside the bread. Then she set it on the river, pushing it out with a twig until the current caught it. It spun round and round three times, then it straightened out, and the river carried it rapidly downstream, the mandrake lying as stiff as a corpse, and the little sacking sail streaming out behind like the banner of a knight.

It was finally over. The mandrake was gone, carried far out to sea, where it could do no more harm. Elena was rid of it for ever. As if she had suddenly been released from a dungeon, she wanted to run and leap and dance like a child.

The air was scrubbed clean like freshly washed linen, perfumed with the rich plum scents of wet earth and crushed grass. The river was gurgling contentedly like a baby, and for the first time Elena noticed that the autumn leaves on the trees were ablaze with scarlet and cherry, amber and topaz, cinnamon and gold. A breeze caught the branches and they shivered with delight, sending a shower of jewelled leaves tumbling through the bright sunlight.

It was like being in love for the very first time. Elena swung her pack over her shoulder and set off. She had no idea where to start looking, but she was sure that her mother's instinct would guide her. She was going to find her son and this time, even if there wasn't a priest left in the world to bless him, she would take him in her arms herself and give her child a name. Raffaele, perhaps, yes, that was a good name for a man.

She was so full of her plans that she didn't notice the small red fox standing at a distance among the trees. It blended into the autumn bracken so perfectly that no mortal eyes would have seen it. But it saw her. It pricked its ears and regarded her for a moment with eyes as dark as a mandrake's skin. Then it turned away as silently as it had appeared and vanished into the undergrowth.

*

It is late, the sun is sinking in the sky and a cold wind is blowing off the river. A woman steps out of her own cottage door and walks towards her neighbour's croft, carrying a small covered cooking pot. Her neighbour, an elderly woman, slipped over at the village well and broke her leg. She was frail even before her fall, and her bones will never heal, not now, not at her age. She won't last the winter. Still, the neighbours do what they can, bringing her a little pottage from their own dinner, and a few turfs from their own meagre stack to burn on her fire. They can't heal her, can't take away her pain, but they can keep her from hunger and cold till death in his mercy comes for her. They know that one day, if please God they live to make old bones, they will be glad of someone to do the same for them. 'Sow as you would reap. Do as you would be done by,' that's the commandment they live by in that village.

The woman pauses as she crosses her garden, calling out to a little girl who squats on the river bank building mice-sized cottages out of pebbles and mud.

'Mary, how many times have I told you not to play so close to the river? Remember what happened to poor little Allan. He played too close to the water and the monstrous mermaid snatched him and took him down to the bottom of the river and gobbled him up with her long sharp teeth. Do you want the mermaids to take you? Inside with you now, keep an eye on the bairn. See he doesn't get into the flour barrel again.'

Mary stands reluctantly, watching her mother walking up the neighbour's path. The child doesn't want to go inside yet, but she dare not disobey. Her mother keeps a switch behind the door. Mary is about to do as she has been told, when in the last rays of the sun, something catches her eye. It is floating towards her down the river. It looks like a little boat. She quickly casts around her, trying to find some way of snaring it before the river carries it away again. She finds a stick, and by lying full stretch on the bank, she just manages to hook the tip of the stick over the edge of the curved bark. The boat is light. It comes towards her easily, eagerly, you might say.

Fearing her mother's return, Mary scurries inside her cottage and sets the dripping boat down on the beaten earth floor. With a grin of delight that almost splits her little face in two she lifts out a tiny, wizened figure.

'A doll!' she exclaims, dancing round the room. 'I can play babies with it.'

It's an ugly little thing. But she doesn't care. To her it is the best toy she's ever had, a little doll all of her own. She already imagines dressing it in scraps of cloth, making it a cradle and feeding it on stolen milk.

A sudden squeal makes her look down. A little boy crawls towards the boat. Mary kneels on the floor and shows her new treasure to him.

'Look, look, it's a dolly.'

Although Mary sometimes becomes impatient, as all little girls do, when she is forced to mind him, she is fond of the child, even though he's not her real brother. Gytha, the cunning woman, brought him for her mother to nurse. There were other nurslings before this one, and Mary supposes there will be others after him. Some day someone will come for him and take him away, as they took away other nurslings when they were old enough to walk and talk. But they won't come yet. He's too little.

The baby grins as she dances the doll in front of him. He reaches out a fat sticky paw, but she pulls the doll back. 'No it's not for you. It's mine!'

The infant crumples up his face as if he is about to cry. Her mother mustn't find him crying or she will tell Mary to give him the doll to quieten him. She will tell Mary that she is too old to play games now and should be minding the bairn if she wants something to nurse. Her mother won't under-stand how much Mary already loves the doll.

Mary drags the little boat out in front of the infant. He is enthralled at once and forgets to cry. He paddles across to it on his chubby little knees and tiny hands. He dabs at the boat with his dimpled fingers, then he sees the bread. He cannot yet say the word, but he knows what it is. And it is just the right size for a tiny mouth. He grabs the piece of bread in his fat little fist and pushes the end of it into his mouth. He sucks frantically, contentedly, gurgling happily like the river which runs on and on outside in the darkness.

One day soon, that little boy will begin to have strange dreams, dreams that will terrify and thrill him. Dreams of blood in far off lands that he cannot begin to understand, but he will know the terror of them. And he will learn to use the power running through his fingers and feel it surging in his veins: the power to hurt, the desire to wound and the passion to murder.

For Gytha the cunning woman did speak the truth about one thing – you cannot rid yourself of a mandrake by casting it away. When Elena finds her son again, I, Yadua, will be waiting for her. The worth of a mandrake is measured in blood and Elena must pay that price, if not with her own life, then with her little son's. There are still thorns left in the little wizened apple and Gytha will use them well. She can wait, she is used to biding her time; she was born into the waiting.

For as Madron so wisely said, 'Yadua will not let you rest in this world or the next, until the price has been paid in full.'

Historical Notes

The Interdict which was imposed on England on 23 March 1208 was formally lifted six years later on 29 June 1214 after King John, in order to avert a papal-backed French invasion, finally agreed to the demands of Pope Innocent III. These were that John should finally accept Stephen Langton as Archbishop of Canterbury and that he should recall all the exiled bishops, priests and laity. John also offered the English Church 100,000 marks in compensation for his confiscation of their property. The Pope agreed to this sum, but the English bishops grumbled it was not nearly enough to compensate them for what he had seized or destroyed, or for their lost revenue whilst the churches were closed.

Both contemporary chroniclers and modern historians differ widely on just what effect the Interdict had on the people. Some eyewitnesses claimed it devastated life in England, others that it had little impact on the ordinary man in the street. Naturally it was in the interests of those on John's side to claim that the Interdict was having no effect. However, the Church and John's critics claimed that the population were on the brink of despair, so distraught were they by the churches being locked against them and being denied the comforts of their faith.

Even in these modern days of instant communication, we hear wildly different reports about the effect of industrial action, depending on whether you're speaking to striking unions or to the management. And allies in war can make contradictory claims about incidents, which in turn bear no relation at all to those reports given by their enemies. In terms of the Interdict, the impact probably varied considerably depending on where you lived, how strictly the clergy in that diocese carried out their instructions and whether or not John had a personal quarrel with your local bishop.

Equally, we shall probably never know the truth about why Richard Cœur-de-Lion massacred the Saracen prisoners at Acre. Deserted only a few days before by his former ally, Philip II of France, Richard was left to supply and finance all the remaining troops. He was anxious to march on Jerusalem and he did not have the resources to feed and guard several thousand prisoners indefinitely. He may have thought that Saladin was deliberately trying to delay the prisoner exchange to buy time in order to reinforce his own army before Richard could reach Jerusalem.

Alternatively, Richard might have believed the rumour that Saladin had already killed the Christian prisoners and had no intention of handing over the ransom Richard was demanding for the Muslim hostages. After all, the terms of the surrender of Acre had been negotiated with the leaders of the city, not Saladin himself, who'd been angered by the surrender. Whatever the reason, when Acre was later retaken by the Muslims, all Christians in the city were then slaughtered, possibly in retaliation for Richard's act.

I've heard people say we should view these events within the context of a very brutal time. Yet what Richard did clearly shocked and outraged Saladin and many contemporary chroniclers, so they must have considered the act unusual even for those times. And whilst, as a novelist, I firmly believe we must try to see medieval events through the prism of medieval morality and belief, I can't help worrying that future generations might look back on the twentieth century and try to excuse the massacres of the Holocaust or of Rwanda and Bosnia and many others, because they were committed in 'the context of a brutal century'. Perhaps the sad truth is that human behaviour really hasn't improved since the Middle Ages.

In the early Christian Church, some devout monks and hermits practised self-castration as a pious act in order to purge their flesh of lust, but by the Middle Ages the Catholic Church had forbidden the castration of monks because of the Old Testament instruction in Deuteronomy 23:1 prohibiting those 'wounded in the stones' from serving in the temple.

Eunuchs and castrati were greatly despised among the general populace, even though castration was used as a 'cure' for hernias. Castration was largely reserved for the punishment of so-called sexual 'crimes', especially of those accused of homosexuality. Noble-born husbands might take revenge on men who had affairs with their wives or daughters by castrating them, as we find in the medieval tale *Parzival*, written around 1200, which was the origin of the opera *Parsifal*.

For centuries, castration was used to humiliate prisoners conquered in battle. In 1282 at Palermo, 2000 French prisoners were castrated then killed after the battle of the Sicilian Vespers. This practice continued for centuries, and even at the Battle of Culloden in 1746 it was reported that the English cut off the genitals of the fallen Scottish Highlanders.

But there was a hidden side to all this. From the very beginning of church music, castrati were employed in the Byzantine church choirs. Since these choirs did not use musical instruments and women were forbidden to sing, they needed a tremendous vocal range and resonance to achieve the effect the composers desired. To this end, boys between the ages of eight and twelve had their testicles removed to preserve their voices and create the angelic vocal range demanded by the music. This left them as adults able to achieve full sexual function, but they were, of course, sterile. Prepubescent castration caused a distinctive physical growth pattern including unusually long limbs, together with a marked gain in body fat in later life.

By the 1100s this practice of using castrati in choirs had been incorporated by both the Armenian and Georgian Churches. In Italy and Sicily the presence of castrati voices in church choirs is documented as far back as the third century, and Bishop Ambrose of Milan (340–97) is credited with the introduction of the Eastern model of singing in his churches. Choir schools to train boys and castrati were set up in the fourth and fifth centuries and one of the most famous, the *schola cantorum,* still operates today to train boy choristers.

Several centres for castration were later established in Italy, and even the monastery at Monte Cassino eventually had its own castration facilities to create castrati for the choir. By the fifteenth century, castrati were well established in all the best Catholic Church choirs in Europe, including the Vatican, but because of the prohibition in Deuteronomy the singers were officially referred to as *sopranos, falsettos* or even *Spagnoletti* – Spanish voices.

By the eighteenth century, castrati were also employed in the opera companies, and many famous operatic arias which are today sung by women were originally written for castrati. Renowned castrati appeared in all the great opera houses of Europe including London, and were fêted as international superstars are today.

Alessandro Moreschi was the last castrato at the Vatican. He is believed to have been castrated around 1865/66. His voice was captured on gramophone recordings made between 1902 and 1904, and he died in 1922.

Gastmere is a fictional village based on those villages in the medieval marshlands between Norwich and Yarmouth. *Gast* in old English means *spirit* and in Middle English *ghost*. *Mere* of course meant marshland.

The beautiful medieval city of Norwich is, of course, real, and you can still visit the streets in Mancroft where Elena walked, as well as have a drink in the Adam and Eve pub, which is one of the oldest inns in England, with a fascinating history of smuggling in centuries past, though now it is entirely law-abiding and respectable.

The town of Great Yarmouth on the Norfolk coast was founded on a sandbank in the mouth of an estuary. In medieval times it was an island, originally inhabited by fishermen who came from the Cinque Ports to fish for the shoals of herring, a staple food of the Middle Ages. The fish were found in great numbers off the coast in autumn. By the 1200s Great Yarmouth was an important international trading post, holding a Free Herring Fair which lasted for forty days from Michaelmas to Martinmas, and the herrings from Yarmouth were sold all over Europe as far as the Middle East.

But unlike many other medieval towns, because it emerged from the 'beach' or coastline, it was owned by the king himself and not by a local lord. Therefore none of the citizens were freemen and were obliged to pay heavy taxes to marry and inherit land. Trade was being crippled by the huge tolls Yarmouth merchants had to pay to do business in neighbouring towns. So knowing that King John was desperate for money to fight against France, in 1209 the men of Yarmouth persuaded John to grant them a charter making them a free port, for which they would pay him 55 pounds a year, a good deal more than he was getting from them in taxes. This charter allowed the citizens of Yarmouth to trade without tax anywhere in England, except London, whilst at the same time they could collect tolls from any outside or foreign merchants who wanted to trade in Yarmouth.

For anyone interested in finding out more about the fascinating and unique history of Yarmouth, the town now has some wonderful museums which have been installed in the old fish smokehouses.

Glossary

Bub – An old Lincolnshire and East Anglian dialect word for an unfledged bird or an inexperienced person.

Cog-ships – were the cargo ships of Europe in the Middle Ages, sailing across the Baltic and the North Sea up as far as Norway. These ships would have been familiar sights in the English Channel and round the coast of Northern Europe and in all the ports. The term *cog* comes from the construction of the vessel, which has square beams of wood protruding from the sides of the hull to enhance its strength. A cog-ship had a single mast with a square sail of about 200sq m or 2050sq ft. There was a raised platform in the stern, which resembled the turret of a castle, from which arrows could be fired to defend the ship, should the need arise. Poisonous gases which built up in the stagnant bilge water in the hold meant it was frequently too dangerous for the crew to sleep below deck when off duty, so they often slept on deck beneath the castle, which provided some protection from wind and rain. From sunken vessels found preserved in the mud, the typical length of a cog-ship was about 24m or 75ft in length with a mast around 25m or 80ft high.

Daul – Dialect word meaning *to weary*, *to wear out* or *to exhaust*. 'Dauled' means worn out, tired and limp.

Dung drag – A three-pronged rake with the metal prongs or tines set at right angles to the long wooden handle. Compass, a mixture of animal dung and soiled straw, was taken out to fields in a cart. A man known as Sir Wag walked behind the cart using the dung drag to pull down the compass on to the field. The long handle ensured he did not get covered in the smelly manure as he raked it down.

Eena, deena, etc. – Many country people, right up to last century, counted in multiples of four or eight when counting livestock or produce. Some say it is because we have four fingers, other have suggested it is easy to pick out four sheep at a glance without counting them individually. Pebbles, beans or notches on a stick would be used to keep track of how many fours had been counted. There has been much speculation as to the origins of the names of the numbers, which vary widely from district to district, but they may be vestiges of older tribal languages which survived long after the language itself ceased to be used.

Frestelles – A musical instrument which looked like panpipes.

Green Mist Babies – A rural expression meaning a baby born in springtime, when the fields and trees appear to be covered with a bright green mist as seeds begin to germinate and buds break open. Babies carried over winter and born in spring were likely to be of low birthweight because of the lack of fresh meat, eggs and vegetables in the mother's diet. Many were stillborn or died within hours, but those that survived the birth had the good warm days of spring and summer when the mother's milk was richer to build up strength before winter. In contrast, autumn babies were often bigger when born, but frequently sickened and died during that first winter.

Herbal – Some readers may query the inclusion of insects, animals and minerals in the *Mandrake's Herbal*. But in the Middle Ages, and indeed even as late as Culpeper (1616–1654), herbals included remedies and cures made from all kinds of things including animals, birds, reptiles, insects, stones, gems and animal excrement, in addition to the herbs and plants we would expect to find in a modern herbal.

Hurdy-gurdy – We think of it as a relatively modern musical instrument, but in fact it was well known in the Middle Ages. It was rested on the knee and played by turning a wheel. Buttons were pressed down on to the strings to produce the notes. Before the twelfth century two people were required to play it, but later designs meant that it could be played by a single musician.

Leet of Mancroft – Norwich was initially divided into four administrative districts known as *leets,* which reflected the Anglo-Saxon development of the town. Most of the properties belonging to Jews were recorded in the Mancroft area immediately to the west of the castle, to which the Jews could flee for protection in times of trouble. This area also contained many of the markets where they did most of their trade. There was a synagogue in Mancroft, but this was not a ghetto, because some Jews lived outside this area, and equally Christians also lived in Mancroft, some of whom may even have rented houses from the Jews.

Nocturns – One of the daily Catholic Church services. Nocturns was the medieval name for the office of *Matins,* which, up to the eleventh century, was known as *vigiliae* or *vigils.* The service of Nocturns originally began at midnight, except for those living under Benedict's rule who celebrated it at the eighth hour of the night – 2 a.m. The name Nocturns comes from the individual unit (a nocturn) which made up the service. Each nocturn consisted of three psalms, the paternoster and the prayer known as the Absolutio, followed by three lessons and a benediction. The number of nocturns or sequences recited in each service varied according to the religious significance of the particular day. On Sundays and feast days three Nocturns were recited in succession, together with other prayers and hymns.

Pike in Galentyne – Pike and lampreys were boiled in ale or vinegar, and spices including pepper, ginger and cloves. The ale or vinegar helped to break down the fine bones. The flesh was removed from the coarser bones, then it was pressed back into a fish shape. The pike was either served cold covered with a hot sauce, or hot with a cold sauce such as *sauce vert*. A hot galentyne sauce was thick and strongly flavoured, more like a relish or condiment than a modern sauce. A typical galentyne consisted of rye breadcrumbs, sweetened white wine, vinegar, oil, onion, cinnamon, pepper and – rather strangely – sandalwood.

Ravel bread – The poorest-quality bread. The best was *wheaten bread* which generally only the rich could afford. Next came *cheat bread*, made of second-quality wheat and generally adulterated with other flours. Cheat bread was usually the bread given as alms to the needy. Worst was *ravel bread*, made from poorest-quality flour mixed with anything people had to hand such as bran, beans, peas, oats, rye, barley or bulrush roots. This was often baked as flat bread in the embers of the fire, or cut into small round discs and fried in lard in a heavy iron pan.

Talbot – As well as being a Christian name, a talbot was also the name for the 'Norman hound', so called because the dogs were thought to have been brought to England by the Normans. It was larger than the modern greyhound, more like a bloodhound, and it was one of a category of dogs known as 'running hounds' which track their quarry by scent and can pursue a stag or boar from dawn to dusk without giving up or becoming tired.

Toft – Old English from the Norse *Topt*. A toft was a small area of land, often surrounding a croft or cottage on which the family grew the vegetables, fruit and herbs they needed to feed themselves. Animals would also be kept on the toft, including bees, poultry and at certain times of the year pigs and a milking goat or cow, when they were not out at pasture. In good years, surplus produce was taken to the market to sell or exchanged for other things the family needed.

Rows – Yarmouth was originally a settlement built on a sandbank at the mouth of three rivers that formed Breydon Water: the Bure,

Yare and Waveney. The sandbank was first colonized by fishermen who built dwellings in narrow parallel strips, to allow the houses to be on higher ground while giving each strip direct access to the sea. This also minimized the effects of flooding. One hundred and forty-five rows were established by the Middle Ages and were densely populated until they were largely destroyed by bombing in the Second World War. The houses in these rows later consisted of one lower room and one upper, and the rows were so narrow it was possible for a man to walk down the middle and touch the walls on either side with outstretched arms.

Sappers – When laying siege to a city, miners or sappers would try to tunnel under the outer walls of the castle or city and lay fires beneath the stones. This, together with the boulders thrown by the siege engines pounding on the walls above, would help to weaken the defensive walls, causing them to collapse. The sapper's work was highly dangerous, for not only was there the risk of the tunnels caving in with the men still inside, but frequently the defenders of the castle would burrow outwards to attack the sappers, and vicious hand-to-hand fighting would take place in the darkness of the narrow tunnels.

Solar – Initially meant any room above ground level. (Derived from the French *sol*, meaning floor, and *solive*, meaning beam.) In the Middle Ages, the solar came to be a common name for the Great Chamber. It was the private living and sleeping quarters of the family who owned the hall. Their servants and retinue would sleep below in the Great Hall. The solar often had a separate staircase and entrance to that of the Great Hall and a wooden partition could be erected at one end of the room to form a private bedchamber, which would have been important if several adult generations of the family had to share the solar.

Thorn apple – (Not to be confused with the herb of the same name, *Datura stramonium*, a powerful narcotic.) The use of an apple studded with twelve thorns or pins as a summoning charm was widely used by those who had the 'gift'. One incident was recorded in Warwickshire as recently as 1929, when a woman demonstrated her powers by using the apple to summon her sister who lived 10 miles away. The sister arrived, even though it was snowing, claiming she had been drawn to come by some force she could not resist.

Undercroft – A basement or cellar under a hall or house used mainly for storage. Often the undercroft was built on the ground floor, rather than below ground, though surviving examples are sometimes now below ground level because the surface levels of streets have risen. The undercroft could be completely enclosed with walls, but was frequently left open on one or more sides to allow carts and wagons to be drawn inside to load and unload. The Great Hall was often built as the upper storey over an undercroft, supported by pillars and arches.

Werecat – Medieval people believed humans could turn themselves into werebeasts that were half human, half animal, including wolves, cats, foxes, crocodiles and tigers. There were two kinds of werebeast: involuntary and voluntary. If you had lived a wicked life, or were cursed, you might be turned into one of these creatures. But men could also *choose* to become werebeasts. There were many ways of doing this: by using ointments or spells, invoking demons or using mandrakes, by drinking the water from the footprint of the animal you wanted to become or by wearing the pelt of the chosen animal as a girdle around the waist. In this way you would gain the power to turn yourself into a half man–half beast, with a savage desire to hurt and kill.

Wolf's head – A term for an outlaw, or a fugitive from justice. Once a man or woman was declared a wolf's head, any citizen was entitled to hunt them down and take them captive or kill them. In fact they had a duty to do so if they discovered their whereabouts. And, like the wolf itself, if a citizen could prove that the fugitive was dead, usually by bringing the corpse or head to the local sheriff, they could claim a bounty or reward.

Yellow Skeggs – A common English name for the Yellow Iris (*Iris pseudacorus*), otherwise known as fleur-de-lis. *Skeggs* is Anglo-Saxon in origin, from *segg*, meaning a small sword, in reference to the leaf shape. In the sixth century Clovis I of France was able to escape the Goths when he noticed a patch of yellow iris growing in the middle of the River Rhine indicating shallow water. In gratitude he took the fleur-de-lis as his emblem. In the twelfth century Louis VII of France adopted it as his emblem during the Crusades. The English called the French soldiers 'flowers', a derogatory nickname which seems to be a reference to the French emblem, the fleur-de-lis, hence Yellow Skeggs.

Read on for an enticing extract from
Karen Maitland's gripping new novel, *Falcons
of Fire and Ice*, coming soon from Michael Joseph . . .

Prologue
Anno Domini 1514 – Iceland

'I killed them, Elísabet, I killed them!'

Elísabet heard the sobs tearing at her husband's throat. She knew Jóhann was desperate for her to comfort him, begging her to assure him that no evil would come from the terrible thing he'd done, but she couldn't speak. She couldn't even bring herself to turn and look at him. She stared at her own hand grasping the iron ladle. She watched her reed-thin fingers stir the dried stock fish in the steaming pot, as if her hand was a strange animal she didn't recognize.

'I had to do it, Elísabet . . . I had no choice.'

Her back snapped upright. 'I begged you not to go. Did you listen? No, as usual you . . .'

But even as she turned to confront him, her eyes glittering with fear and rage, her words died away in a horrified gasp. Jóhann was standing close behind her in the tiny cottage, bathed in the mustard light of the fish-oil lamp. But if she hadn't heard his voice, Elísabet would never have recognized the creature staring down at her as her husband.

His face was a mask of blood. It ran down his cheeks, and pooled in the creases of his skin, staining his pale beard crimson. Blood oozed too from numerous deep gashes on his arms and hands. Even his hair was soaked and matted with gore. If it hadn't been for his clothes, which she had woven and stitched with her own hand, Elísabet would have sworn he was the ghost of some ancient Viking who'd perished in battle.

Jóhann's legs buckled beneath him and he sank down on the wooden platform that served as both bed and chairs in the tiny room. That was enough to jerk Elísabet into action.

Although her belly was swollen with child, she moved with a swiftness that she had not managed for weeks, hurrying to dip a handful of raw wool into the water pail and return with it, dripping, to her husband's side. Gently she began to wipe the scarlet stains from his face, but even as she washed the blood away more ran from the wounds to cover the blanched skin. Jóhann, wincing, caught her wrist and, pulling the hank of wet wool from her fingers, pressed it to his forehead. He closed his eyes and for a moment, Elísabet thought he was going to pass out, but he didn't fall.

'Did you . . .' She swallowed hard. 'Did you get the foreigner what he wanted?'

Jóhann reached beneath his shirt, flinching as the coarse woollen cloth rasped over the cuts on his hand. He pulled out a leather draw-string purse and let it fall on to the bed. The purse looked well stuffed, but that told Elísabet little about the value of the coins inside.

'He has the chicks, both of them,' Jóhann said wearily. 'They're alive . . . and strong enough to survive the sea voyage back to Portugal.'

'But to kill the white falcons . . . the last white falcons on this mountain . . . Don't you understand what you've done? Anyone who kills that bird is cursed until the day they die. You promised me, Jóhann, you promised that no harm would come to the adult falcons . . . You took an oath on the life of our unborn child.'

Elísabet touched her rounded belly where only the night before her husband had laid his own warm hand, as he'd sworn to her he would not hurt the birds.

'The foreigner will pay good money for the chicks,' he had told her. 'The falcons will have more young next year and I'll see to it that nothing disturbs them, even if I have to guard their nest day and night. But I must do this. I have to pay back the money I borrowed for the cattle, and with the baby coming, this is the only way we can survive. What else would you have me do?'

He meant the *dead* cattle, which had all perished the same summer he'd bought them when the cloud of gas from the volcano had poisoned the grass. Four years of misery and hunger for man and falcons alike, when the grass had withered and the ptarmigan, the prey of the white falcons, did not venture into the high valley. Before the poison cloud swept over them, a dozen white falcons had circled in the skies above the river of blue ice. But they had starved to death or flown away to the north, and the single pair that still soared over the frozen river had not laid eggs for three years.

'Don't you see? It's a good omen,' Jóhann had told her. 'The falcons have bred once more, that means they know the ptarmigan are returning and the grass is sweet again. With the money I'll get for the chicks we'll be able to buy more cattle. The foreigners will give a heavy purse for the white falcons they sell to the royal houses of Europe.' He laughed. 'They say that kings will pay more for a single white falcon than for a whole palace.'

Elísabet stared down at her husband's bloodied head. Last night Jóhann had been so sure that their luck was changing. Now look at him – was this the change of fortune he'd promised her?

'But you swore to me, Jóhann, on our child's life . . . Why . . . why have you done this to us? What possessed you to call down such evil on us . . . on your own family?'

Jóhann opened his eyes, but he didn't look at his wife. He gazed fixedly into the flames of the cooking fire as a despairing man stares down at the sea before he drowns himself. Finally, and in a voice that barely rose above a whisper, he answered her.

'We waited until the adults had gone hunting. I've never climbed so high up the cliff face before. It was a long, slow climb. Then, just as I was within a man's length of the nest, the adult falcons returned. They began diving at me, slashing me with their talons, screaming at me till I was so deafened I couldn't think. My arms were stinging from the gashes and my fingers were so slippery with my blood that a dozen times I nearly fell from the rock face. I realized I'd plunge to my death if I tried to carry on, so I climbed back down.

'The foreigner was yelling at me. I didn't know what he was saying, but I didn't need words to understand he was furious. The Icelander who had brought him to me told me that if I didn't go back up and get the chicks, they would tell our Danish masters that they'd caught me trying to raid the nest. He said the Danes would hang me on the spot.'

Jóhann looked up at his wife, his tired blue eyes pleading for understanding. 'I didn't want to do it, Elísabet, but . . . if I was to have any chance of capturing the chicks and getting back down safely, I had to drive the adults off. I thought if I shot an arrow at one of them, the other would fly away. I aimed for the male which was flying low. I only meant to clip his wing feathers, but he crashed down on to the rocks. The female circled higher and higher, till I could no longer see her. I was certain she'd taken fright and had gone.

'I started to climb back up to the nest, but just as I reached it she dived at me again. I was slashing at her with my knife, trying to keep a grip with my other hand on the rock. As if she knew I'd killed her mate, she fastened her claws on my shoulder, stabbing at my head with her beak. I was in agony and terrified she would blind me. I lashed out wildly with my knife. I didn't mean to kill her, just to make her let go. Then I felt her collapse against me. But even though she was dead, her talons gripped my shoulder as fiercely as ever.

'When I carried her chicks down from the nest her claws were still locked deep into my flesh. Her dead body was swinging from my shoulder. Even when I reached the bottom, her talons were still embedded in me. They had to cut them out of me, before they could tear her body off me . . . But I can still feel her talons gripping me. She won't let go of me. She'll never let go of me.'

He was sobbing, and Elísabet knew she should go to him and put her arms around him, but she couldn't. She could see the white bird beating its wings against her husband's face. She could hear its cry of fury. The whole room was suddenly full of flailing wings and the screams of *murder, murder!*

Elísabet fought her way out of the tiny cottage and ran as fast as her swollen belly would allow, but too soon she was forced to stop and gasp for breath. It was summer, but the great river of blue ice that lay below the cottage never melted, never moved. And now the chill, damp air rose up as if every breath she took sucked the cold towards her, turning her lungs to ice. She stared up at the clear blue sky above, but it was empty. Not a single bird flew, not a single cry was heard, as if every creature in the world had died with those falcons, the last falcons in the valley.

A boom echoed round the mountains, louder than a thunder clap. Startled, she stared down at the ice. A huge crack had opened in the frozen river, leaving a hollow in the ice like the inside of a giant white egg. Even as she gazed at it, Elísabet saw a great black shadow running down the valley, staining the sparkling blue-white ice until it was as dark as the bog pools. Terrified, she glanced up. It was only a cloud passing over the sun . . . only a cloud creeping out from behind the mountain . . . only a cloud where there had been none before.

Elísabet gasped as the child in her belly kicked. Tiny fists punched into her, thrashing furiously as if her child was trying to fight its way out. She could sense its fear, feel the small heart fluttering and racing like the heartbeat of a snared bird. But even as she listened to the tiny frantic pounding, she realized there was not just one heart beating in her belly, but two. Two little heads butted her. Two pairs of minute arms thrashed about inside her in their terror. She sank to the ground, pressing her hands to her belly, gently rubbing their little limbs through her skin, trying to comfort them as if she could grasp those frightened, angry little fists and calm them.

'They know,' a voice said behind her.

Elísabet twisted herself around as best she could. A young

woman was standing in the shadow of a rocky outcrop. She was taller even than Jóhann and she held her back as straight as a birch tree.

'An oath sworn on the life of an unborn child cannot be broken without a terrible price being paid. You should not have let him swear on the infants in your womb. If an oath was to be made, it should have been on your own heads, not on innocent lives. Your daughters are marked now. The spirits of the falcons have entered your belly. But I will do all I can to protect them if you entrust them to me.'

Elísabet stared aghast into the eyes of the stranger, eyes that were as grey and dark as a winter's storm. She saw something else too in that handsome face, a tiny ridge beneath the nose where a groove should have been.

'Get away from me,' she screamed, desperately trying to scramble to her feet. 'I know who your people are. You're evil, wicked, every last one of your tribe. You're child killers. Everyone knows what happens to the children you steal from decent people like us. I won't let you near my babies. I won't let you take them, do you hear? Get away from us!'

Her eyes wide in terror, Elísabet backed away, desperately making the sign of the cross over herself and her belly as if this would drive the stranger off.

But the woman regarded her impassively as she might have watched a screeching gull riding the wind. After a long moment, she reached beneath her shawl and unlooped a long, knotted cord of white and red wool from about her waist. She drew the cord three times through her right hand, before holding it out to Elísabet.

'This will help ease the birth and undo some of the harm that has been done. Loosen one knot each time the pains come upon you.'

Elísabet backed away, holding her hands behind her as if she feared the cord might fly into them unbidden. 'I don't want it! I won't have it in my house. I'd never take anything you or your filthy brood have touched.'

The stranger's placid expression did not change, but she tossed the cord on the ground between them. The scarlet and white cord lay among the rusty grass stalks, limp, inert. Then the stranger lifted her hand and without warning the cord reared up in front of Elísabet and slithered towards her. But even as she cried out, it burst into flame and vanished into smoke.

The woman lifted her head and her eyes were as sharp and hard as the black rocks on the mountains of fire. 'Remember this – in the days that are coming it is not my people you should fear. You have cursed your own babies and day by day, as they grow, so will your dread of them, until you and all your people will become more terrified of your daughters than of any other creatures on this earth. When that day comes, we will be waiting!'

Chapter One
Anno Domini 1539

The queen of Spain once had a dream, that a white falcon flew out of the mountains towards her and in its talons it held the flaming ball of the sun and icy sphere of the moon. The queen opened her hand and the falcon dropped the sun and the moon into her outstretched palm and she grasped them.

The falcon perched upon her arm and spread its wings. And, as it stretched them, the white feathers grew longer and wider until they enveloped the queen like a royal mantle.

Then the queen dreamt that a traitor had entered her presence and at once the white falcon rose and flew to him. It alighted on the man's shoulders and the talons of the falcon were so strong and sharp they severed the man's arms from his body. Streams of blood poured out from his body and the queen knelt and drank the blood of the traitor.

Lisbon, Portugal

Enter – *a term meaning to give a falcon the first sight of the prey which the falconer wants it to hunt and kill.*

On a bleak winter's morning in Lisbon, in front of a howling mob, Manuel da Costa was burned alive. Only he died that day, a lone, pathetic figure on the pyre. He was a poor man, an insignificant man, a man that few would have troubled to mourn. But hundreds of men and women who even then were huddling behind closed doors would have chilling cause to remember Manuel's death. And all through the bitter, blood-soaked years to come they would whisper into the darkness how on that winter's day and in that very hour the devils of hell were made flesh and dwelt on earth.

If young Manuel had only kept his head down, averted his eyes, held his tongue, if he had just kept walking, he might have stayed alive. And if he had survived, who knows, maybe the thousands of others who came after him might have lived too. But Manuel had no warning of the nightmare that was about to ensnare him. How could he?

So, just as he did every day, one February morning, shortly after dawn, he closed the door of the tiny room he rented and hurried through the narrow, twisting streets of Lisbon. Even a passing stranger would have spotted Manuel's occupation at once, for though he was only in his twenties his chest was already as round as a barrel from years of blowing glass and his olive hands scarred with a hundred healed burns.

With his head hunched down against the wetted wind, Manuel would never have noticed the small crowd gathered at the far end of the square in front of the church had it not been for a small boy who ran headlong into him. With a curse worthy of a sailor the brat dodged around him and scampered across the square. Only then did Manuel lift his head to see what was attracting the lad. The crowd was swelling fast, with men, women and children hurrying towards it in twos and threes. As they joined the gathering, they simply stood and gazed at the church as if it was the most astounding thing they had ever seen.

Manuel hesitated, torn between curiosity and his fear of being late for work. Curiosity won. He hurried across the square and joined the back of the crowd. An old woman, dressed in widow's black, was trying to elbow her way to the front. Manuel knew her. She occupied one of the tiny squalid rooms two houses down from his own lodgings. He wasn't surprised to see her here. If there was any trouble or misfortune anywhere in the neighbourhood she was always the first on the scene. He sidled closer to her.

'What's everyone looking so thunderstruck for?' he whispered, then, just to bait her, he added with a grin, 'You'd think the Virgin Mary had farted in the middle of Mass.'

The old crone turned and glared furiously at him, crossing herself rapidly.

'How dare you speak so of the Blessed Virgin? If your poor mother was alive today it would kill her to hear such wicked words on your lips.'

She hobbled around to the other side of the crowd, darting poisonous glances at him. Manuel grinned broadly at the outraged expression on her face. That would give the old witch something to complain about.

A man standing on the other side of Manuel pointed through the heads of the crowd to a notice pinned to the door of the church.

'What's it say?' he demanded.

Manuel shrugged. He'd never learned to read much more than his own name, but even if he had been a scholar, at that distance it would have been impossible to make out the words.

The question was taken up by others who were unable to get close to the door. They began insisting that those at the front should either move aside or tell them what had been nailed up there. So in scandalized tones, the ripple of the words spread back through the crowd, passing from mouth to mouth until it reached Manuel's ears.

The Messiah has not yet come. Jesus is not the Messiah.

Manuel was as shocked as any in that crowd. It was one thing to make jokes, but what was nailed on that door was nothing short of blasphemy. Even as the words spread through the crowd, an angry buzzing began. Strangers and neighbours alike were demanding to know who could have committed such an outrage.

Manuel felt a cold shiver of unease. It never took much to inflame a crowd in Lisbon. If a few hotheads started whipping up the anger of the mob, they would turn violent in minutes. And he knew only too well who the crowd would turn on first. Somehow, the Old Christians of Lisbon could always tell if you were a Jewish convert. They could scent the presence of a New Christian and would attack with the savagery of a pack of wild dogs.

He broke away and hurried off in the direction of the glass-blowers' works. As he scuttled through the streets he passed two more churches and saw to his disquiet the same heresy nailed to their doors and other angry mobs beginning to gather around them.

By noon everyone in the city knew that the blasphemous proclamation had been pinned not only to every church door in Lisbon, but also on the very door of the great Cathedral itself, and King João had offered a reward of 10,000 silver crusados to anyone who could discover the author of this evil.

That night when Manuel returned to his lodgings, he found the house packed to the rafters with frightened men and women. Men and women like himself who were *Cristianos Nuevos*, New Christians, or, as the Old Christians mockingly called them, *Marranos*, meaning pigs. They were Jews fled from Spain, or their descendants, who had been forced to convert to Christianity, and now practised the Catholic faith. But to the Old Christians they were filthy foreigners come here to take their jobs, their homes and their women, and no matter how much the New Christians swore they were now good Catholics, they still remained what they had always been in the eyes of the Old Christians – Christ killers.

Manuel squashed himself into the darkened doorway of one of the rooms. Jorge, the physician, was holding forth amid a crowd of men all murmuring nearly as loudly as the crowd outside the churches.

Jorge held up his hands for silence, raising his voice to make himself heard.

'There is no cause for fear. The Pope issued a bull declaring all New Christians free and cancelling all the charges brought against us. He's forbidden the Inquistion to act against those of us who were forcibly converted or against the children of converts.'

'But for three years only.' Benito's white beard trembled as he rasped for breath. 'Those three years are now ended. I have lived through it all before in Spain, trust me, you cannot rely on the promises of kings or popes. It will happen here, as it did there. Our people will be rounded up and murdered one by one till not so much as a newborn infant remains alive.'

He swept his clawed hand around the room. 'Are you all so blind? Don't you see they will blame us for these notices on the churches; who else will they blame? Who else do they ever blame? Every Catholic in Portugal will soon be screaming for our blood. The king will have all the backing he needs to unleash the dogs of the Inquisition. It is no secret he hates us. He is looking for any excuse to purge Portugal of us. Who knows, maybe King João himself nailed the notices to the churches deliberately to turn his people against us.'

At that, several of the men leapt to their feet, shouting at the old man to be quiet. Weren't they in enough danger already without him adding the charge of slandering the king to their troubles? They glanced anxiously over at the shutters. They were fastened tightly, but all the same, you never knew who was listening outside on the street.

'Enough, enough.' Jorge waved the men back to their seats. 'Benito has a point. There are some who will try to blame us. So it is up to us to make certain we are not blamed. Now listen,' he said, lowering his voice to a whisper, 'tonight . . .'

But Manuel did not wait to hear what they would do tonight. He'd grown up in this community and he knew that the old men would still be arguing about what they would do 'tonight' come daybreak. All he wanted to do was sleep. Dawn would come only too quickly and, with luck, by then the people of Lisbon would have found some new scandal to divert them.

But the following morning found another notice pinned to the Cathedral door. This time the crowd that rapidly gathered around it read the proclamation:

I, as the author, declare that I am neither Spanish nor Portuguese, but I am an Englishman and even if 20,000 gold escudos were offered, my name will never be discovered.

The crowd read it, but they did not believe a single word of it.

Two nights later, Manuel woke with a start as the light from a lantern shone full into his face. Even as his mind registered the fact that this was the middle of the night, a wave of cold fear washed over him. As his eyes struggled to adjust to the light, he was dimly aware of four hooded figures looming over him. He could hear their breathing like the hissing of snakes.

Manuel tried to scramble out of bed, but his legs became entangled in the bedclothes and he tripped, sprawling at the feet of one of the black-robed figures. The man stared down at him as if he was a beggar whining for alms. His face was concealed by a pointed black hood, and in the lamp-light his eyes glittered through the slits, the eyes of a cobra rising to strike.

'Manuel da Costa, by order of the Grand Inquisitor you are to accompany us for questioning.'

Sheer terror washed through Manuel, almost emptying his bowels. 'No, no, please, you have the wrong man. It's a mistake. Why would you want to question me? I know nothing . . . I swear, by all the Holy Saints, by . . . I . . . I am a good Catholic. I go to church regularly every week. I never miss Mass. Never miss confession, you ask anyone.'

'A good Catholic does not blaspheme the Holy Virgin.' The hooded man raised a warning hand as Manuel opened his mouth to protest. 'We have a dozen witnesses who will swear they heard you mocking the Virgin even as you denied with your own hand that her Son was the true Messiah.'

They dragged Manuel down the stairs – they had to, for his legs had buckled and he couldn't manage to stand, much less walk. From behind the many doors they passed along the street there came only the sound of silence as heavy as a stone coffin lid. All lights were extinguished. All shutters closed. All doors barred.

Only the old widow, her eye pressed to a crack in the wood, watched and chuckled. Ten thousand crusados they'd promised her. It was a fortune, more than enough to move away from this street of pigs into a respectable district and live in comfort for the rest of her life. They had explained that she would only get her reward if the accused confessed his guilt, but she didn't have the slightest twinge of concern about that.

And Manuel did confess, of course . . . after his muscles and tendons had been ripped from his bones on the rack; after every joint in his limbs had been slowly dislocated by the ropes biting into his thighs, shins, wrists and ankles. Day and night without sleep, they whispered, shouted and cajoled, until they had even him believing that he must have nailed those notices to the church doors.

But, as his inquisitors said, his admission of guilt was not enough, not nearly enough to demonstrate his repentance, for how could one man alone have nailed those notices to the churches all over Lisbon in one night without being seen? Manuel must have had accomplices, unless the Devil himself aided him. He had only to name those men and his suffering would be over, his pain ended. They would let him rest.

Give us a name, any name, that is all we want – JUST ONE NAME.

He could have named his friends, his acquaintances, even his enemies, especially his enemies, most did. He could have uttered any name at all that surfaced in his pain-crazed mind, uttered it without even knowing if he was dreaming or speaking it aloud. But although Manuel prayed with every fibre of his being for an end to his torment, his inquisitors could not make him name another soul. Now, that kind of defiance takes a rare courage.

In the end, they carried him to the square. There, in front of a blood-crazed mob, they sliced through his wrists, separating skin and flesh, muscle and bone, severing the hands with which those foul words had been written. In truth he scarcely recognized the pain of the knife, for what was left of his limbs was already half-dead from the rack. He had thought himself in so much anguish that he could feel no greater torment, but when they tied him to the stake, and he felt the burning flames licking around his body, he knew that he could. The Inquisition had, as always, left the most exquisite agony to the last.

KAREN MAITLAND

COMPANY OF LIARS

The year is 1348 and the first plague victim has reached English shores. Panic erupts around the country and a small band of travellers comes together to outrun the deadly disease, unaware that something far more deadly is – in fact – travelling with them.

The ill-assorted company – a scarred trader in holy relics, a conjurer, two musicians, a healer and a deformed storyteller – are all concealing secrets and lies. And at their heart is the strange, cold child – Narigorm – who reads the runes.

But as law and order breaks down across the country and the battle for survival becomes ever more fierce, Narigorm mercilessly compels each of her fellow travellers to reveal the truth … and each in turn is driven to a cruel and unnatural death.

'A richly evocative page-turner which brings to life a lost and terrible period of British history, with a disturbing final twist worthy of a master of the spine-tingler, such as Henry James' *Daily Express*

'An engrossing fireside read . . . a compelling mystery' *Daily Mail*

'Combines the storytelling traditions of The Canterbury Tales with the supernatural suspense of Mosse's Sepulchre in this atmospheric tale of treachery and magic' *Marie Claire*